Title: Pandemonium

Author: Chris Wooding

Illustrator: Cassandra Diaz

Publication Date: February 2012

Format: Jacketed Hardcover & Paperback

ISBN (Hardcover): 978-0-545-25221-8
ISBN (Paperback): 978-0-439-87759-6

Retail Price (Hardcover): $22.99 US
Retail Price (Paperback): $12.99 US

Ages: 8–12

Grades: 3–7

LOC Number: Available

Length: 160 pages

Trim: 6 x 9 inches

Classification: Comics & Graphic Novels (F),
Science Fiction, Fantasy, Magic (F)

The illustrations in this advance galley appear in both color and black-and-white. In the final book, all the illustrations will be in full color throughout.

graphix

An Imprint of Scholastic Inc.
557 Broadway, New York, NY 10012

For information, contact us at: tradepublicity@scholastic.com

UNCORRECTED PROOF — NOT FOR SALE
If any material is to be quoted, it should be checked against the bound book.
CIP information to be included in bound book.

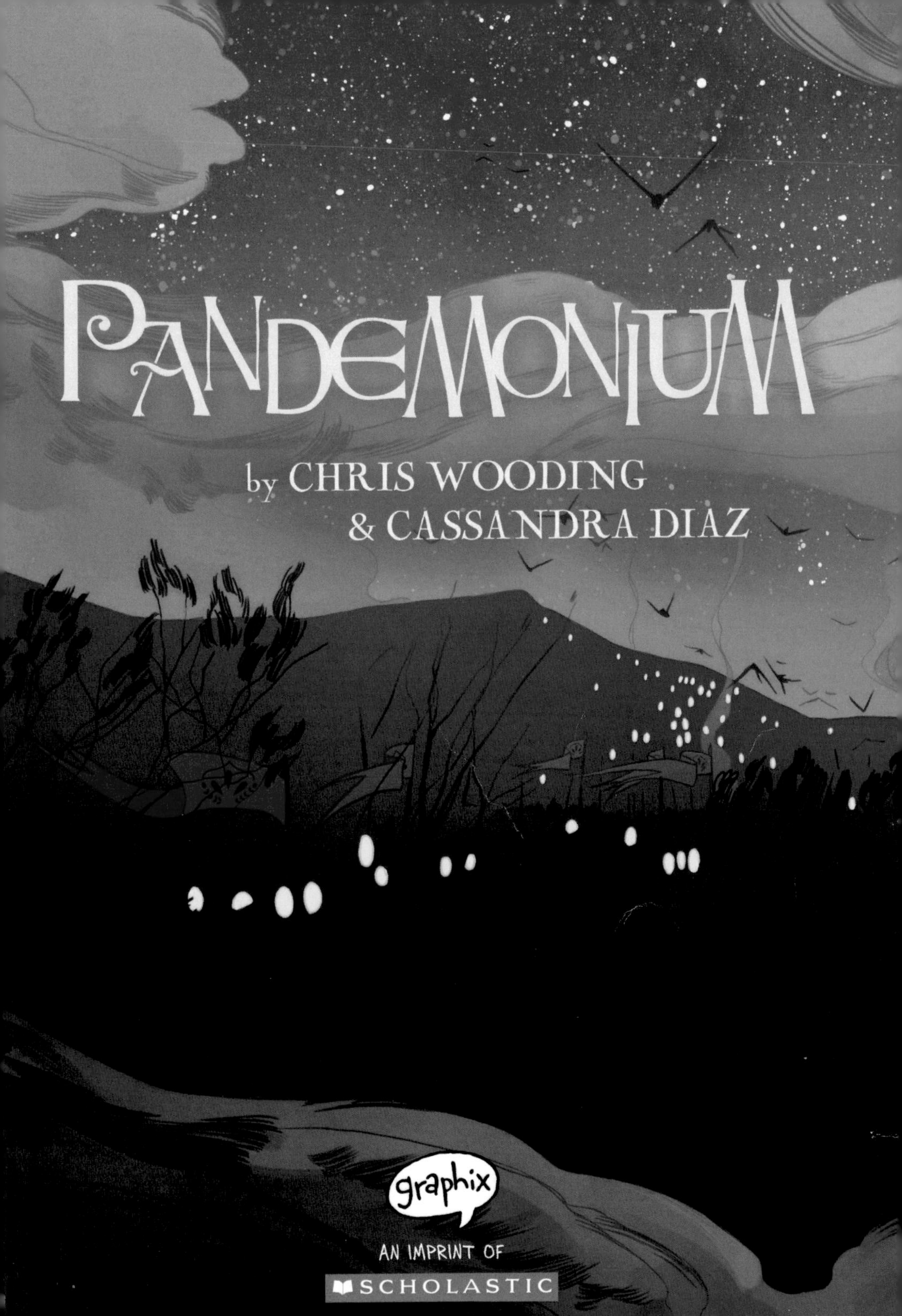

PANDEMONIUM

by CHRIS WOODING
& CASSANDRA DIAZ

graphix

AN IMPRINT OF

SCHOLASTIC

NEW YORK TORONTO LONDON AUCKLAND SYDNEY MEXICO CITY NEW DELHI HONG KONG

Text copyright © 2012 by Chris Wooding
Art copyright © 2012 by Cassandra Diaz

Library of Congress Cataloging-in-Publication Data Available

ISBN 978-0-545-25221-8 (hardcover)
ISBN 978-0-439-87759-6 (paperback)

10 9 8 7 6 5 4 3 2 1   12 13 14 15 16

Printed in USA   66

First edition, February 2012

Creative Director: David Saylor
Designed by Phil Falco
Edited by Nick Eliopulos

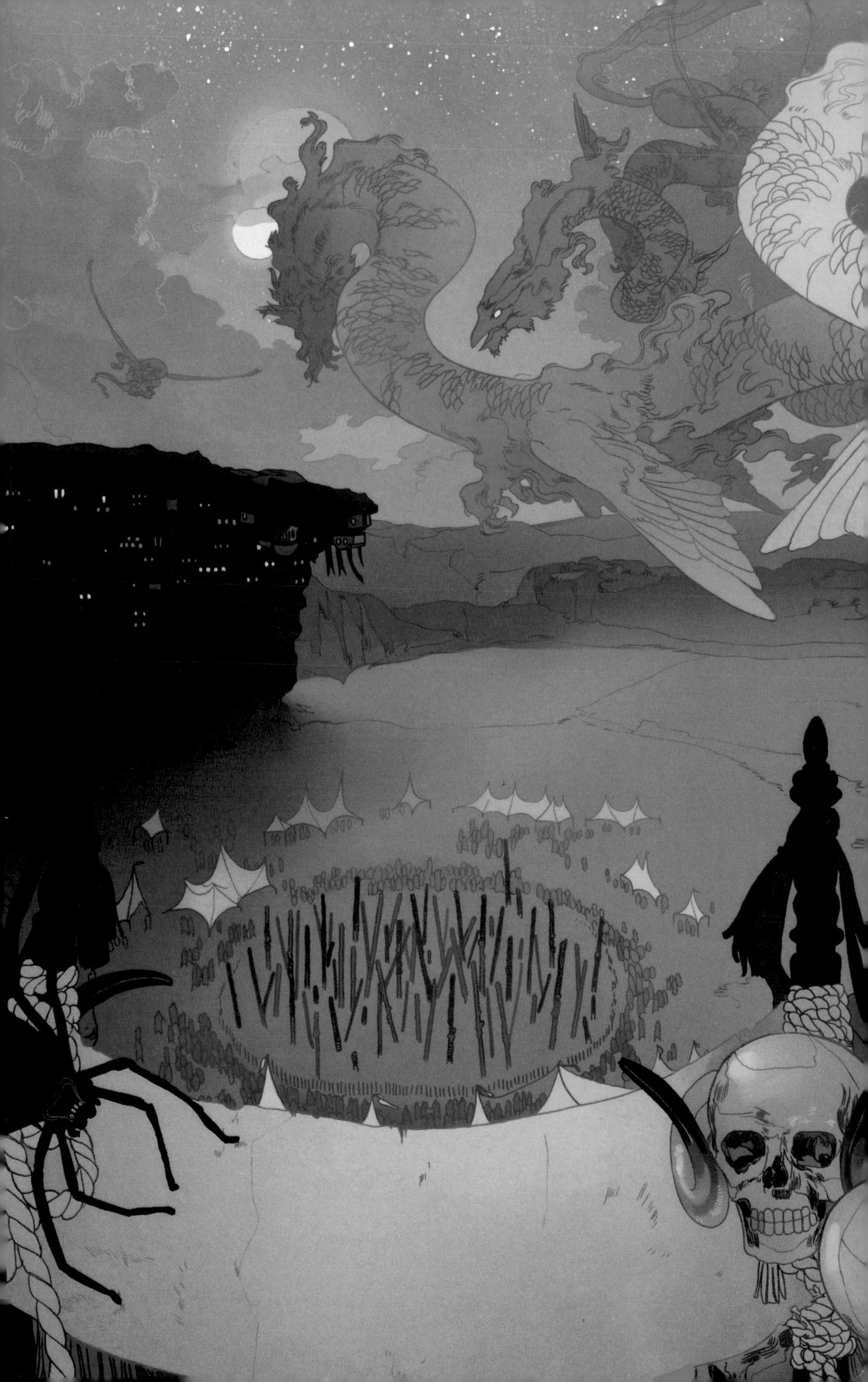

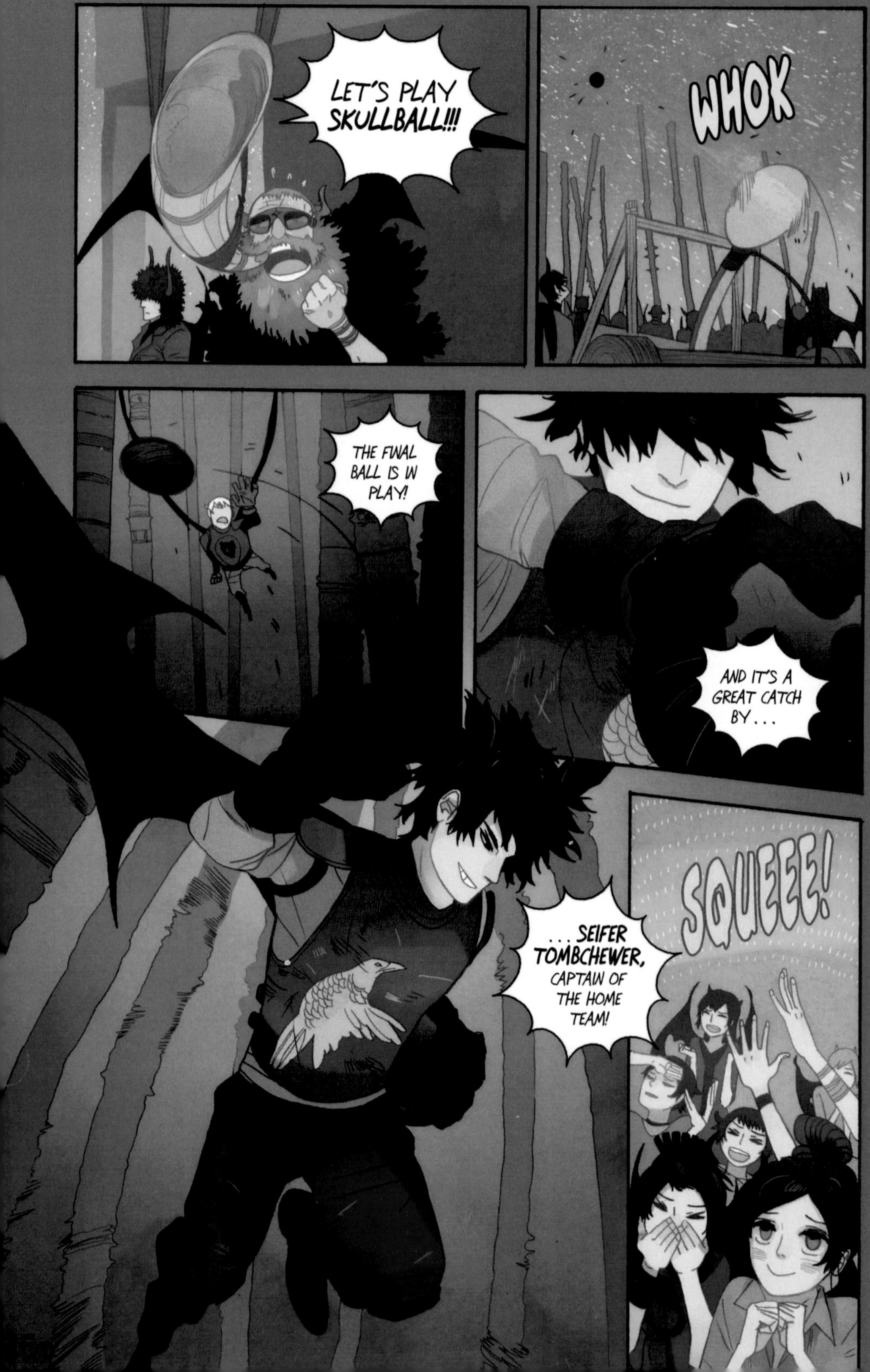
LET'S PLAY SKULLBALL!!!
WHOK
THE FINAL BALL IS IN PLAY!
AND IT'S A GREAT CATCH BY . . .
. . . SEIFER TOMBCHEWER, CAPTAIN OF THE HOME TEAM!
SQUEEE!

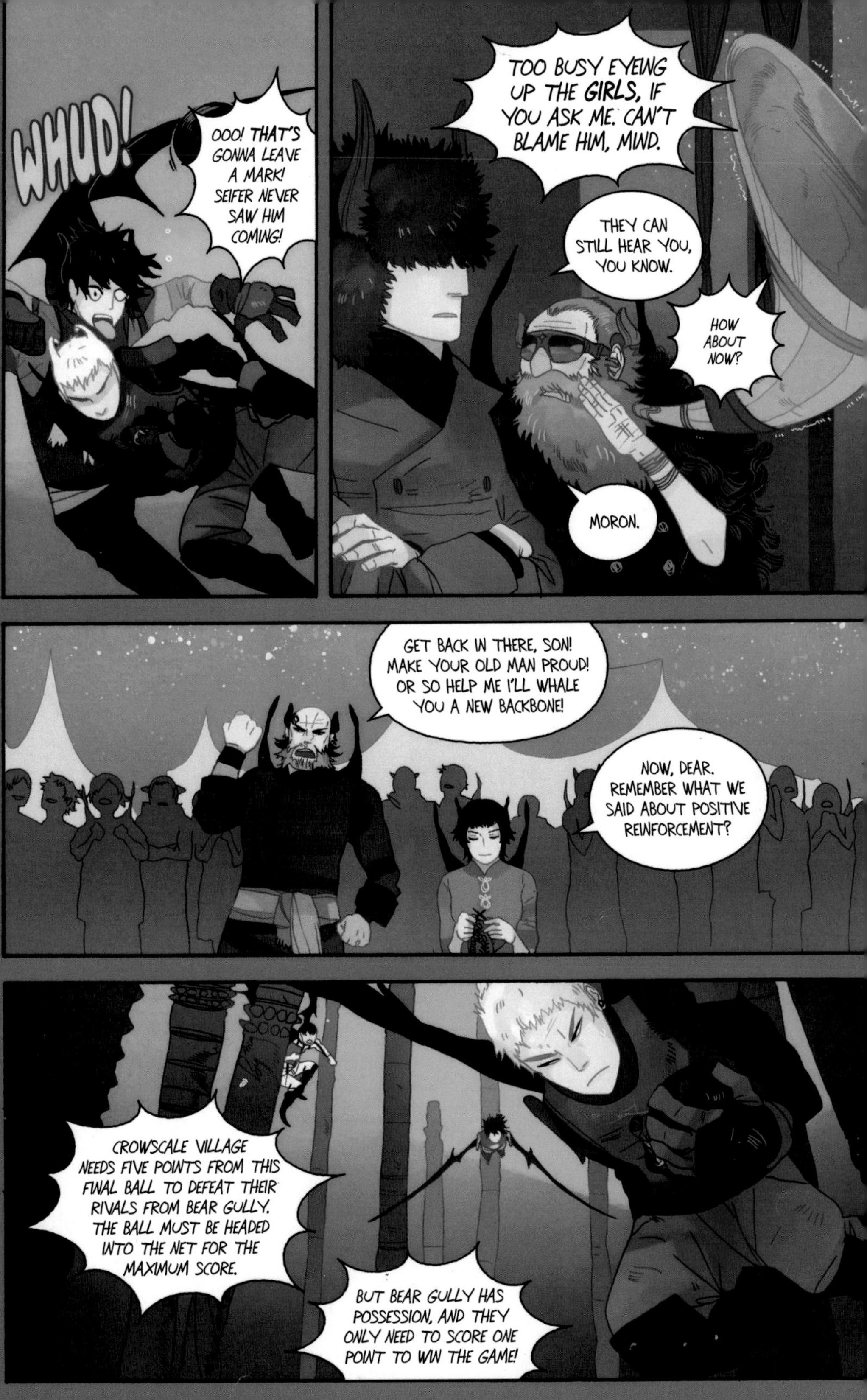
WHUD!
OOO! THAT'S GONNA LEAVE A MARK! SEIFER NEVER SAW HIM COMING!
TOO BUSY EYEING UP THE GIRLS, IF YOU ASK ME. CAN'T BLAME HIM, MIND.
THEY CAN STILL HEAR YOU, YOU KNOW.
HOW ABOUT NOW?
MORON.
GET BACK IN THERE, SON! MAKE YOUR OLD MAN PROUD! OR SO HELP ME I'LL WHALE YOU A NEW BACKBONE!
NOW, DEAR. REMEMBER WHAT WE SAID ABOUT POSITIVE REINFORCEMENT?
CROWSCALE VILLAGE NEEDS FIVE POINTS FROM THIS FINAL BALL TO DEFEAT THEIR RIVALS FROM BEAR GULLY. THE BALL MUST BE HEADED INTO THE NET FOR THE MAXIMUM SCORE.
BUT BEAR GULLY HAS POSSESSION, AND THEY ONLY NEED TO SCORE ONE POINT TO WIN THE GAME!

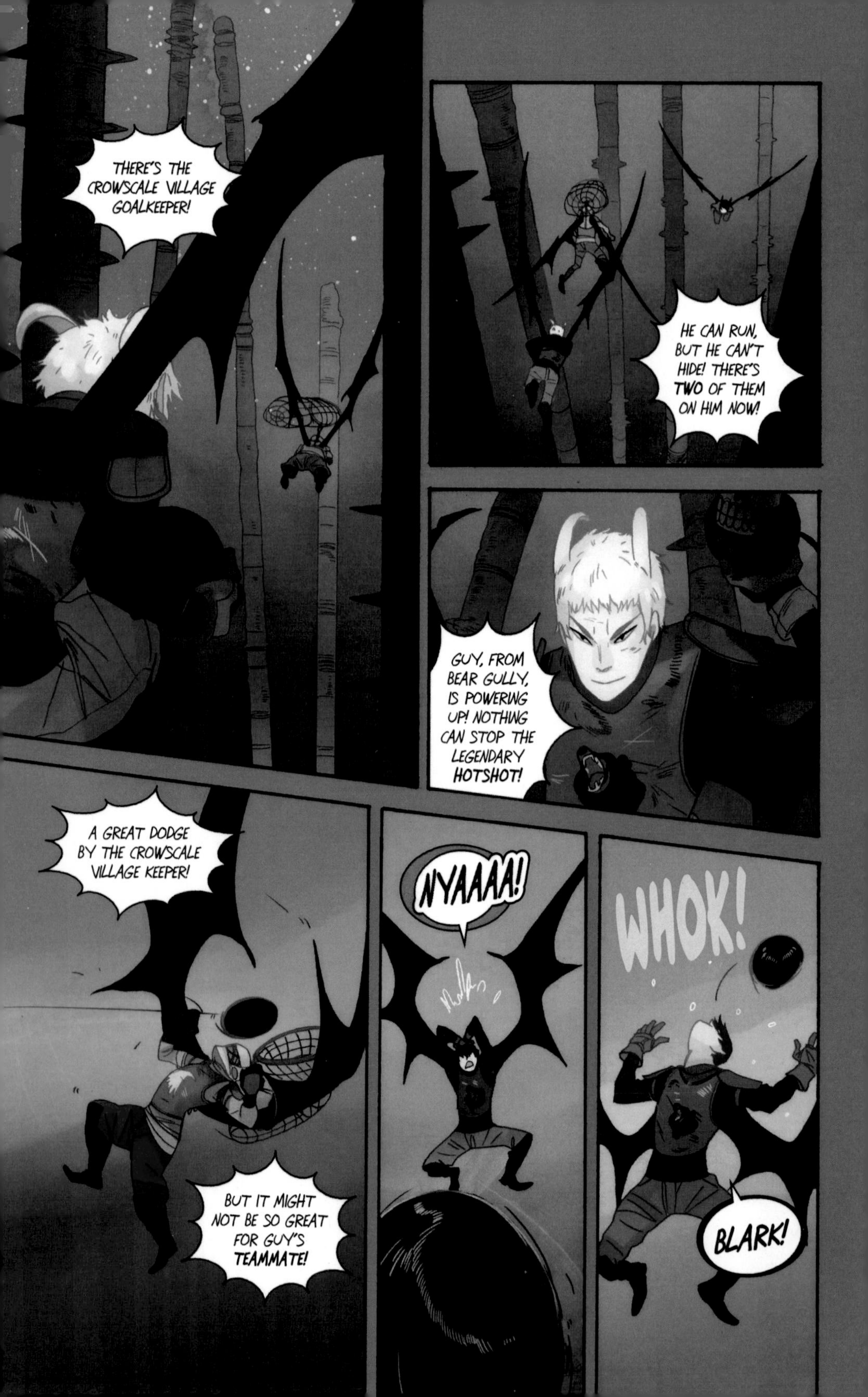

THERE'S THE CROWSCALE VILLAGE GOALKEEPER!
HE CAN RUN, BUT HE CAN'T HIDE! THERE'S TWO OF THEM ON HIM NOW!
GUY, FROM BEAR GULLY, IS POWERING UP! NOTHING CAN STOP THE LEGENDARY HOTSHOT!
A GREAT DODGE BY THE CROWSCALE VILLAGE KEEPER!
BUT IT MIGHT NOT BE SO GREAT FOR GUY'S TEAMMATE!
NYAAAA!
WHOK!
BLARK!

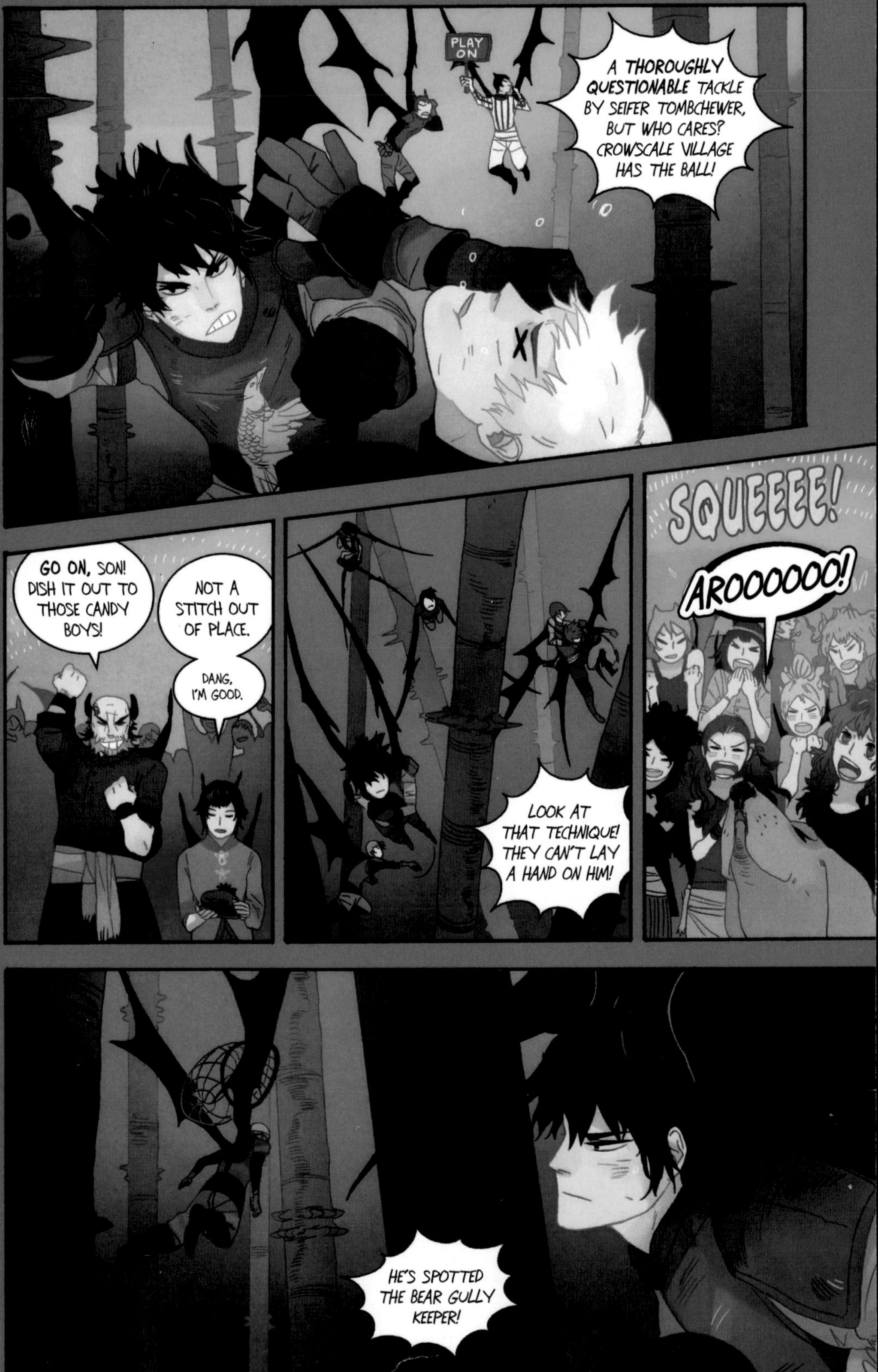
PLAY ON
A THOROUGHLY QUESTIONABLE TACKLE BY SEIFER TOMBCHEWER, BUT WHO CARES? CROWSCALE VILLAGE HAS THE BALL!
GO ON, SON! DISH IT OUT TO THOSE CANDY BOYS!
NOT A STITCH OUT OF PLACE.
DANG, I'M GOOD.
LOOK AT THAT TECHNIQUE! THEY CAN'T LAY A HAND ON HIM!
SQUEEEE!
AROOOOOO!
HE'S SPOTTED THE BEAR GULLY KEEPER!

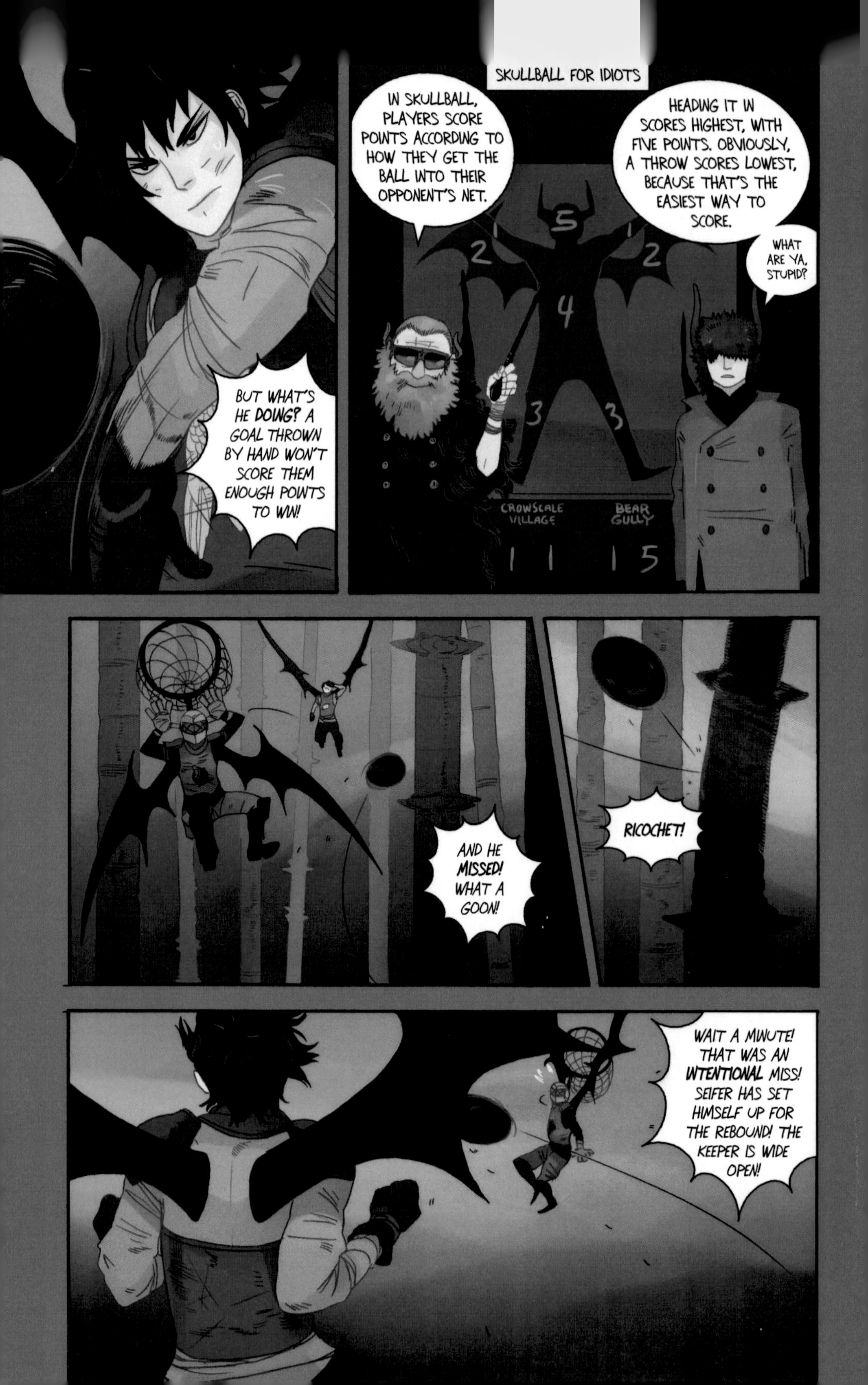
BUT WHAT'S HE DOING? A GOAL THROWN BY HAND WON'T SCORE THEM ENOUGH POINTS TO WIN!
SKULLBALL FOR IDIOTS
IN SKULLBALL, PLAYERS SCORE POINTS ACCORDING TO HOW THEY GET THE BALL INTO THEIR OPPONENT'S NET.
HEADING IT IN SCORES HIGHEST, WITH FIVE POINTS. OBVIOUSLY, A THROW SCORES LOWEST, BECAUSE THAT'S THE EASIEST WAY TO SCORE.
WHAT ARE YA, STUPID?
1 5 1
2 2
4
3 3
CROWSCALE VILLAGE
BEAR GULLY
1 1 1 5
AND HE MISSED! WHAT A GOON!
RICOCHET!
WAIT A MINUTE! THAT WAS AN INTENTIONAL MISS! SEIFER HAS SET HIMSELF UP FOR THE REBOUND! THE KEEPER IS WIDE OPEN!

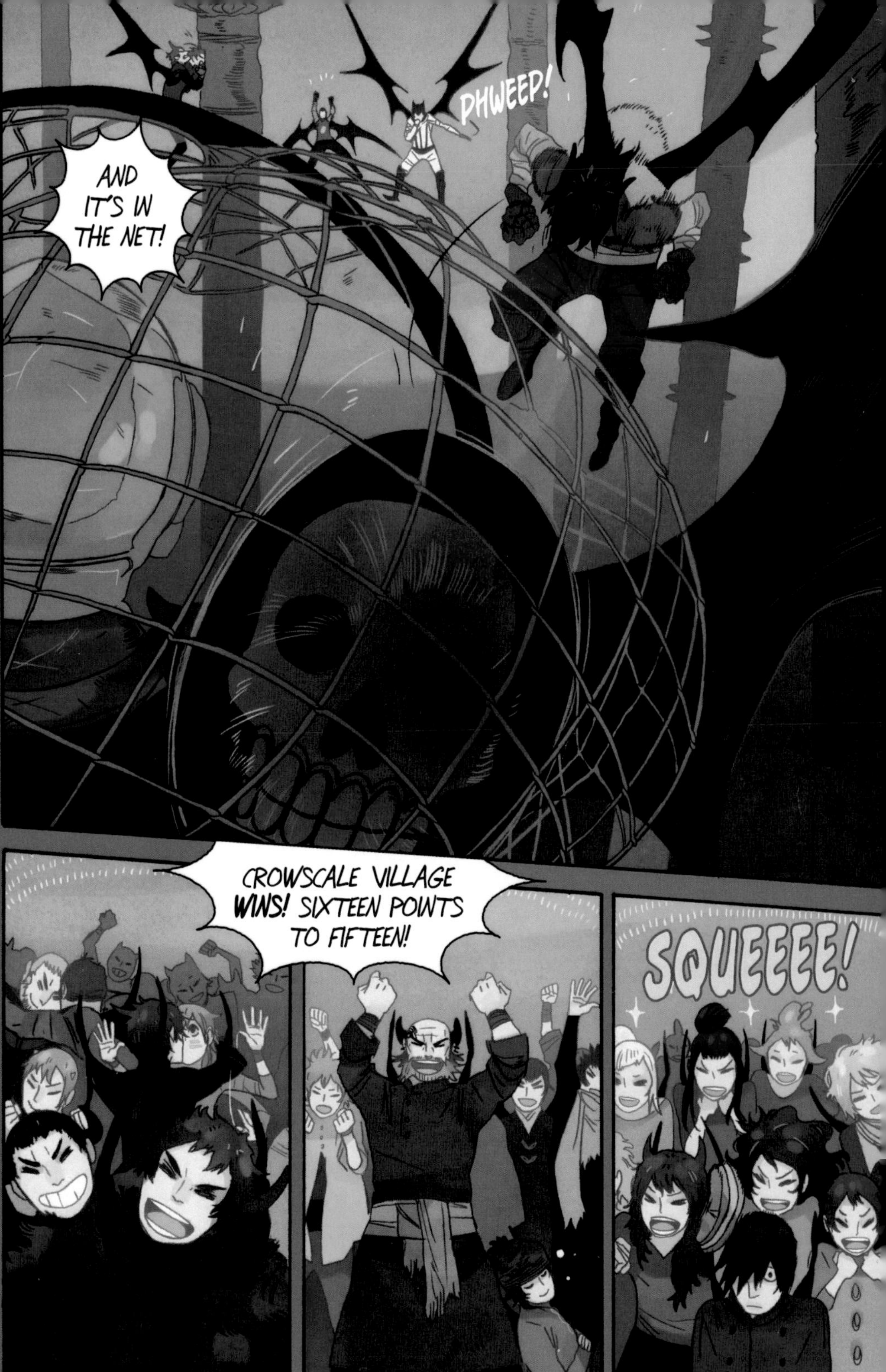
PHWEEP!
AND IT'S IN THE NET!
CROWSCALE VILLAGE WINS! SIXTEEN POINTS TO FIFTEEN!
SQUEEEE!

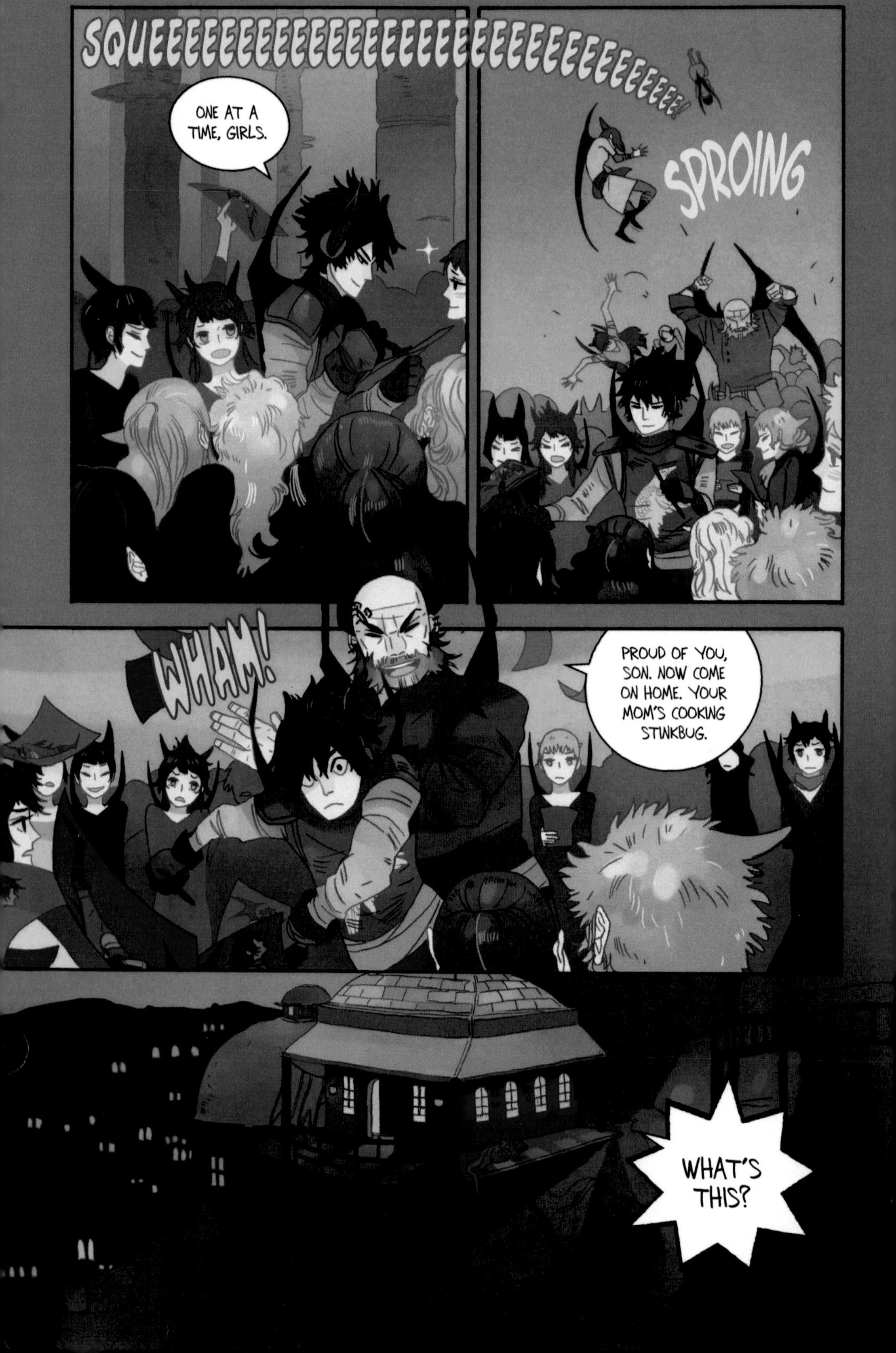
SQUEEEEEEEEEEEEEEEEEEEEEEEEEEEEEEEEEEE!
ONE AT A TIME, GIRLS.
SPROING
WHAM!
PROUD OF YOU, SON. NOW COME ON HOME. YOUR MOM'S COOKING STINKBUG.
WHAT'S THIS?

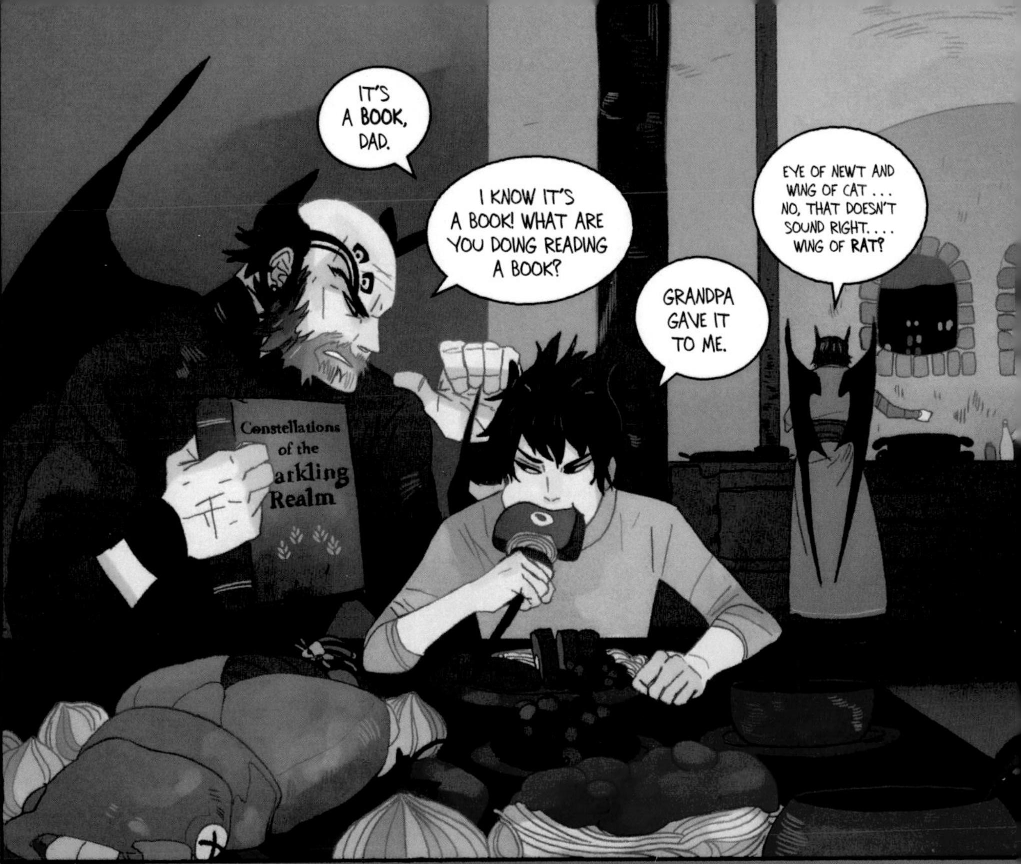
IT'S A BOOK, DAD.
I KNOW IT'S A BOOK! WHAT ARE YOU DOING READING A BOOK?
Constellations of the Sparkling Realm
GRANDPA GAVE IT TO ME.
EYE OF NEWT AND WING OF CAT . . . NO, THAT DOESN'T SOUND RIGHT. . . . WING OF RAT?

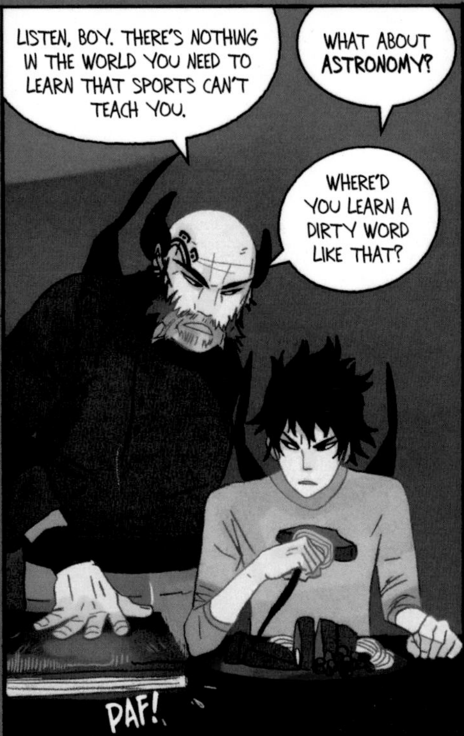
LISTEN, BOY. THERE'S NOTHING IN THE WORLD YOU NEED TO LEARN THAT SPORTS CAN'T TEACH YOU.
WHAT ABOUT ASTRONOMY?
WHERE'D YOU LEARN A DIRTY WORD LIKE THAT?
PAF!

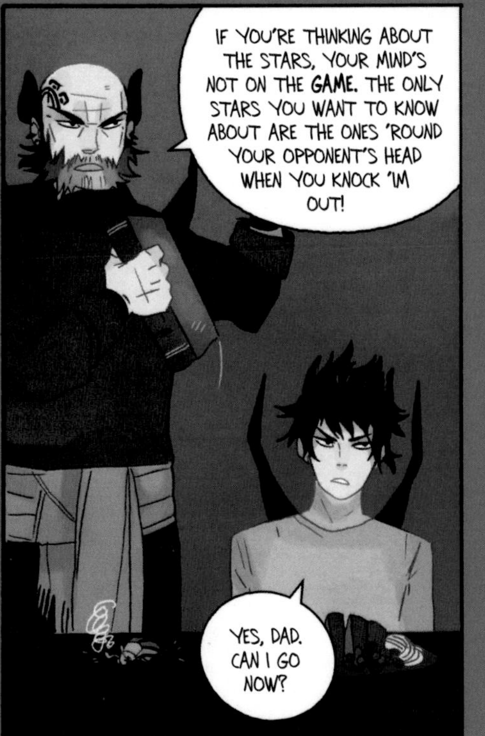
IF YOU'RE THINKING ABOUT THE STARS, YOUR MIND'S NOT ON THE GAME. THE ONLY STARS YOU WANT TO KNOW ABOUT ARE THE ONES 'ROUND YOUR OPPONENT'S HEAD WHEN YOU KNOCK 'IM OUT!
YES, DAD. CAN I GO NOW?

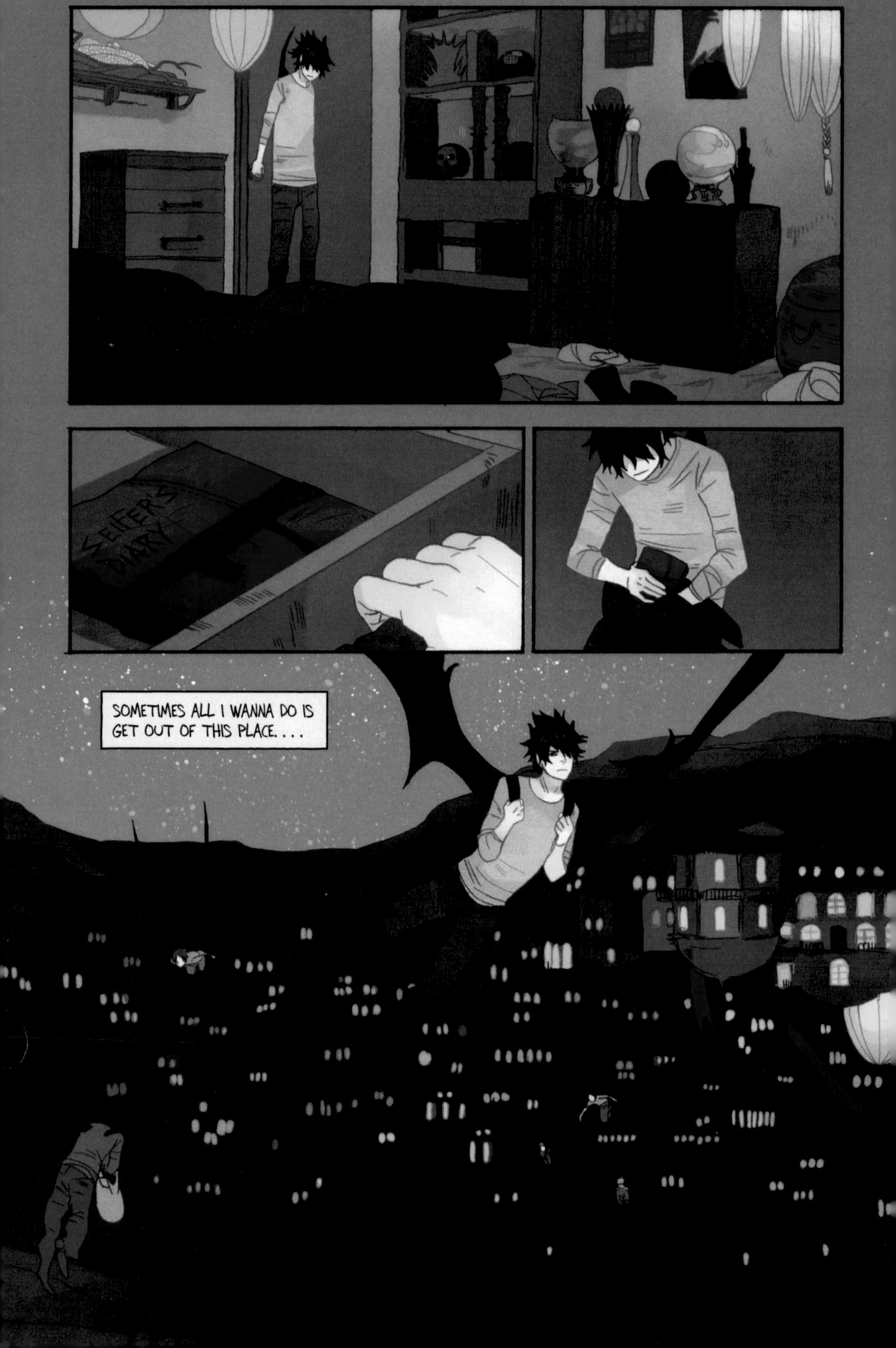
SEIFER'S DIARY
SOMETIMES ALL I WANNA DO IS GET OUT OF THIS PLACE. . . .

THE MOUNTAINS ARE ALL I'VE EVER KNOWN. THEY SEEM TO GO ON FOREVER, BUT I KNOW THEY DON'T.

I'VE SEEN **MAPS**.

I COULD SPEND MY LIFE HERE. FIND A GIRL AND SETTLE DOWN. MAYBE BUY A FARM.

JUST **THINKING** IT MAKES ME FEEL EMPTY.

I'LL NEVER BE HAPPY HERE UNTIL I'VE SEEN WHAT'S OUT THERE.

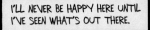

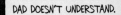

DAD DOESN'T UNDERSTAND.

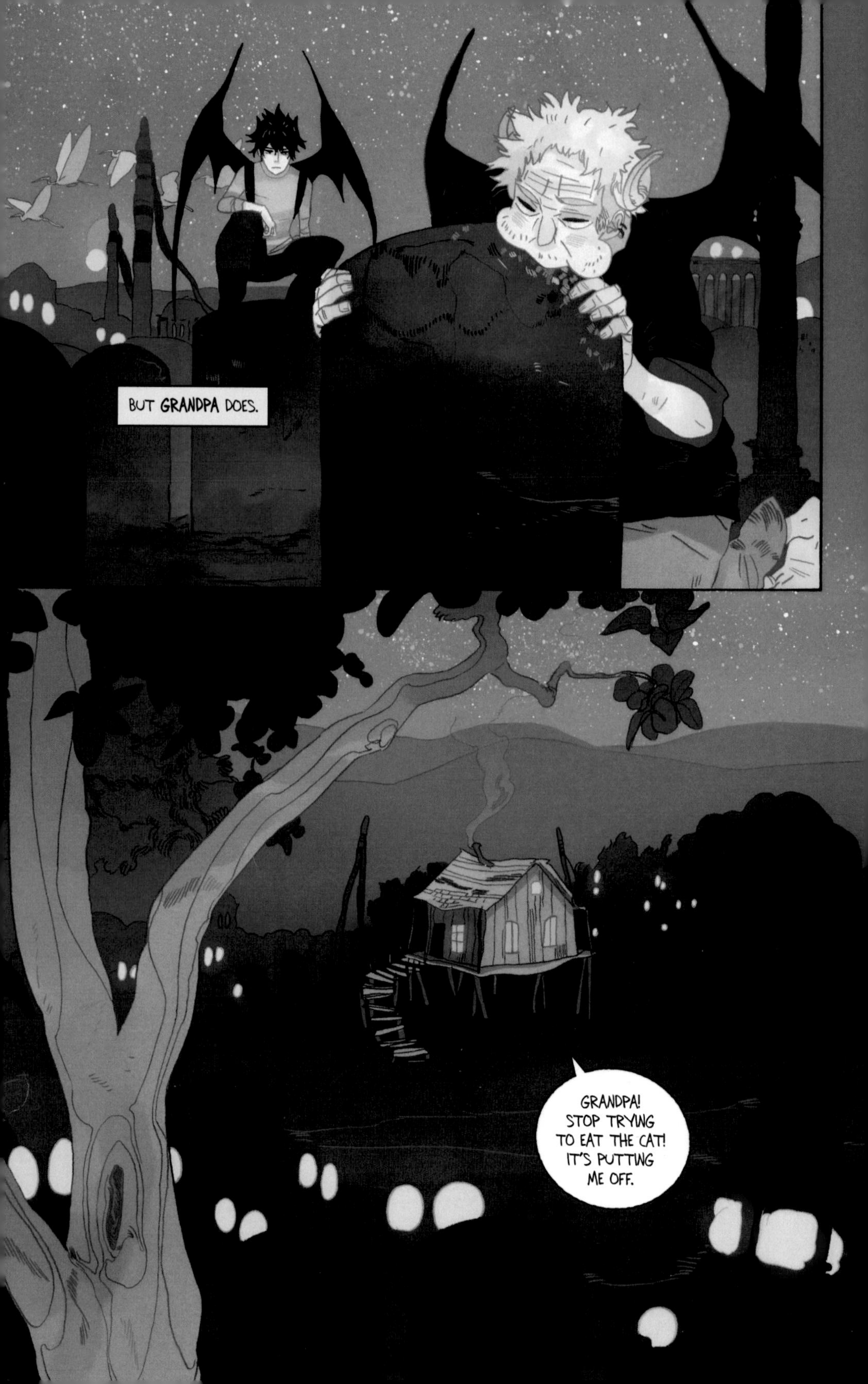
BUT GRANDPA DOES.
GRANDPA! STOP TRYING TO EAT THE CAT! IT'S PUTTING ME OFF.

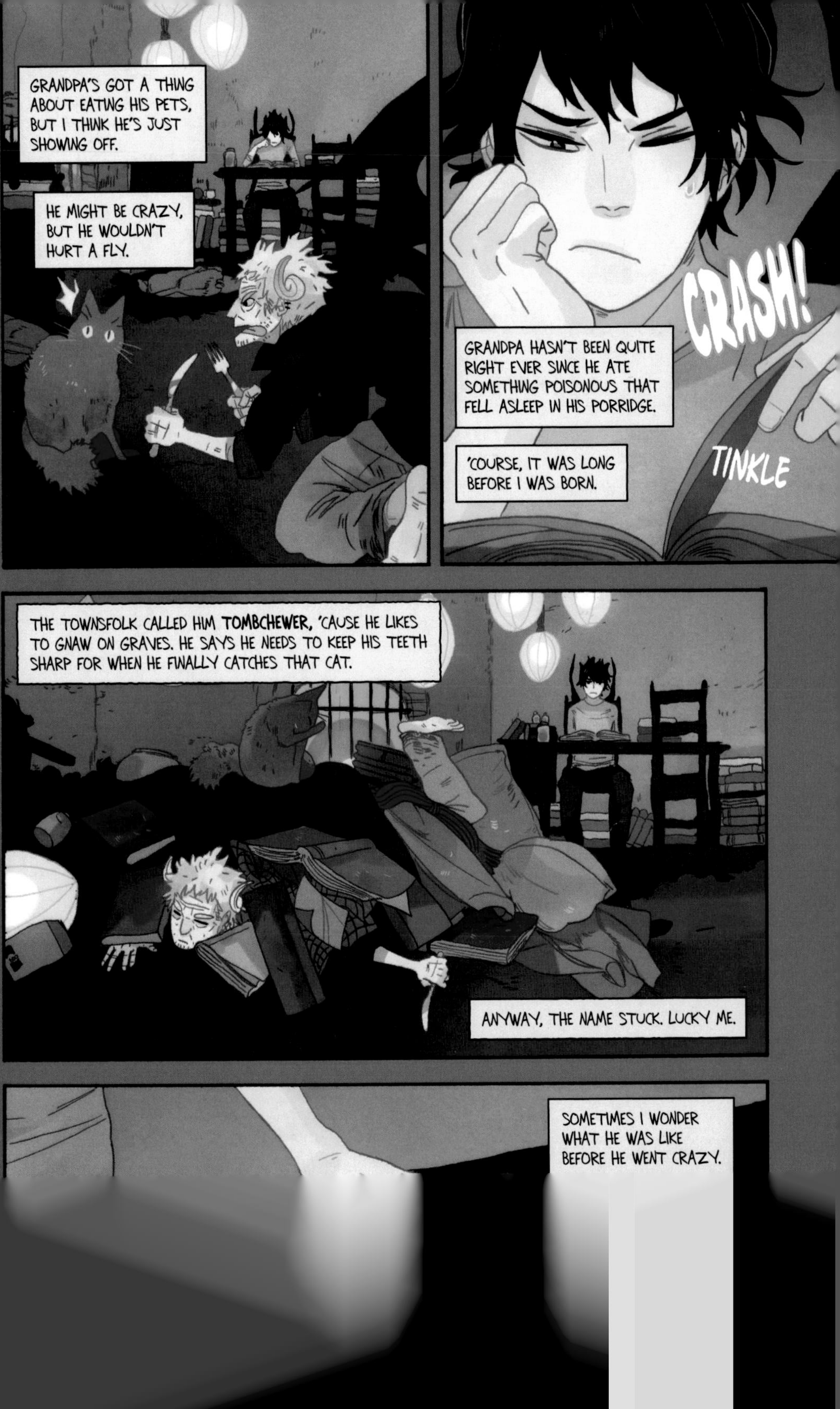
GRANDPA'S GOT A THING ABOUT EATING HIS PETS, BUT I THINK HE'S JUST SHOWING OFF.
HE MIGHT BE CRAZY, BUT HE WOULDN'T HURT A FLY.
GRANDPA HASN'T BEEN QUITE RIGHT EVER SINCE HE ATE SOMETHING POISONOUS THAT FELL ASLEEP IN HIS PORRIDGE.
'COURSE, IT WAS LONG BEFORE I WAS BORN.
CRASH!
TINKLE
THE TOWNSFOLK CALLED HIM **TOMBCHEWER**, 'CAUSE HE LIKES TO GNAW ON GRAVES. HE SAYS HE NEEDS TO KEEP HIS TEETH SHARP FOR WHEN HE FINALLY CATCHES THAT CAT.
ANYWAY, THE NAME STUCK. LUCKY ME.
SOMETIMES I WONDER WHAT HE WAS LIKE BEFORE HE WENT CRAZY.

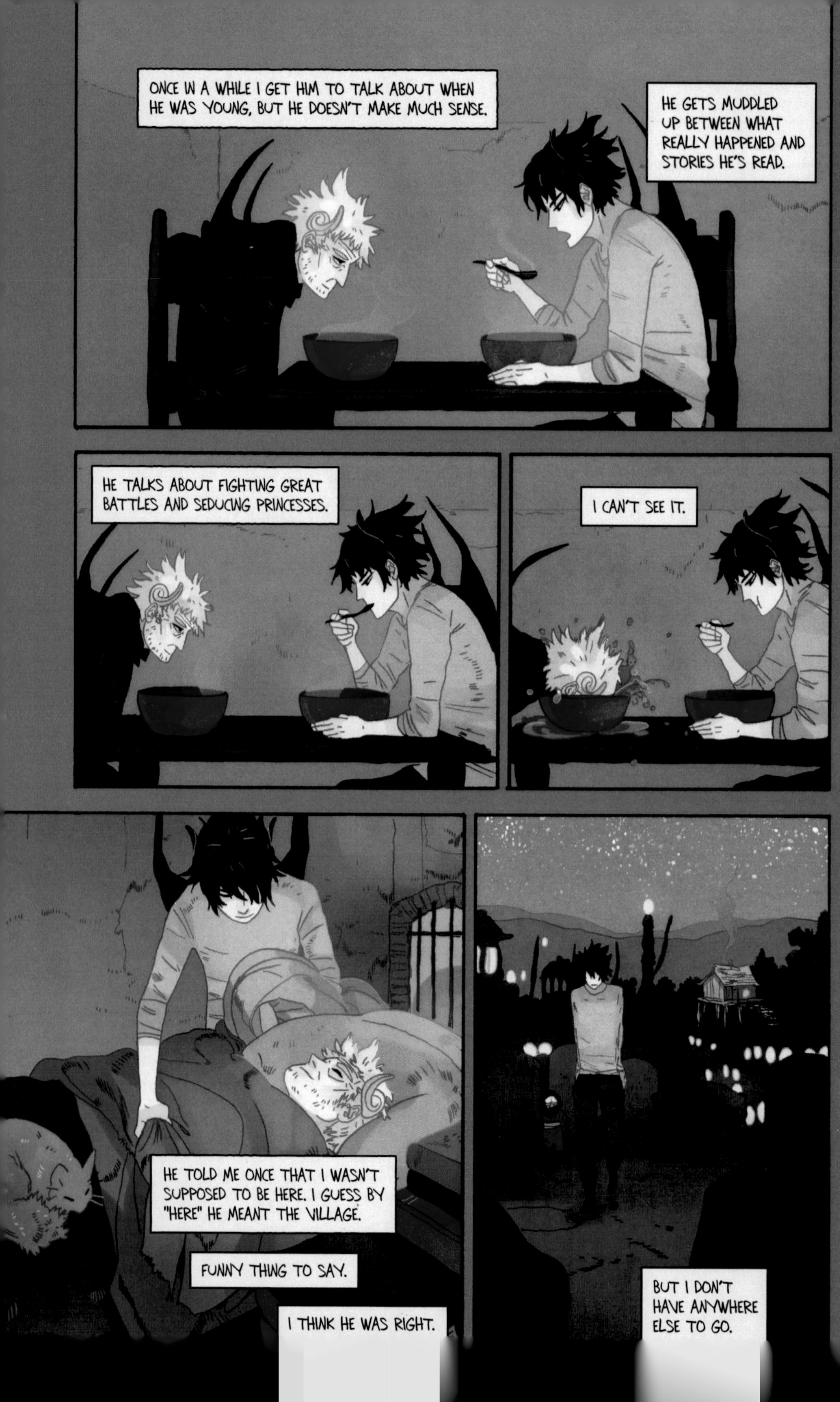
ONCE IN A WHILE I GET HIM TO TALK ABOUT WHEN HE WAS YOUNG, BUT HE DOESN'T MAKE MUCH SENSE.
HE GETS MUDDLED UP BETWEEN WHAT REALLY HAPPENED AND STORIES HE'S READ.
HE TALKS ABOUT FIGHTING GREAT BATTLES AND SEDUCING PRINCESSES.
I CAN'T SEE IT.
HE TOLD ME ONCE THAT I WASN'T SUPPOSED TO BE HERE. I GUESS BY "HERE" HE MEANT THE VILLAGE.
FUNNY THING TO SAY.
I THINK HE WAS RIGHT.
BUT I DON'T HAVE ANYWHERE ELSE TO GO.

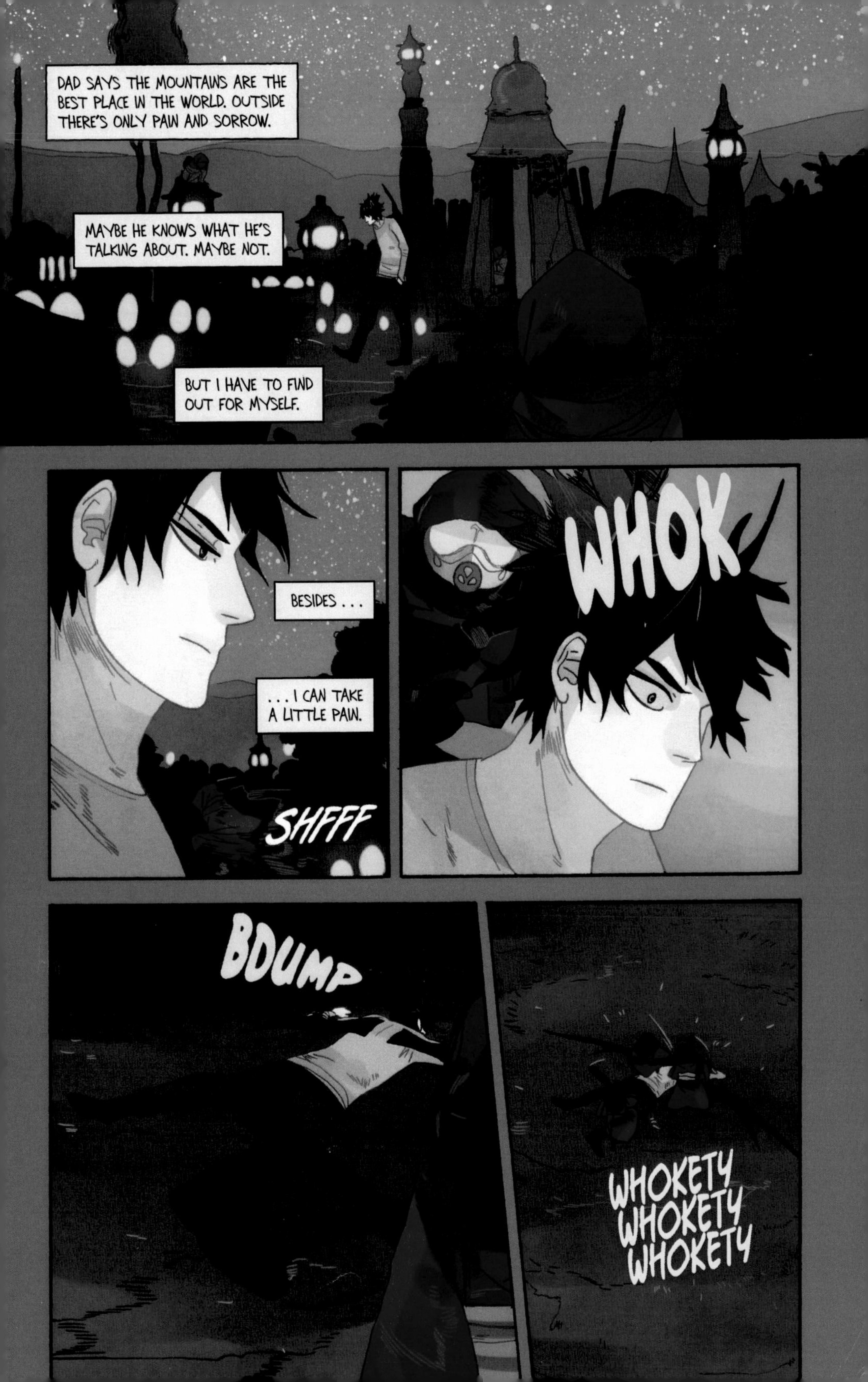
DAD SAYS THE MOUNTAINS ARE THE BEST PLACE IN THE WORLD. OUTSIDE THERE'S ONLY PAIN AND SORROW.
MAYBE HE KNOWS WHAT HE'S TALKING ABOUT. MAYBE NOT.
BUT I HAVE TO FIND OUT FOR MYSELF.
BESIDES . . .
. . . I CAN TAKE A LITTLE PAIN.
SHFFF
WHOK
BDUMP
WHOKETY
WHOKETY
WHOKETY

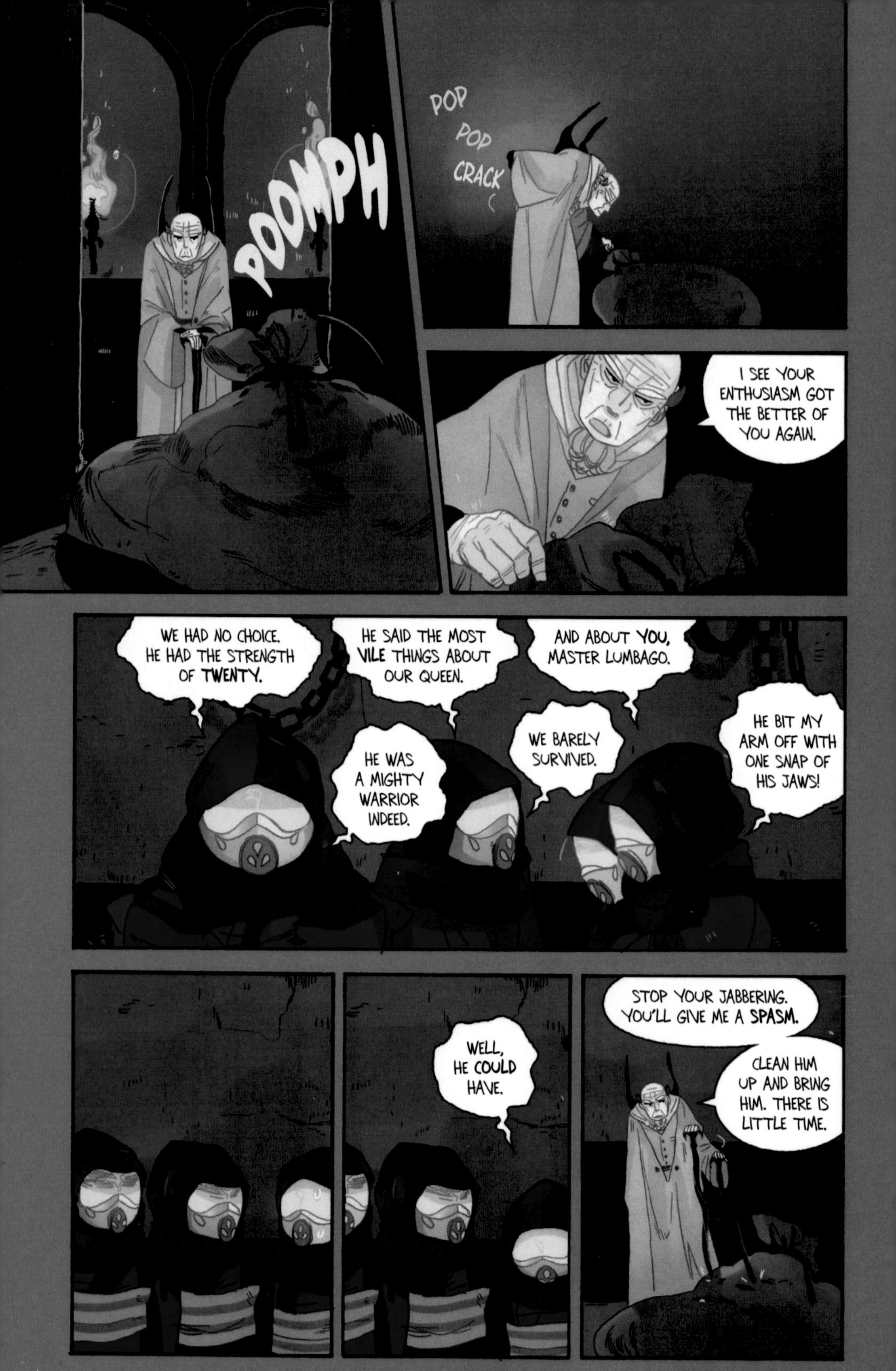
POOMPH
POP
POP
CRACK
I SEE YOUR ENTHUSIASM GOT THE BETTER OF YOU AGAIN.
WE HAD NO CHOICE. HE HAD THE STRENGTH OF TWENTY.
HE SAID THE MOST VILE THINGS ABOUT OUR QUEEN.
AND ABOUT YOU, MASTER LUMBAGO.
HE WAS A MIGHTY WARRIOR INDEED.
WE BARELY SURVIVED.
HE BIT MY ARM OFF WITH ONE SNAP OF HIS JAWS!
WELL, HE COULD HAVE.
STOP YOUR JABBERING. YOU'LL GIVE ME A SPASM.
CLEAN HIM UP AND BRING HIM. THERE IS LITTLE TIME.

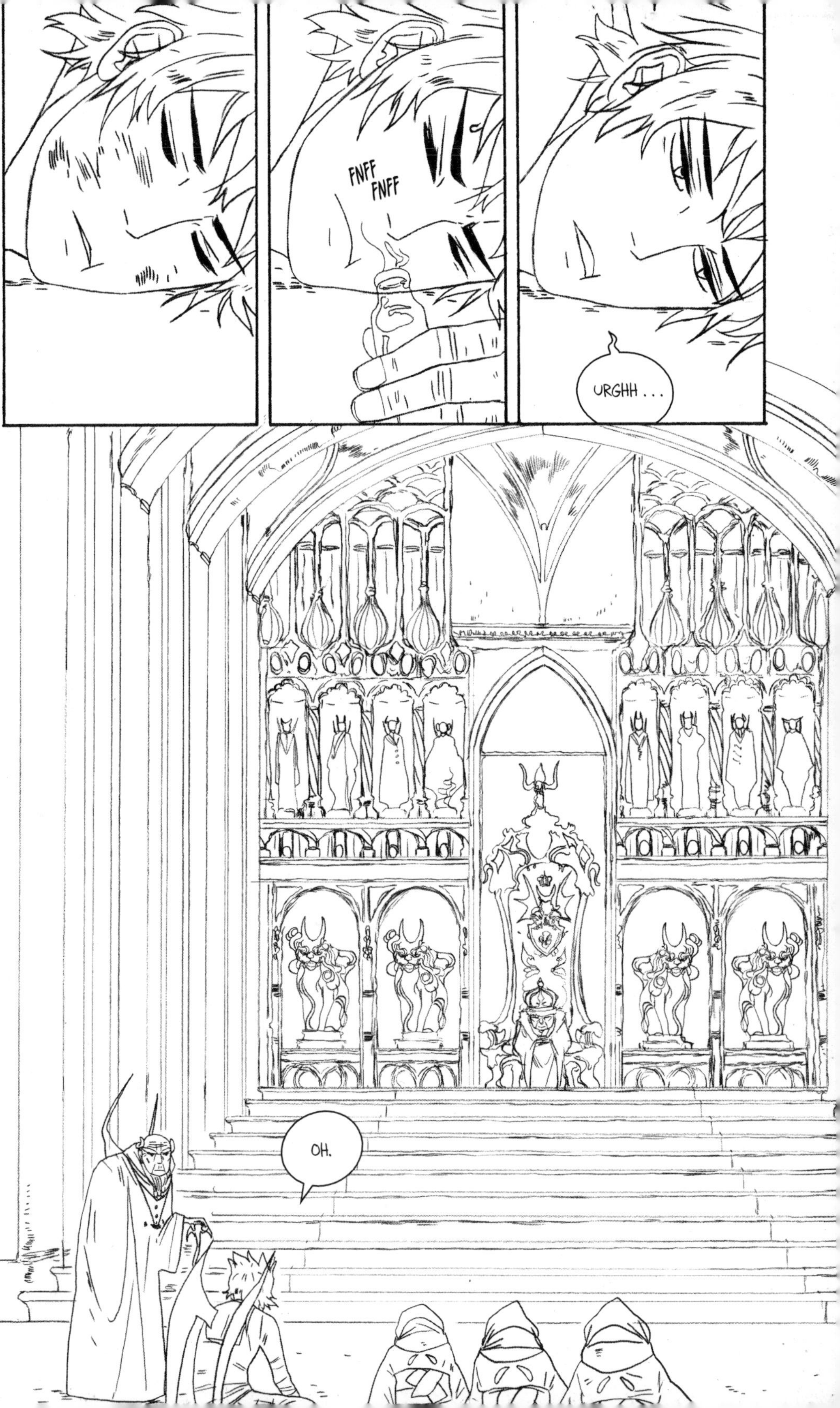
FNFF FNFF
URGHH . . .
OH.

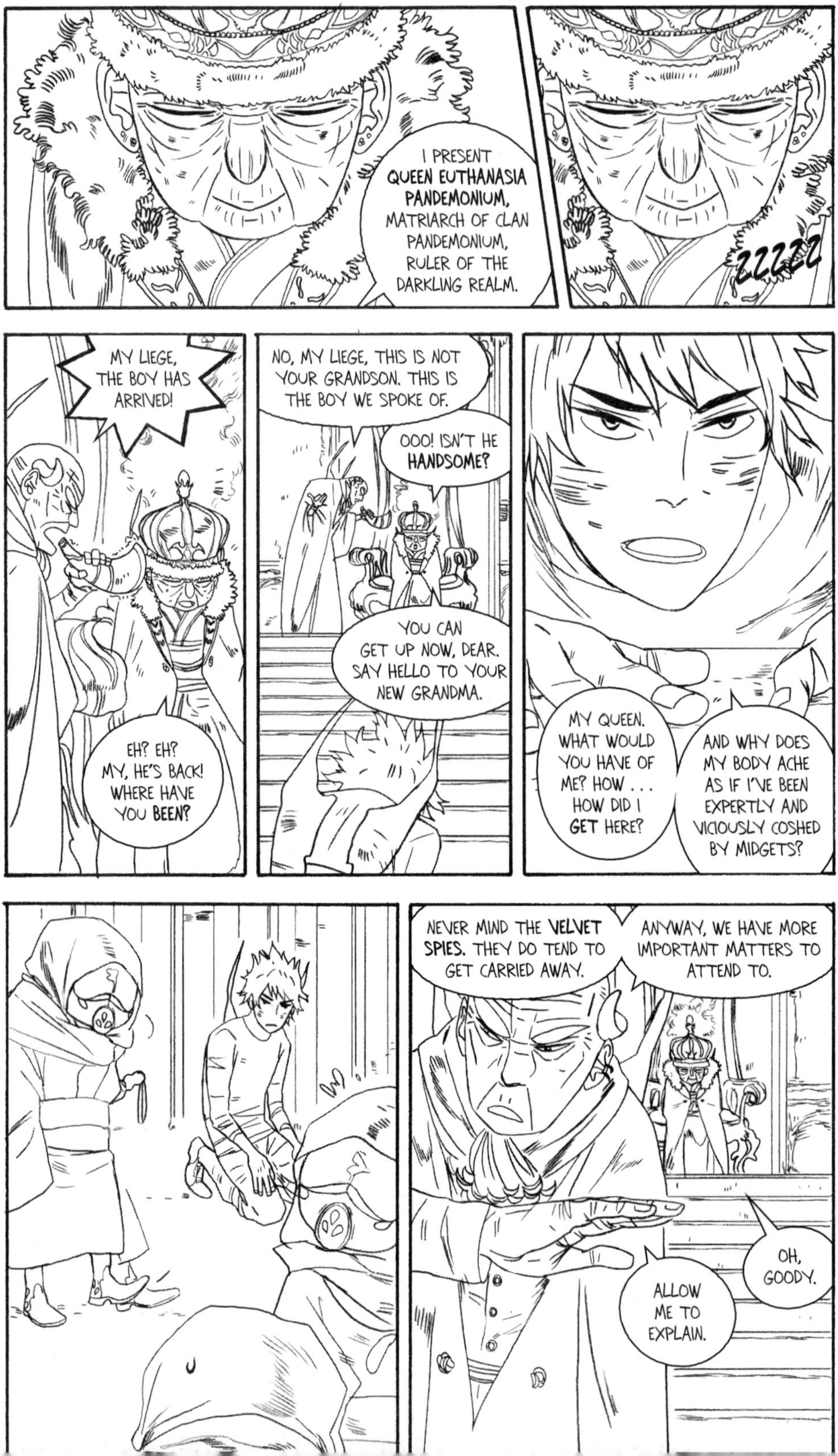
I PRESENT **QUEEN EUTHANASIA PANDEMONIUM,** MATRIARCH OF CLAN PANDEMONIUM, RULER OF THE DARKLING REALM.
ZZZZZ
MY LIEGE, THE BOY HAS ARRIVED!
EH? EH? MY, HE'S BACK! WHERE HAVE YOU **BEEN?**
NO, MY LIEGE, THIS IS NOT YOUR GRANDSON. THIS IS THE BOY WE SPOKE OF.
OOO! ISN'T HE **HANDSOME?**
YOU CAN GET UP NOW, DEAR. SAY HELLO TO YOUR NEW GRANDMA.
MY QUEEN. WHAT WOULD YOU HAVE OF ME? HOW . . . HOW DID I **GET** HERE?
AND WHY DOES MY BODY ACHE AS IF I'VE BEEN EXPERTLY AND VICIOUSLY COSHED BY MIDGETS?
NEVER MIND THE **VELVET SPIES.** THEY DO TEND TO GET CARRIED AWAY.
ANYWAY, WE HAVE MORE IMPORTANT MATTERS TO ATTEND TO.
OH, GOODY.
ALLOW ME TO EXPLAIN.

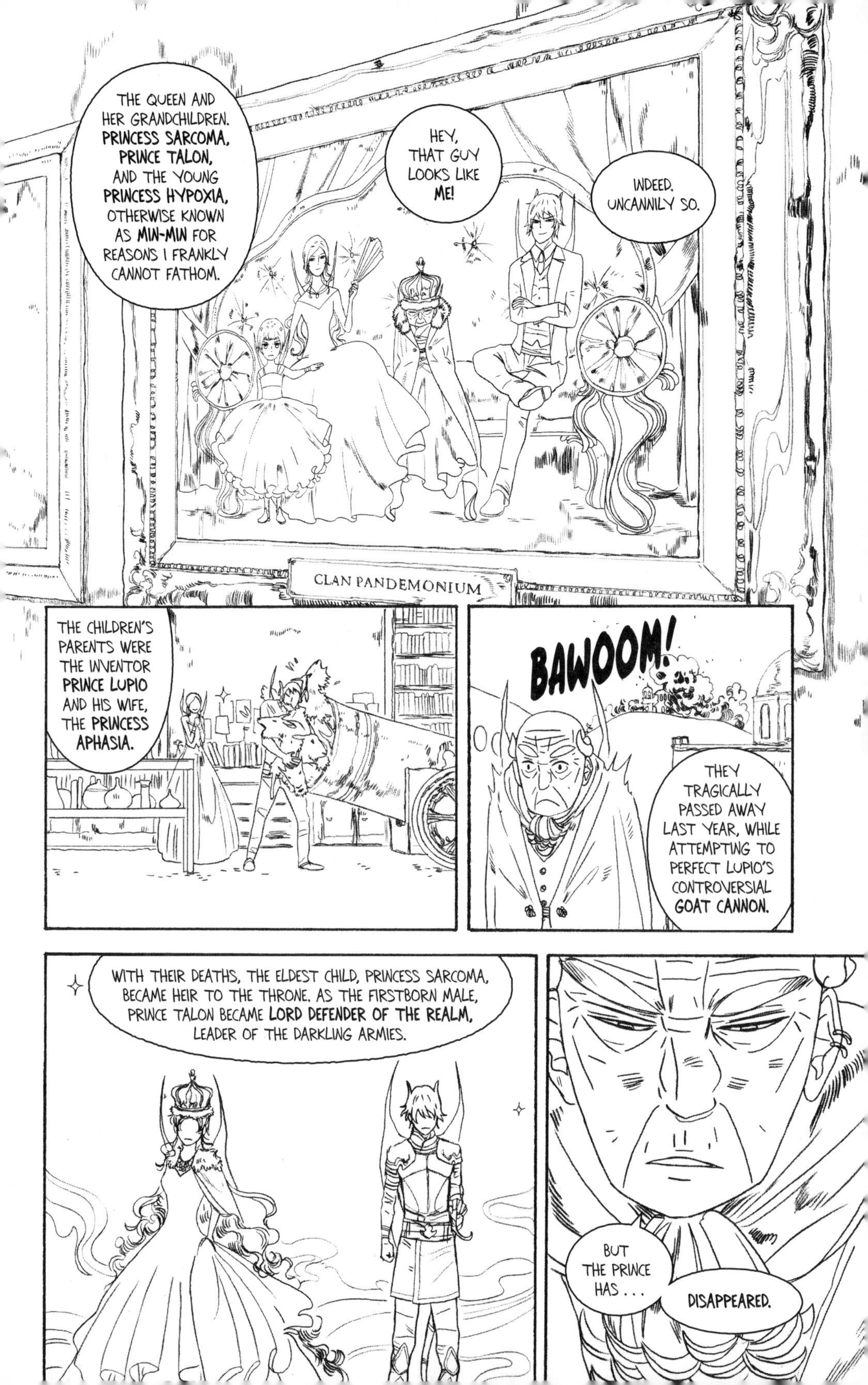
THE QUEEN AND HER GRANDCHILDREN. PRINCESS SARCOMA, PRINCE TALON, AND THE YOUNG PRINCESS HYPOXIA, OTHERWISE KNOWN AS MIN-MIN FOR REASONS I FRANKLY CANNOT FATHOM.
HEY, THAT GUY LOOKS LIKE ME!
INDEED. UNCANNILY SO.
CLAN PANDEMONIUM
THE CHILDREN'S PARENTS WERE THE INVENTOR PRINCE LUPIO AND HIS WIFE, THE PRINCESS APHASIA.
BAWOOM!
THEY TRAGICALLY PASSED AWAY LAST YEAR, WHILE ATTEMPTING TO PERFECT LUPIO'S CONTROVERSIAL GOAT CANNON.
WITH THEIR DEATHS, THE ELDEST CHILD, PRINCESS SARCOMA, BECAME HEIR TO THE THRONE. AS THE FIRSTBORN MALE, PRINCE TALON BECAME LORD DEFENDER OF THE REALM, LEADER OF THE DARKLING ARMIES.
BUT THE PRINCE HAS . . .
DISAPPEARED.

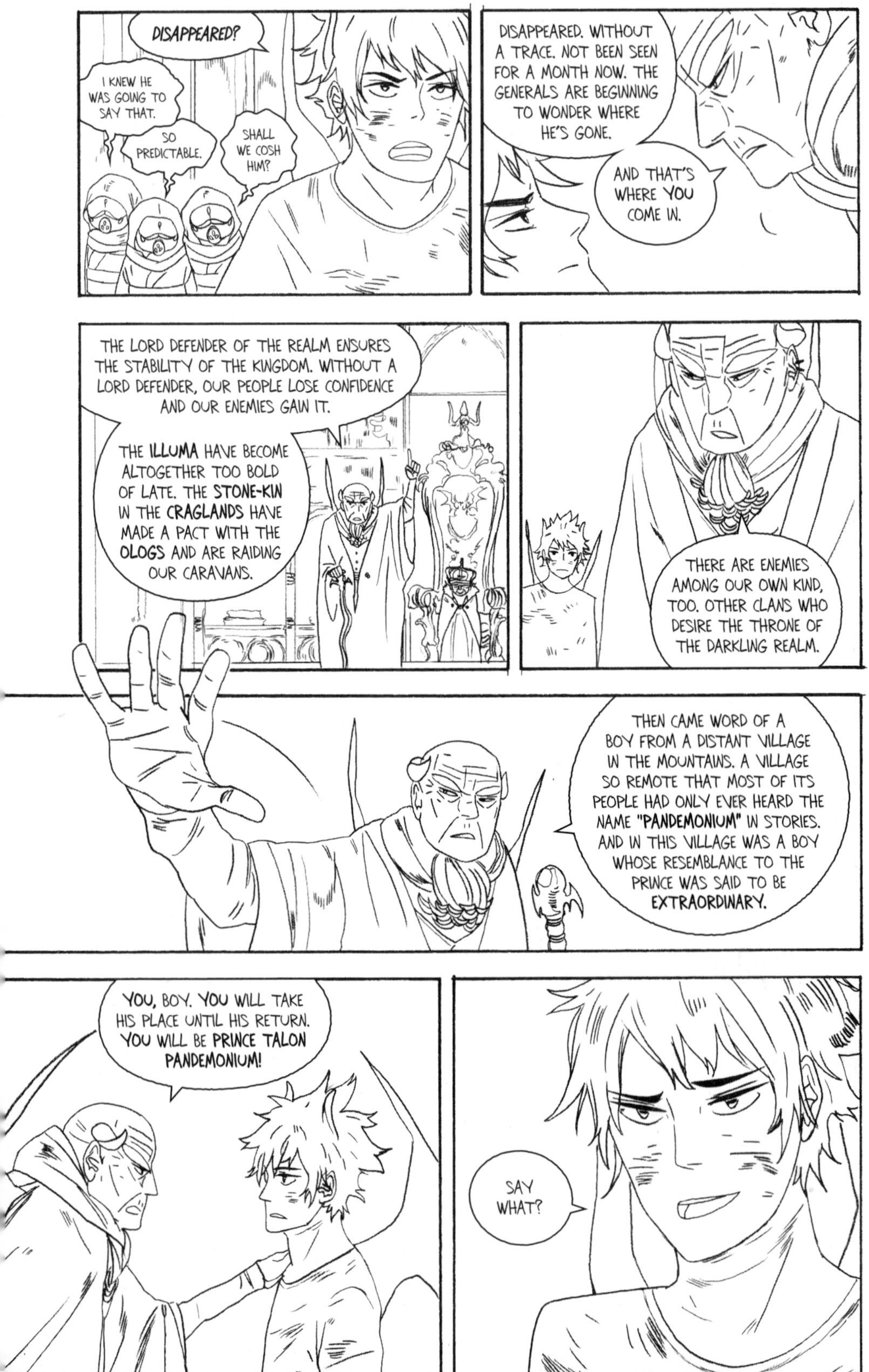
DISAPPEARED?
I KNEW HE WAS GOING TO SAY THAT.
SO PREDICTABLE.
SHALL WE COSH HIM?
DISAPPEARED. WITHOUT A TRACE. NOT BEEN SEEN FOR A MONTH NOW. THE GENERALS ARE BEGINNING TO WONDER WHERE HE'S GONE.
AND THAT'S WHERE YOU COME IN.
THE LORD DEFENDER OF THE REALM ENSURES THE STABILITY OF THE KINGDOM. WITHOUT A LORD DEFENDER, OUR PEOPLE LOSE CONFIDENCE AND OUR ENEMIES GAIN IT.
THE ILLUMA HAVE BECOME ALTOGETHER TOO BOLD OF LATE. THE STONE-KIN IN THE CRAGLANDS HAVE MADE A PACT WITH THE OLOGS AND ARE RAIDING OUR CARAVANS.
THERE ARE ENEMIES AMONG OUR OWN KIND, TOO. OTHER CLANS WHO DESIRE THE THRONE OF THE DARKLING REALM.
THEN CAME WORD OF A BOY FROM A DISTANT VILLAGE IN THE MOUNTAINS. A VILLAGE SO REMOTE THAT MOST OF ITS PEOPLE HAD ONLY EVER HEARD THE NAME "PANDEMONIUM" IN STORIES. AND IN THIS VILLAGE WAS A BOY WHOSE RESEMBLANCE TO THE PRINCE WAS SAID TO BE EXTRAORDINARY.
YOU, BOY. YOU WILL TAKE HIS PLACE UNTIL HIS RETURN. YOU WILL BE PRINCE TALON PANDEMONIUM!
SAY WHAT?

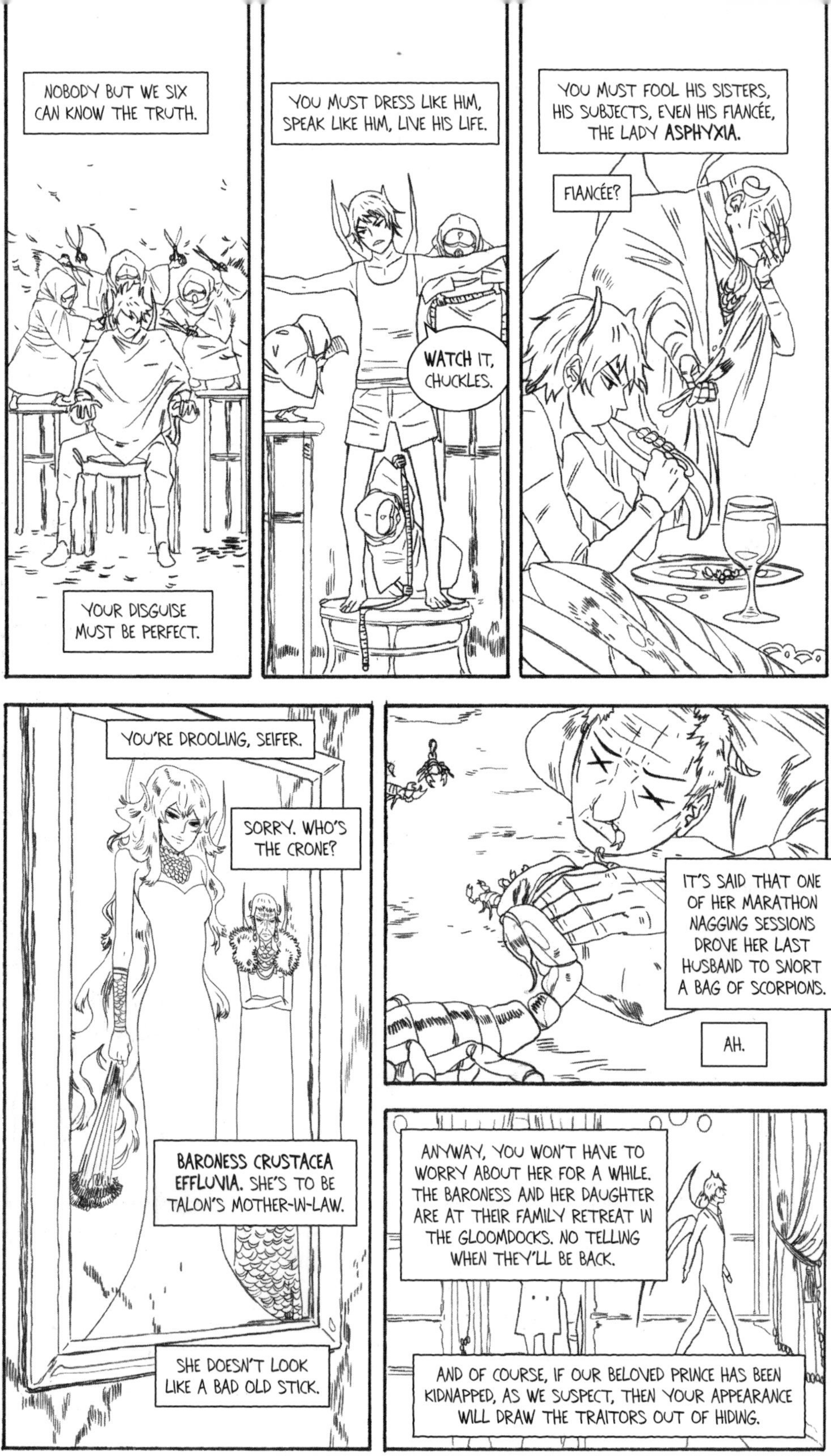
NOBODY BUT WE SIX CAN KNOW THE TRUTH.
YOUR DISGUISE MUST BE PERFECT.
YOU MUST DRESS LIKE HIM, SPEAK LIKE HIM, LIVE HIS LIFE.
WATCH IT, CHUCKLES.
YOU MUST FOOL HIS SISTERS, HIS SUBJECTS, EVEN HIS FIANCÉE, THE LADY ASPHYXIA.
FIANCÉE?
YOU'RE DROOLING, SEIFER.
SORRY. WHO'S THE CRONE?
BARONESS CRUSTACEA EFFLUVIA. SHE'S TO BE TALON'S MOTHER-IN-LAW.
SHE DOESN'T LOOK LIKE A BAD OLD STICK.
IT'S SAID THAT ONE OF HER MARATHON NAGGING SESSIONS DROVE HER LAST HUSBAND TO SNORT A BAG OF SCORPIONS.
AH.
ANYWAY, YOU WON'T HAVE TO WORRY ABOUT HER FOR A WHILE. THE BARONESS AND HER DAUGHTER ARE AT THEIR FAMILY RETREAT IN THE GLOOMDOCKS. NO TELLING WHEN THEY'LL BE BACK.
AND OF COURSE, IF OUR BELOVED PRINCE HAS BEEN KIDNAPPED, AS WE SUSPECT, THEN YOUR APPEARANCE WILL DRAW THE TRAITORS OUT OF HIDING.

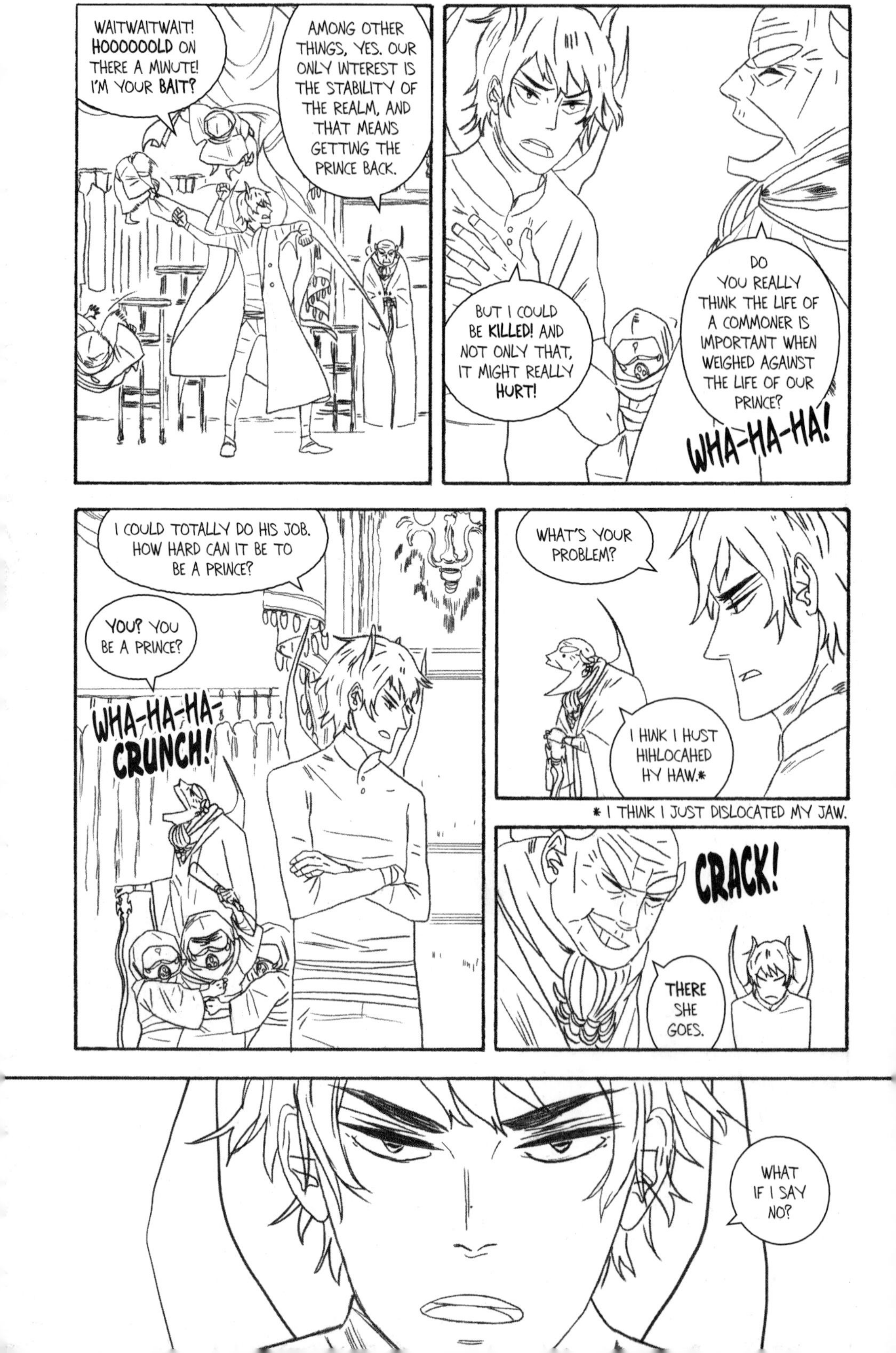
WAITWAITWAIT! HOOOOOOLD ON THERE A MINUTE! I'M YOUR BAIT?
AMONG OTHER THINGS, YES. OUR ONLY INTEREST IS THE STABILITY OF THE REALM, AND THAT MEANS GETTING THE PRINCE BACK.
BUT I COULD BE KILLED! AND NOT ONLY THAT, IT MIGHT REALLY HURT!
DO YOU REALLY THINK THE LIFE OF A COMMONER IS IMPORTANT WHEN WEIGHED AGAINST THE LIFE OF OUR PRINCE?
WHA-HA-HA!
I COULD TOTALLY DO HIS JOB. HOW HARD CAN IT BE TO BE A PRINCE?
YOU? YOU BE A PRINCE?
WHA-HA-HA-CRUNCH!
WHAT'S YOUR PROBLEM?
I HINK I HUST HIHLOCAHED HY HAW.*
* I THINK I JUST DISLOCATED MY JAW.
CRACK!
THERE SHE GOES.
WHAT IF I SAY NO?

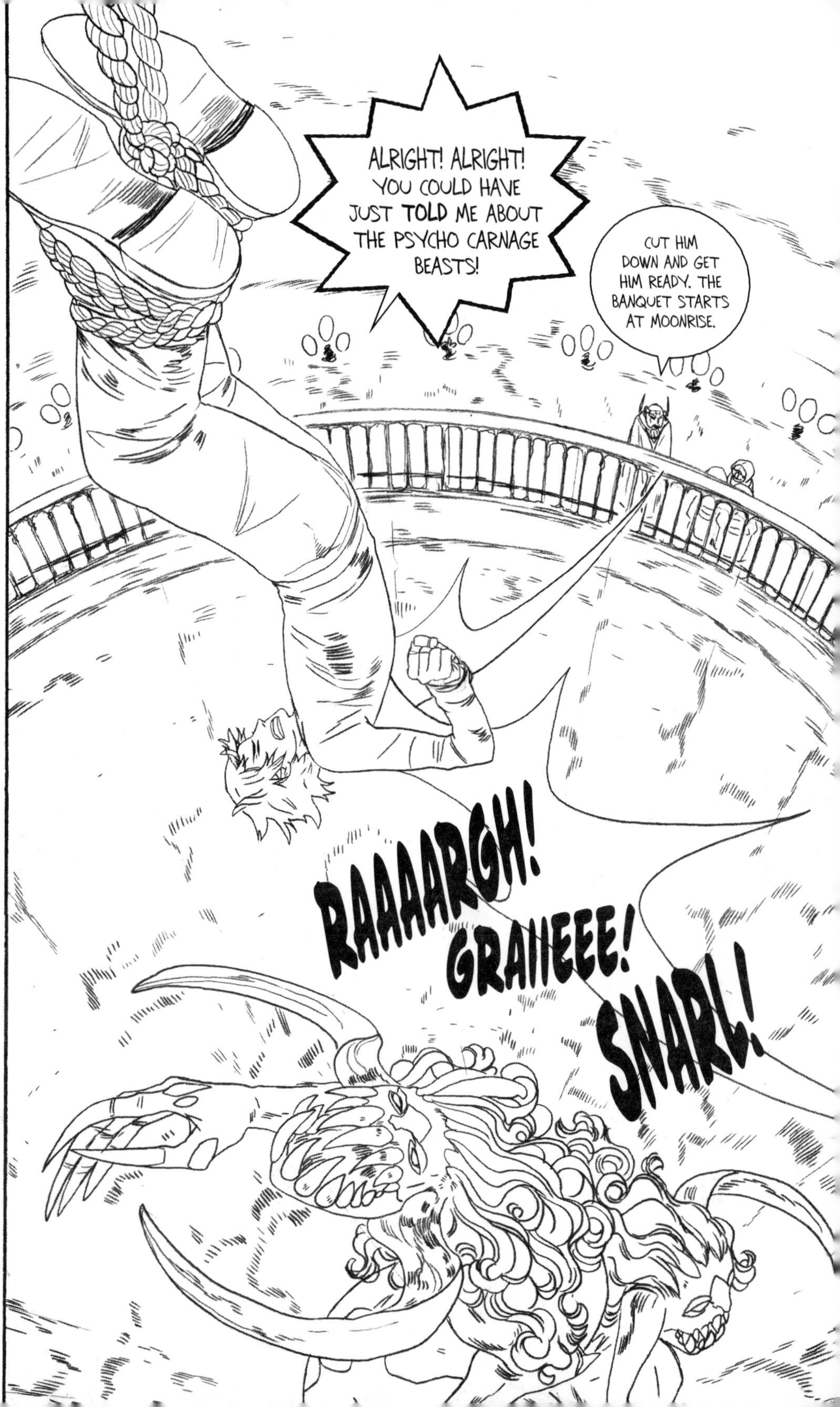
ALRIGHT! ALRIGHT! YOU COULD HAVE JUST TOLD ME ABOUT THE PSYCHO CARNAGE BEASTS!
CUT HIM DOWN AND GET HIM READY. THE BANQUET STARTS AT MOONRISE.
RAAAARGH!
GRAIIEEE!
SNARL!

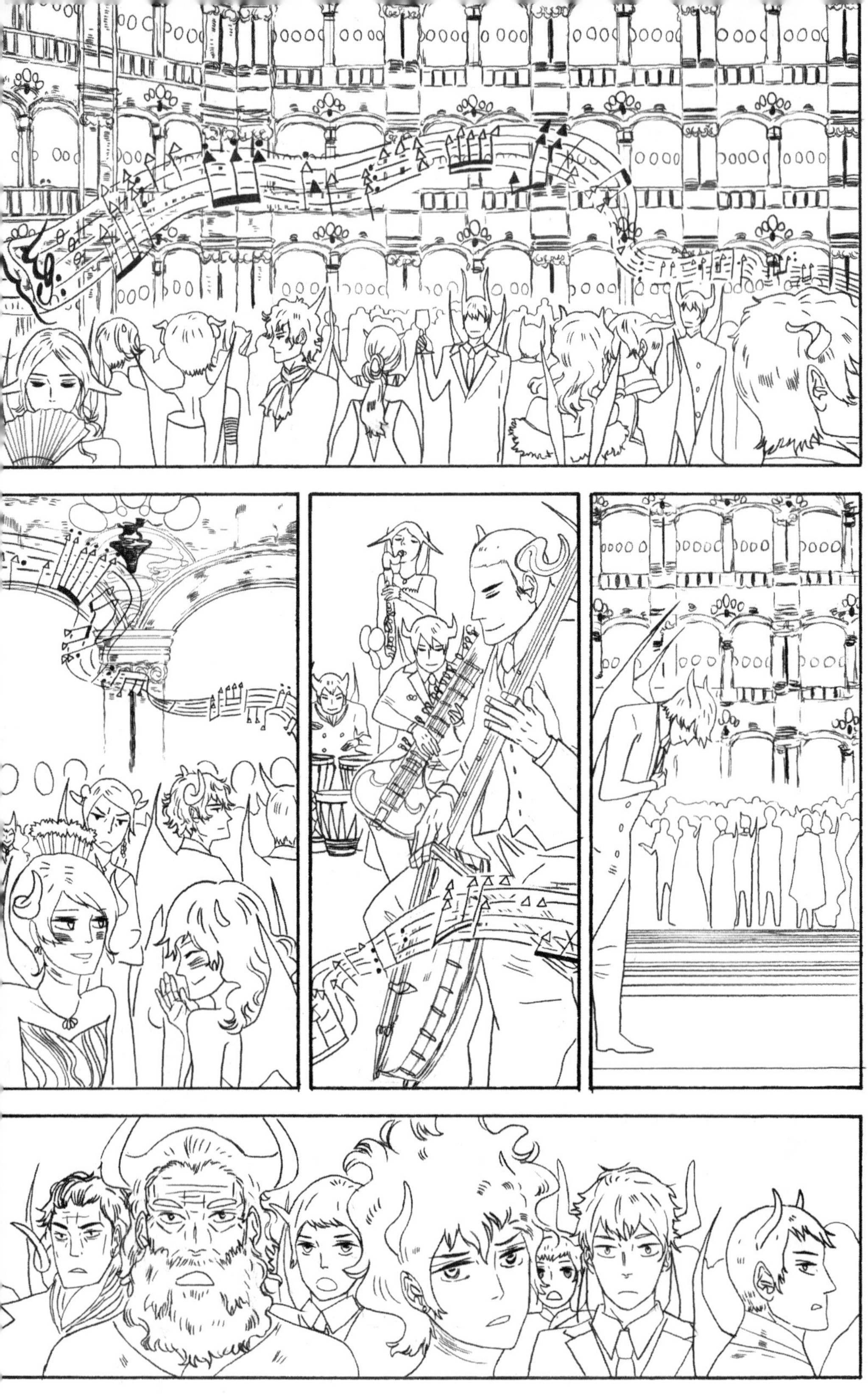

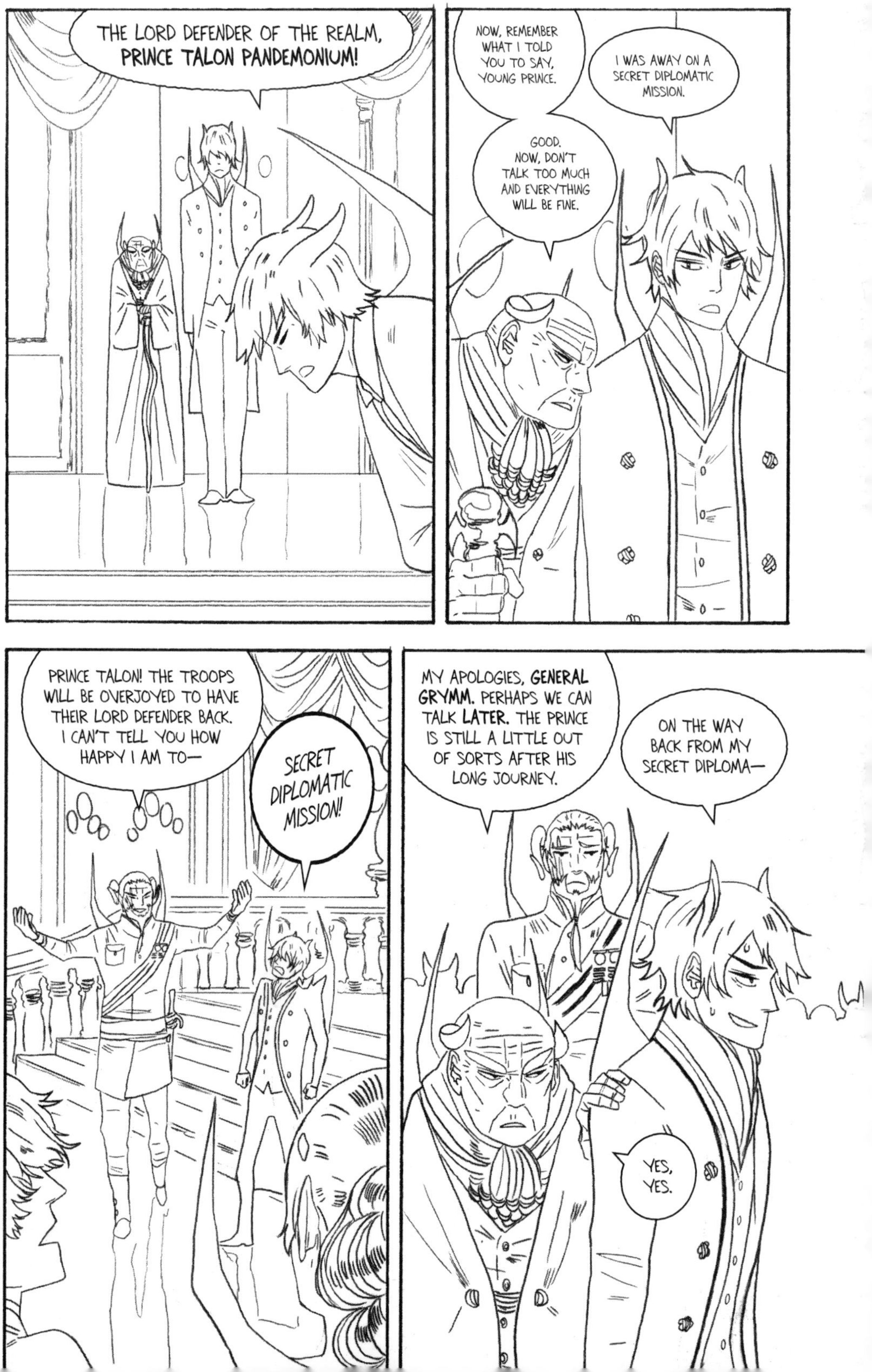
THE LORD DEFENDER OF THE REALM, **PRINCE TALON PANDEMONIUM!**
NOW, REMEMBER WHAT I TOLD YOU TO SAY, YOUNG PRINCE.
I WAS AWAY ON A SECRET DIPLOMATIC MISSION.
GOOD. NOW, DON'T TALK TOO MUCH AND EVERYTHING WILL BE FINE.
PRINCE TALON! THE TROOPS WILL BE OVERJOYED TO HAVE THEIR LORD DEFENDER BACK. I CAN'T TELL YOU HOW HAPPY I AM TO—
SECRET DIPLOMATIC MISSION!
MY APOLOGIES, **GENERAL GRYMM.** PERHAPS WE CAN TALK **LATER.** THE PRINCE IS STILL A LITTLE OUT OF SORTS AFTER HIS LONG JOURNEY.
ON THE WAY BACK FROM MY SECRET DIPLOMA—
YES, YES.

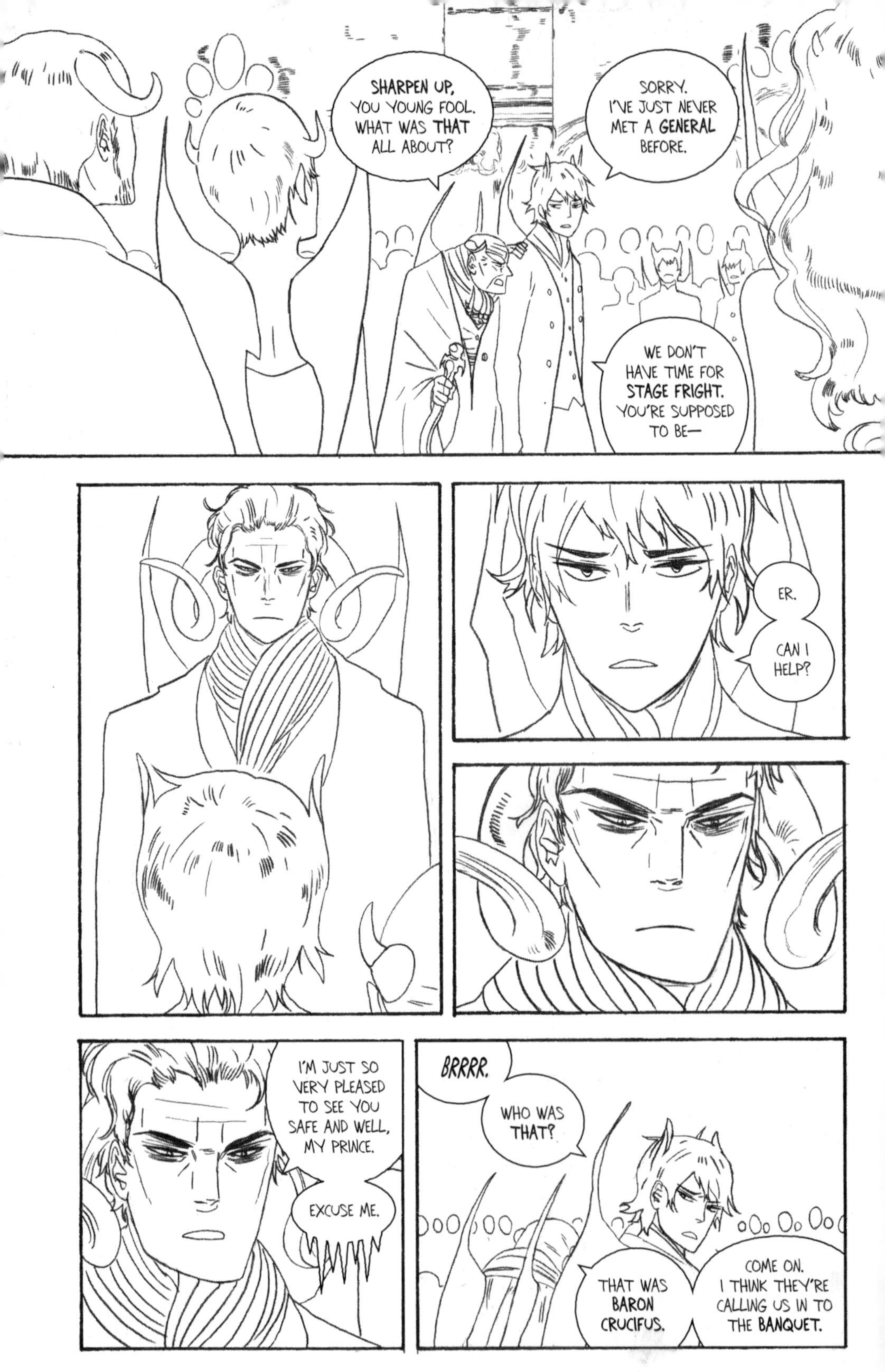
SHARPEN UP, YOU YOUNG FOOL. WHAT WAS THAT ALL ABOUT?
SORRY. I'VE JUST NEVER MET A GENERAL BEFORE.
WE DON'T HAVE TIME FOR STAGE FRIGHT. YOU'RE SUPPOSED TO BE—
ER.
CAN I HELP?
I'M JUST SO VERY PLEASED TO SEE YOU SAFE AND WELL, MY PRINCE.
EXCUSE ME.
BRRRR.
WHO WAS THAT?
THAT WAS BARON CRUCIFUS.
COME ON. I THINK THEY'RE CALLING US IN TO THE BANQUET.

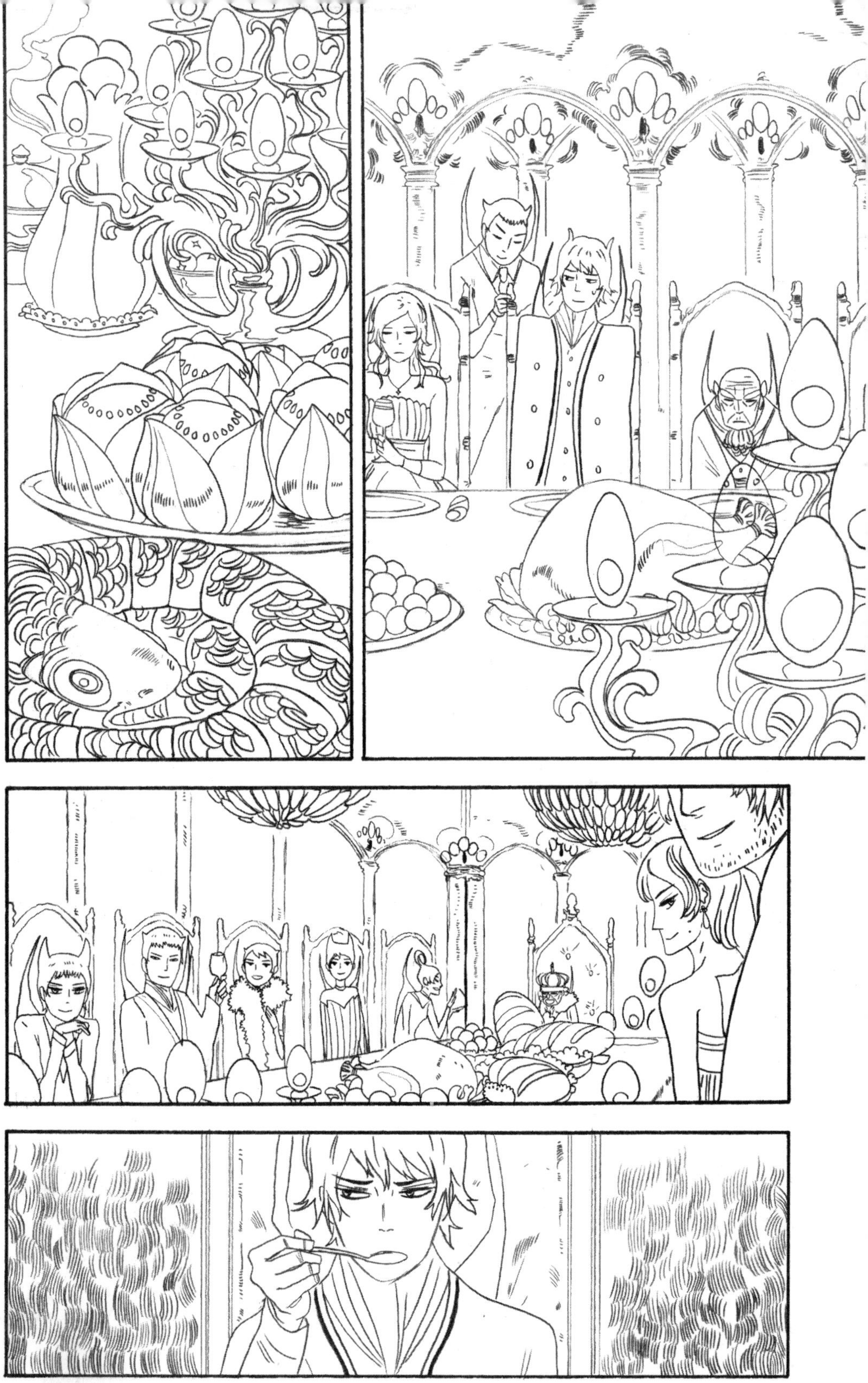

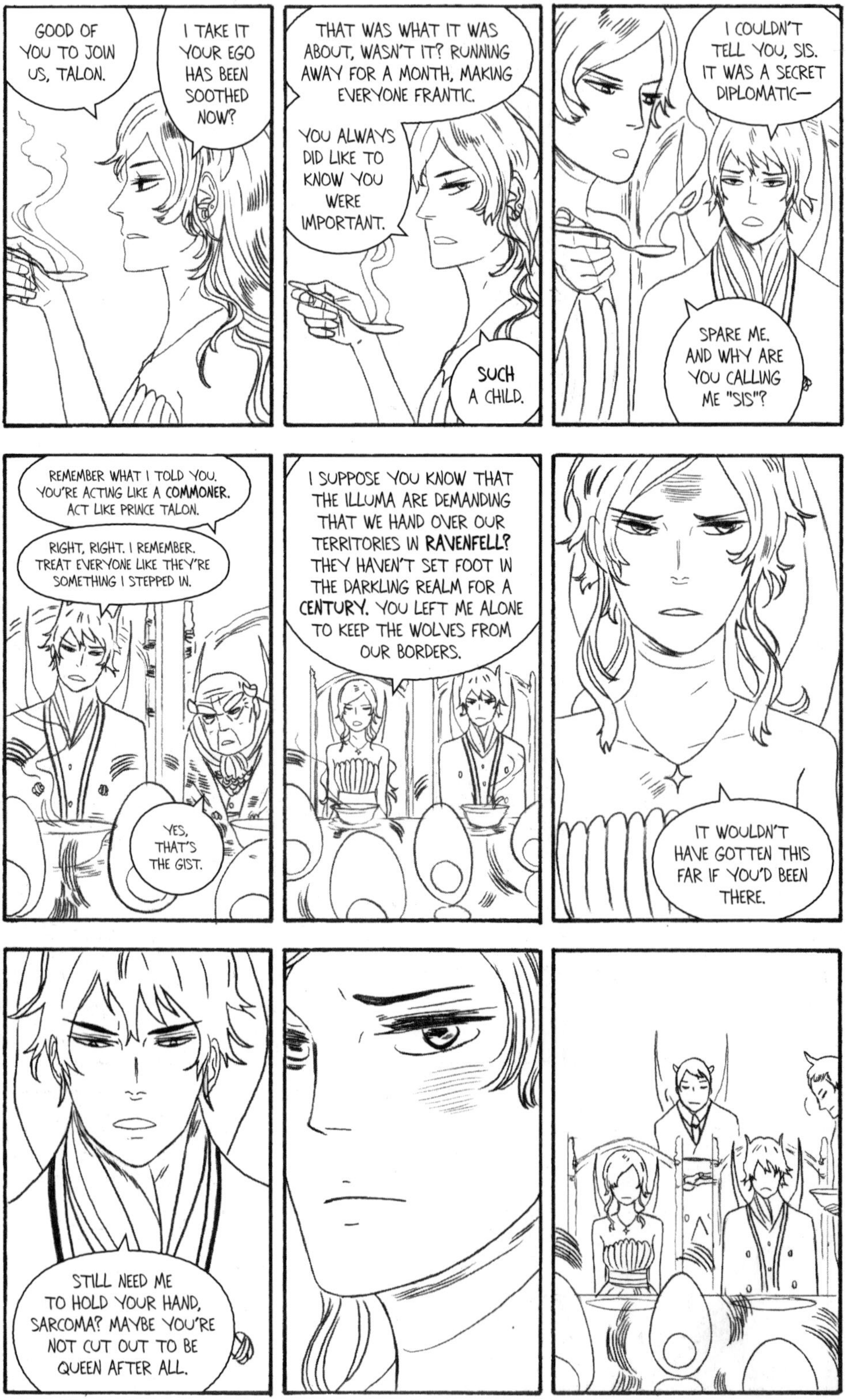
GOOD OF YOU TO JOIN US, TALON.
I TAKE IT YOUR EGO HAS BEEN SOOTHED NOW?
THAT WAS WHAT IT WAS ABOUT, WASN'T IT? RUNNING AWAY FOR A MONTH, MAKING EVERYONE FRANTIC.
YOU ALWAYS DID LIKE TO KNOW YOU WERE IMPORTANT.
SUCH A CHILD.
I COULDN'T TELL YOU, SIS. IT WAS A SECRET DIPLOMATIC—
SPARE ME. AND WHY ARE YOU CALLING ME "SIS"?
REMEMBER WHAT I TOLD YOU. YOU'RE ACTING LIKE A COMMONER. ACT LIKE PRINCE TALON.
RIGHT, RIGHT. I REMEMBER. TREAT EVERYONE LIKE THEY'RE SOMETHING I STEPPED IN.
YES, THAT'S THE GIST.
I SUPPOSE YOU KNOW THAT THE ILLUMA ARE DEMANDING THAT WE HAND OVER OUR TERRITORIES IN RAVENFELL? THEY HAVEN'T SET FOOT IN THE DARKLING REALM FOR A CENTURY. YOU LEFT ME ALONE TO KEEP THE WOLVES FROM OUR BORDERS.
IT WOULDN'T HAVE GOTTEN THIS FAR IF YOU'D BEEN THERE.
STILL NEED ME TO HOLD YOUR HAND, SARCOMA? MAYBE YOU'RE NOT CUT OUT TO BE QUEEN AFTER ALL.

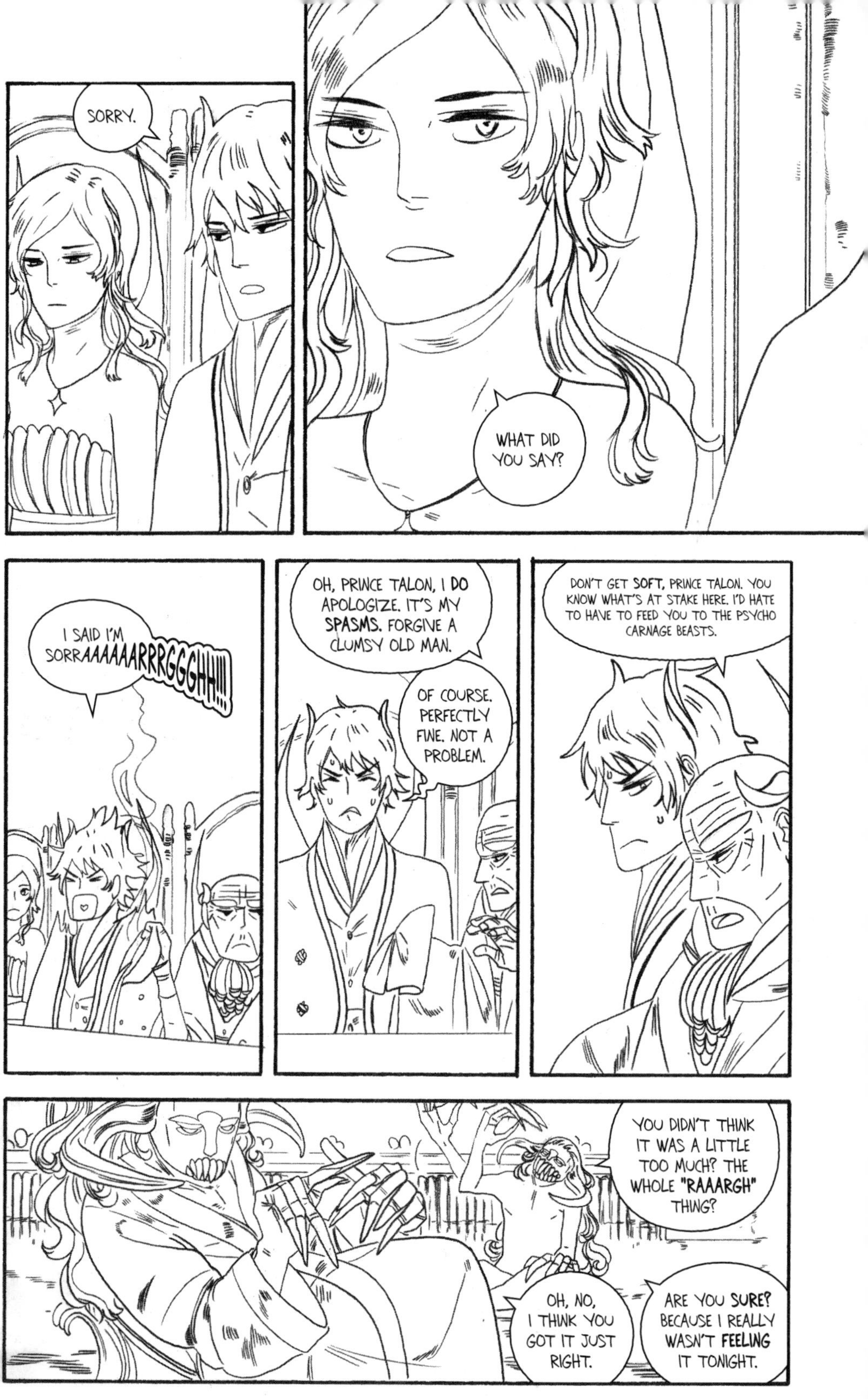
SORRY.
WHAT DID YOU SAY?
I SAID I'M SORRAAAAAARRRGGGHH!!!!
OH, PRINCE TALON, I DO APOLOGIZE. IT'S MY SPASMS. FORGIVE A CLUMSY OLD MAN.
OF COURSE. PERFECTLY FINE. NOT A PROBLEM.
DON'T GET SOFT, PRINCE TALON. YOU KNOW WHAT'S AT STAKE HERE. I'D HATE TO HAVE TO FEED YOU TO THE PSYCHO CARNAGE BEASTS.
YOU DIDN'T THINK IT WAS A LITTLE TOO MUCH? THE WHOLE "RAAARGH" THING?
ARE YOU SURE? BECAUSE I REALLY WASN'T FEELING IT TONIGHT.
OH, NO, I THINK YOU GOT IT JUST RIGHT.

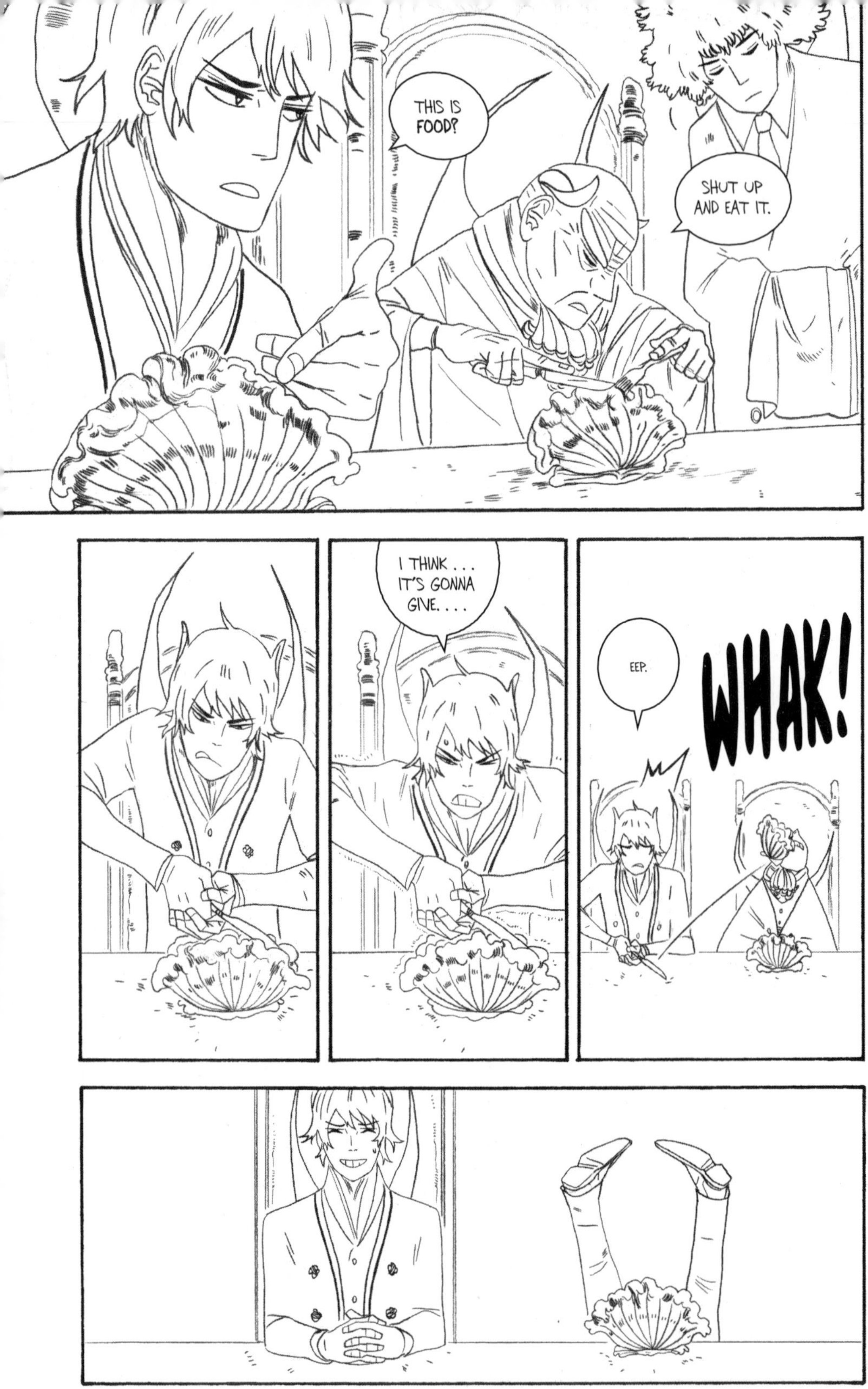
THIS IS FOOD?
SHUT UP AND EAT IT.
I THINK . . . IT'S GONNA GIVE. . . .
EEP.
WHAK!

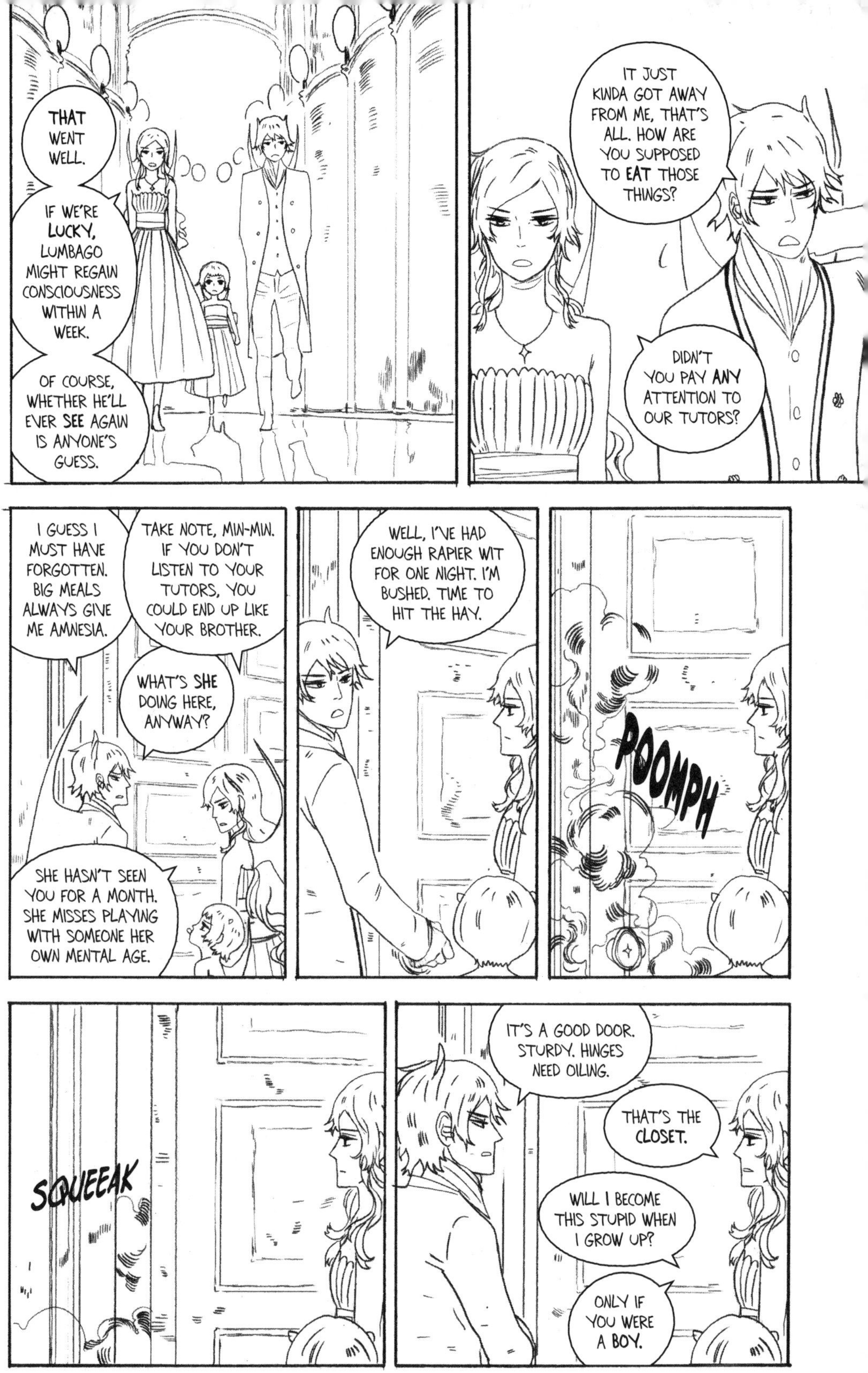
THAT WENT WELL.
IF WE'RE LUCKY, LUMBAGO MIGHT REGAIN CONSCIOUSNESS WITHIN A WEEK.
OF COURSE, WHETHER HE'LL EVER SEE AGAIN IS ANYONE'S GUESS.
IT JUST KINDA GOT AWAY FROM ME, THAT'S ALL. HOW ARE YOU SUPPOSED TO EAT THOSE THINGS?
DIDN'T YOU PAY ANY ATTENTION TO OUR TUTORS?
I GUESS I MUST HAVE FORGOTTEN. BIG MEALS ALWAYS GIVE ME AMNESIA.
TAKE NOTE, MIN-MIN. IF YOU DON'T LISTEN TO YOUR TUTORS, YOU COULD END UP LIKE YOUR BROTHER.
WHAT'S SHE DOING HERE, ANYWAY?
SHE HASN'T SEEN YOU FOR A MONTH. SHE MISSES PLAYING WITH SOMEONE HER OWN MENTAL AGE.
WELL, I'VE HAD ENOUGH RAPIER WIT FOR ONE NIGHT. I'M BUSHED. TIME TO HIT THE HAY.
POOMPH
SQUEEEAK
IT'S A GOOD DOOR. STURDY. HINGES NEED OILING.
THAT'S THE CLOSET.
WILL I BECOME THIS STUPID WHEN I GROW UP?
ONLY IF YOU WERE A BOY.

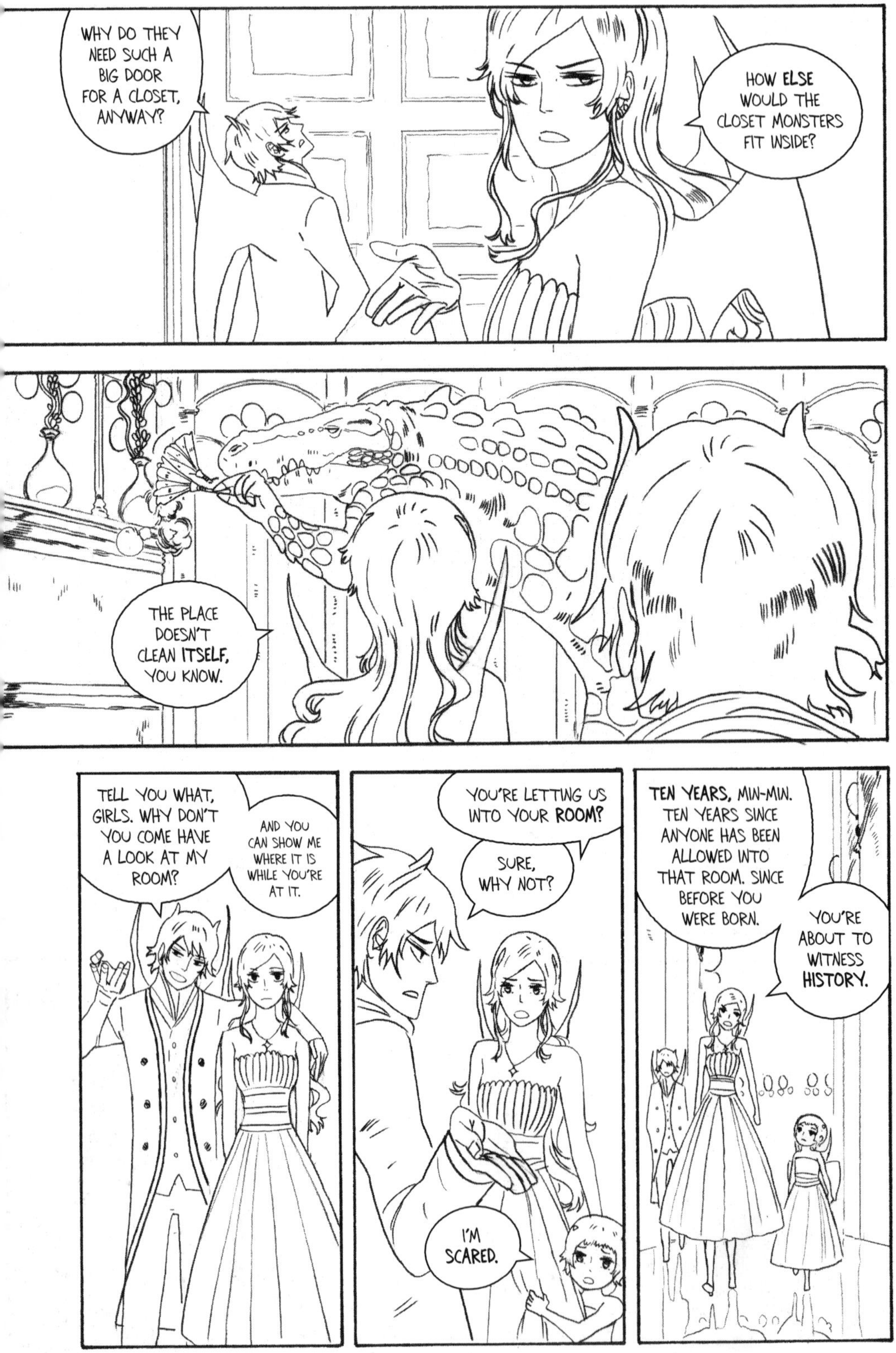
WHY DO THEY NEED SUCH A BIG DOOR FOR A CLOSET, ANYWAY?
HOW **ELSE** WOULD THE CLOSET MONSTERS FIT INSIDE?
THE PLACE DOESN'T CLEAN **ITSELF,** YOU KNOW.
TELL YOU WHAT, GIRLS. WHY DON'T YOU COME HAVE A LOOK AT MY ROOM?
AND YOU CAN SHOW ME WHERE IT IS WHILE YOU'RE AT IT.
YOU'RE LETTING US INTO YOUR **ROOM?**
SURE, WHY NOT?
I'M **SCARED.**
TEN YEARS, MIN-MIN. TEN YEARS SINCE ANYONE HAS BEEN ALLOWED INTO THAT ROOM. SINCE BEFORE YOU WERE BORN.
YOU'RE ABOUT TO WITNESS **HISTORY.**

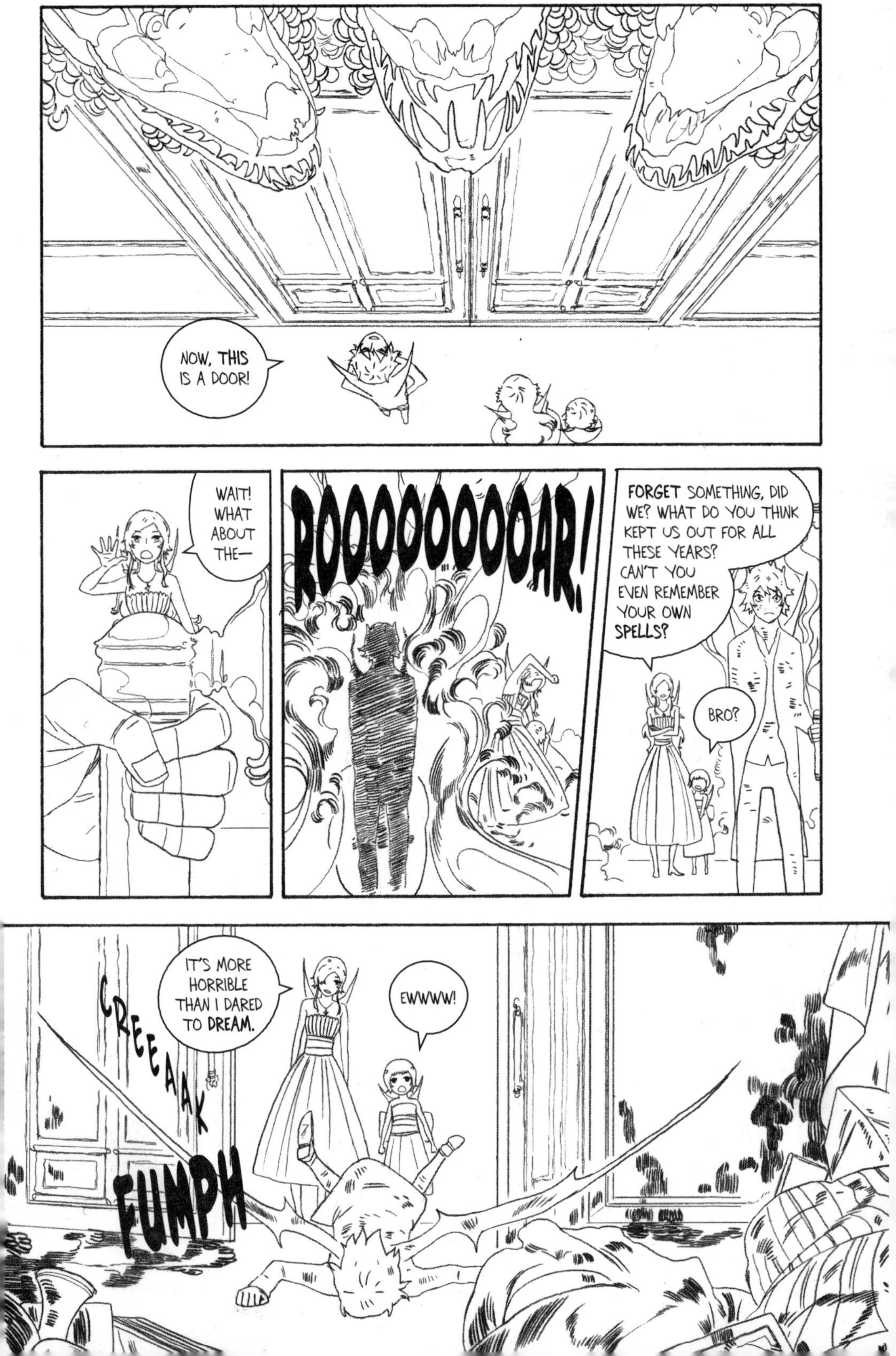
NOW, THIS IS A DOOR!
WAIT! WHAT ABOUT THE—
ROOOOOOOOAR!
FORGET SOMETHING, DID WE? WHAT DO YOU THINK KEPT US OUT FOR ALL THESE YEARS? CAN'T YOU EVEN REMEMBER YOUR OWN SPELLS?
BRO?
CREEEAAAK
FUMPH
IT'S MORE HORRIBLE THAN I DARED TO DREAM.
EWWWW!

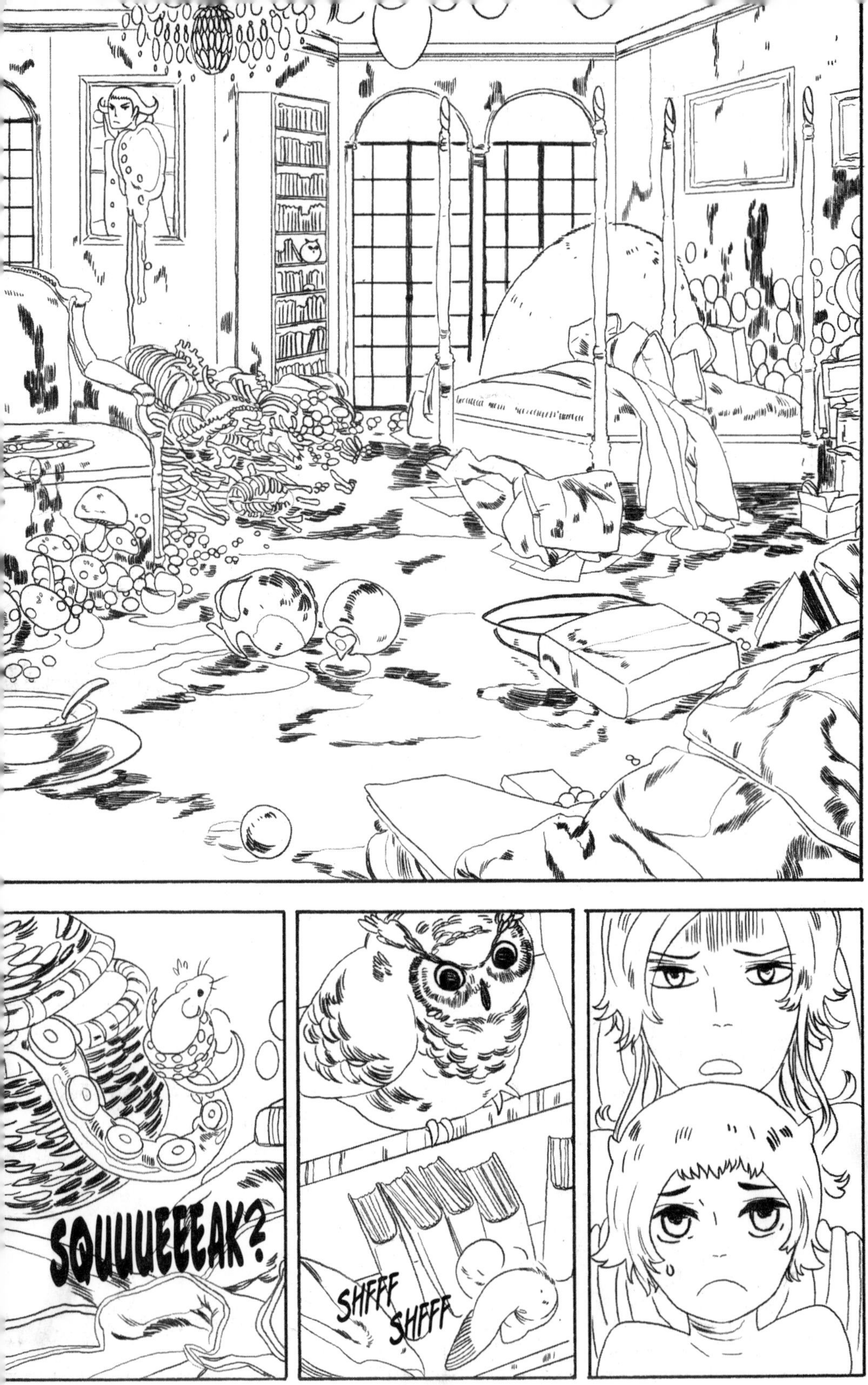
SQUUUEEEAK?
SHFFF
SHFFF

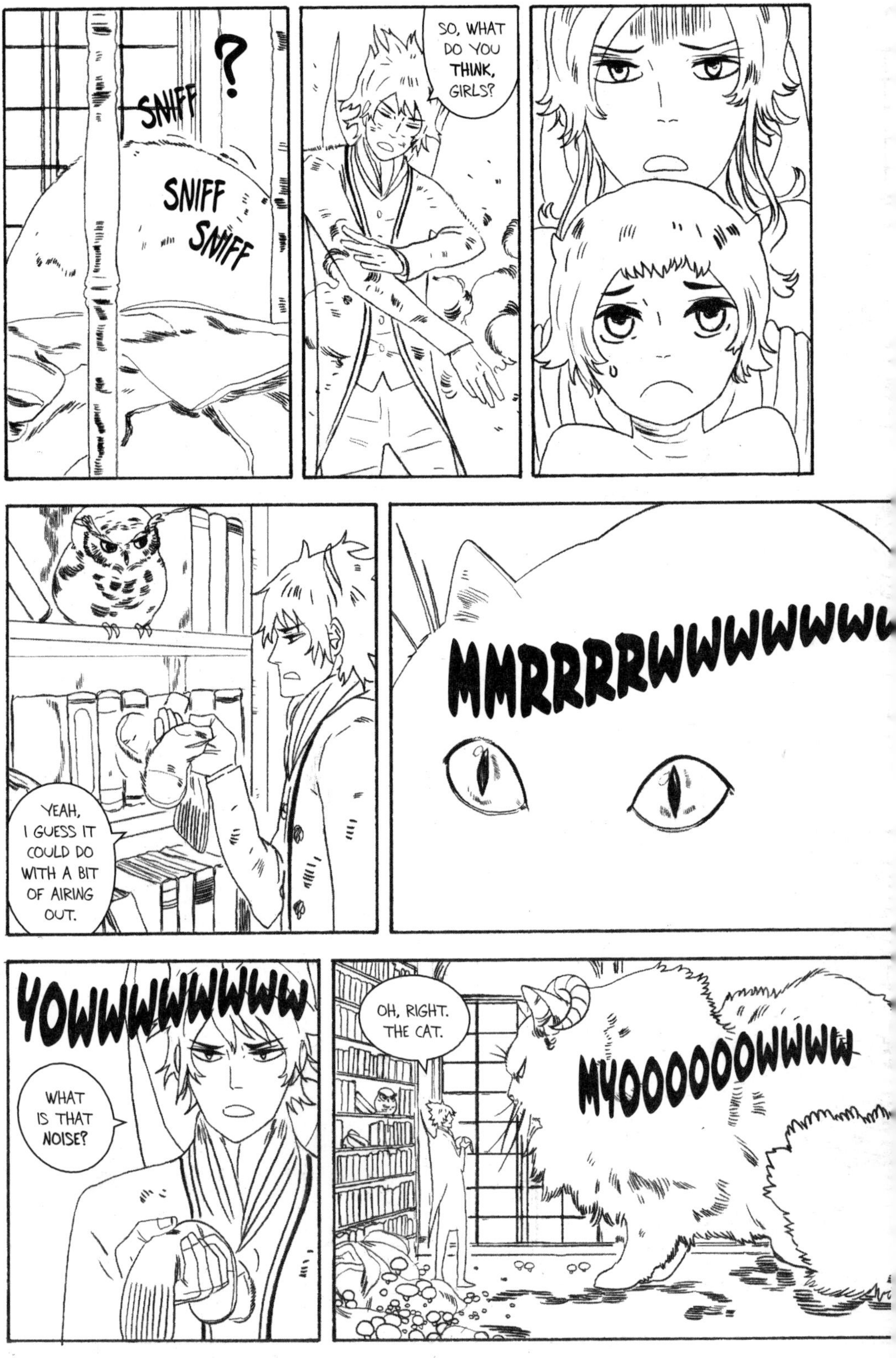
SNIFF
?
SNIFF
SNIFF
SO, WHAT DO YOU THINK, GIRLS?
YEAH, I GUESS IT COULD DO WITH A BIT OF AIRING OUT.
MMRRRRWWWWWW
YOWWWWWWWW
WHAT IS THAT NOISE?
OH, RIGHT. THE CAT.
MYOOOOOOWWWW

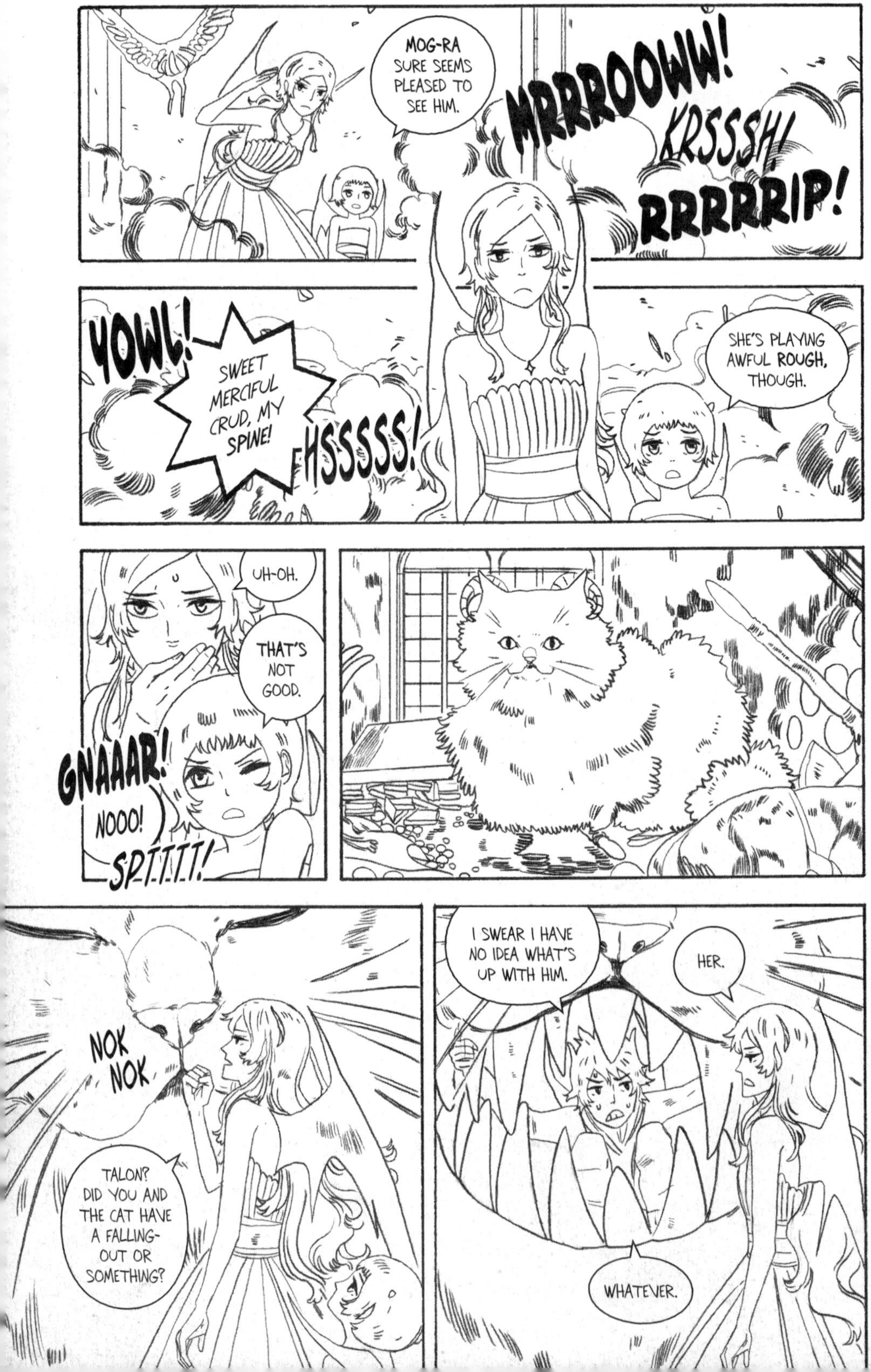
MOG-RA SURE SEEMS PLEASED TO SEE HIM.
MRRROOWW!
KRSSSH!
RRRRRIP!
YOWL!
SWEET MERCIFUL CRUD, MY SPINE!
HSSSSS!
SHE'S PLAYING AWFUL ROUGH, THOUGH.
UH-OH.
THAT'S NOT GOOD.
GNAAAR!
NOOO!
SPTTTTT!
NOK NOK
TALON? DID YOU AND THE CAT HAVE A FALLING-OUT OR SOMETHING?
I SWEAR I HAVE NO IDEA WHAT'S UP WITH HIM.
HER.
WHATEVER.

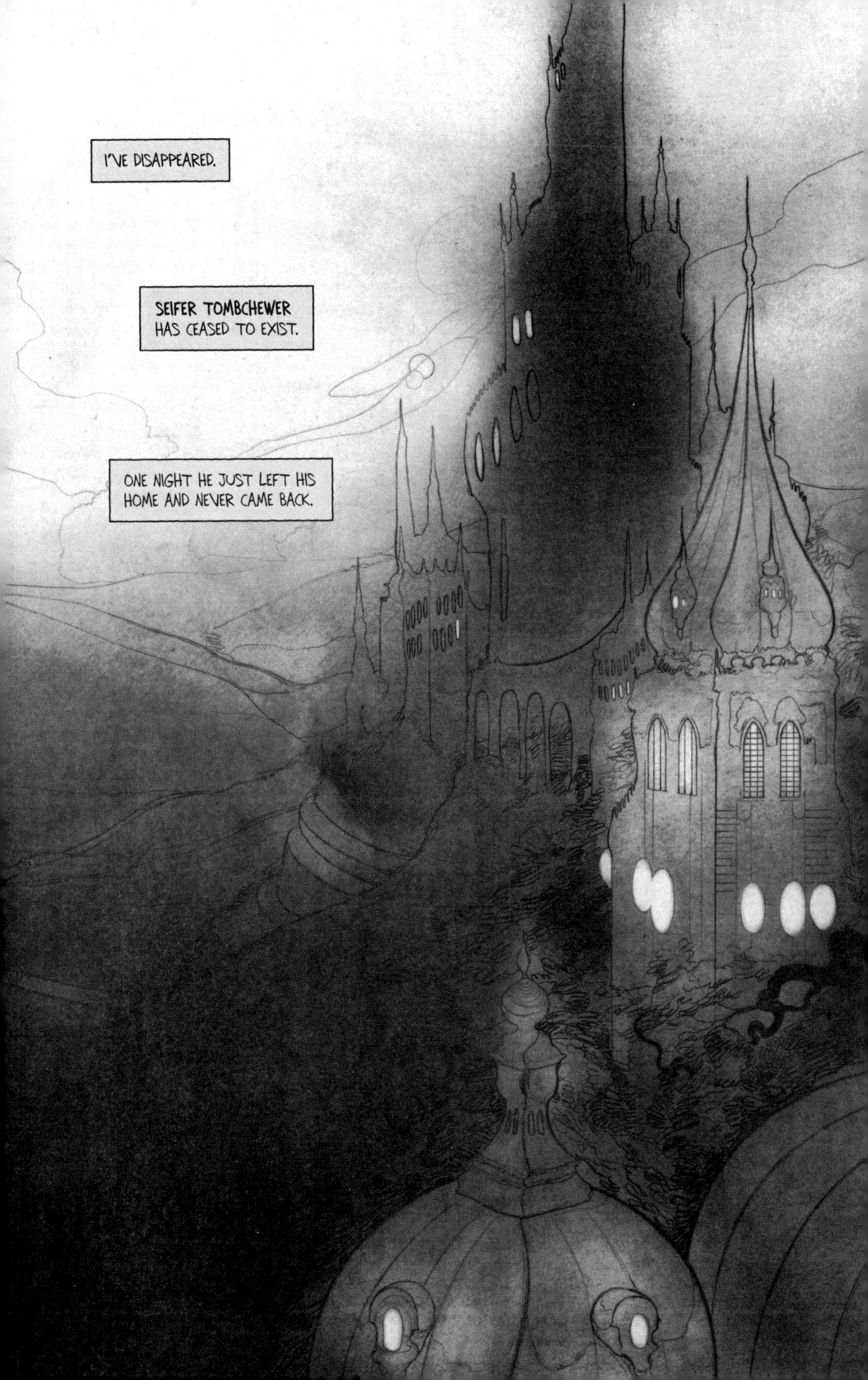
I'VE DISAPPEARED.
SEIFER TOMBCHEWER HAS CEASED TO EXIST.
ONE NIGHT HE JUST LEFT HIS HOME AND NEVER CAME BACK.

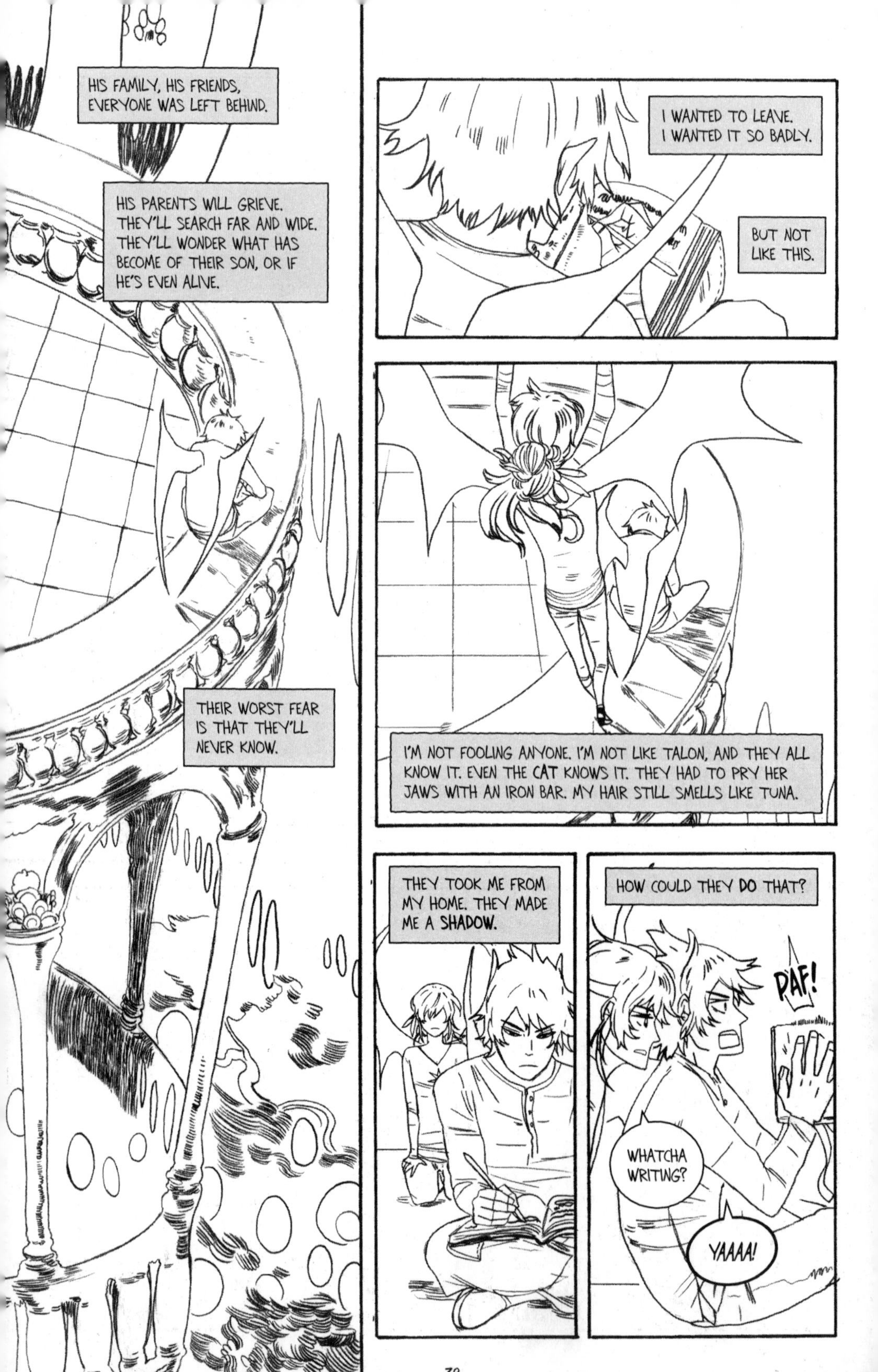
HIS FAMILY, HIS FRIENDS, EVERYONE WAS LEFT BEHIND.
HIS PARENTS WILL GRIEVE. THEY'LL SEARCH FAR AND WIDE. THEY'LL WONDER WHAT HAS BECOME OF THEIR SON, OR IF HE'S EVEN ALIVE.
THEIR WORST FEAR IS THAT THEY'LL NEVER KNOW.
I WANTED TO LEAVE. I WANTED IT SO BADLY.
BUT NOT LIKE THIS.
I'M NOT FOOLING ANYONE. I'M NOT LIKE TALON, AND THEY ALL KNOW IT. EVEN THE CAT KNOWS IT. THEY HAD TO PRY HER JAWS WITH AN IRON BAR. MY HAIR STILL SMELLS LIKE TUNA.
THEY TOOK ME FROM MY HOME. THEY MADE ME A SHADOW.
HOW COULD THEY DO THAT?
PAF!
WHATCHA WRITING?
YAAAA!

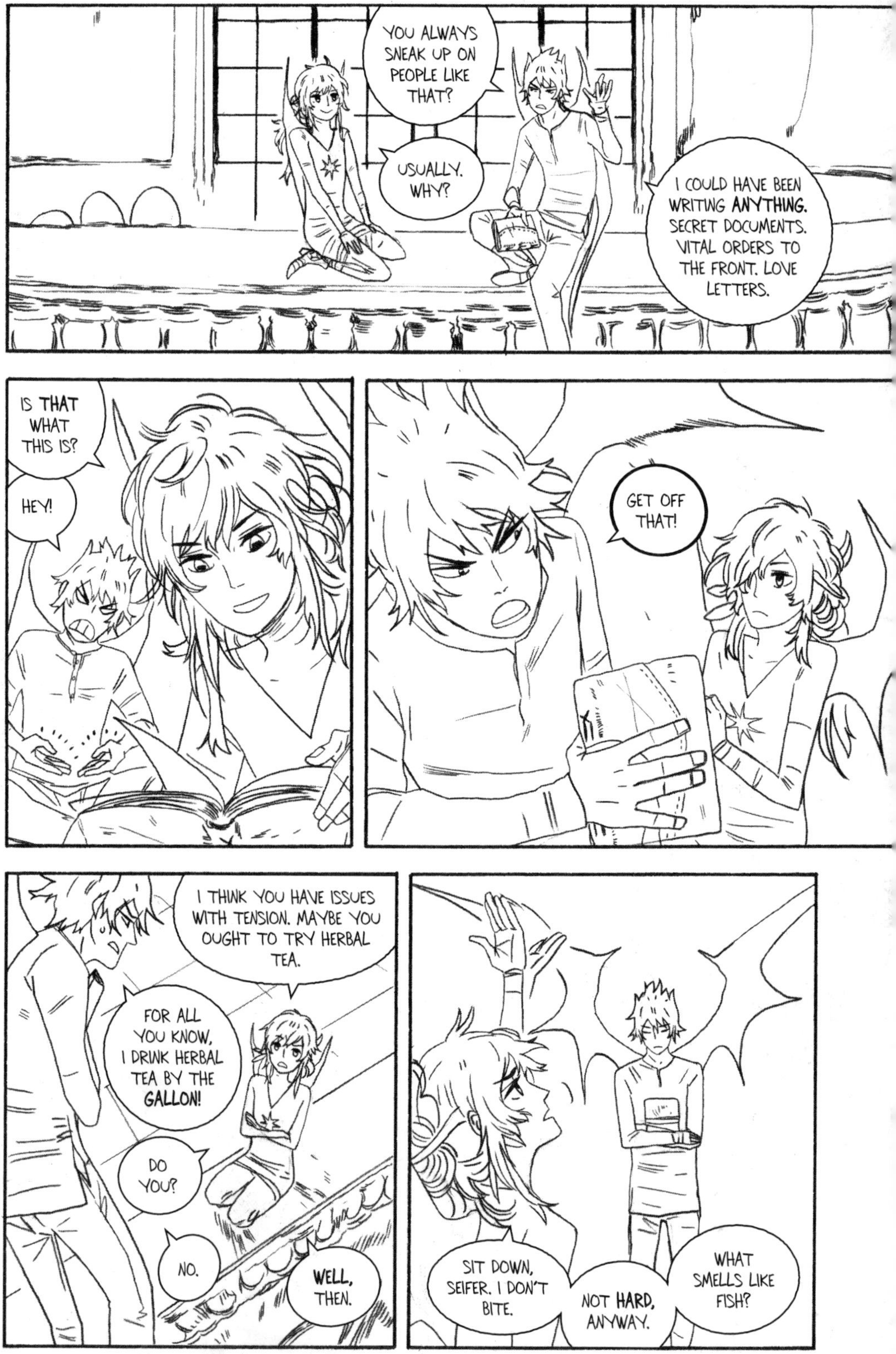
YOU ALWAYS SNEAK UP ON PEOPLE LIKE THAT?
USUALLY. WHY?
I COULD HAVE BEEN WRITING ANYTHING. SECRET DOCUMENTS. VITAL ORDERS TO THE FRONT. LOVE LETTERS.
IS THAT WHAT THIS IS?
HEY!
GET OFF THAT!
I THINK YOU HAVE ISSUES WITH TENSION. MAYBE YOU OUGHT TO TRY HERBAL TEA.
FOR ALL YOU KNOW, I DRINK HERBAL TEA BY THE GALLON!
DO YOU?
NO.
WELL, THEN.
SIT DOWN, SEIFER. I DON'T BITE.
NOT HARD, ANYWAY.
WHAT SMELLS LIKE FISH?

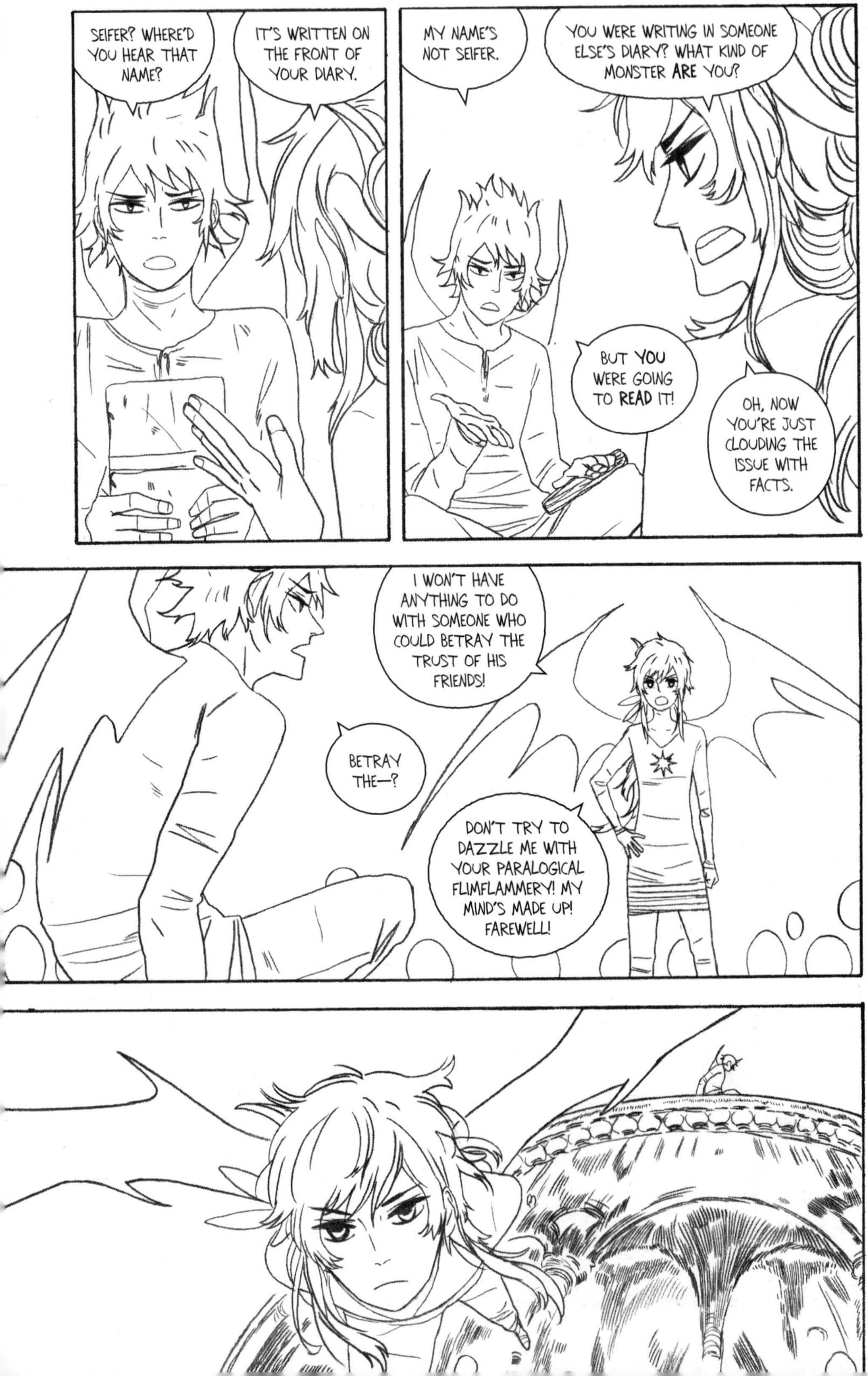
SEIFER? WHERE'D YOU HEAR THAT NAME?
IT'S WRITTEN ON THE FRONT OF YOUR DIARY.
MY NAME'S NOT SEIFER.
YOU WERE WRITING IN SOMEONE ELSE'S DIARY? WHAT KIND OF MONSTER ARE YOU?
BUT YOU WERE GOING TO READ IT!
OH, NOW YOU'RE JUST CLOUDING THE ISSUE WITH FACTS.
I WON'T HAVE ANYTHING TO DO WITH SOMEONE WHO COULD BETRAY THE TRUST OF HIS FRIENDS!
BETRAY THE—?
DON'T TRY TO DAZZLE ME WITH YOUR PARALOGICAL FLIMFLAMMERY! MY MIND'S MADE UP! FAREWELL!

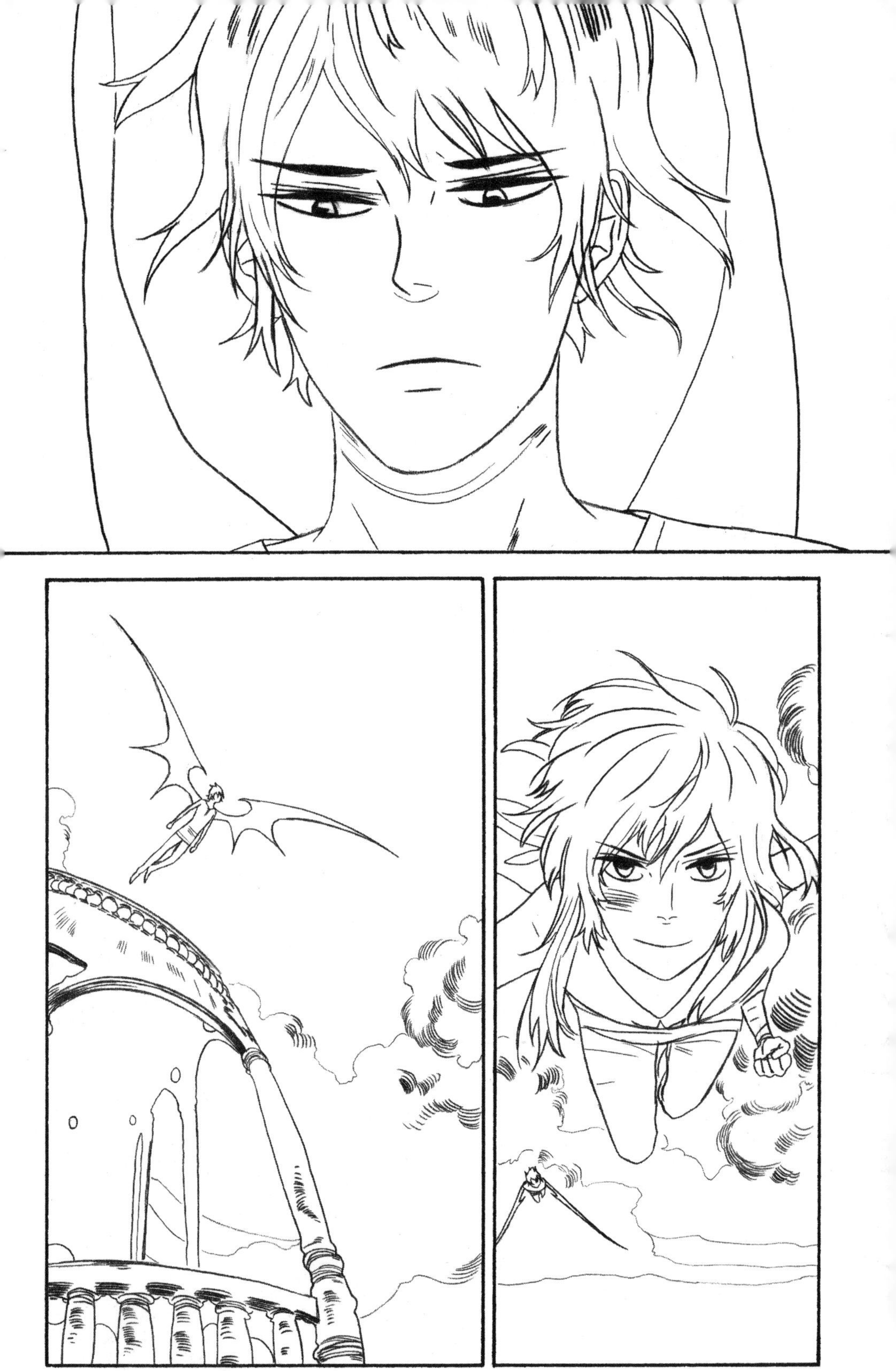

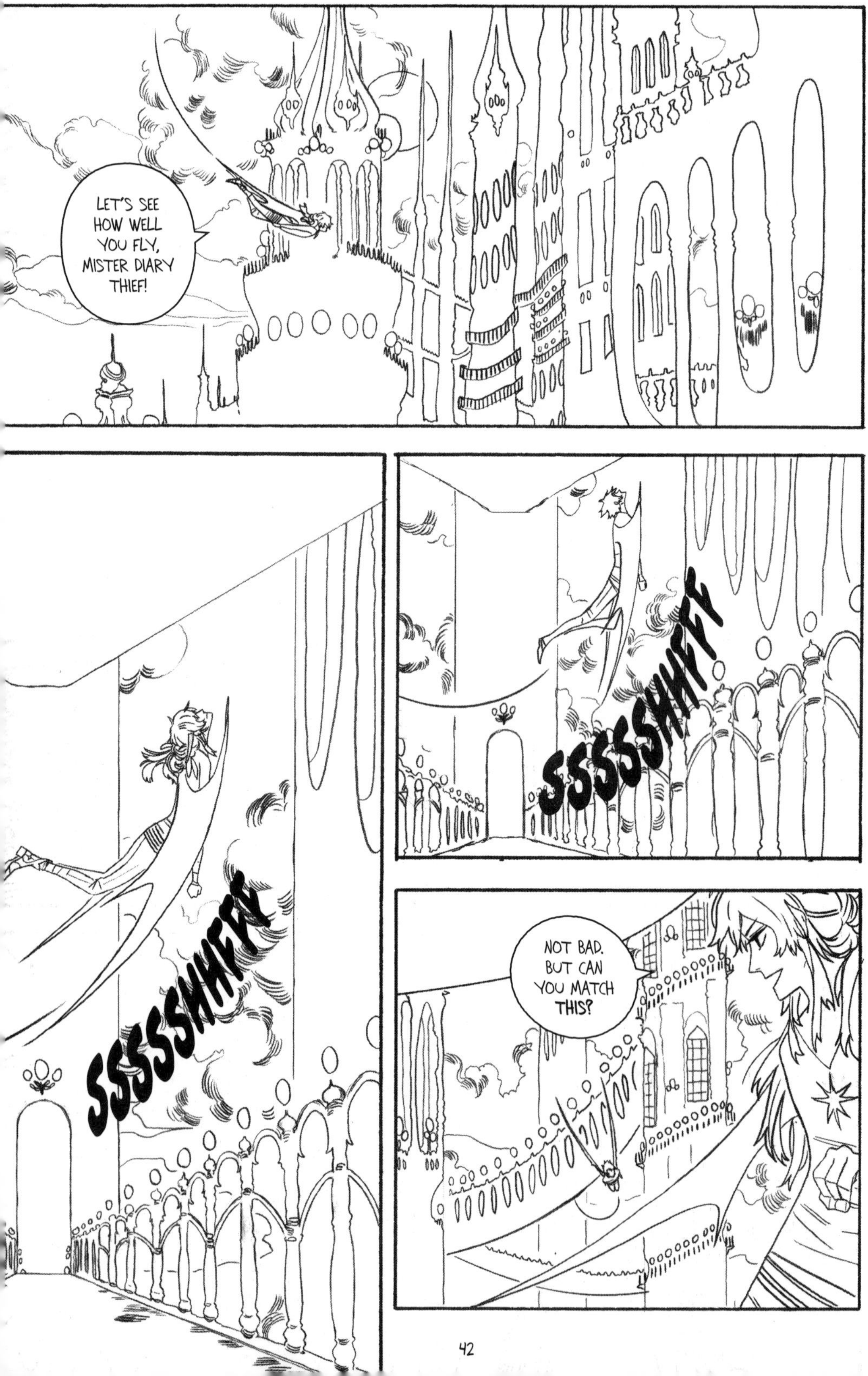
LET'S SEE HOW WELL YOU FLY, MISTER DIARY THIEF!
SSSSSHHFFF
SSSSSHHFFF
NOT BAD. BUT CAN YOU MATCH **THIS?**

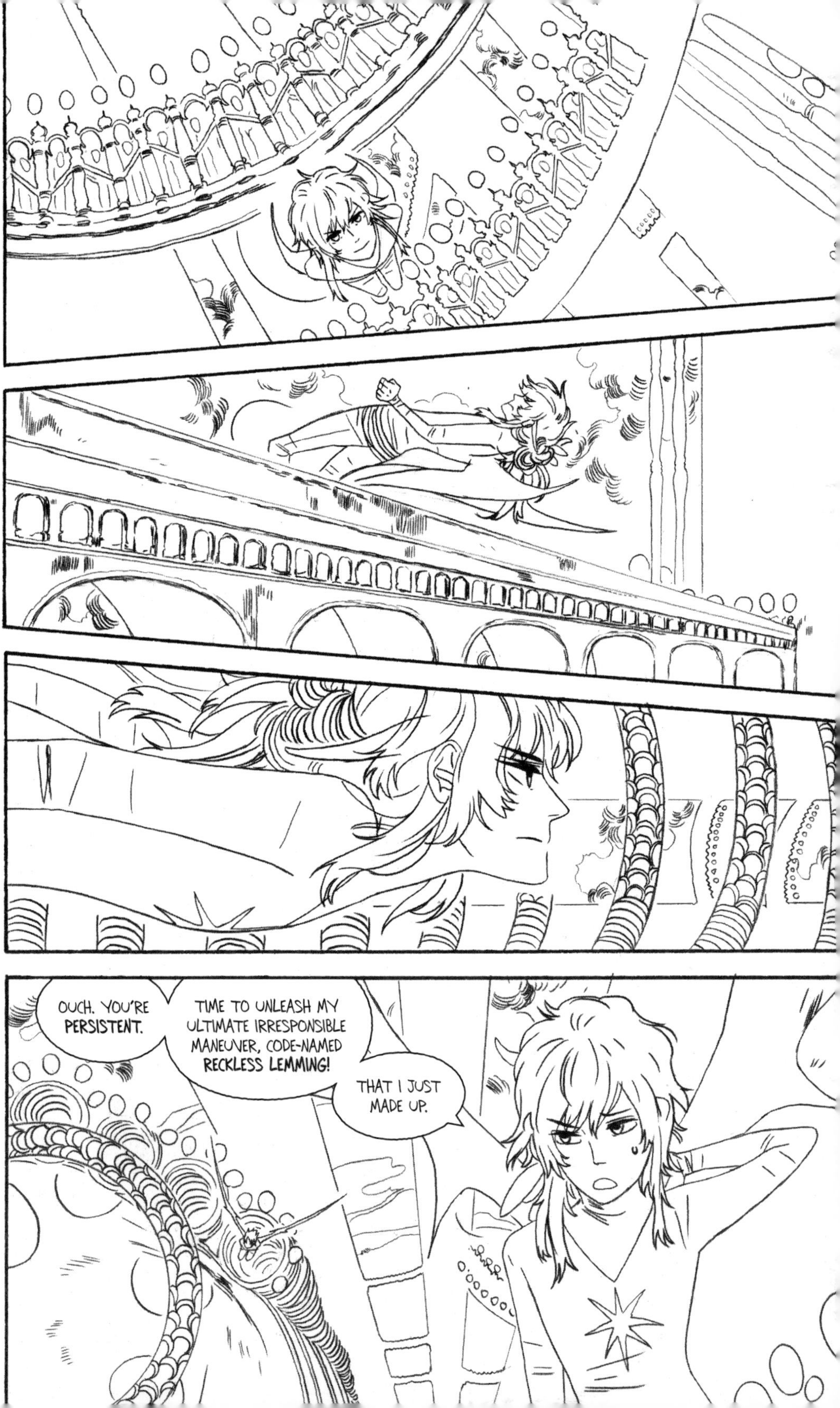
OUCH. YOU'RE **PERSISTENT.**
TIME TO UNLEASH MY ULTIMATE IRRESPONSIBLE MANEUVER, CODE-NAMED **RECKLESS LEMMING!**
THAT I JUST MADE UP.

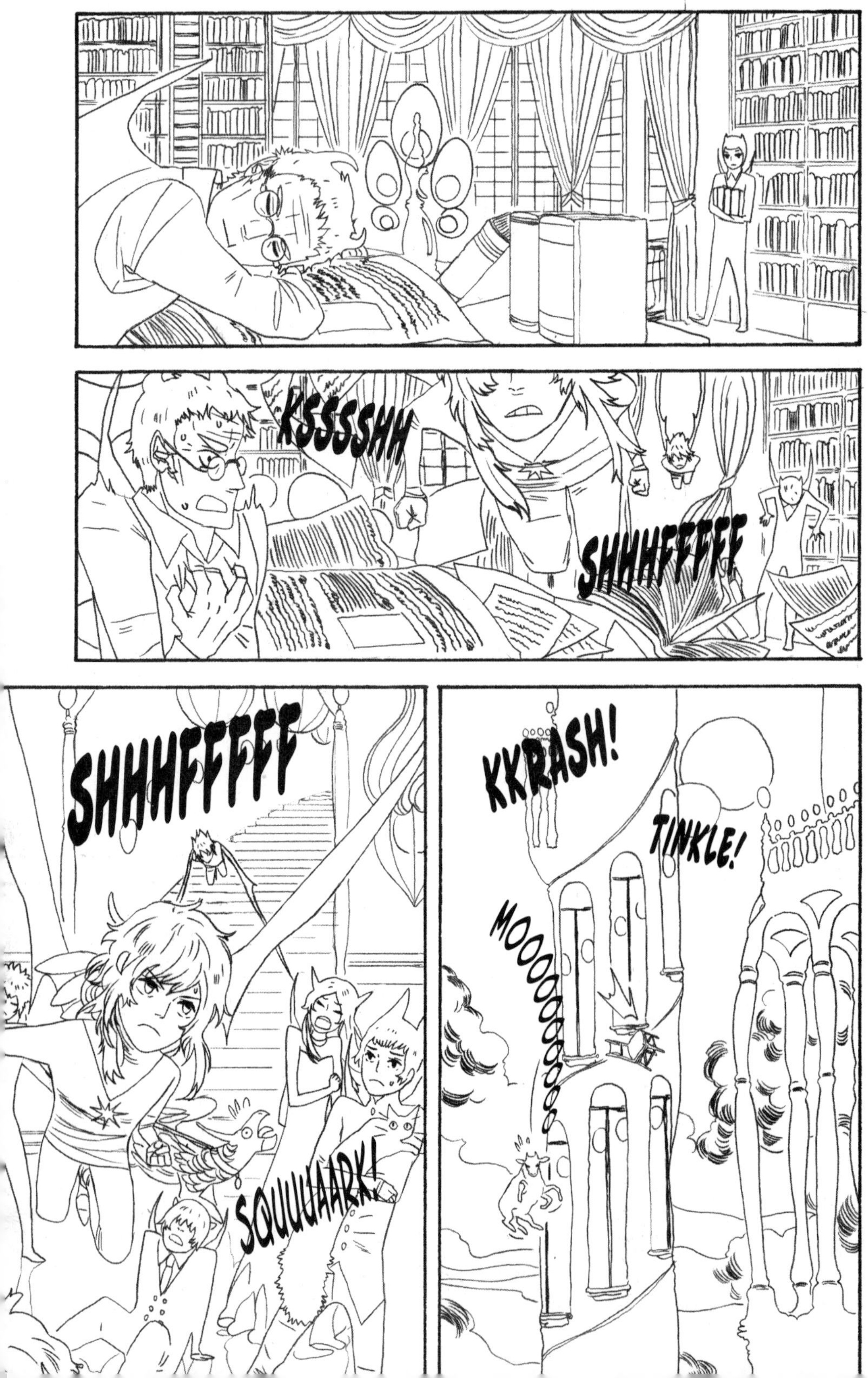
KSSSSHH
SHHHFFFFF
SHHHFFFFF
SQUUUAARK!
KKRASH!
TINKLE!
MOOOOOOOOOO

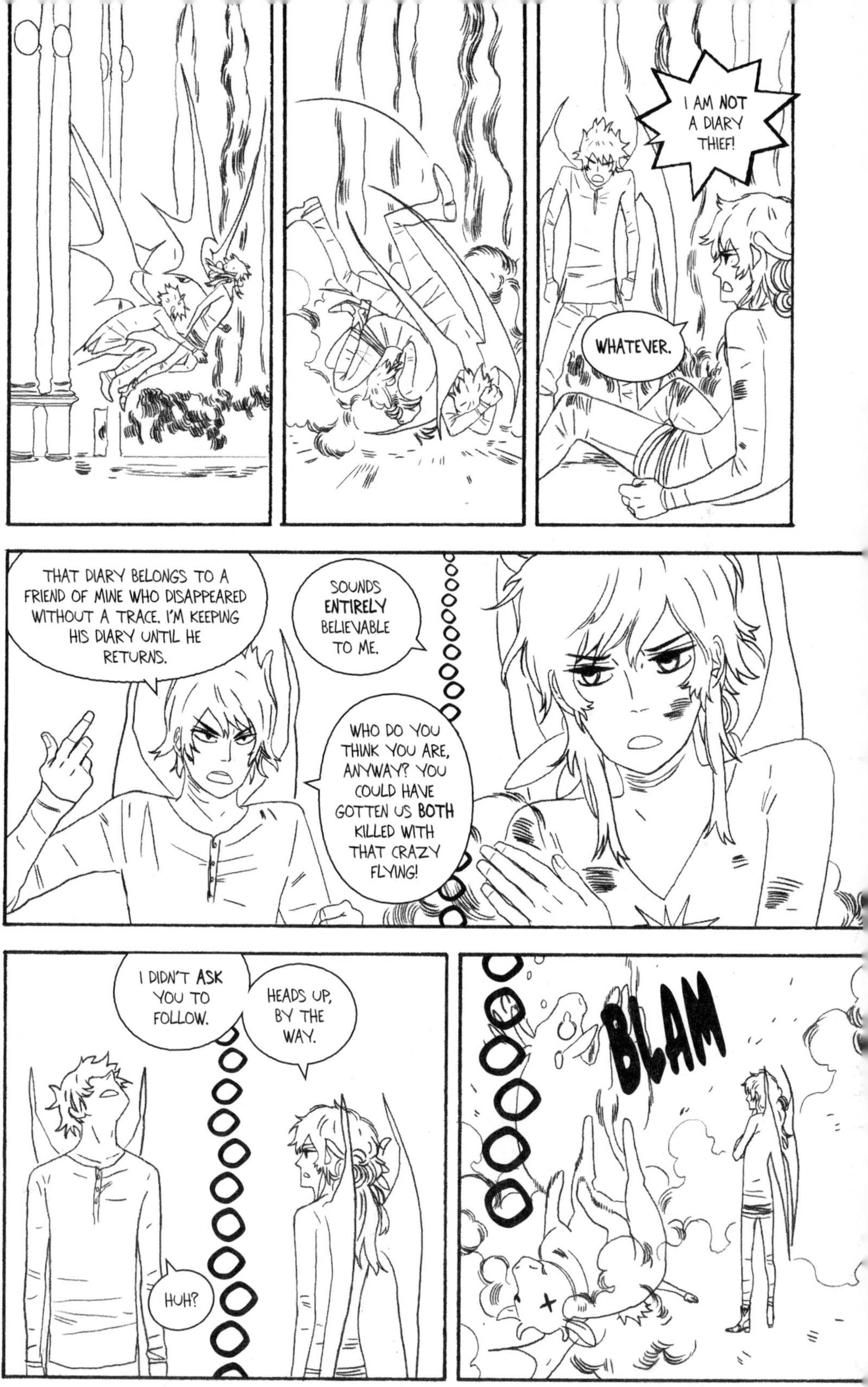
I AM NOT A DIARY THIEF!
WHATEVER.
THAT DIARY BELONGS TO A FRIEND OF MINE WHO DISAPPEARED WITHOUT A TRACE. I'M KEEPING HIS DIARY UNTIL HE RETURNS.
SOUNDS ENTIRELY BELIEVABLE TO ME.
WHO DO YOU THINK YOU ARE, ANYWAY? YOU COULD HAVE GOTTEN US BOTH KILLED WITH THAT CRAZY FLYING!
I DIDN'T ASK YOU TO FOLLOW.
HEADS UP, BY THE WAY.
HUH?
BLAM

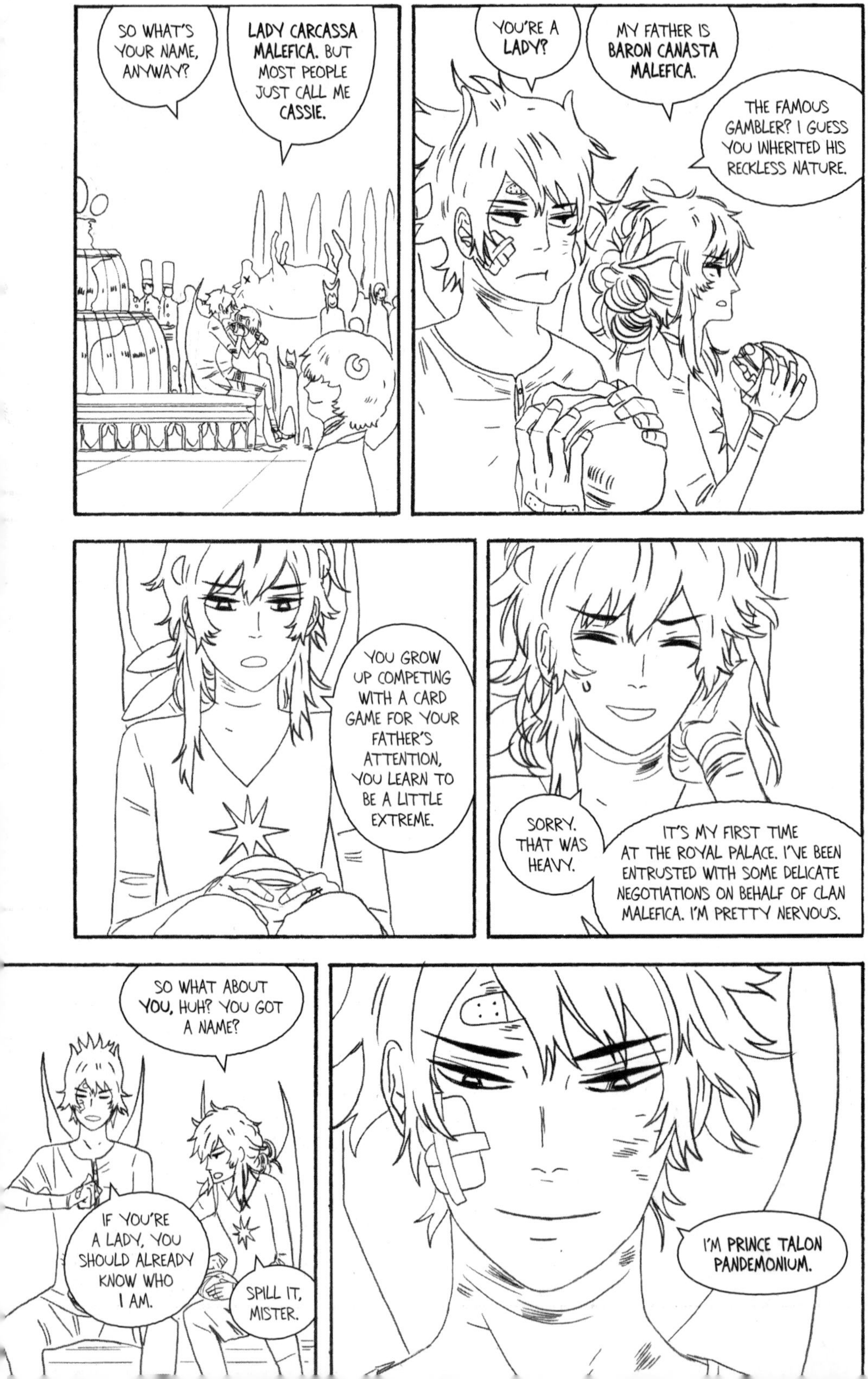
SO WHAT'S YOUR NAME, ANYWAY?
LADY CARCASSA MALEFICA. BUT MOST PEOPLE JUST CALL ME CASSIE.
YOU'RE A LADY?
MY FATHER IS BARON CANASTA MALEFICA.
THE FAMOUS GAMBLER? I GUESS YOU INHERITED HIS RECKLESS NATURE.
YOU GROW UP COMPETING WITH A CARD GAME FOR YOUR FATHER'S ATTENTION, YOU LEARN TO BE A LITTLE EXTREME.
SORRY. THAT WAS HEAVY.
IT'S MY FIRST TIME AT THE ROYAL PALACE. I'VE BEEN ENTRUSTED WITH SOME DELICATE NEGOTIATIONS ON BEHALF OF CLAN MALEFICA. I'M PRETTY NERVOUS.
SO WHAT ABOUT YOU, HUH? YOU GOT A NAME?
IF YOU'RE A LADY, YOU SHOULD ALREADY KNOW WHO I AM.
SPILL IT, MISTER.
I'M PRINCE TALON PANDEMONIUM.

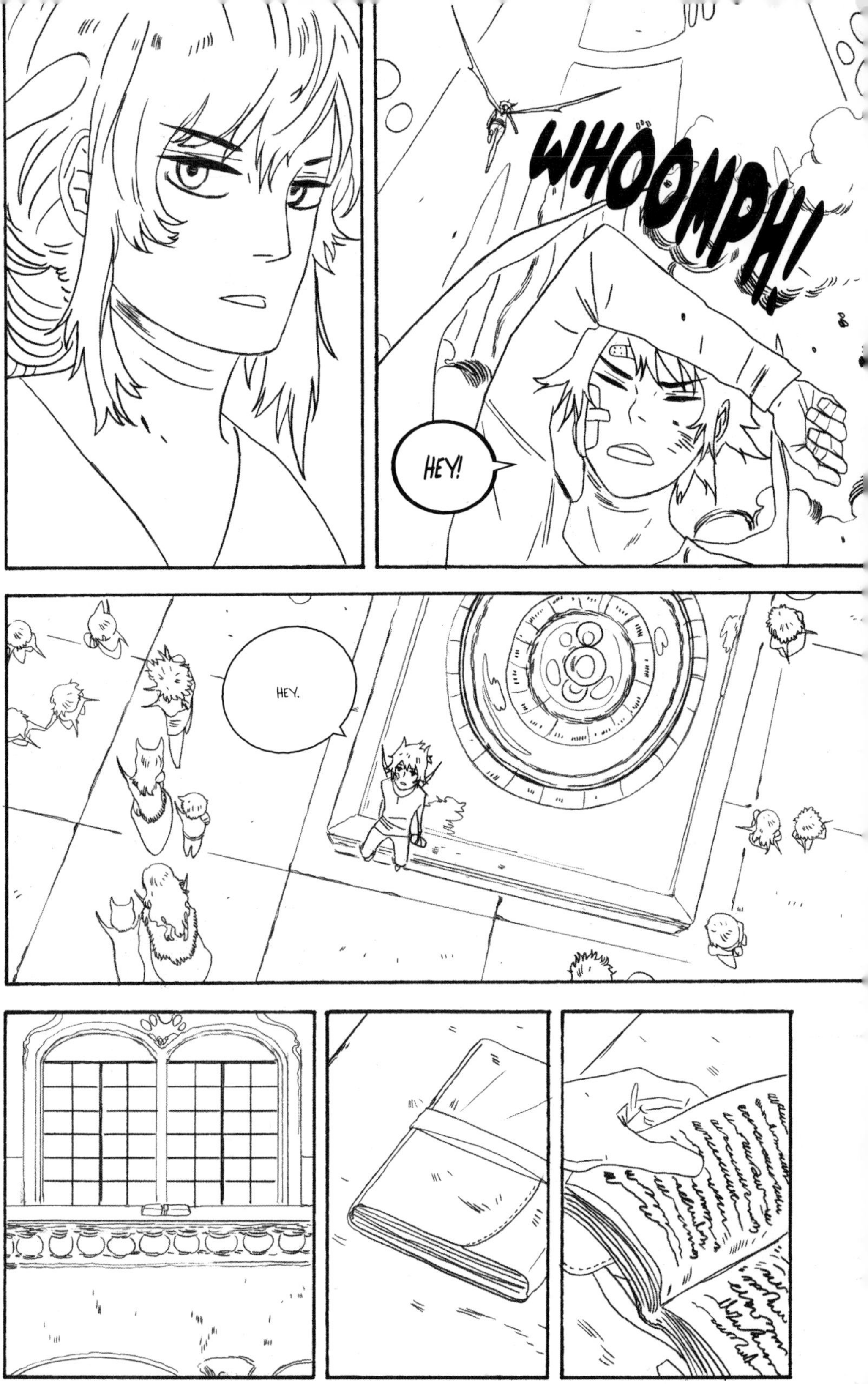
WHOOOMPH!
HEY!
HEY.

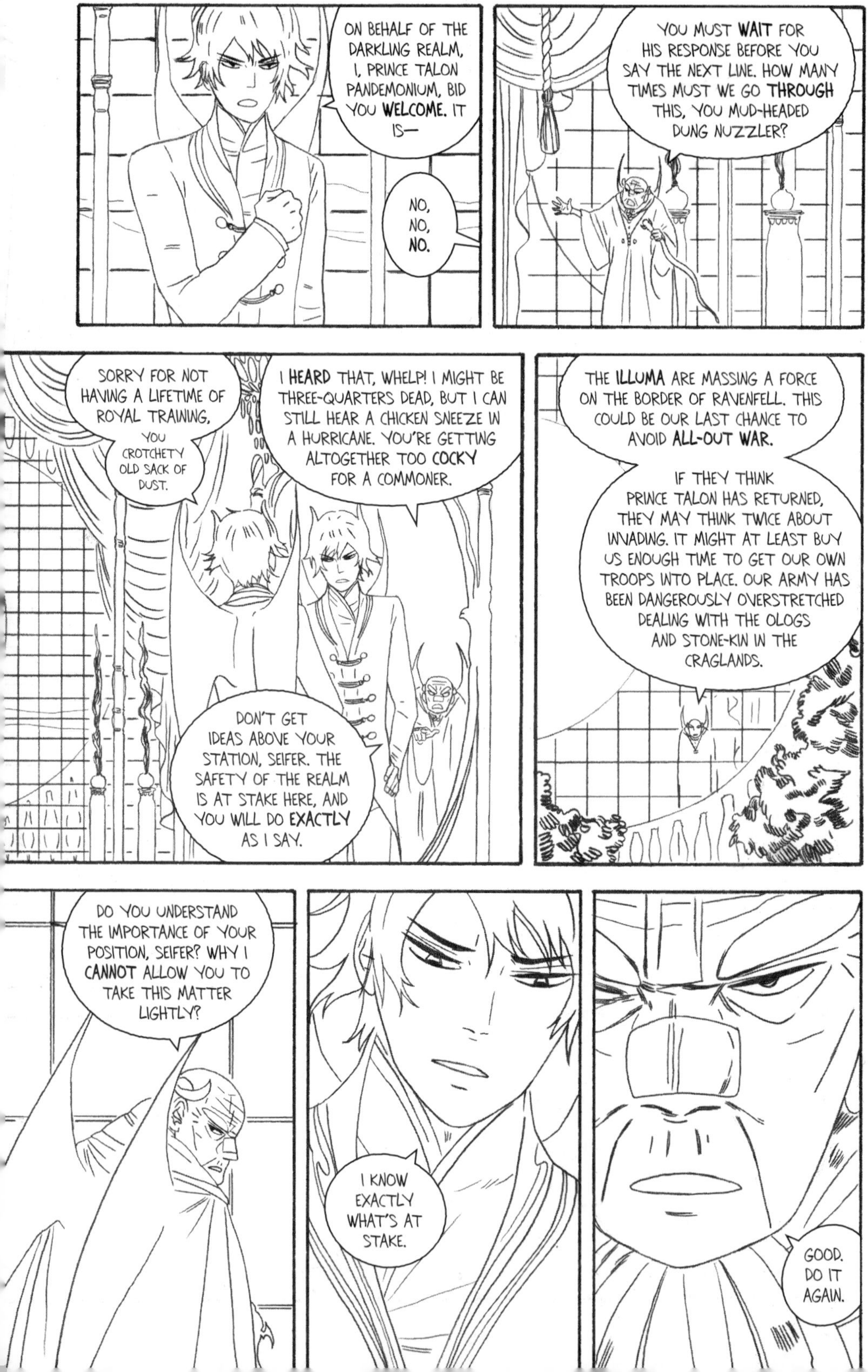
ON BEHALF OF THE DARKLING REALM, I, PRINCE TALON PANDEMONIUM, BID YOU WELCOME. IT IS—
NO, NO, NO.
YOU MUST WAIT FOR HIS RESPONSE BEFORE YOU SAY THE NEXT LINE. HOW MANY TIMES MUST WE GO THROUGH THIS, YOU MUD-HEADED DUNG NUZZLER?
SORRY FOR NOT HAVING A LIFETIME OF ROYAL TRAINING,
YOU CROTCHETY OLD SACK OF DUST.
I HEARD THAT, WHELP! I MIGHT BE THREE-QUARTERS DEAD, BUT I CAN STILL HEAR A CHICKEN SNEEZE IN A HURRICANE. YOU'RE GETTING ALTOGETHER TOO COCKY FOR A COMMONER.
DON'T GET IDEAS ABOVE YOUR STATION, SEIFER. THE SAFETY OF THE REALM IS AT STAKE HERE, AND YOU WILL DO EXACTLY AS I SAY.
THE ILLUMA ARE MASSING A FORCE ON THE BORDER OF RAVENFELL. THIS COULD BE OUR LAST CHANCE TO AVOID ALL-OUT WAR.
IF THEY THINK PRINCE TALON HAS RETURNED, THEY MAY THINK TWICE ABOUT INVADING. IT MIGHT AT LEAST BUY US ENOUGH TIME TO GET OUR OWN TROOPS INTO PLACE. OUR ARMY HAS BEEN DANGEROUSLY OVERSTRETCHED DEALING WITH THE OLOGS AND STONE-KIN IN THE CRAGLANDS.
DO YOU UNDERSTAND THE IMPORTANCE OF YOUR POSITION, SEIFER? WHY I CANNOT ALLOW YOU TO TAKE THIS MATTER LIGHTLY?
I KNOW EXACTLY WHAT'S AT STAKE.
GOOD. DO IT AGAIN.

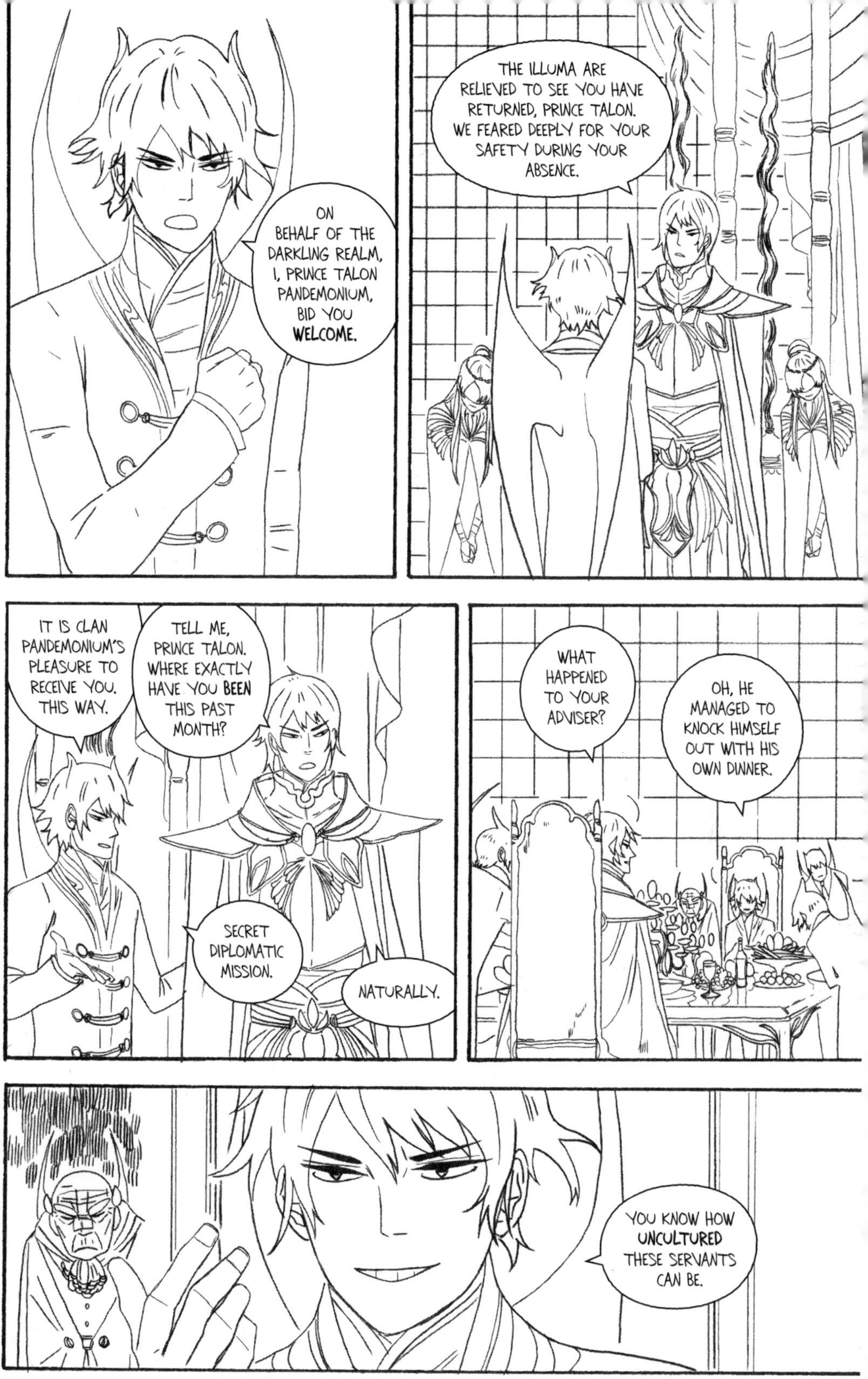
ON BEHALF OF THE DARKLING REALM, I, PRINCE TALON PANDEMONIUM, BID YOU **WELCOME.**
THE ILLUMA ARE RELIEVED TO SEE YOU HAVE RETURNED, PRINCE TALON. WE FEARED DEEPLY FOR YOUR SAFETY DURING YOUR ABSENCE.
IT IS CLAN PANDEMONIUM'S PLEASURE TO RECEIVE YOU. THIS WAY.
TELL ME, PRINCE TALON. WHERE EXACTLY HAVE YOU **BEEN** THIS PAST MONTH?
SECRET DIPLOMATIC MISSION.
NATURALLY.
WHAT HAPPENED TO YOUR ADVISER?
OH, HE MANAGED TO KNOCK HIMSELF OUT WITH HIS OWN DINNER.
YOU KNOW HOW **UNCULTURED** THESE SERVANTS CAN BE.

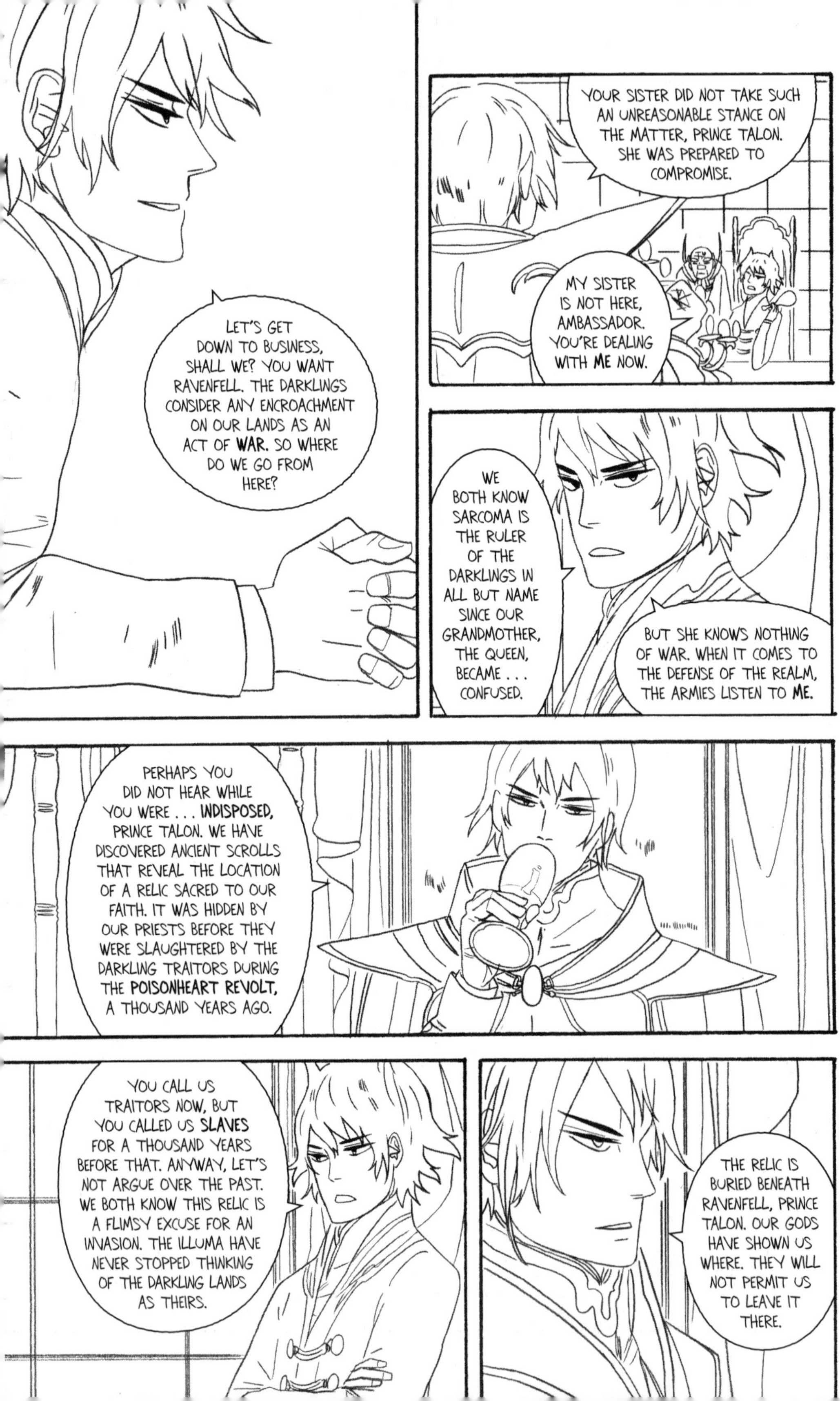
LET'S GET DOWN TO BUSINESS, SHALL WE? YOU WANT RAVENFELL. THE DARKLINGS CONSIDER ANY ENCROACHMENT ON OUR LANDS AS AN ACT OF **WAR.** SO WHERE DO WE GO FROM HERE?
YOUR SISTER DID NOT TAKE SUCH AN UNREASONABLE STANCE ON THE MATTER, PRINCE TALON. SHE WAS PREPARED TO COMPROMISE.
MY SISTER IS NOT HERE, AMBASSADOR. YOU'RE DEALING WITH **ME** NOW.
WE BOTH KNOW SARCOMA IS THE RULER OF THE DARKLINGS IN ALL BUT NAME SINCE OUR GRANDMOTHER, THE QUEEN, BECAME . . . CONFUSED.
BUT SHE KNOWS NOTHING OF WAR. WHEN IT COMES TO THE DEFENSE OF THE REALM, THE ARMIES LISTEN TO **ME.**
PERHAPS YOU DID NOT HEAR WHILE YOU WERE . . . **INDISPOSED,** PRINCE TALON. WE HAVE DISCOVERED ANCIENT SCROLLS THAT REVEAL THE LOCATION OF A RELIC SACRED TO OUR FAITH. IT WAS HIDDEN BY OUR PRIESTS BEFORE THEY WERE SLAUGHTERED BY THE DARKLING TRAITORS DURING THE **POISONHEART REVOLT,** A THOUSAND YEARS AGO.
YOU CALL US TRAITORS NOW, BUT YOU CALLED US **SLAVES** FOR A THOUSAND YEARS BEFORE THAT. ANYWAY, LET'S NOT ARGUE OVER THE PAST. WE BOTH KNOW THIS RELIC IS A FLIMSY EXCUSE FOR AN INVASION. THE ILLUMA HAVE NEVER STOPPED THINKING OF THE DARKLING LANDS AS THEIRS.
THE RELIC IS BURIED BENEATH RAVENFELL, PRINCE TALON. OUR GODS HAVE SHOWN US WHERE. THEY WILL NOT PERMIT US TO LEAVE IT THERE.

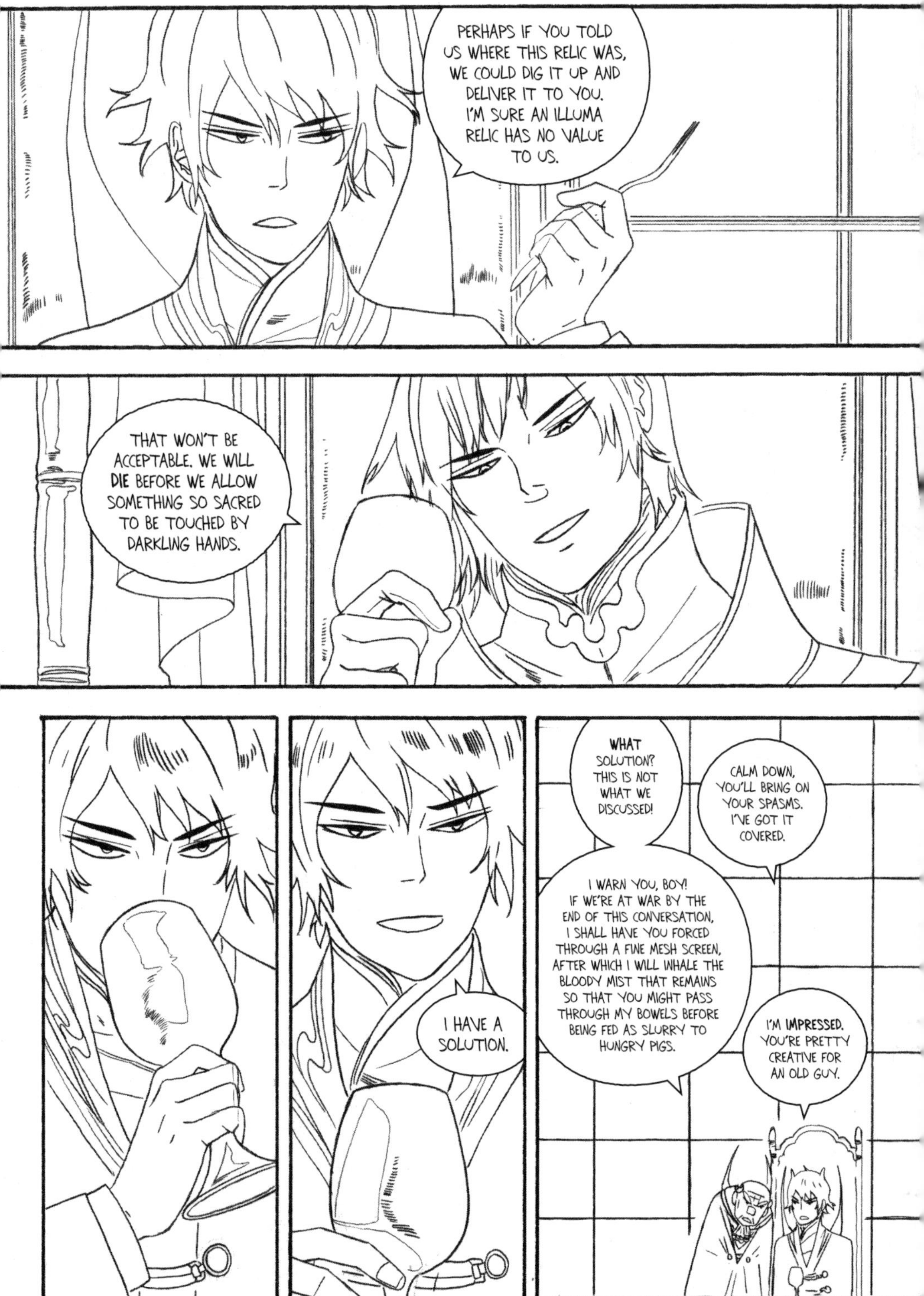
PERHAPS IF YOU TOLD US WHERE THIS RELIC WAS, WE COULD DIG IT UP AND DELIVER IT TO YOU. I'M SURE AN ILLUMA RELIC HAS NO VALUE TO US.
THAT WON'T BE ACCEPTABLE. WE WILL **DIE** BEFORE WE ALLOW SOMETHING SO SACRED TO BE TOUCHED BY DARKLING HANDS.
I HAVE A SOLUTION.
WHAT SOLUTION? THIS IS NOT WHAT WE DISCUSSED!
CALM DOWN, YOU'LL BRING ON YOUR SPASMS. I'VE GOT IT COVERED.
I WARN YOU, BOY! IF WE'RE AT WAR BY THE END OF THIS CONVERSATION, I SHALL HAVE YOU FORCED THROUGH A FINE MESH SCREEN, AFTER WHICH I WILL WHALE THE BLOODY MIST THAT REMAINS SO THAT YOU MIGHT PASS THROUGH MY BOWELS BEFORE BEING FED AS SLURRY TO HUNGRY PIGS.
I'M **IMPRESSED.** YOU'RE PRETTY CREATIVE FOR AN OLD GUY.

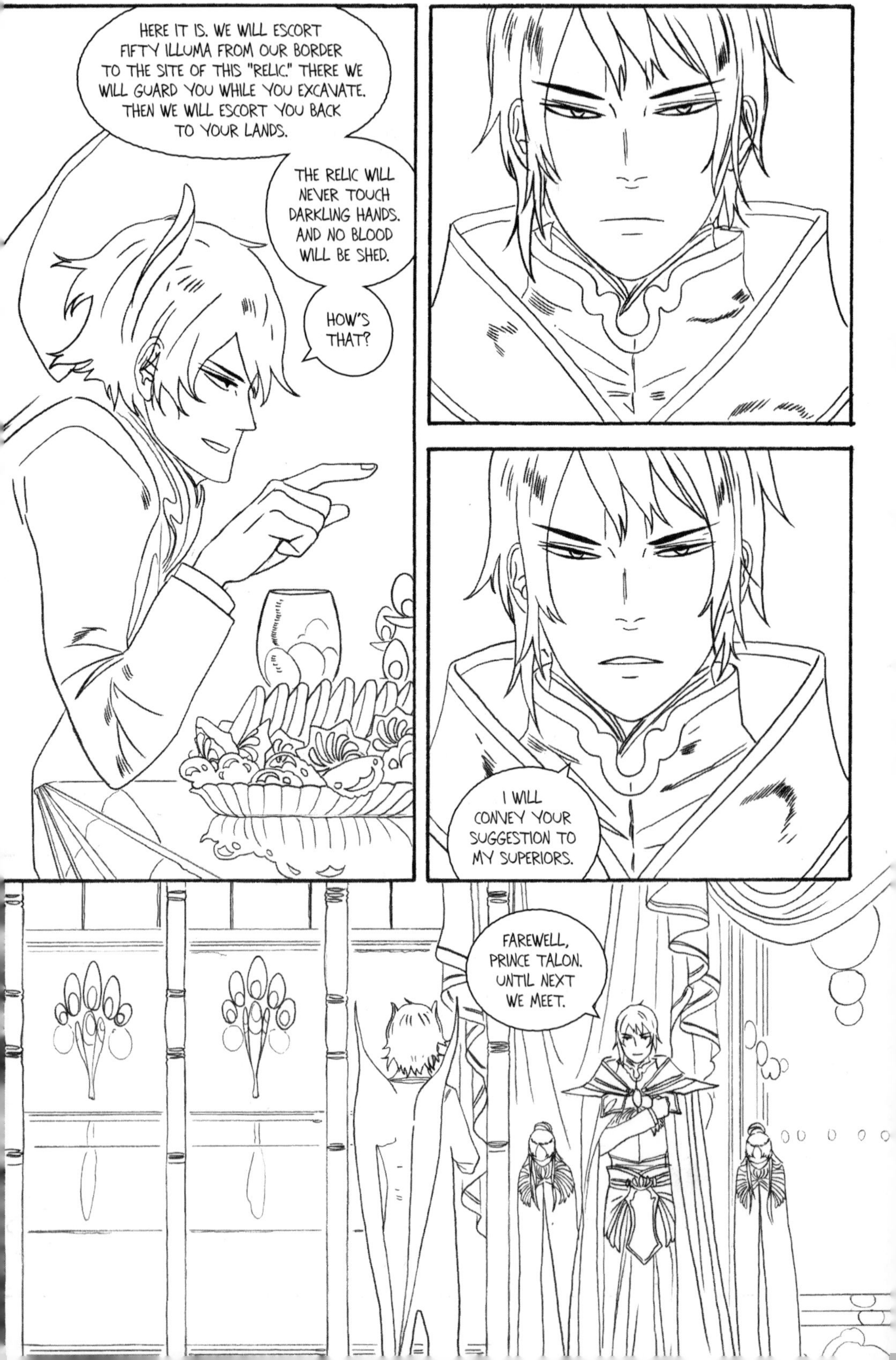
HERE IT IS. WE WILL ESCORT FIFTY ILLUMA FROM OUR BORDER TO THE SITE OF THIS "RELIC." THERE WE WILL GUARD YOU WHILE YOU EXCAVATE. THEN WE WILL ESCORT YOU BACK TO YOUR LANDS.
THE RELIC WILL NEVER TOUCH DARKLING HANDS. AND NO BLOOD WILL BE SHED.
HOW'S THAT?
I WILL CONVEY YOUR SUGGESTION TO MY SUPERIORS.
FAREWELL, PRINCE TALON. UNTIL NEXT WE MEET.

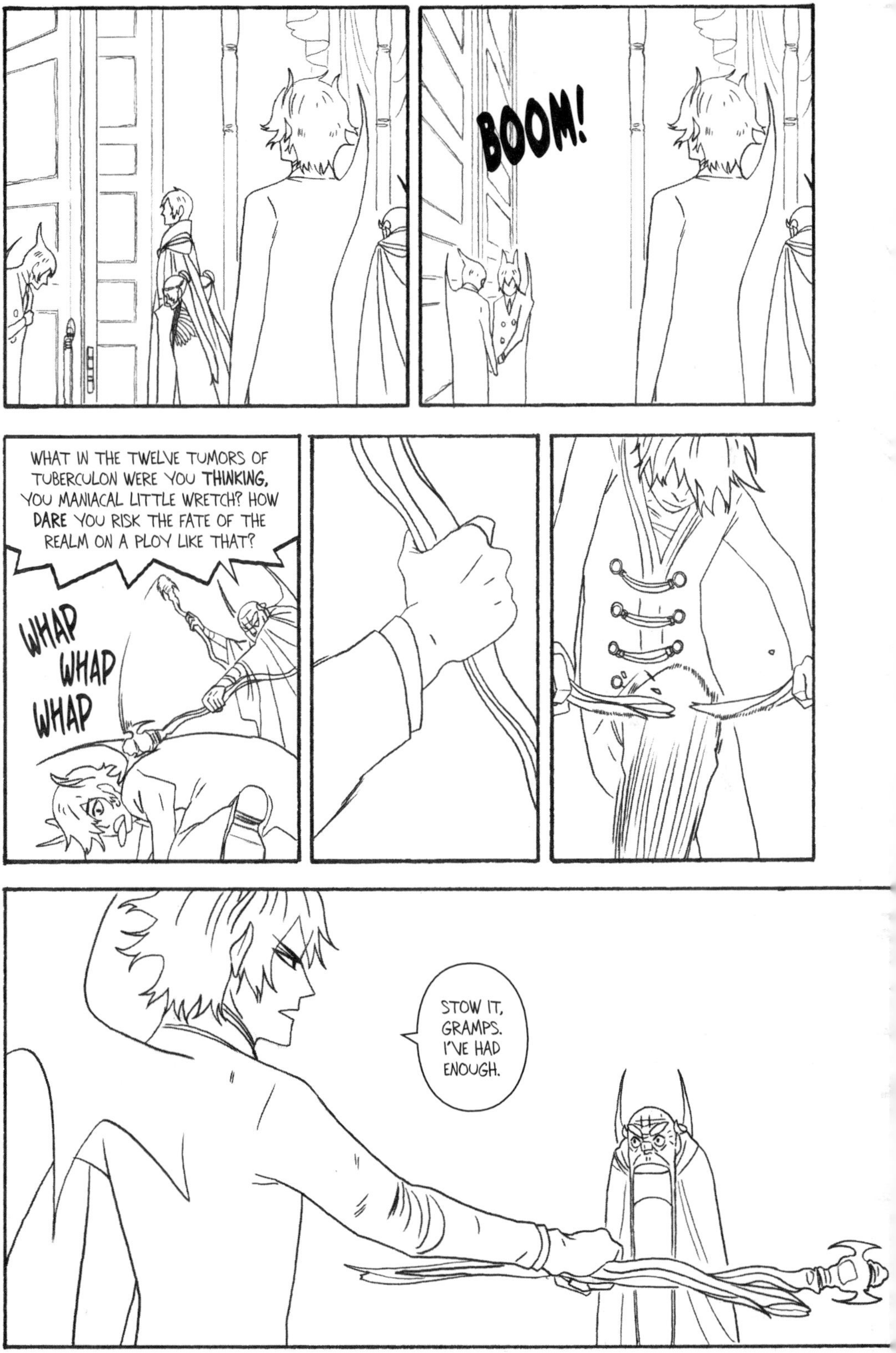
BOOM!
WHAT IN THE TWELVE TUMORS OF TUBERCULON WERE YOU THINKING, YOU MANIACAL LITTLE WRETCH? HOW DARE YOU RISK THE FATE OF THE REALM ON A PLOY LIKE THAT?
WHAP WHAP WHAP
STOW IT, GRAMPS. I'VE HAD ENOUGH.

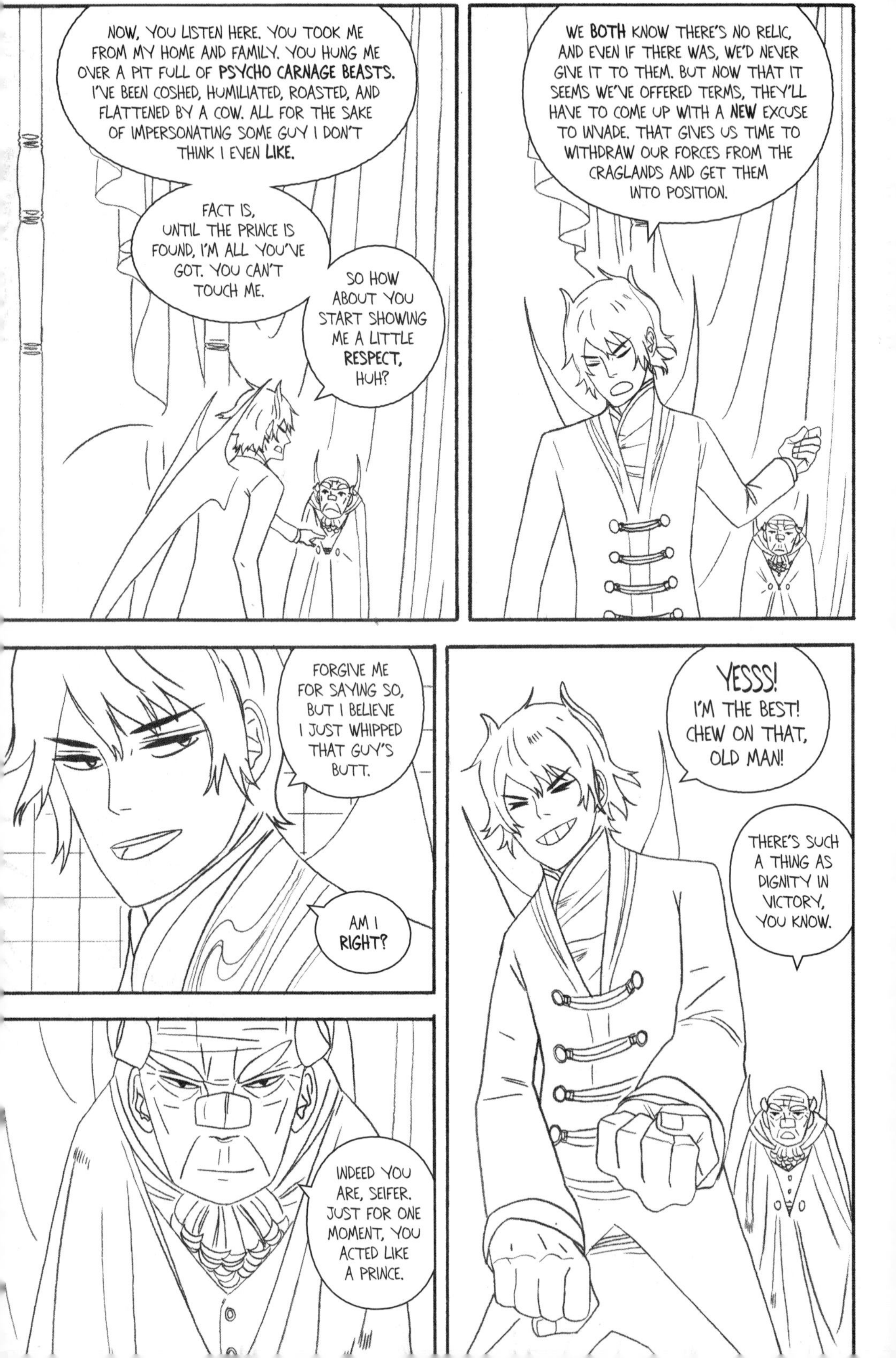
NOW, YOU LISTEN HERE. YOU TOOK ME FROM MY HOME AND FAMILY. YOU HUNG ME OVER A PIT FULL OF **PSYCHO CARNAGE BEASTS.** I'VE BEEN COSHED, HUMILIATED, ROASTED, AND FLATTENED BY A COW. ALL FOR THE SAKE OF IMPERSONATING SOME GUY I DON'T THINK I EVEN **LIKE.**
FACT IS, UNTIL THE PRINCE IS FOUND, I'M ALL YOU'VE GOT. YOU CAN'T TOUCH ME.
SO HOW ABOUT YOU START SHOWING ME A LITTLE **RESPECT,** HUH?
WE **BOTH** KNOW THERE'S NO RELIC, AND EVEN IF THERE WAS, WE'D NEVER GIVE IT TO THEM. BUT NOW THAT IT SEEMS WE'VE OFFERED TERMS, THEY'LL HAVE TO COME UP WITH A **NEW** EXCUSE TO INVADE. THAT GIVES US TIME TO WITHDRAW OUR FORCES FROM THE CRAGLANDS AND GET THEM INTO POSITION.
FORGIVE ME FOR SAYING SO, BUT I BELIEVE I JUST WHIPPED THAT GUY'S BUTT.
AM I **RIGHT?**
INDEED YOU ARE, SEIFER. JUST FOR ONE MOMENT, YOU ACTED LIKE A PRINCE.
YESSS! I'M THE BEST! CHEW ON THAT, OLD MAN!
THERE'S SUCH A THING AS DIGNITY IN VICTORY, YOU KNOW.

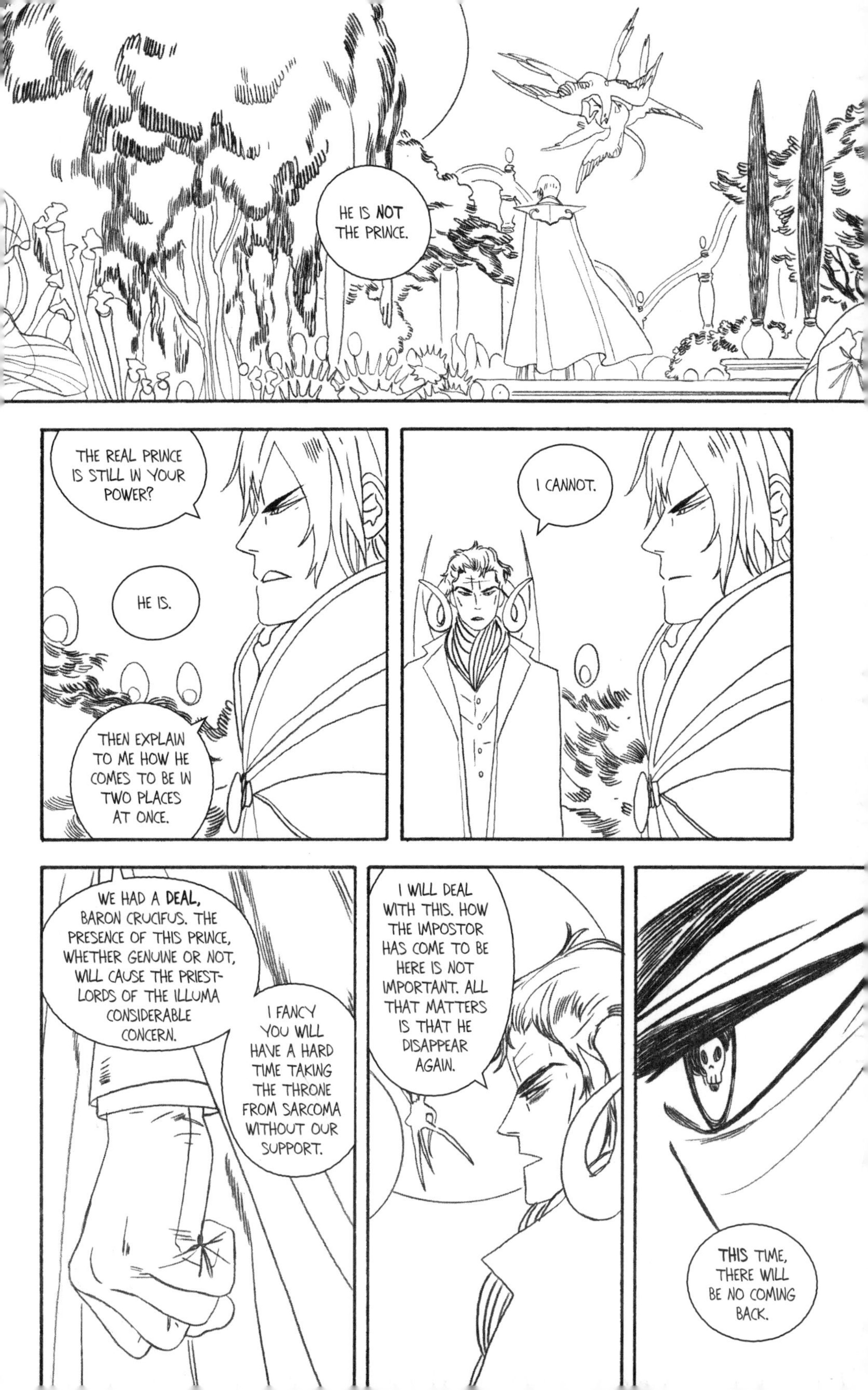
HE IS **NOT** THE PRINCE.
THE REAL PRINCE IS STILL IN YOUR POWER?
HE IS.
THEN EXPLAIN TO ME HOW HE COMES TO BE IN TWO PLACES AT ONCE.
I CANNOT.
WE HAD A **DEAL,** BARON CRUCIFUS. THE PRESENCE OF THIS PRINCE, WHETHER GENUINE OR NOT, WILL CAUSE THE PRIEST-LORDS OF THE ILLUMA CONSIDERABLE CONCERN.
I FANCY YOU WILL HAVE A HARD TIME TAKING THE THRONE FROM SARCOMA WITHOUT OUR SUPPORT.
I WILL DEAL WITH THIS. HOW THE IMPOSTOR HAS COME TO BE HERE IS NOT IMPORTANT. ALL THAT MATTERS IS THAT HE DISAPPEAR AGAIN.
THIS TIME, THERE WILL BE NO COMING BACK.

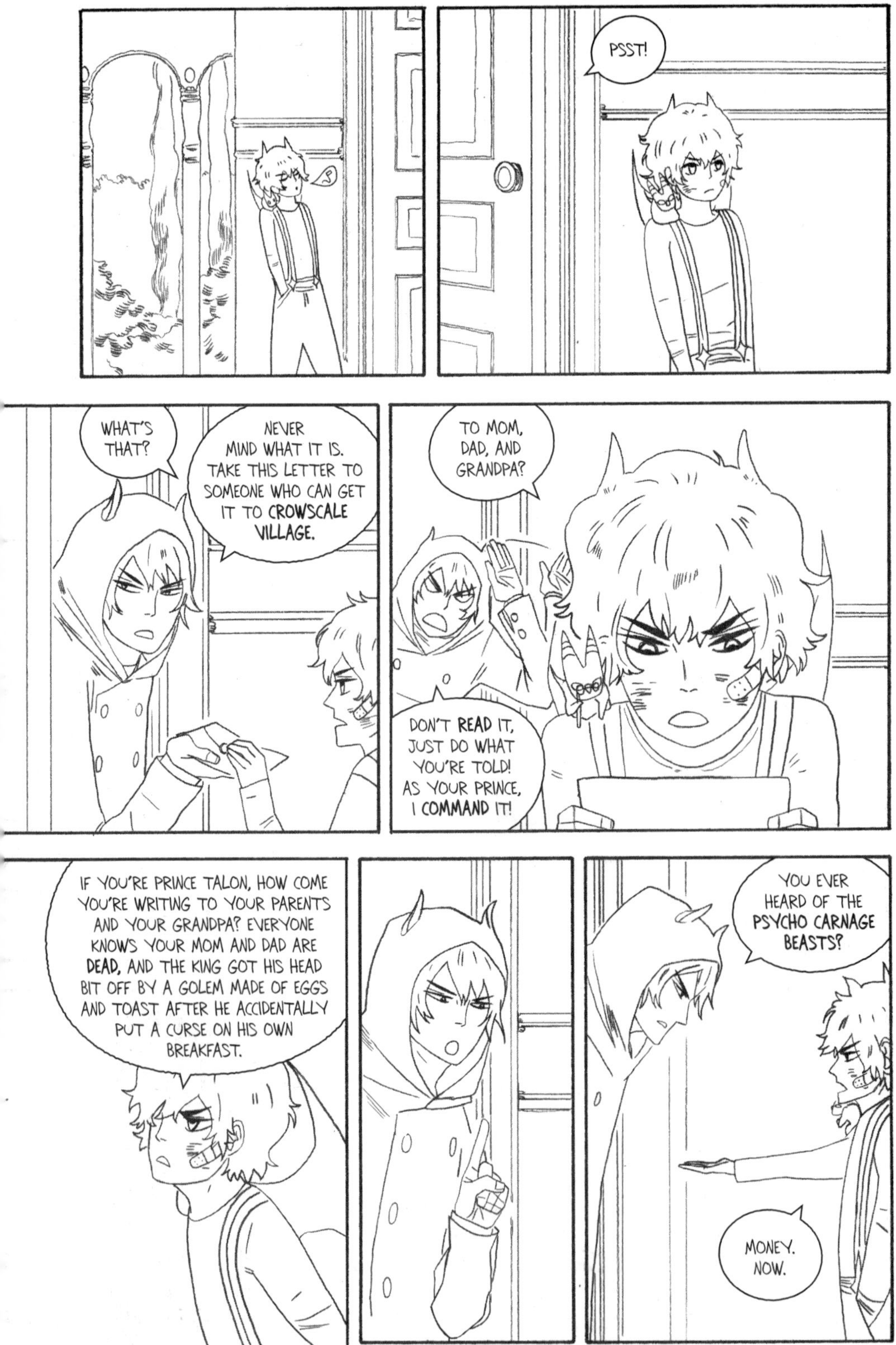
PSST!
WHAT'S THAT?
NEVER MIND WHAT IT IS. TAKE THIS LETTER TO SOMEONE WHO CAN GET IT TO CROWSCALE VILLAGE.
TO MOM, DAD, AND GRANDPA?
DON'T READ IT, JUST DO WHAT YOU'RE TOLD! AS YOUR PRINCE, I COMMAND IT!
IF YOU'RE PRINCE TALON, HOW COME YOU'RE WRITING TO YOUR PARENTS AND YOUR GRANDPA? EVERYONE KNOWS YOUR MOM AND DAD ARE DEAD, AND THE KING GOT HIS HEAD BIT OFF BY A GOLEM MADE OF EGGS AND TOAST AFTER HE ACCIDENTALLY PUT A CURSE ON HIS OWN BREAKFAST.
YOU EVER HEARD OF THE PSYCHO CARNAGE BEASTS?
MONEY. NOW.

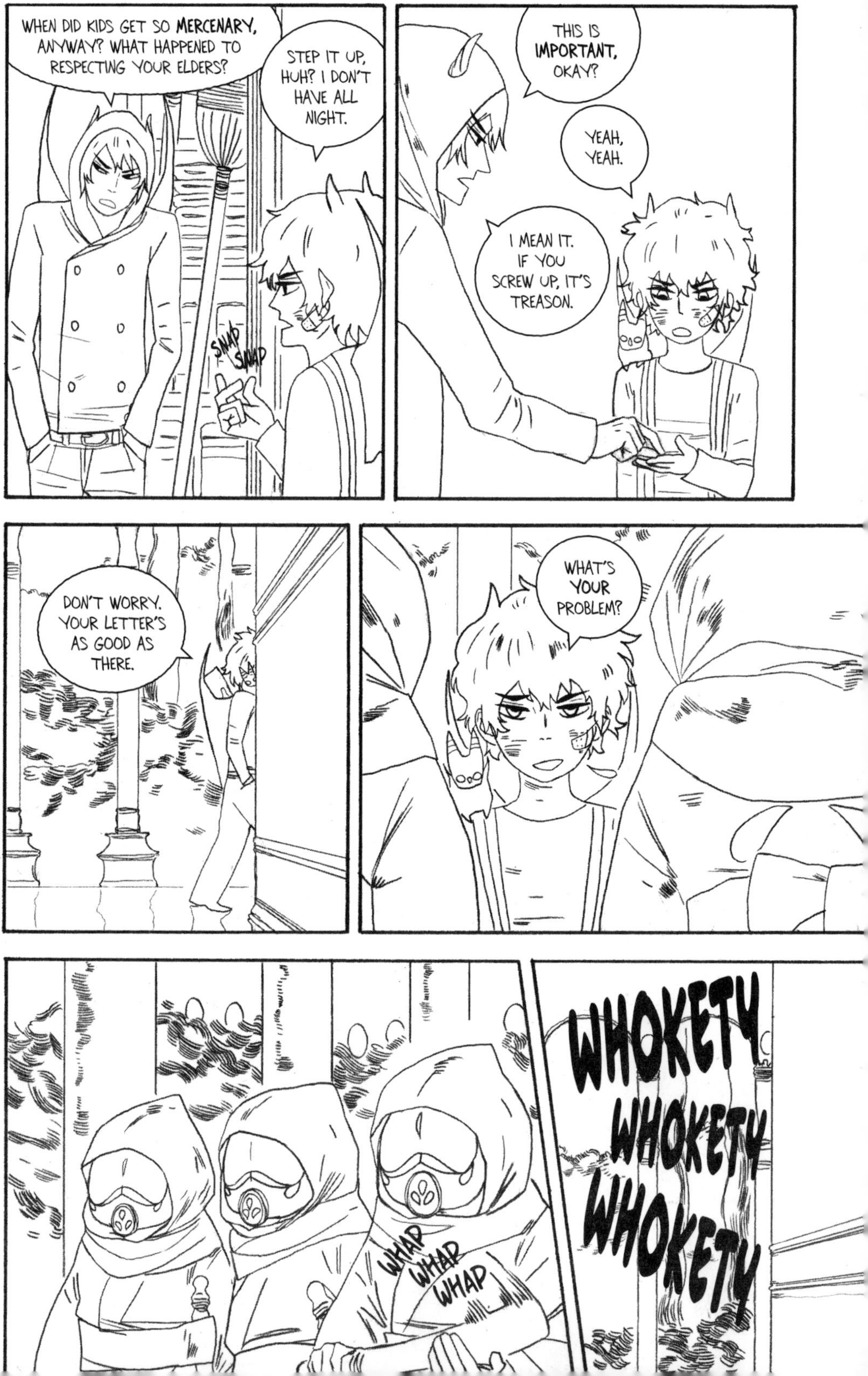
WHEN DID KIDS GET SO MERCENARY, ANYWAY? WHAT HAPPENED TO RESPECTING YOUR ELDERS?
STEP IT UP, HUH? I DON'T HAVE ALL NIGHT.
SNAP SNAP
THIS IS IMPORTANT, OKAY?
YEAH, YEAH.
I MEAN IT. IF YOU SCREW UP, IT'S TREASON.
DON'T WORRY. YOUR LETTER'S AS GOOD AS THERE.
WHAT'S YOUR PROBLEM?
WHAP WHAP WHAP
WHOKETY WHOKETY WHOKETY

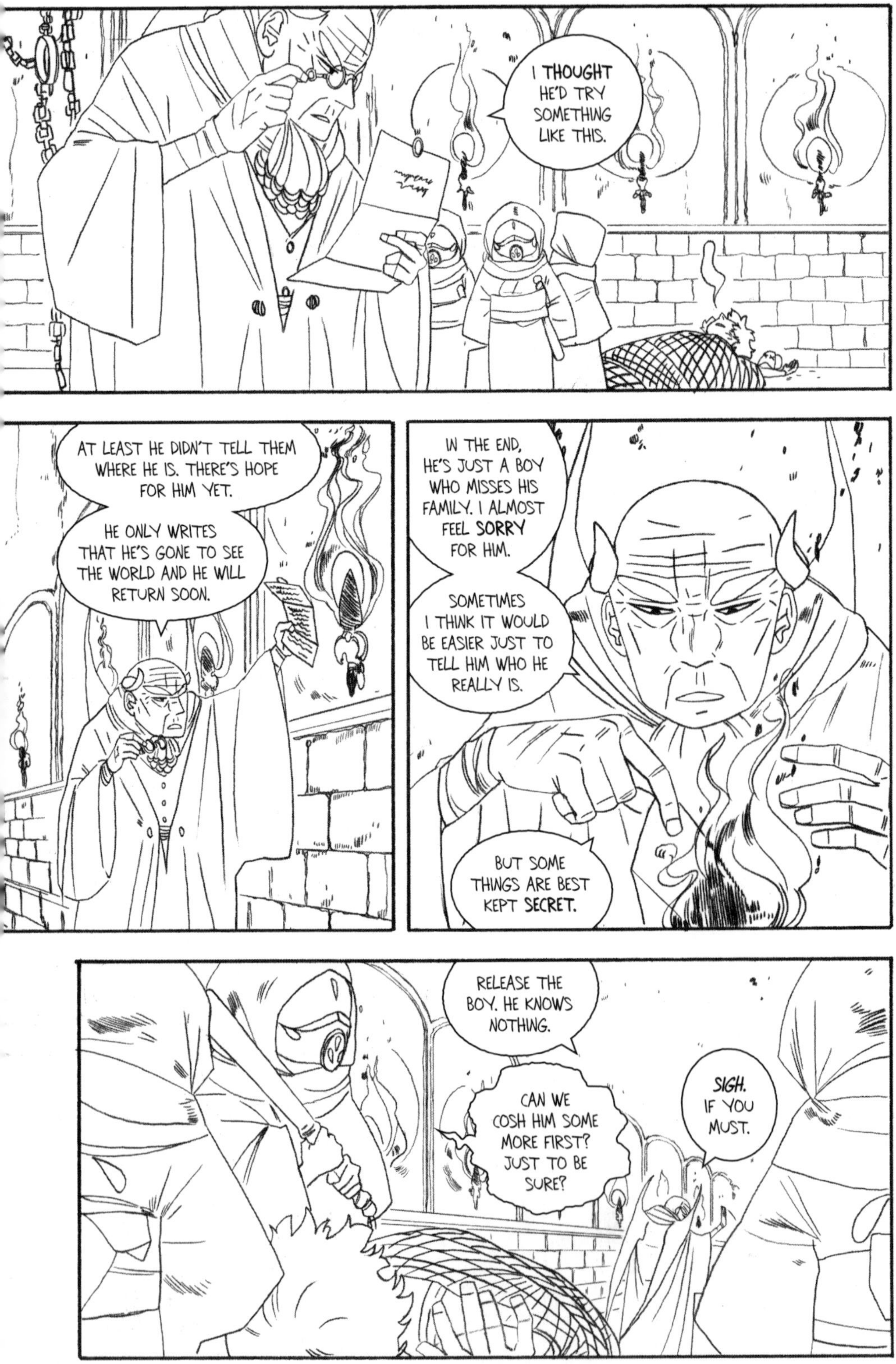
I THOUGHT HE'D TRY SOMETHING LIKE THIS.
AT LEAST HE DIDN'T TELL THEM WHERE HE IS. THERE'S HOPE FOR HIM YET.
HE ONLY WRITES THAT HE'S GONE TO SEE THE WORLD AND HE WILL RETURN SOON.
IN THE END, HE'S JUST A BOY WHO MISSES HIS FAMILY. I ALMOST FEEL SORRY FOR HIM.
SOMETIMES I THINK IT WOULD BE EASIER JUST TO TELL HIM WHO HE REALLY IS.
BUT SOME THINGS ARE BEST KEPT SECRET.
RELEASE THE BOY. HE KNOWS NOTHING.
CAN WE COSH HIM SOME MORE FIRST? JUST TO BE SURE?
SIGH. IF YOU MUST.

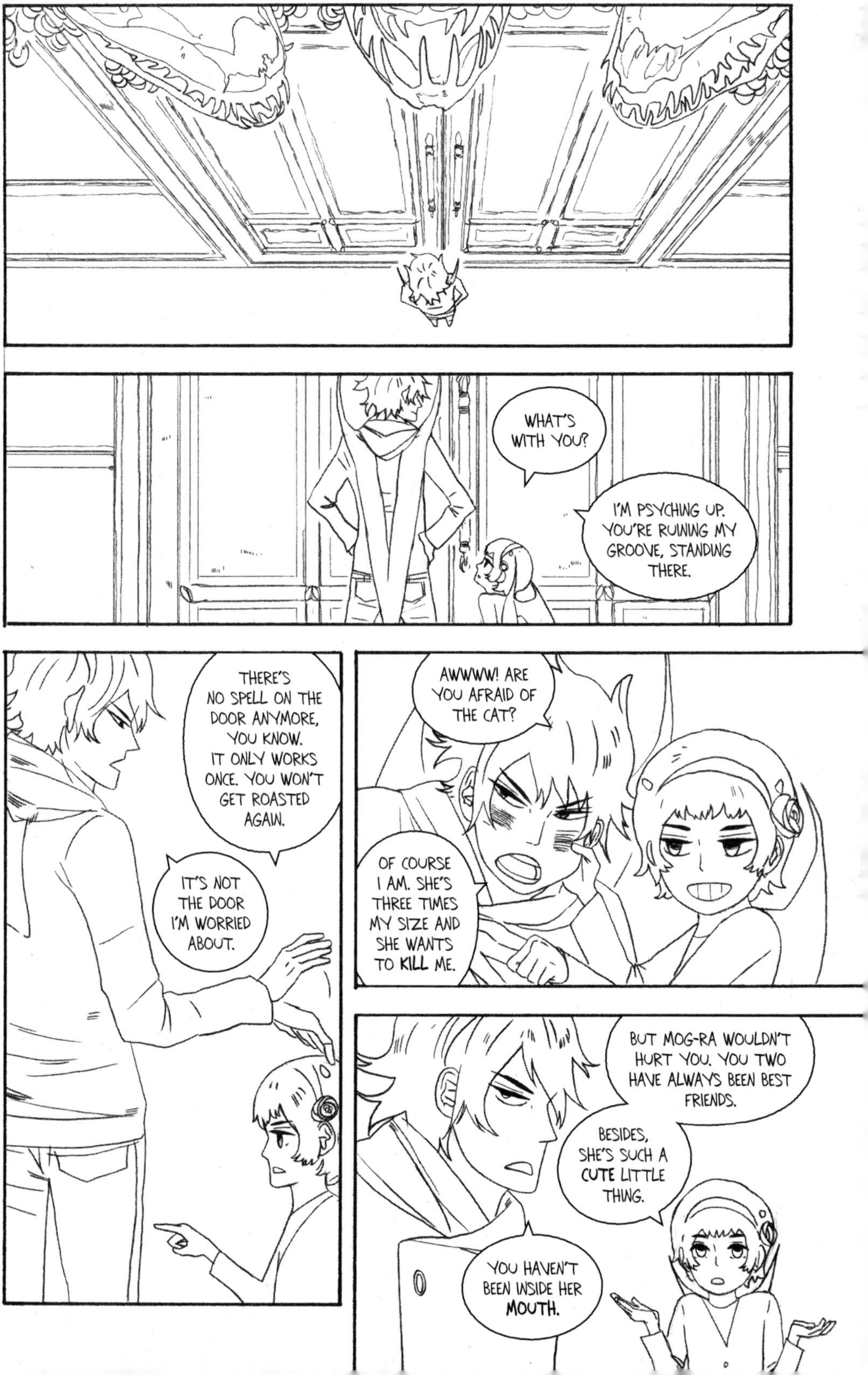
WHAT'S WITH YOU?
I'M PSYCHING UP. YOU'RE RUINING MY GROOVE, STANDING THERE.
THERE'S NO SPELL ON THE DOOR ANYMORE, YOU KNOW. IT ONLY WORKS ONCE. YOU WON'T GET ROASTED AGAIN.
IT'S NOT THE DOOR I'M WORRIED ABOUT.
AWWWW! ARE YOU AFRAID OF THE CAT?
OF COURSE I AM. SHE'S THREE TIMES MY SIZE AND SHE WANTS TO **KILL** ME.
BUT MOG-RA WOULDN'T HURT YOU. YOU TWO HAVE ALWAYS BEEN BEST FRIENDS.
BESIDES, SHE'S SUCH A **CUTE** LITTLE THING.
YOU HAVEN'T BEEN INSIDE HER **MOUTH.**

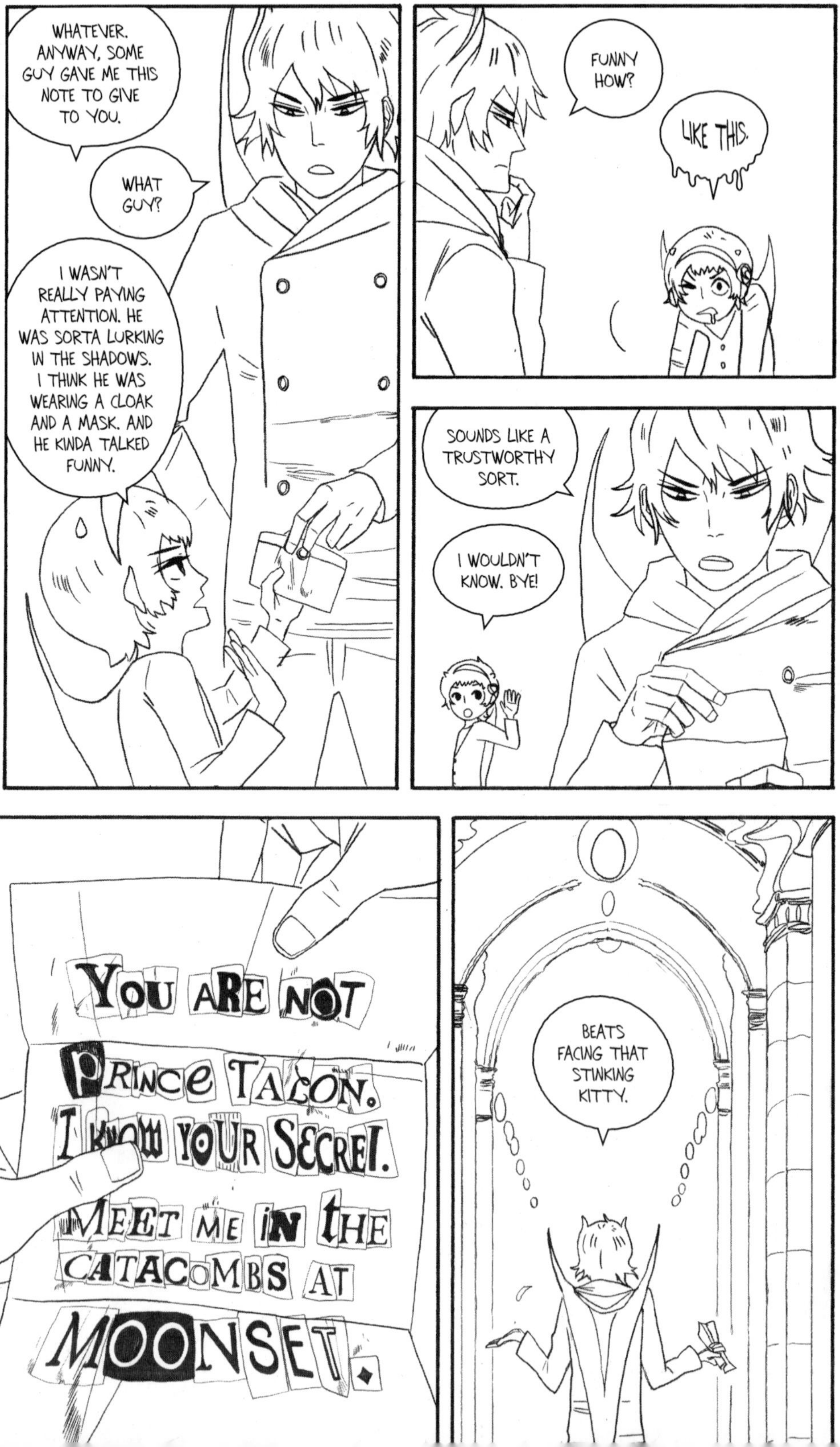
WHATEVER. ANYWAY, SOME GUY GAVE ME THIS NOTE TO GIVE TO YOU.
WHAT GUY?
I WASN'T REALLY PAYING ATTENTION. HE WAS SORTA LURKING IN THE SHADOWS. I THINK HE WAS WEARING A CLOAK AND A MASK. AND HE KINDA TALKED FUNNY.
FUNNY HOW?
LIKE THIS.
SOUNDS LIKE A TRUSTWORTHY SORT.
I WOULDN'T KNOW. BYE!
YOU ARE NOT PRINCE TALON. I KNOW YOUR SECRET. MEET ME IN THE CATACOMBS AT MOONSET.
BEATS FACING THAT STINKING KITTY.

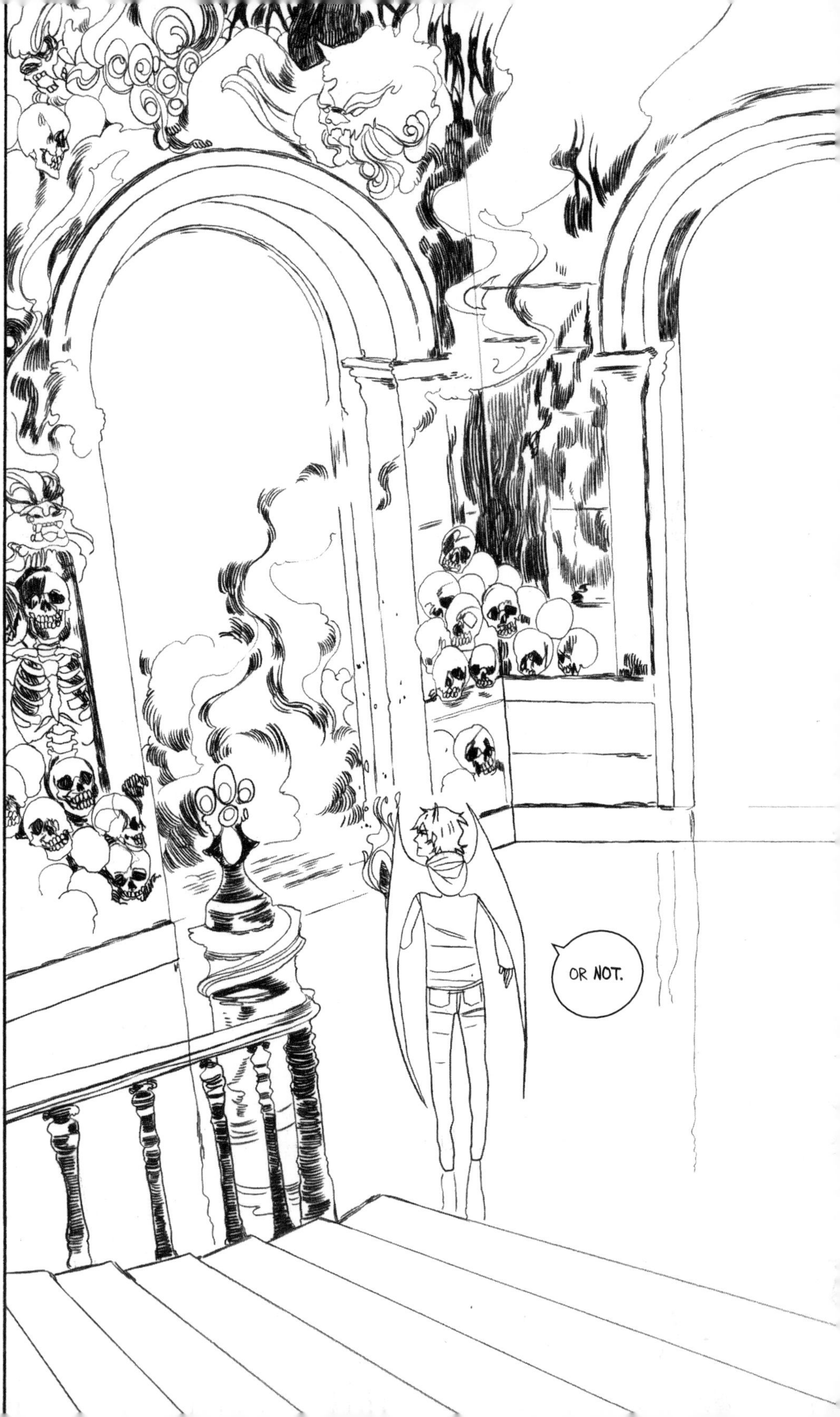
OR NOT.

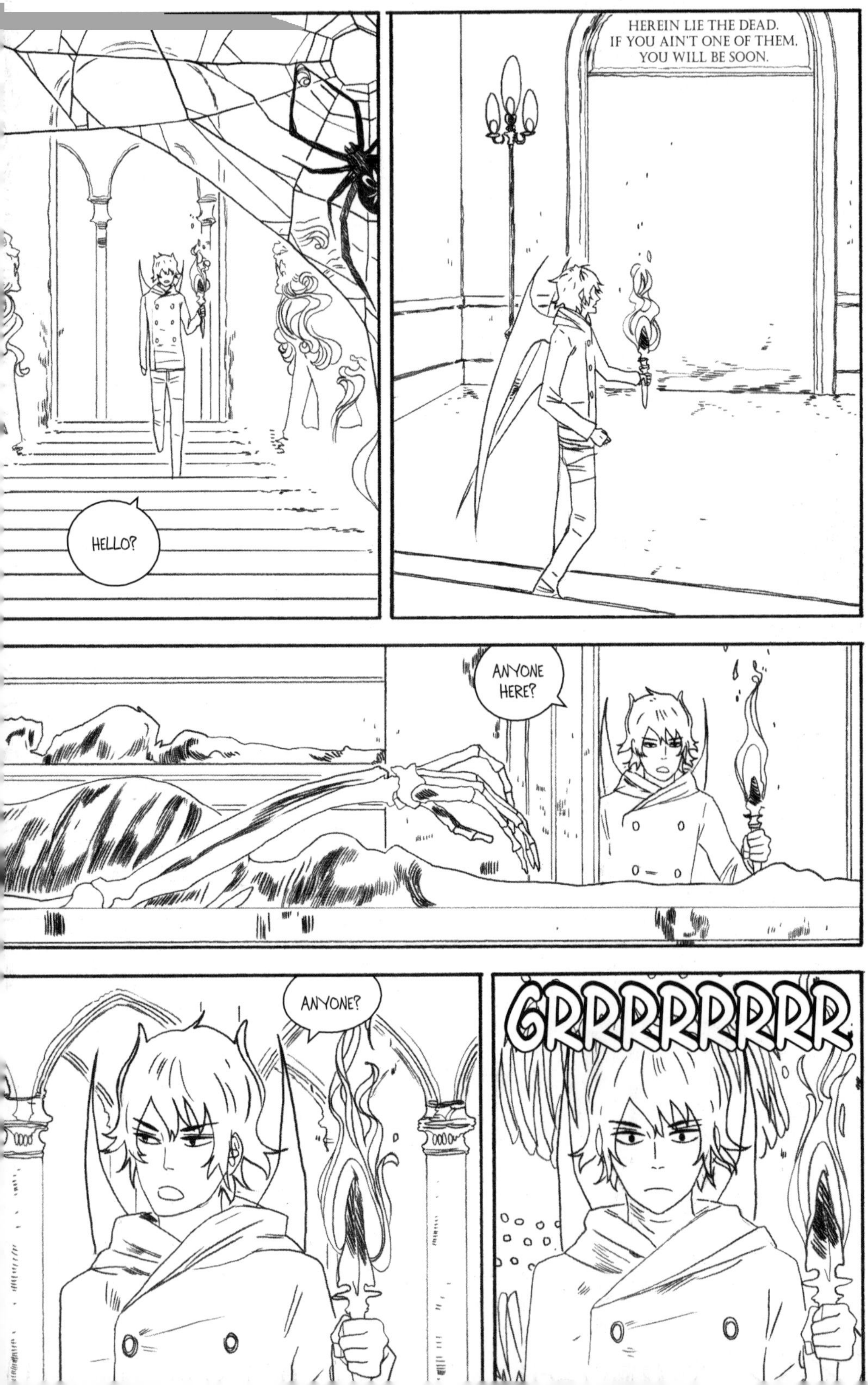
HELLO?
HEREIN LIE THE DEAD.
IF YOU AIN'T ONE OF THEM,
YOU WILL BE SOON.
ANYONE HERE?
ANYONE?
GRRRRRRRR

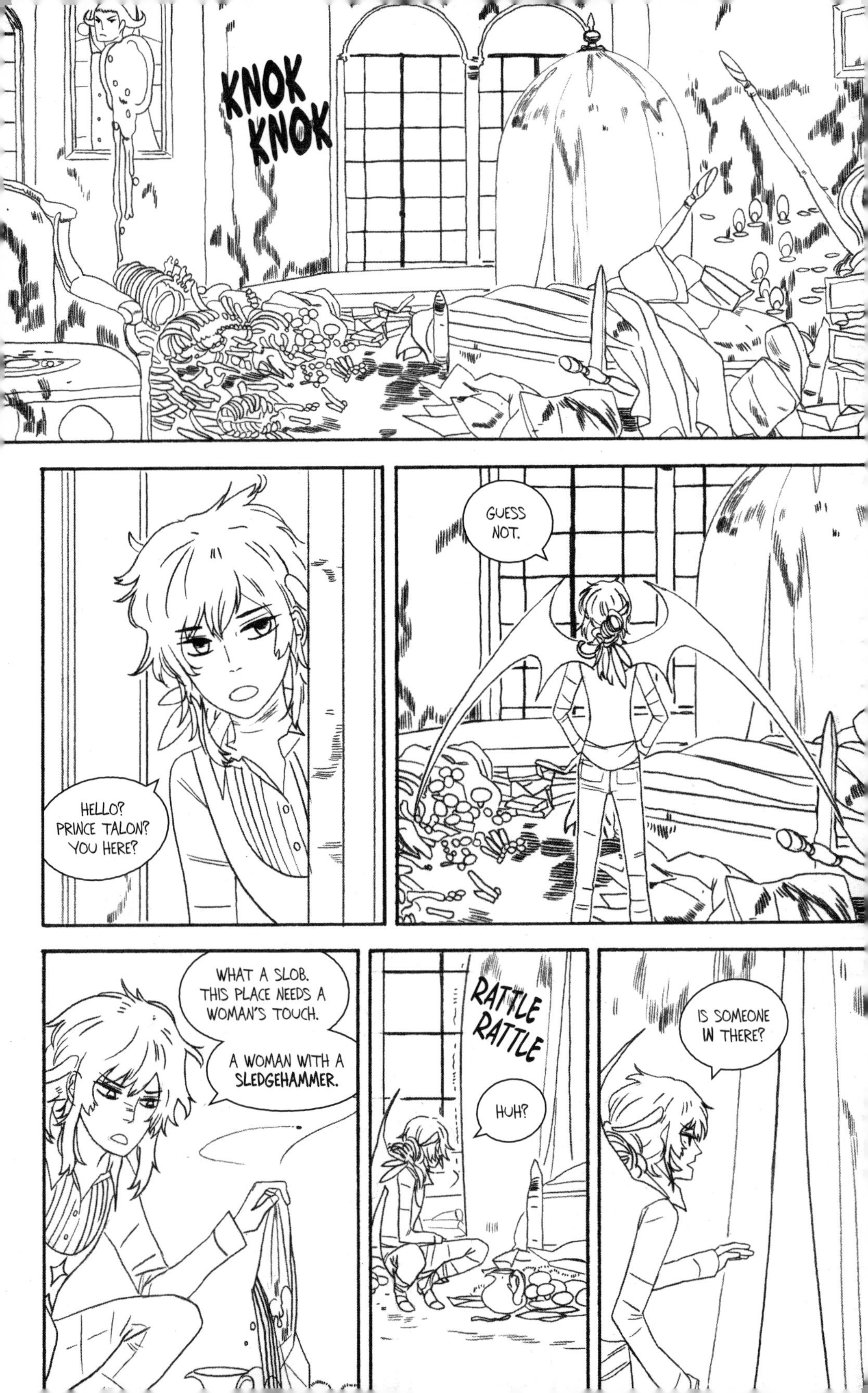
KNOK KNOK
HELLO? PRINCE TALON? YOU HERE?
GUESS NOT.
WHAT A SLOB. THIS PLACE NEEDS A WOMAN'S TOUCH.
A WOMAN WITH A SLEDGEHAMMER.
RATTLE RATTLE
HUH?
IS SOMEONE IN THERE?

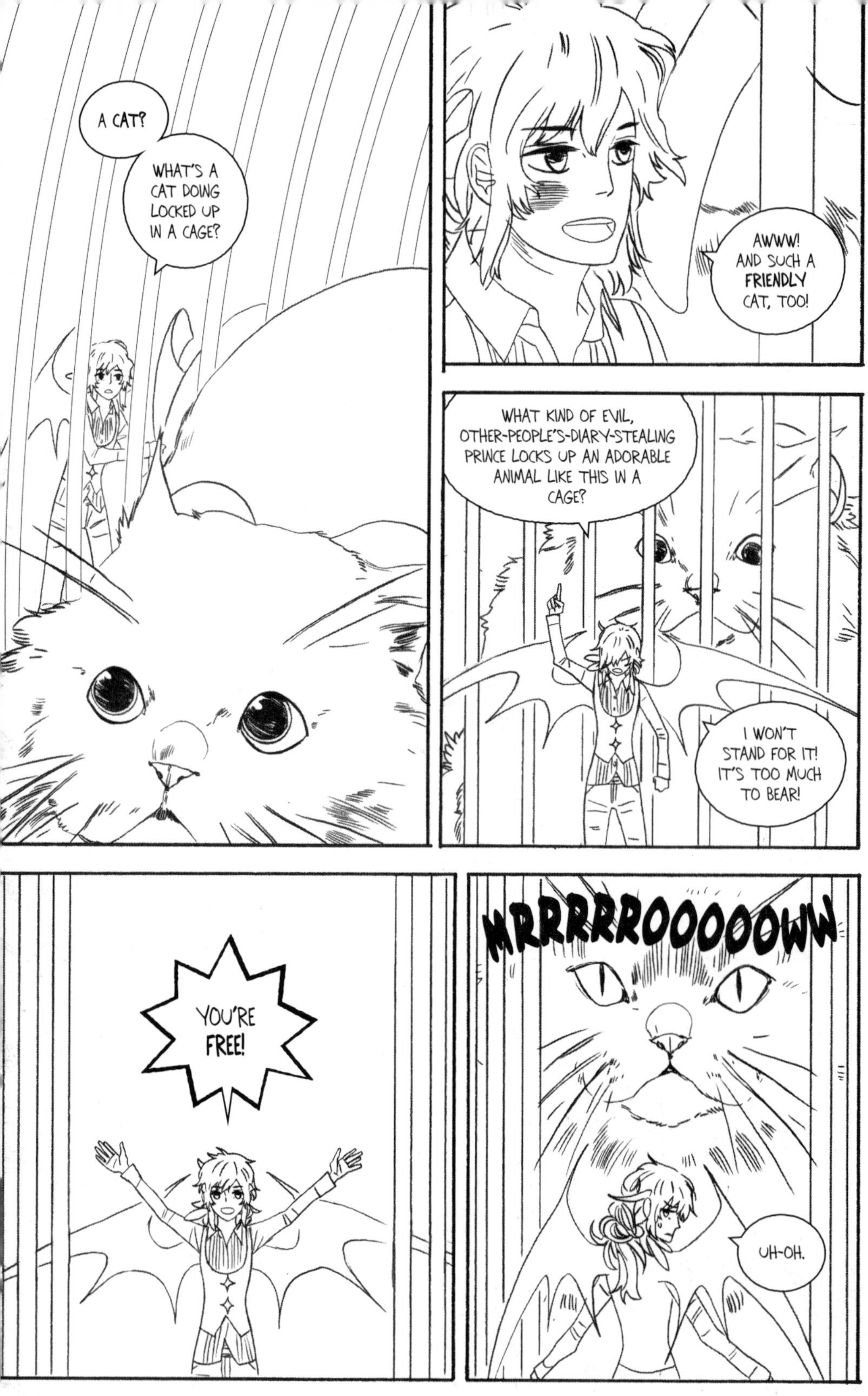
A CAT?
WHAT'S A CAT DOING LOCKED UP IN A CAGE?
AWWW! AND SUCH A FRIENDLY CAT, TOO!
WHAT KIND OF EVIL, OTHER-PEOPLE'S-DIARY-STEALING PRINCE LOCKS UP AN ADORABLE ANIMAL LIKE THIS IN A CAGE?
I WON'T STAND FOR IT! IT'S TOO MUCH TO BEAR!
YOU'RE FREE!
MRRRRROOOOOWW
UH-OH.

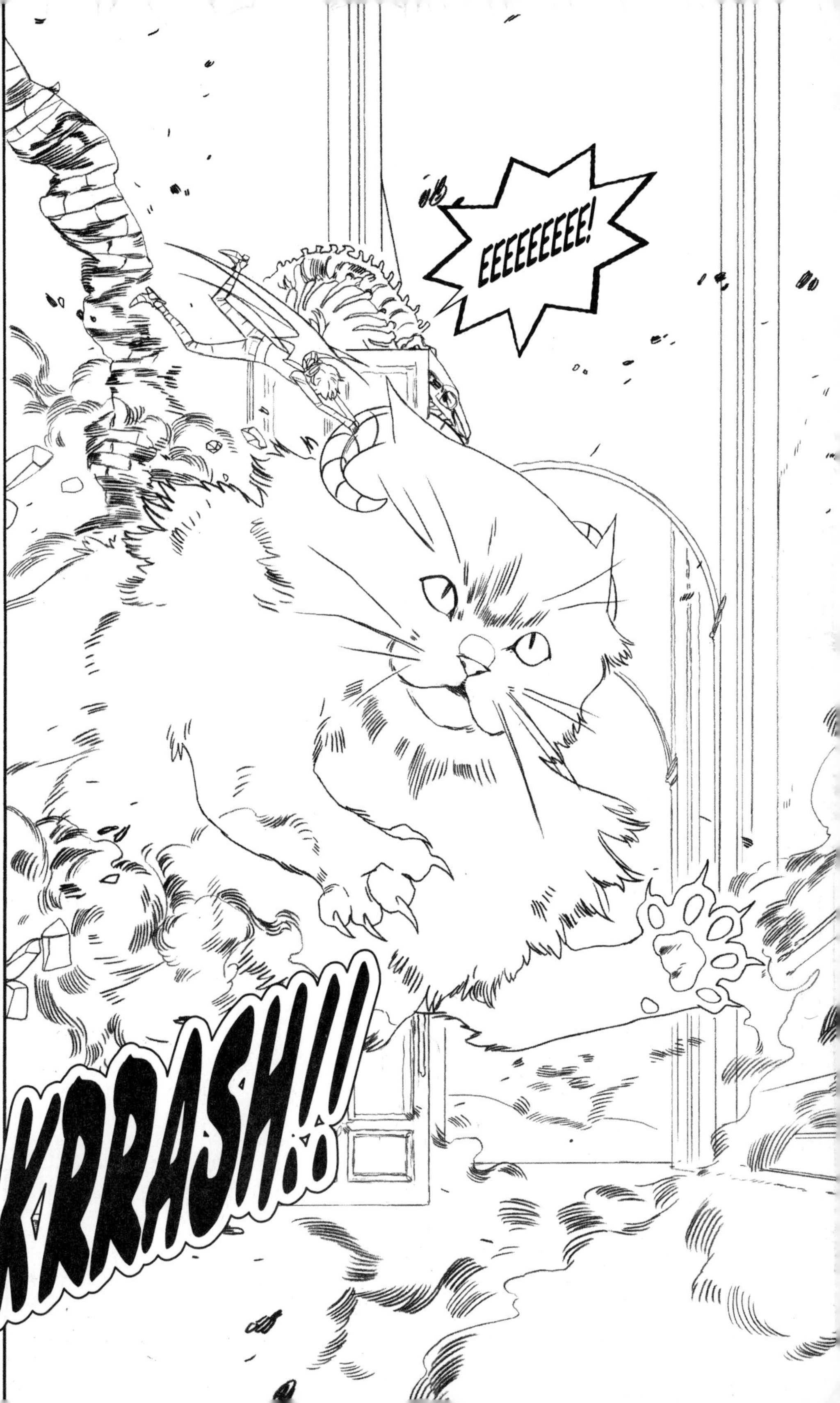
EEEEEEEEE!
KRRASH!!

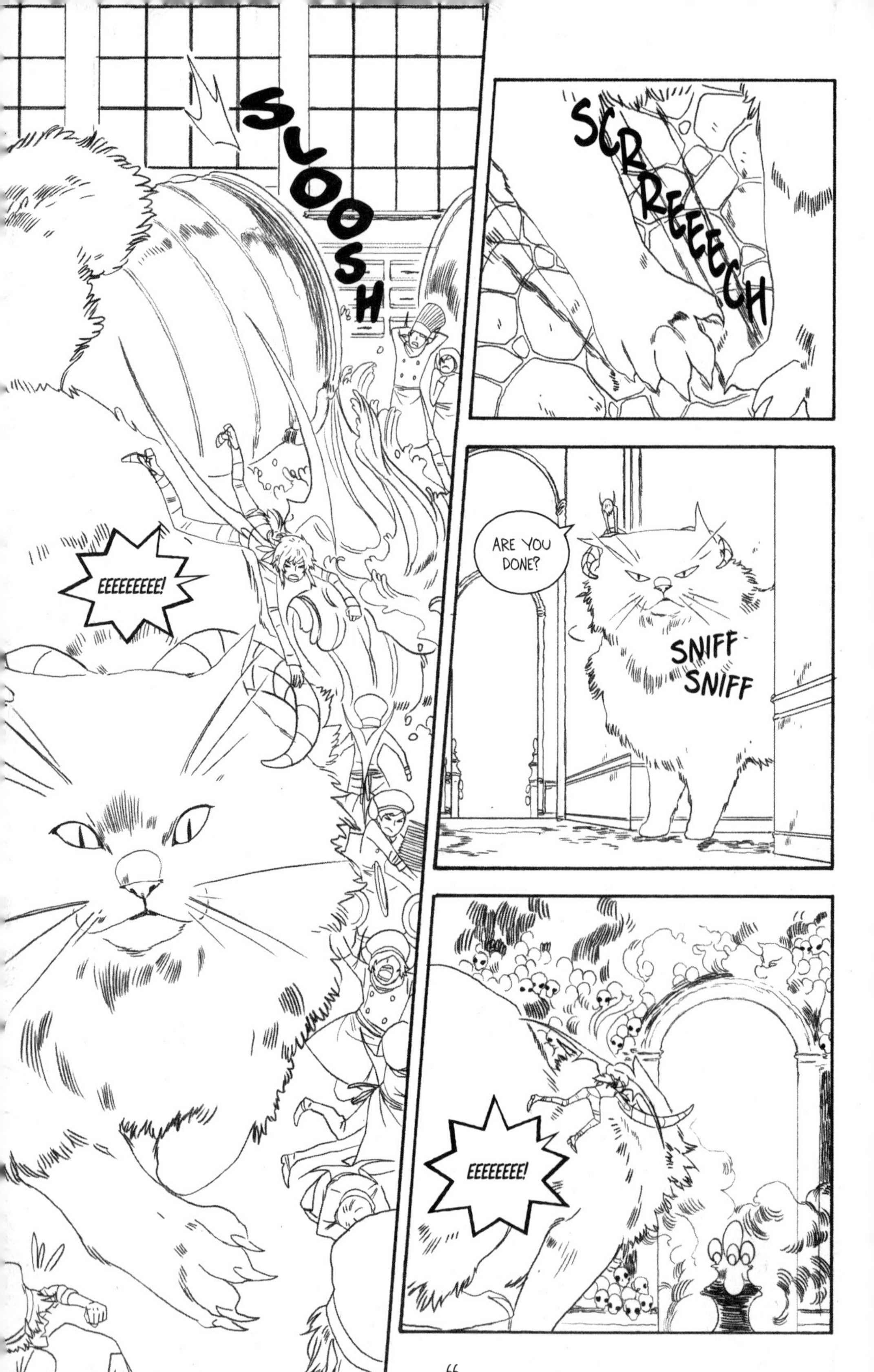
SLOOSH
EEEEEEEEE!
SCRREEEECH
ARE YOU DONE?
SNIFF SNIFF
EEEEEEEE!

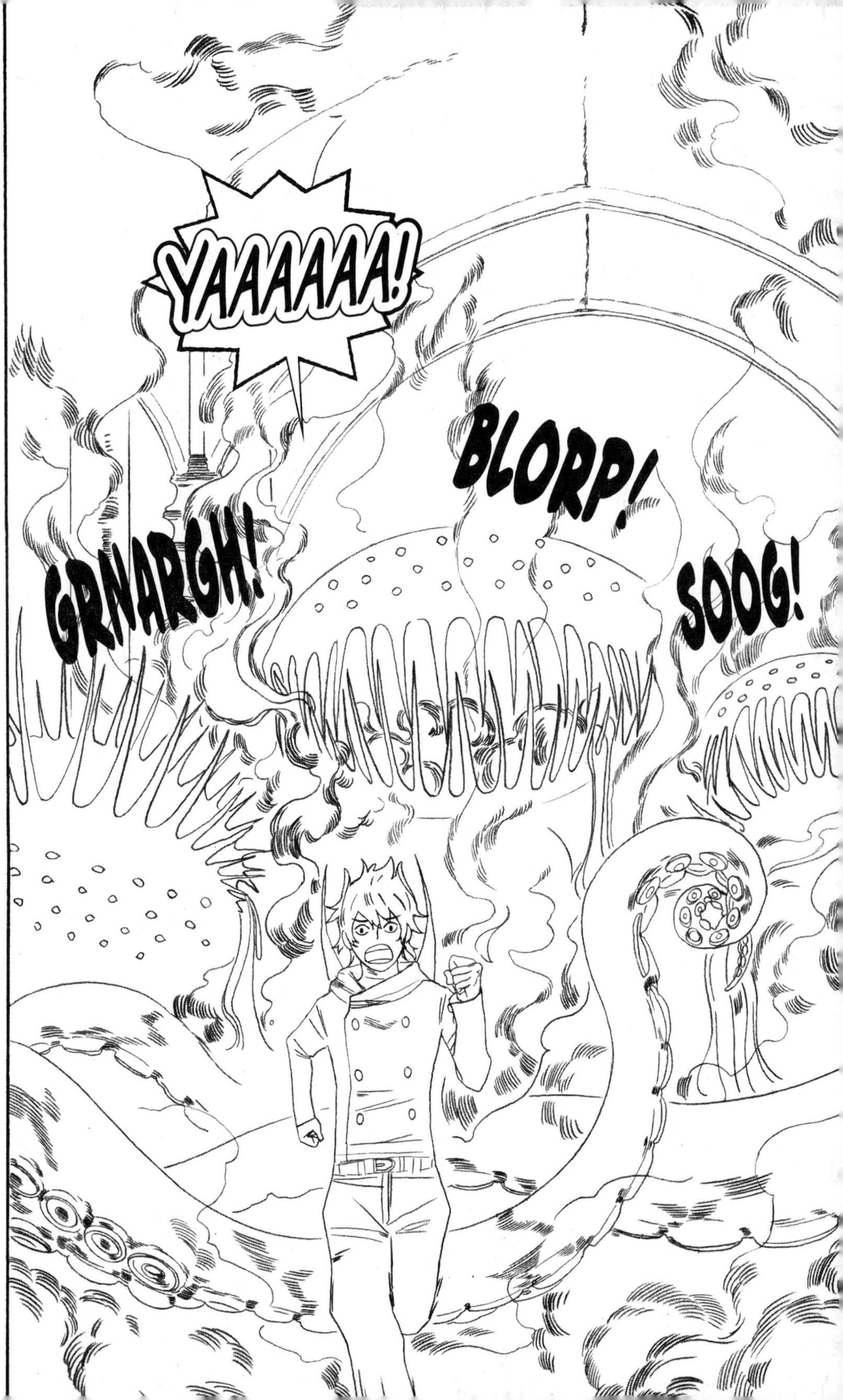
YAAAAAA!
BLORP!
GRNARGH!
SOOG!

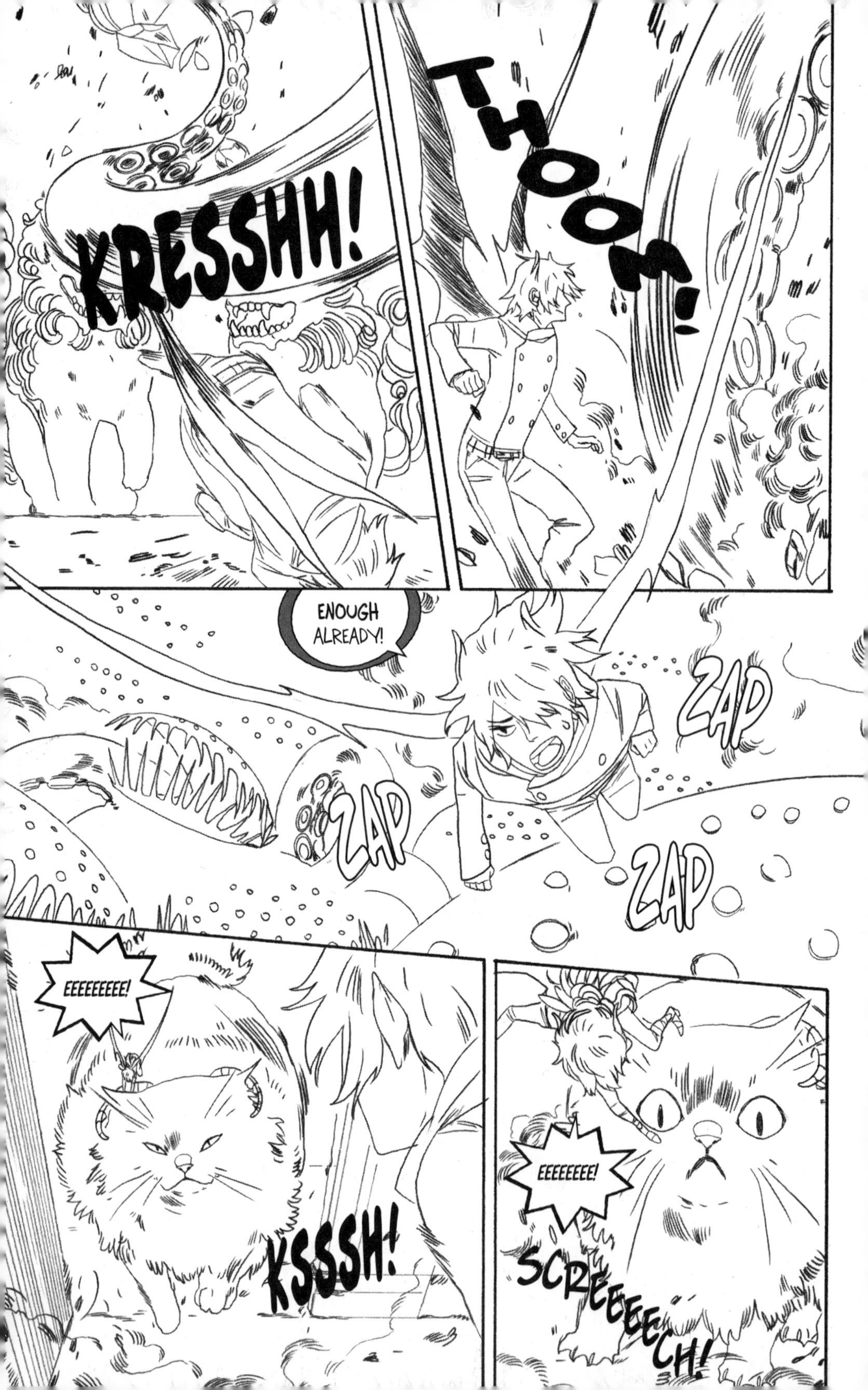
KRESSHH!
THOOM!
ENOUGH ALREADY!
ZAP
ZAP
ZAP
EEEEEEEEE!
KSSSH!
EEEEEEEE!
SCREEEEECH!

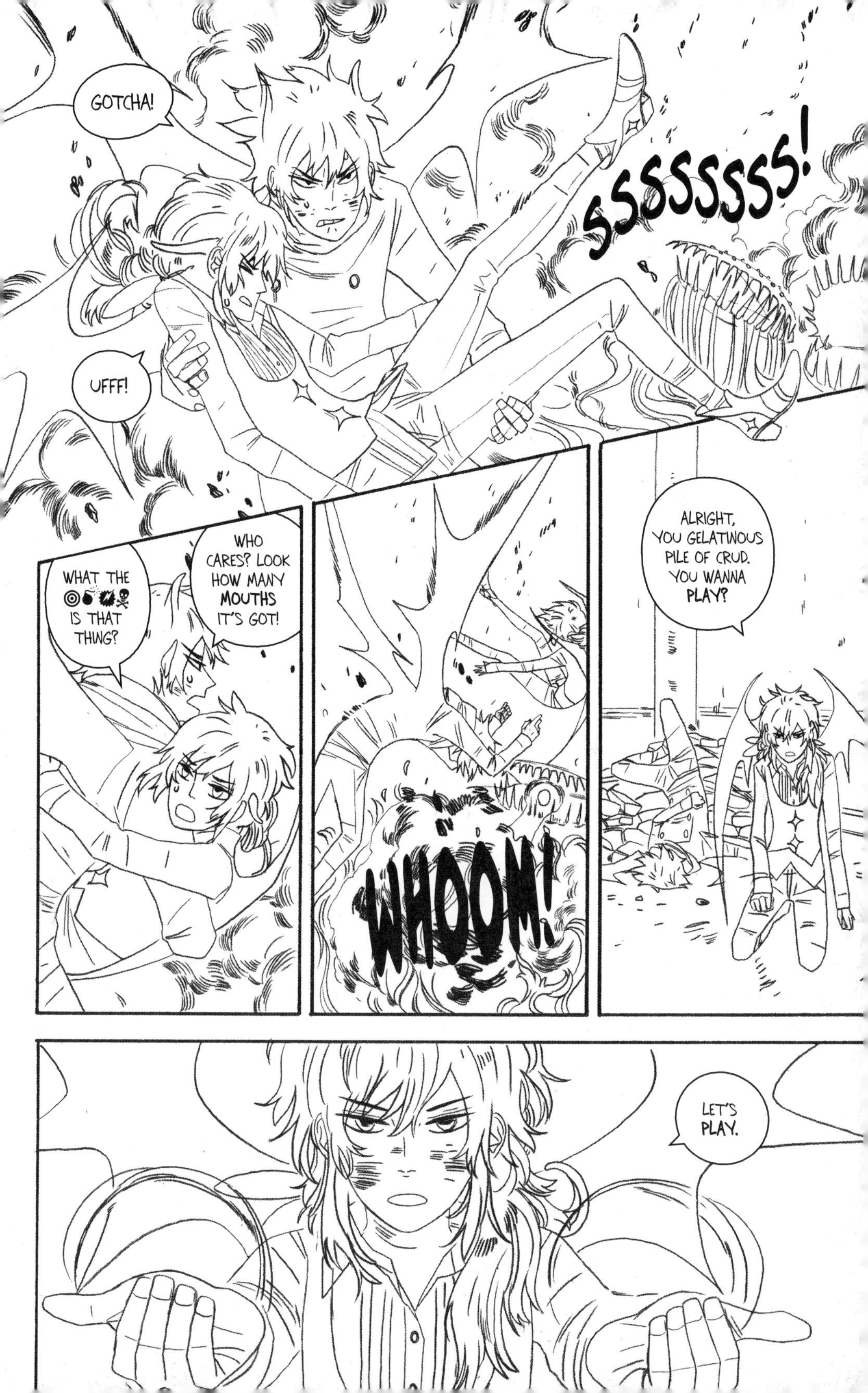
GOTCHA!
UFFF!
SSSSSSSS!
WHAT THE IS THAT THING?
WHO CARES? LOOK HOW MANY MOUTHS IT'S GOT!
WHOOM!
ALRIGHT, YOU GELATINOUS PILE OF CRUD. YOU WANNA PLAY?
LET'S PLAY.

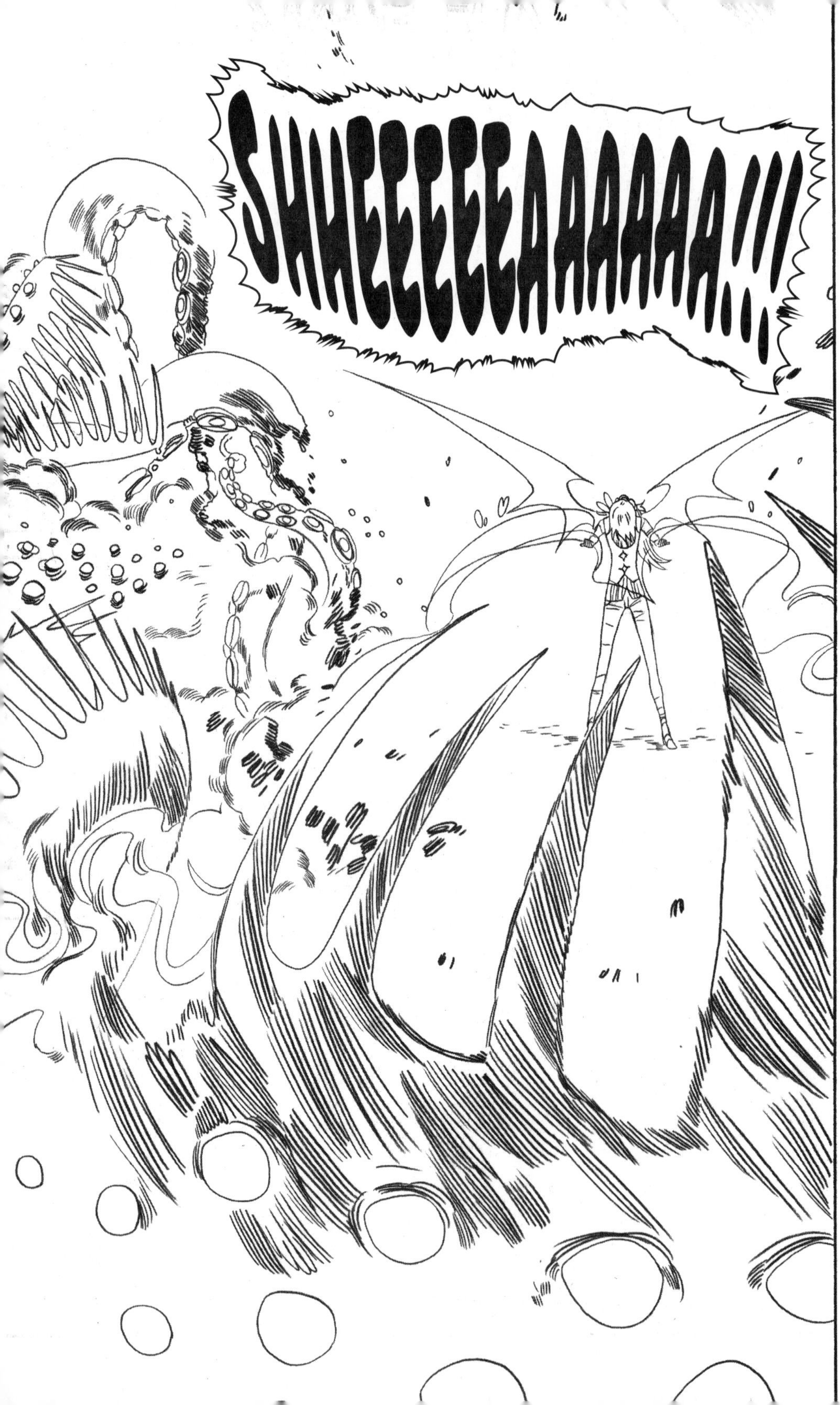
SHWEEEEEAAAAAA!!!

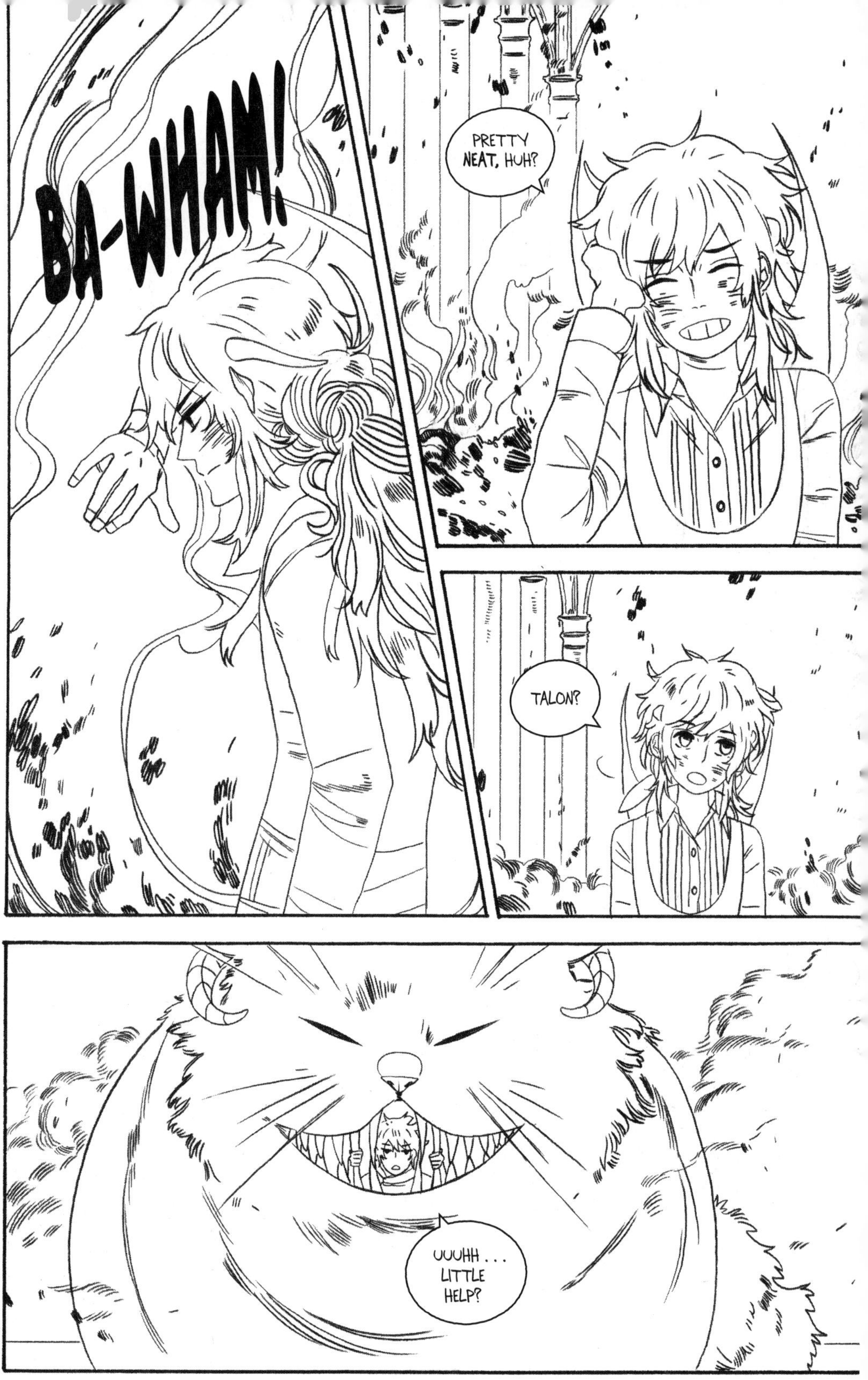
BA-WHAM!
PRETTY NEAT, HUH?
TALON?
UUUHH . . . LITTLE HELP?

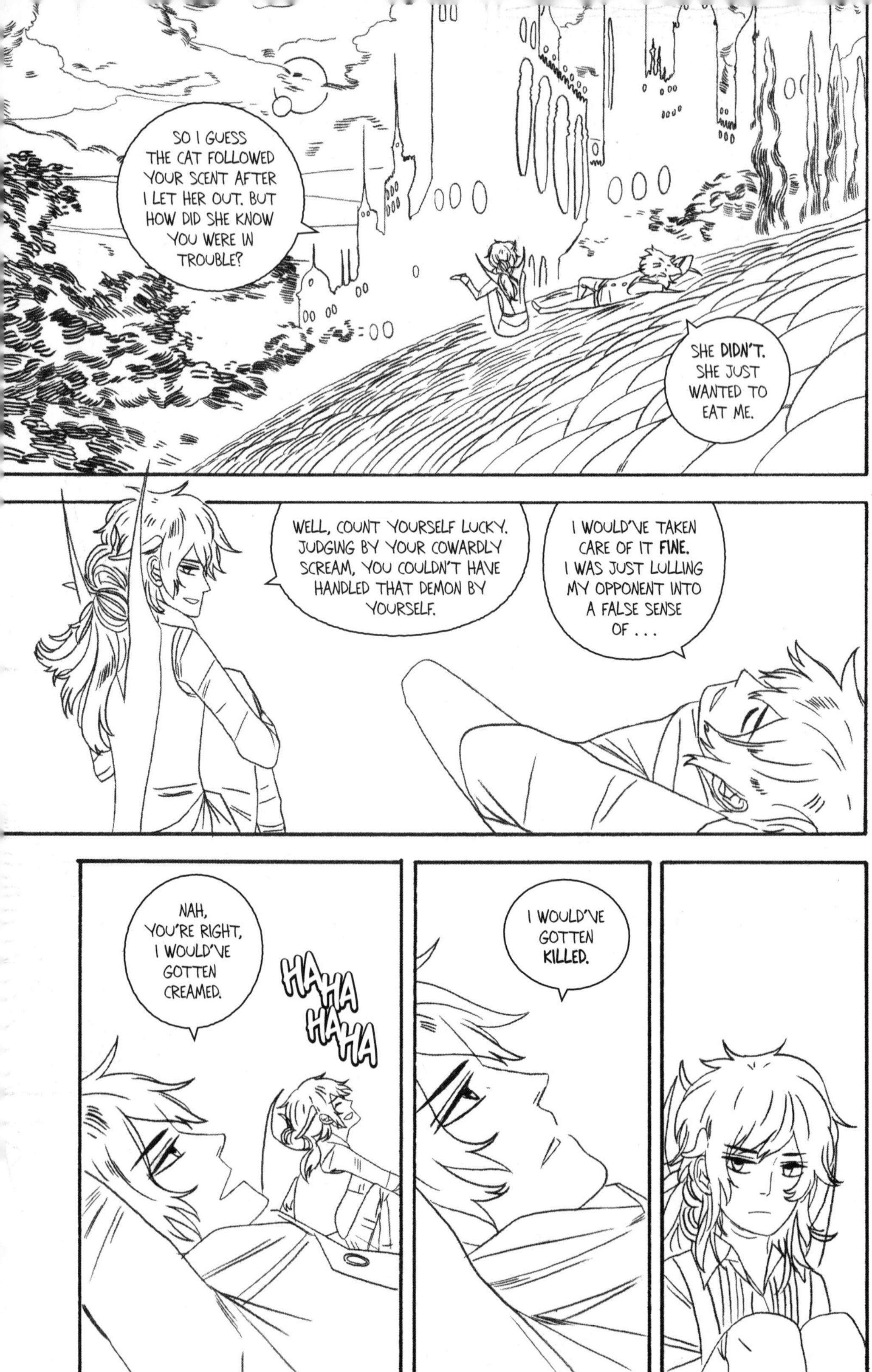
SO I GUESS THE CAT FOLLOWED YOUR SCENT AFTER I LET HER OUT. BUT HOW DID SHE KNOW YOU WERE IN TROUBLE?
SHE **DIDN'T.** SHE JUST WANTED TO EAT ME.
WELL, COUNT YOURSELF LUCKY. JUDGING BY YOUR COWARDLY SCREAM, YOU COULDN'T HAVE HANDLED THAT DEMON BY YOURSELF.
I WOULD'VE TAKEN CARE OF IT **FINE.** I WAS JUST LULLING MY OPPONENT INTO A FALSE SENSE OF . . .
NAH, YOU'RE RIGHT, I WOULD'VE GOTTEN CREAMED.
HAHA HAHA
I WOULD'VE GOTTEN **KILLED.**

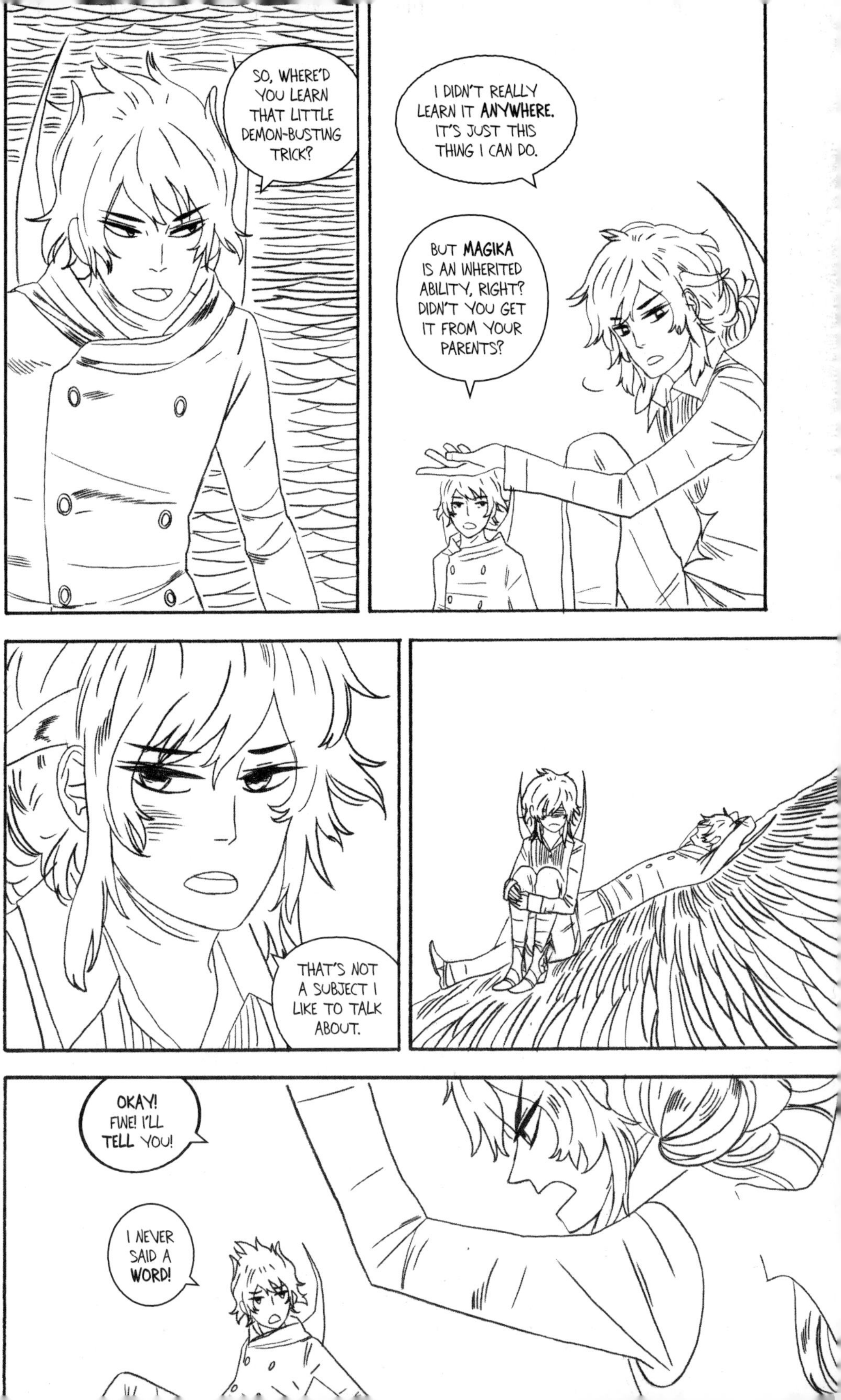
SO, WHERE'D YOU LEARN THAT LITTLE DEMON-BUSTING TRICK?
I DIDN'T REALLY LEARN IT **ANYWHERE.** IT'S JUST THIS THING I CAN DO.
BUT **MAGIKA** IS AN INHERITED ABILITY, RIGHT? DIDN'T YOU GET IT FROM YOUR PARENTS?
THAT'S NOT A SUBJECT I LIKE TO TALK ABOUT.
OKAY! FINE! I'LL **TELL** YOU!
I NEVER SAID A **WORD!**

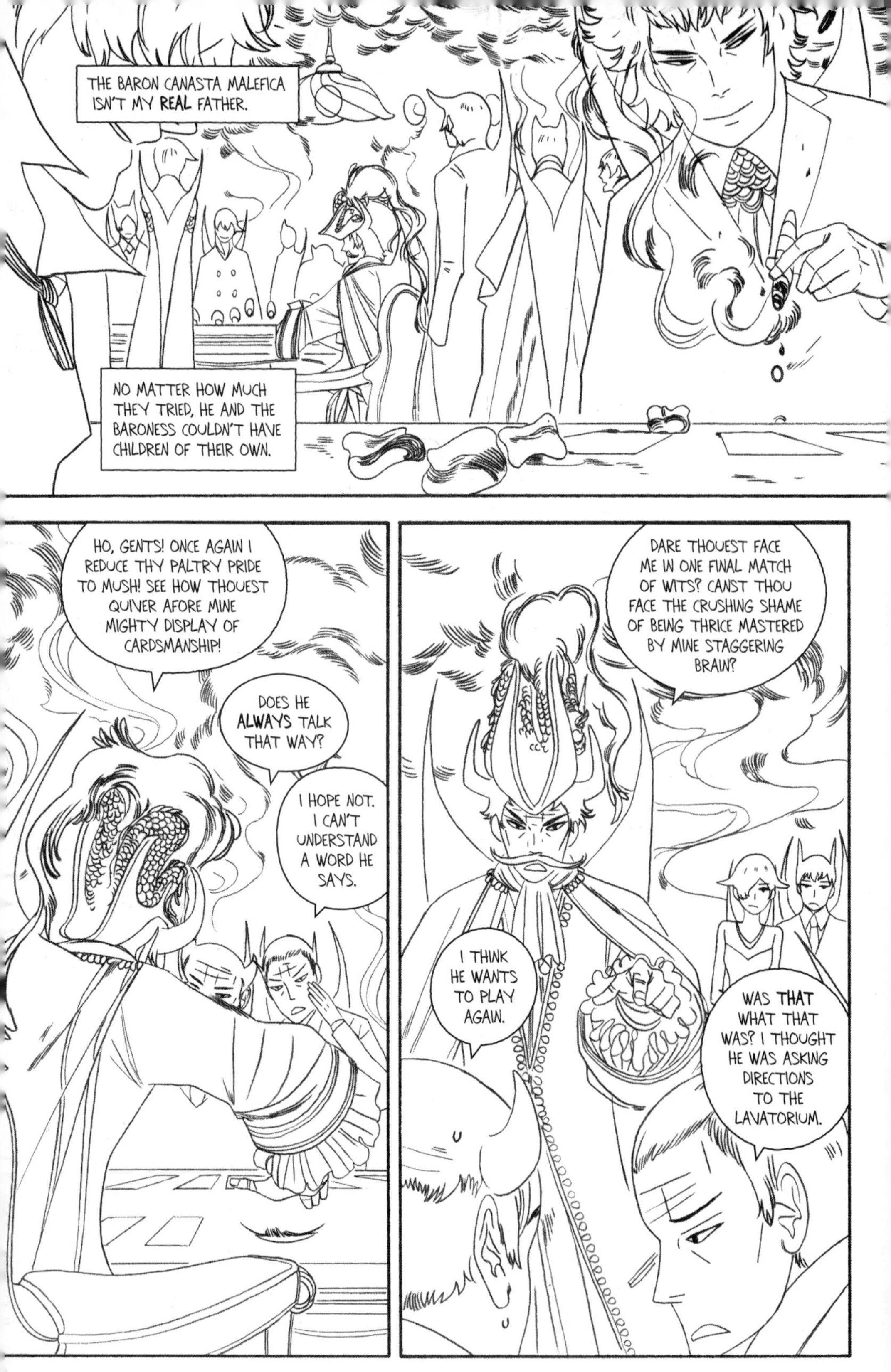
THE BARON CANASTA MALEFICA ISN'T MY **REAL** FATHER.
NO MATTER HOW MUCH THEY TRIED, HE AND THE BARONESS COULDN'T HAVE CHILDREN OF THEIR OWN.
HO, GENTS! ONCE AGAIN I REDUCE THY PALTRY PRIDE TO MUSH! SEE HOW THOUEST QUIVER AFORE MINE MIGHTY DISPLAY OF CARDSMANSHIP!
DOES HE **ALWAYS** TALK THAT WAY?
I HOPE NOT. I CAN'T UNDERSTAND A WORD HE SAYS.
DARE THOUEST FACE ME IN ONE FINAL MATCH OF WITS? CANST THOU FACE THE CRUSHING SHAME OF BEING THRICE MASTERED BY MINE STAGGERING BRAIN?
I THINK HE WANTS TO PLAY AGAIN.
WAS **THAT** WHAT THAT WAS? I THOUGHT HE WAS ASKING DIRECTIONS TO THE LAVATORIUM.

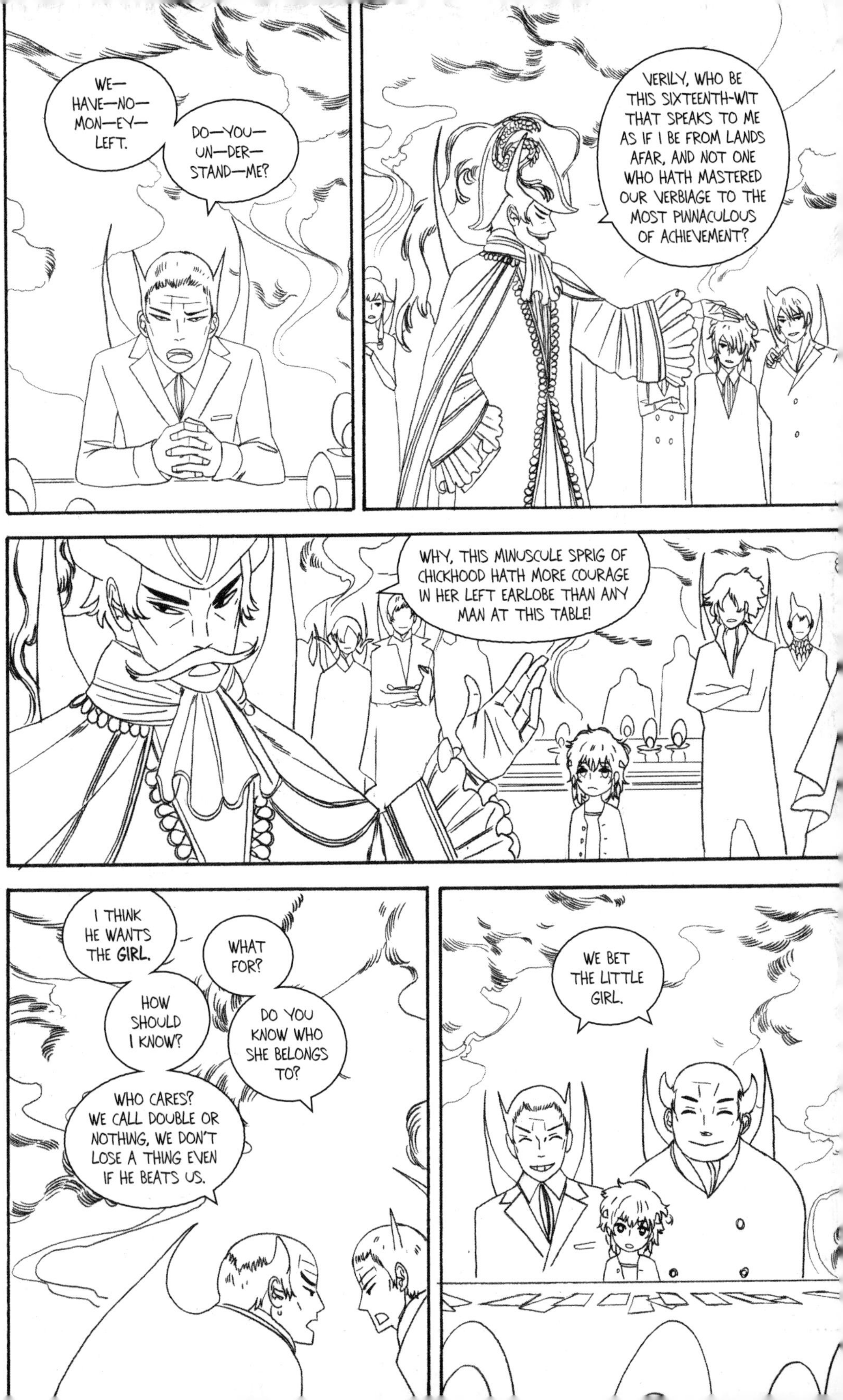
WE—HAVE—NO—MON—EY—LEFT.
DO—YOU—UN—DER—STAND—ME?
VERILY, WHO BE THIS SIXTEENTH-WIT THAT SPEAKS TO ME AS IF I BE FROM LANDS AFAR, AND NOT ONE WHO HATH MASTERED OUR VERBIAGE TO THE MOST PINNACULOUS OF ACHIEVEMENT?
WHY, THIS MINUSCULE SPRIG OF CHICKHOOD HATH MORE COURAGE IN HER LEFT EARLOBE THAN ANY MAN AT THIS TABLE!
I THINK HE WANTS THE **GIRL.**
WHAT FOR?
HOW SHOULD I KNOW?
DO YOU KNOW WHO SHE BELONGS TO?
WHO CARES? WE CALL DOUBLE OR NOTHING, WE DON'T LOSE A THING EVEN IF HE BEATS US.
WE BET THE LITTLE GIRL.

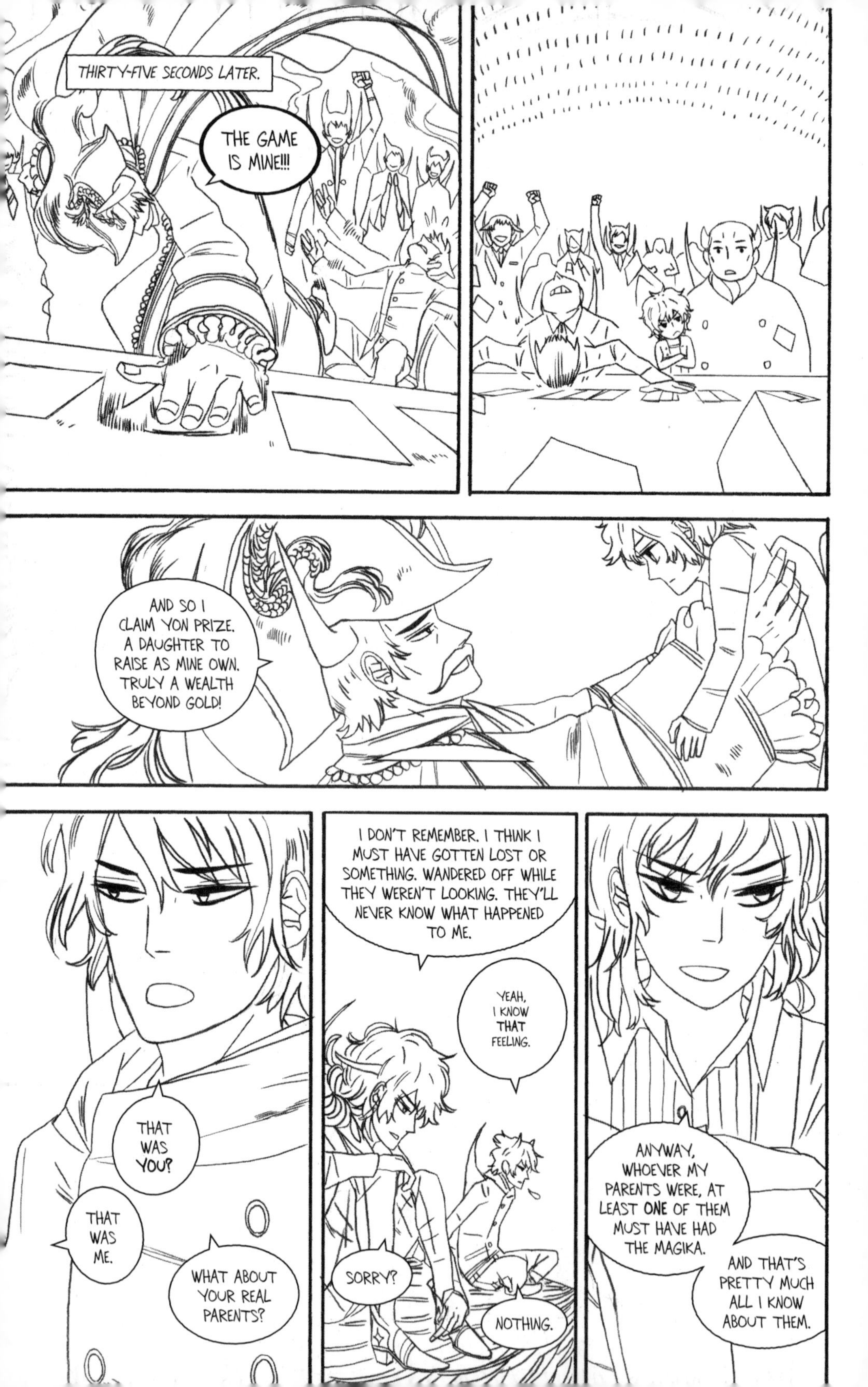
THIRTY-FIVE SECONDS LATER.
THE GAME IS MINE!!!
AND SO I CLAIM YON PRIZE. A DAUGHTER TO RAISE AS MINE OWN. TRULY A WEALTH BEYOND GOLD!
THAT WAS YOU?
THAT WAS ME.
WHAT ABOUT YOUR REAL PARENTS?
I DON'T REMEMBER. I THINK I MUST HAVE GOTTEN LOST OR SOMETHING. WANDERED OFF WHILE THEY WEREN'T LOOKING. THEY'LL NEVER KNOW WHAT HAPPENED TO ME.
YEAH, I KNOW **THAT** FEELING.
SORRY?
NOTHING.
ANYWAY, WHOEVER MY PARENTS WERE, AT LEAST **ONE** OF THEM MUST HAVE HAD THE MAGIKA.
AND THAT'S PRETTY MUCH ALL I KNOW ABOUT THEM.

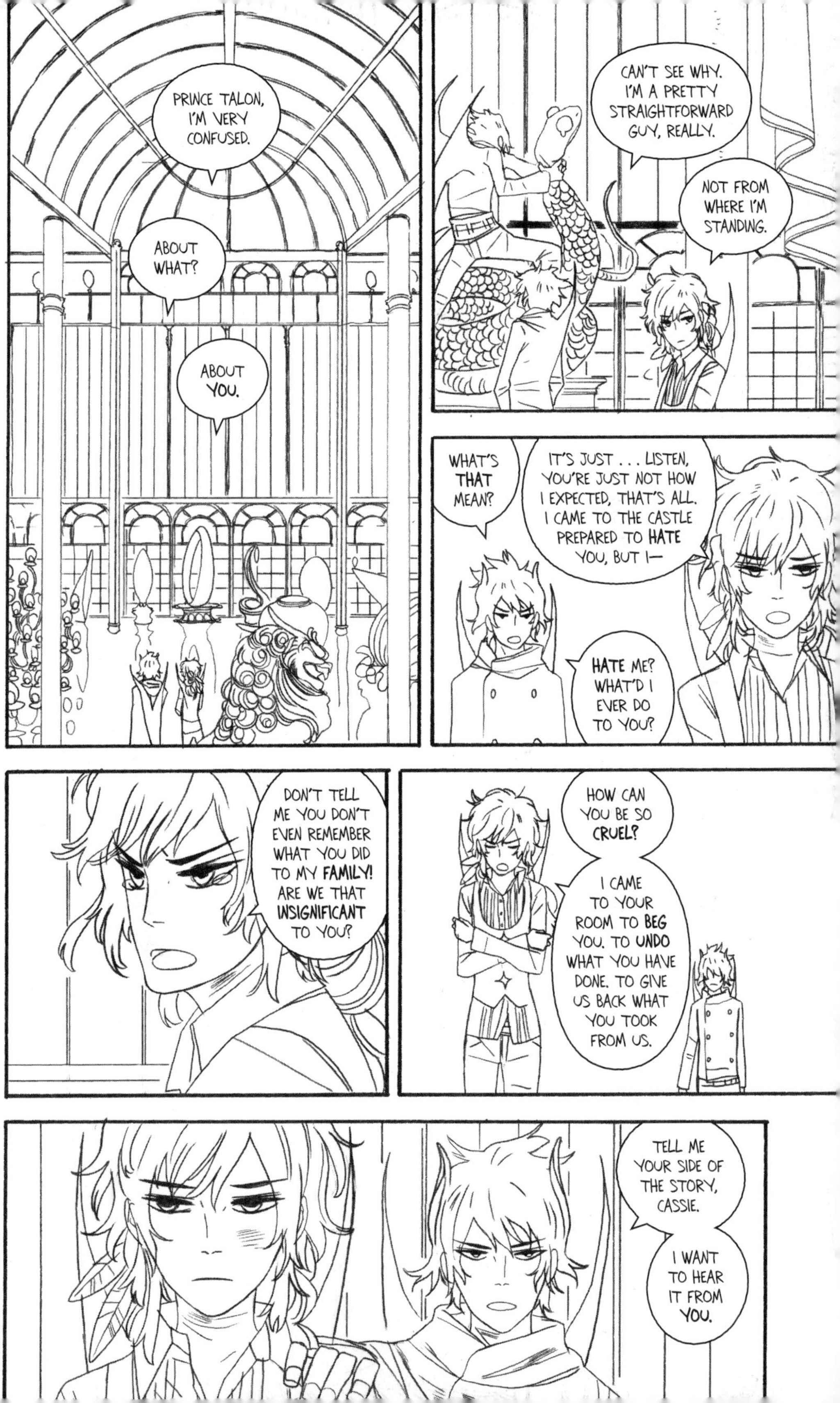
PRINCE TALON, I'M VERY CONFUSED.
ABOUT WHAT?
ABOUT **YOU.**
CAN'T SEE WHY. I'M A PRETTY STRAIGHTFORWARD GUY, REALLY.
NOT FROM WHERE I'M STANDING.
WHAT'S **THAT** MEAN?
IT'S JUST . . . LISTEN, YOU'RE JUST NOT HOW I EXPECTED, THAT'S ALL. I CAME TO THE CASTLE PREPARED TO **HATE** YOU, BUT I—
HATE ME? WHAT'D I EVER DO TO YOU?
DON'T TELL ME YOU DON'T EVEN REMEMBER WHAT YOU DID TO MY **FAMILY!** ARE WE THAT **INSIGNIFICANT** TO YOU?
HOW CAN YOU BE SO **CRUEL?**
I CAME TO YOUR ROOM TO **BEG** YOU. TO **UNDO** WHAT YOU HAVE DONE. TO GIVE US BACK WHAT YOU TOOK FROM US.
TELL ME YOUR SIDE OF THE STORY, CASSIE.
I WANT TO HEAR IT FROM **YOU.**

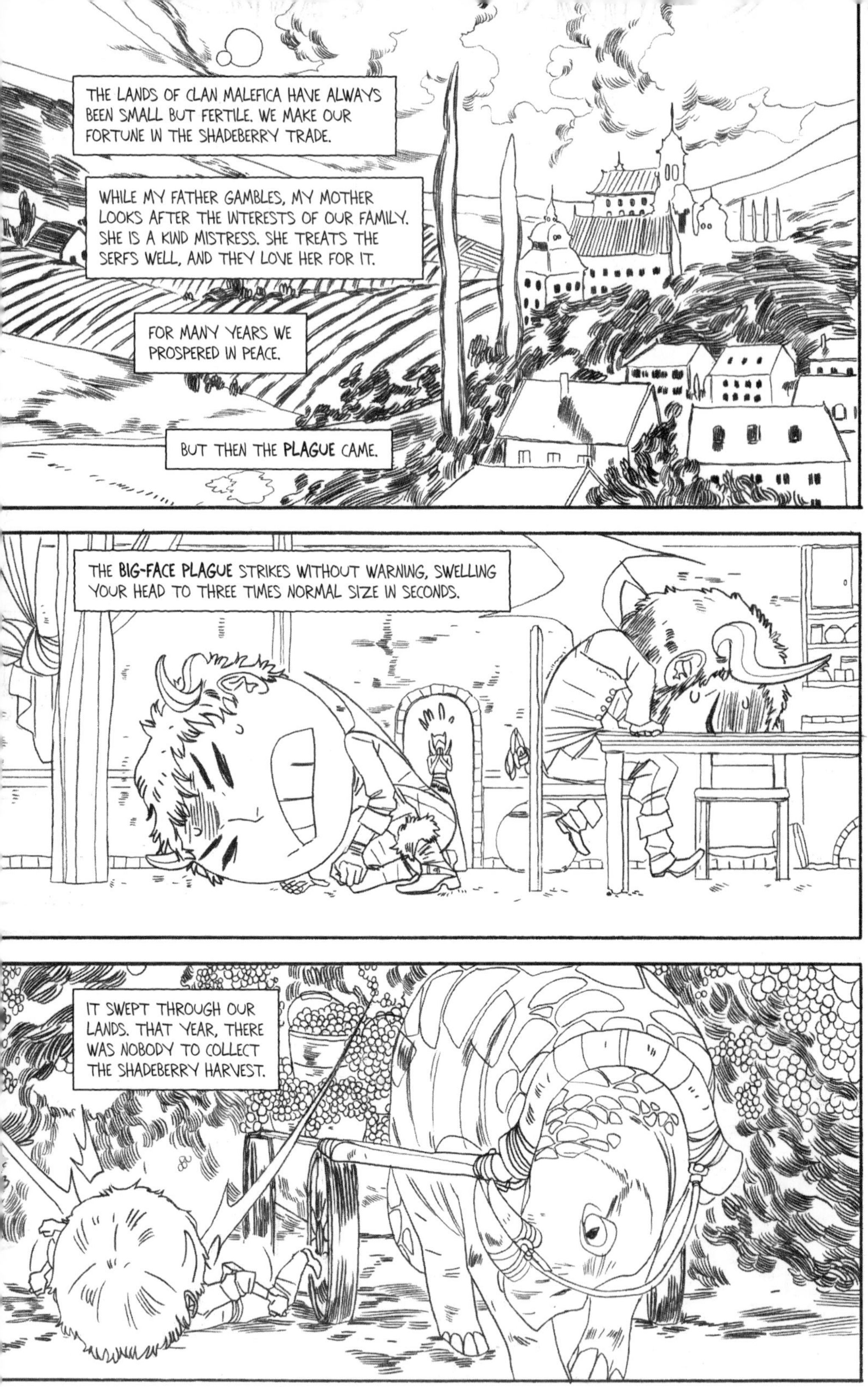
THE LANDS OF CLAN MALEFICA HAVE ALWAYS BEEN SMALL BUT FERTILE. WE MAKE OUR FORTUNE IN THE SHADEBERRY TRADE.
WHILE MY FATHER GAMBLES, MY MOTHER LOOKS AFTER THE INTERESTS OF OUR FAMILY. SHE IS A KIND MISTRESS. SHE TREATS THE SERFS WELL, AND THEY LOVE HER FOR IT.
FOR MANY YEARS WE PROSPERED IN PEACE.
BUT THEN THE PLAGUE CAME.
THE BIG-FACE PLAGUE STRIKES WITHOUT WARNING, SWELLING YOUR HEAD TO THREE TIMES NORMAL SIZE IN SECONDS.
IT SWEPT THROUGH OUR LANDS. THAT YEAR, THERE WAS NOBODY TO COLLECT THE SHADEBERRY HARVEST.

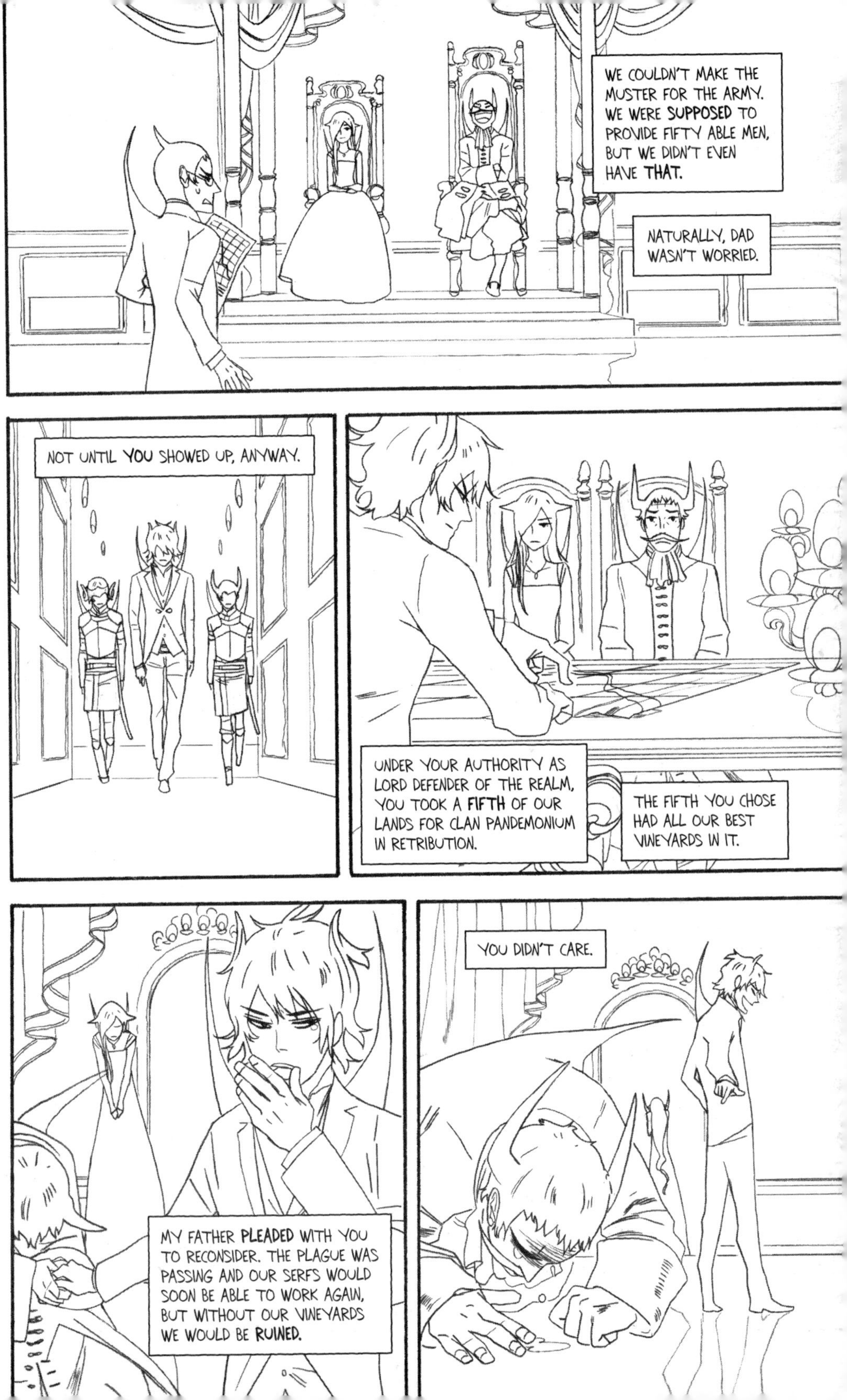
WE COULDN'T MAKE THE MUSTER FOR THE ARMY. WE WERE **SUPPOSED** TO PROVIDE FIFTY ABLE MEN, BUT WE DIDN'T EVEN HAVE **THAT.**
NATURALLY, DAD WASN'T WORRIED.
NOT UNTIL **YOU** SHOWED UP, ANYWAY.
UNDER YOUR AUTHORITY AS LORD DEFENDER OF THE REALM, YOU TOOK A **FIFTH** OF OUR LANDS FOR CLAN PANDEMONIUM IN RETRIBUTION.
THE FIFTH YOU CHOSE HAD ALL OUR BEST VINEYARDS IN IT.
MY FATHER **PLEADED** WITH YOU TO RECONSIDER. THE PLAGUE WAS PASSING AND OUR SERFS WOULD SOON BE ABLE TO WORK AGAIN, BUT WITHOUT OUR VINEYARDS WE WOULD BE **RUINED.**
YOU DIDN'T CARE.

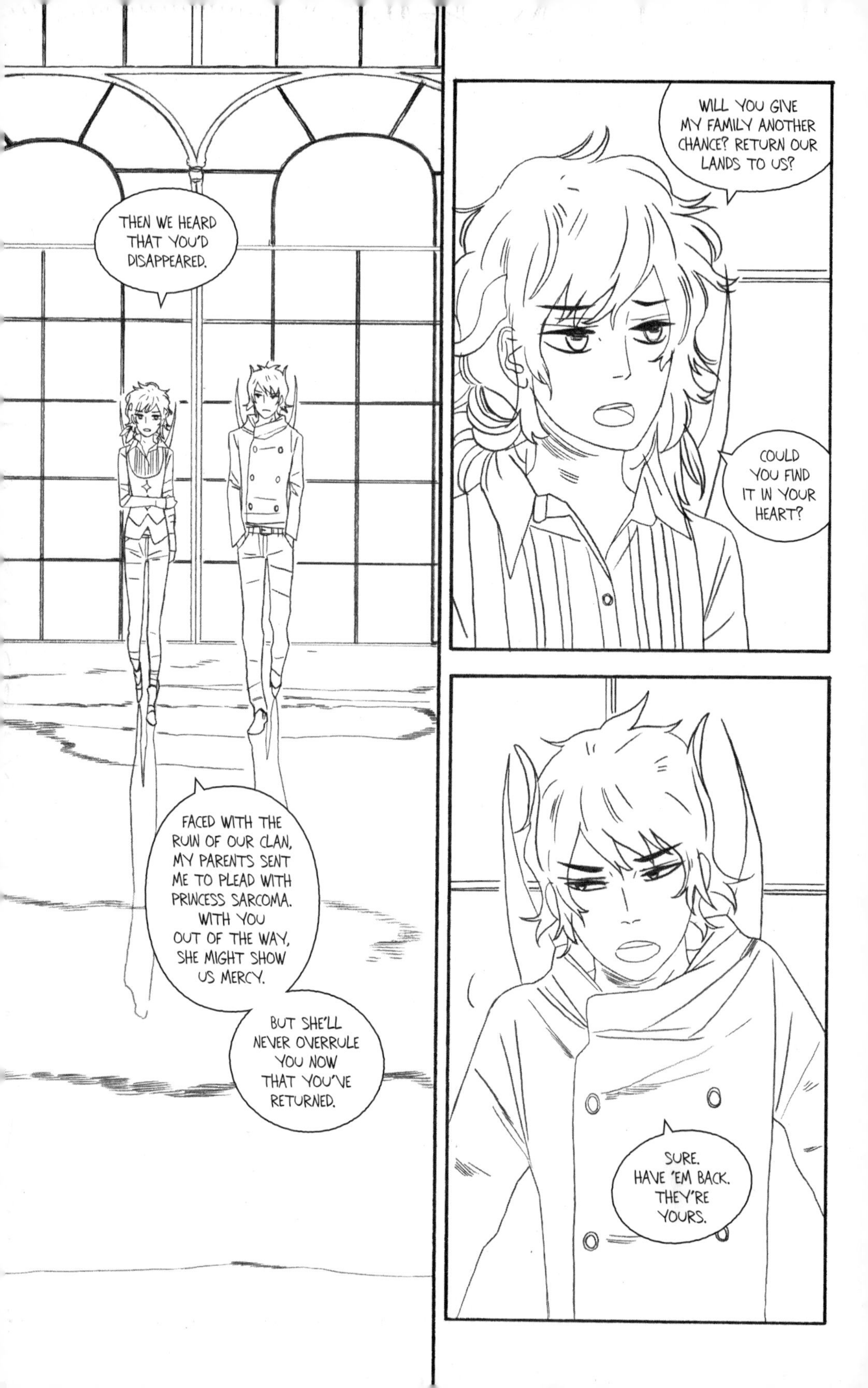
THEN WE HEARD THAT YOU'D DISAPPEARED.
FACED WITH THE RUIN OF OUR CLAN, MY PARENTS SENT ME TO PLEAD WITH PRINCESS SARCOMA. WITH YOU OUT OF THE WAY, SHE MIGHT SHOW US MERCY.
BUT SHE'LL NEVER OVERRULE YOU NOW THAT YOU'VE RETURNED.
WILL YOU GIVE MY FAMILY ANOTHER CHANCE? RETURN OUR LANDS TO US?
COULD YOU FIND IT IN YOUR HEART?
SURE. HAVE 'EM BACK. THEY'RE YOURS.

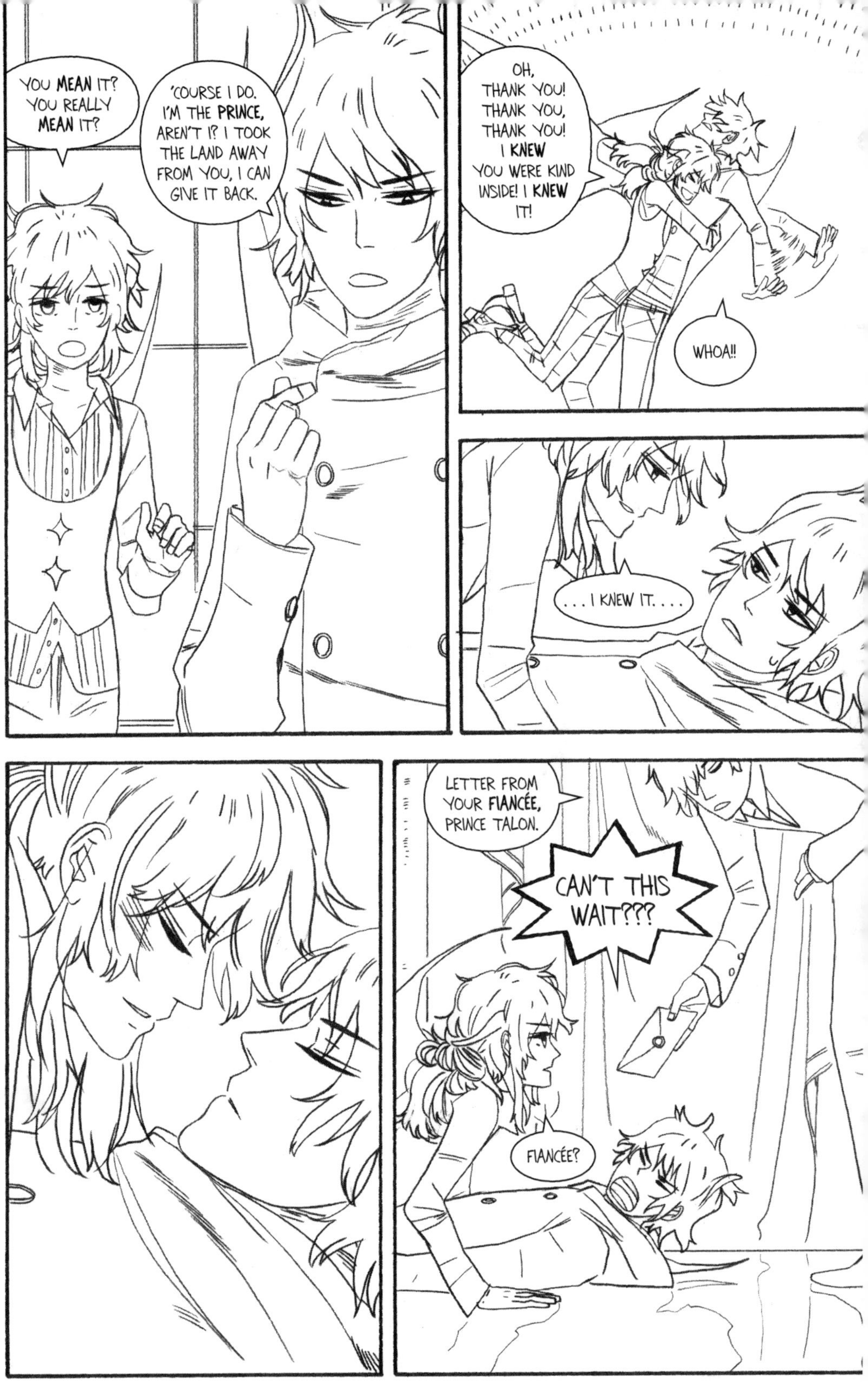

YOU MEAN IT? YOU REALLY MEAN IT?
'COURSE I DO. I'M THE PRINCE, AREN'T I? I TOOK THE LAND AWAY FROM YOU, I CAN GIVE IT BACK.
OH, THANK YOU! THANK YOU, THANK YOU! I KNEW YOU WERE KIND INSIDE! I KNEW IT!
WHOA!!
. . . I KNEW IT. . . .
LETTER FROM YOUR FIANCÉE, PRINCE TALON.
CAN'T THIS WAIT???
FIANCÉE?

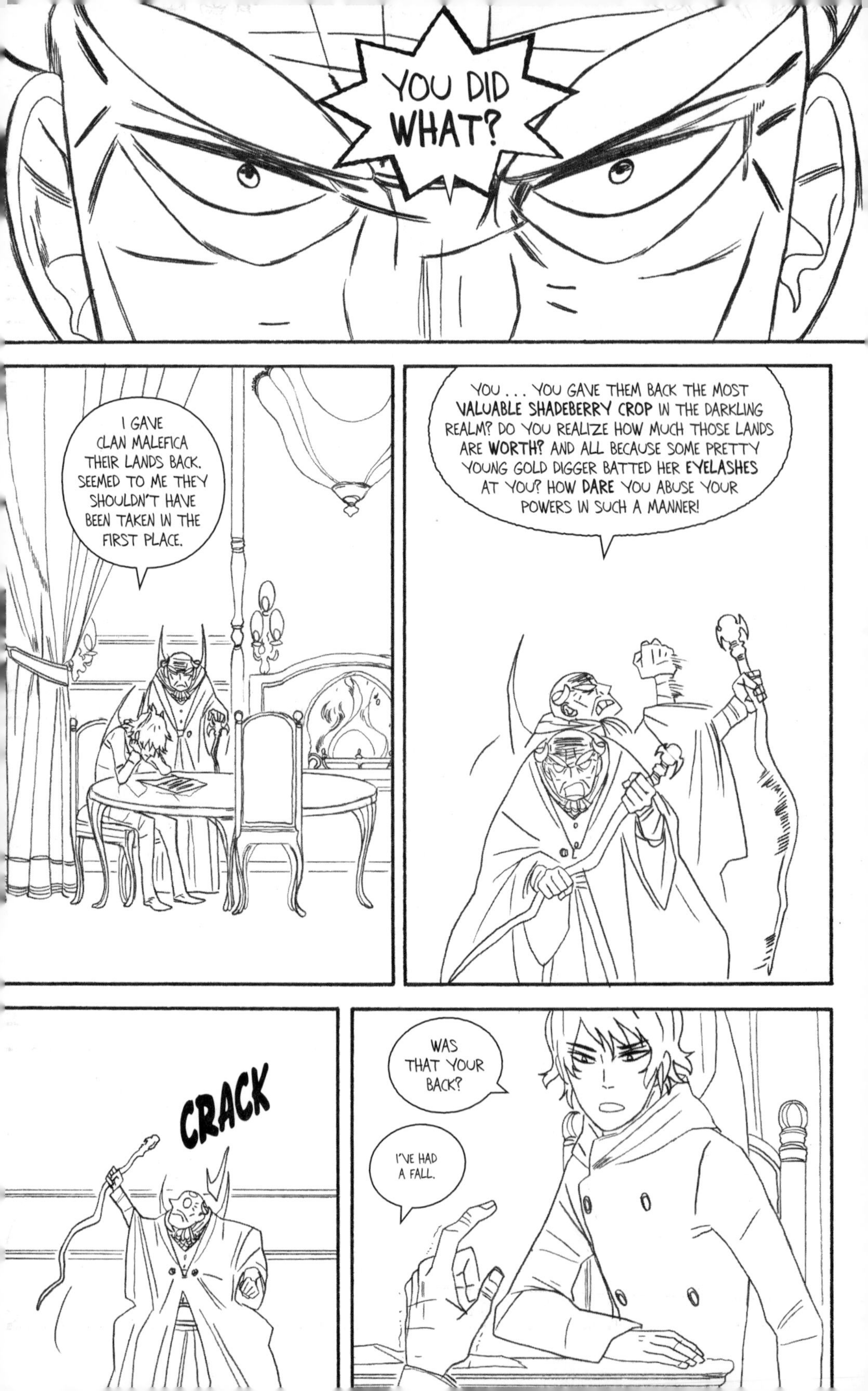
YOU DID WHAT?
I GAVE CLAN MALEFICA THEIR LANDS BACK. SEEMED TO ME THEY SHOULDN'T HAVE BEEN TAKEN IN THE FIRST PLACE.
YOU . . . YOU GAVE THEM BACK THE MOST VALUABLE SHADEBERRY CROP IN THE DARKLING REALM? DO YOU REALIZE HOW MUCH THOSE LANDS ARE WORTH? AND ALL BECAUSE SOME PRETTY YOUNG GOLD DIGGER BATTED HER EYELASHES AT YOU? HOW DARE YOU ABUSE YOUR POWERS IN SUCH A MANNER!
CRACK
WAS THAT YOUR BACK?
I'VE HAD A FALL.

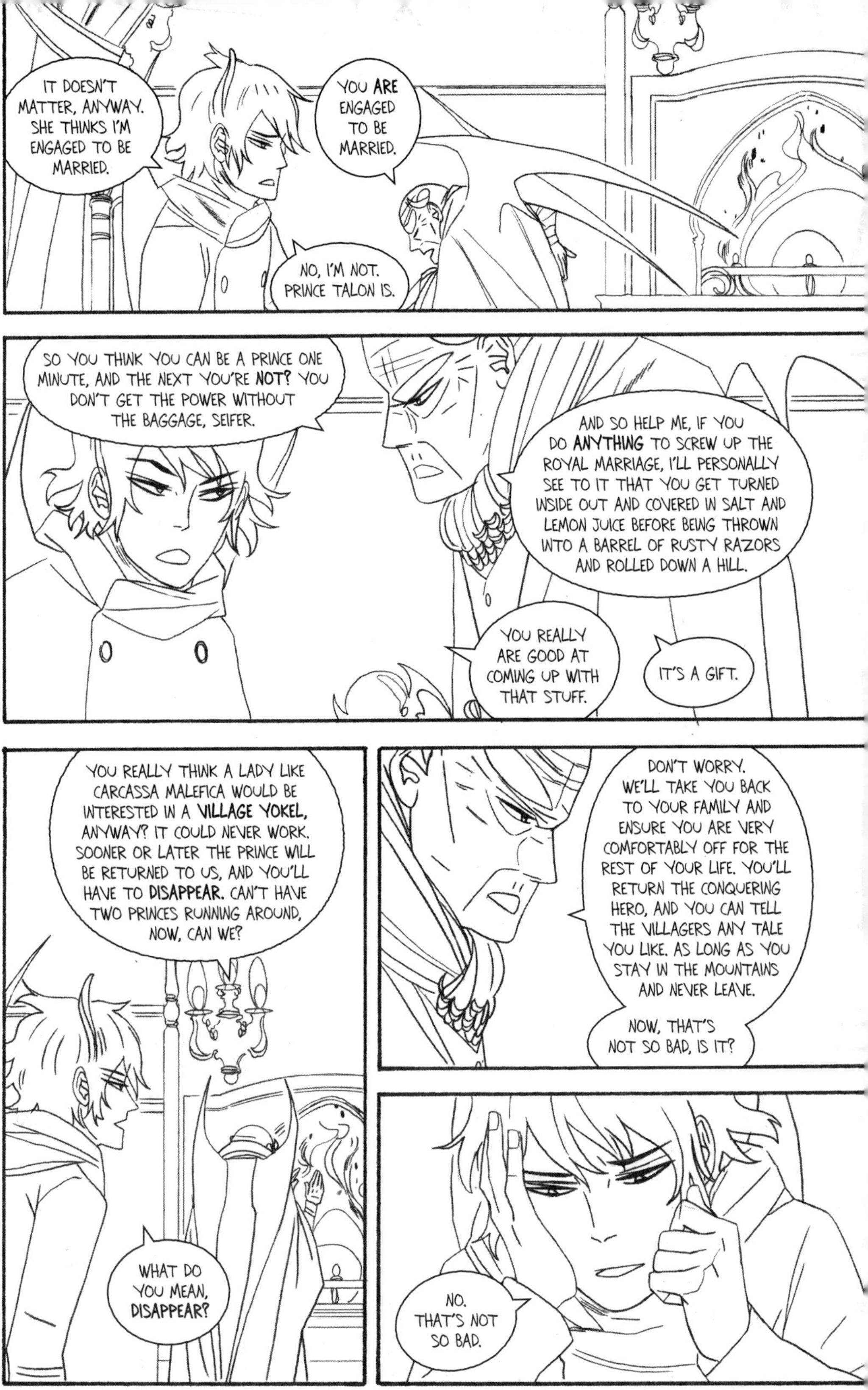
IT DOESN'T MATTER, ANYWAY. SHE THINKS I'M ENGAGED TO BE MARRIED.
YOU **ARE** ENGAGED TO BE MARRIED.
NO, I'M NOT. PRINCE TALON IS.
SO YOU THINK YOU CAN BE A PRINCE ONE MINUTE, AND THE NEXT YOU'RE **NOT?** YOU DON'T GET THE POWER WITHOUT THE BAGGAGE, SEIFER.
AND SO HELP ME, IF YOU DO **ANYTHING** TO SCREW UP THE ROYAL MARRIAGE, I'LL PERSONALLY SEE TO IT THAT YOU GET TURNED INSIDE OUT AND COVERED IN SALT AND LEMON JUICE BEFORE BEING THROWN INTO A BARREL OF RUSTY RAZORS AND ROLLED DOWN A HILL.
YOU REALLY ARE GOOD AT COMING UP WITH THAT STUFF.
IT'S A GIFT.
YOU REALLY THINK A LADY LIKE CARCASSA MALEFICA WOULD BE INTERESTED IN A **VILLAGE YOKEL,** ANYWAY? IT COULD NEVER WORK. SOONER OR LATER THE PRINCE WILL BE RETURNED TO US, AND YOU'LL HAVE TO **DISAPPEAR.** CAN'T HAVE TWO PRINCES RUNNING AROUND, NOW, CAN WE?
WHAT DO YOU MEAN, **DISAPPEAR?**
DON'T WORRY. WE'LL TAKE YOU BACK TO YOUR FAMILY AND ENSURE YOU ARE VERY COMFORTABLY OFF FOR THE REST OF YOUR LIFE. YOU'LL RETURN THE CONQUERING HERO, AND YOU CAN TELL THE VILLAGERS ANY TALE YOU LIKE. AS LONG AS YOU STAY IN THE MOUNTAINS AND NEVER LEAVE.
NOW, THAT'S NOT SO BAD, IS IT?
NO. THAT'S NOT SO BAD.

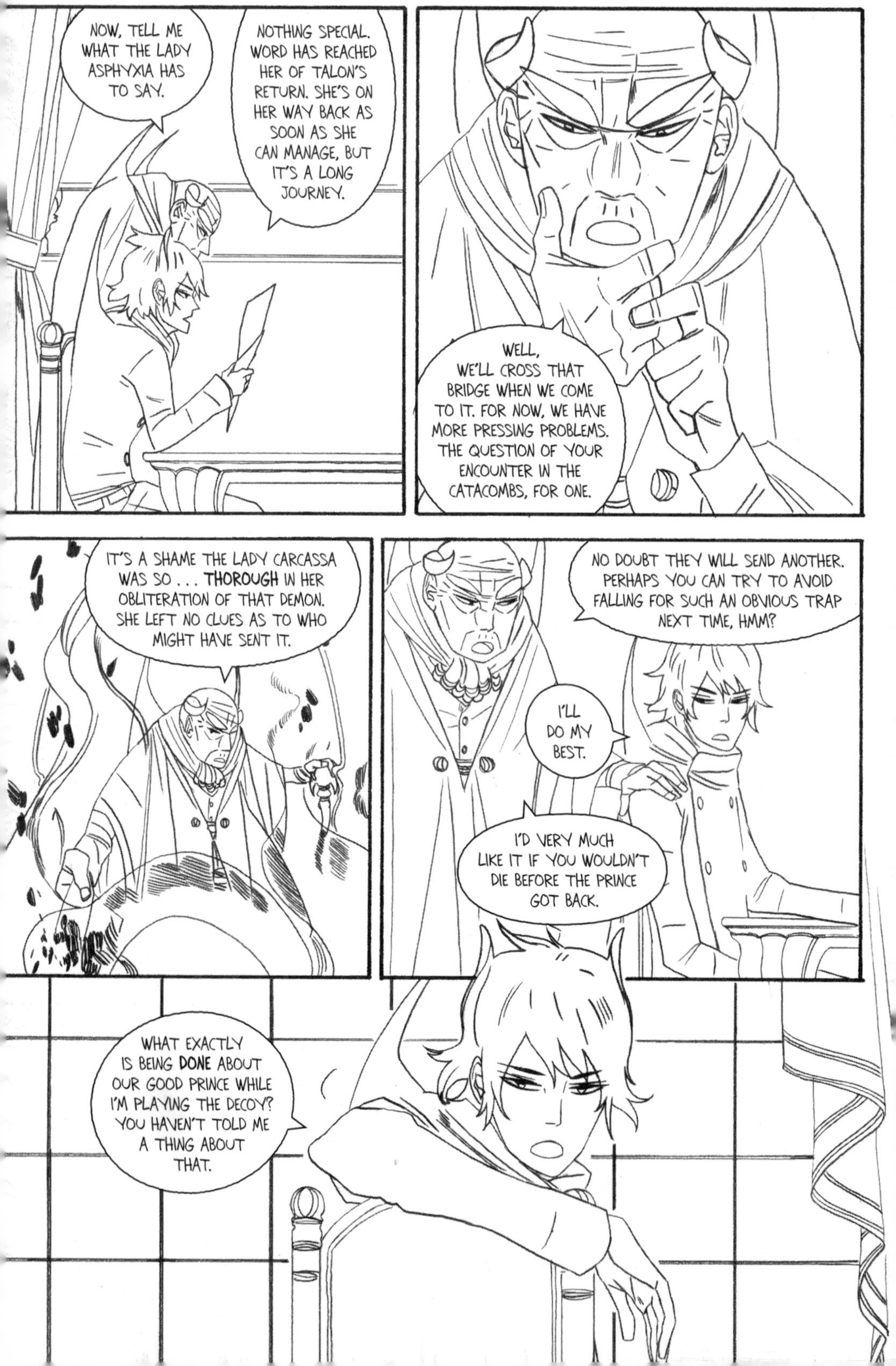

NOW, TELL ME WHAT THE LADY ASPHYXIA HAS TO SAY.
NOTHING SPECIAL. WORD HAS REACHED HER OF TALON'S RETURN. SHE'S ON HER WAY BACK AS SOON AS SHE CAN MANAGE, BUT IT'S A LONG JOURNEY.
WELL, WE'LL CROSS THAT BRIDGE WHEN WE COME TO IT. FOR NOW, WE HAVE MORE PRESSING PROBLEMS. THE QUESTION OF YOUR ENCOUNTER IN THE CATACOMBS, FOR ONE.
IT'S A SHAME THE LADY CARCASSA WAS SO . . . **THOROUGH** IN HER OBLITERATION OF THAT DEMON. SHE LEFT NO CLUES AS TO WHO MIGHT HAVE SENT IT.
NO DOUBT THEY WILL SEND ANOTHER. PERHAPS YOU CAN TRY TO AVOID FALLING FOR SUCH AN OBVIOUS TRAP NEXT TIME, HMM?
I'LL DO MY BEST.
I'D VERY MUCH LIKE IT IF YOU WOULDN'T DIE BEFORE THE PRINCE GOT BACK.
WHAT EXACTLY IS BEING **DONE** ABOUT OUR GOOD PRINCE WHILE I'M PLAYING THE DECOY? YOU HAVEN'T TOLD ME A THING ABOUT THAT.

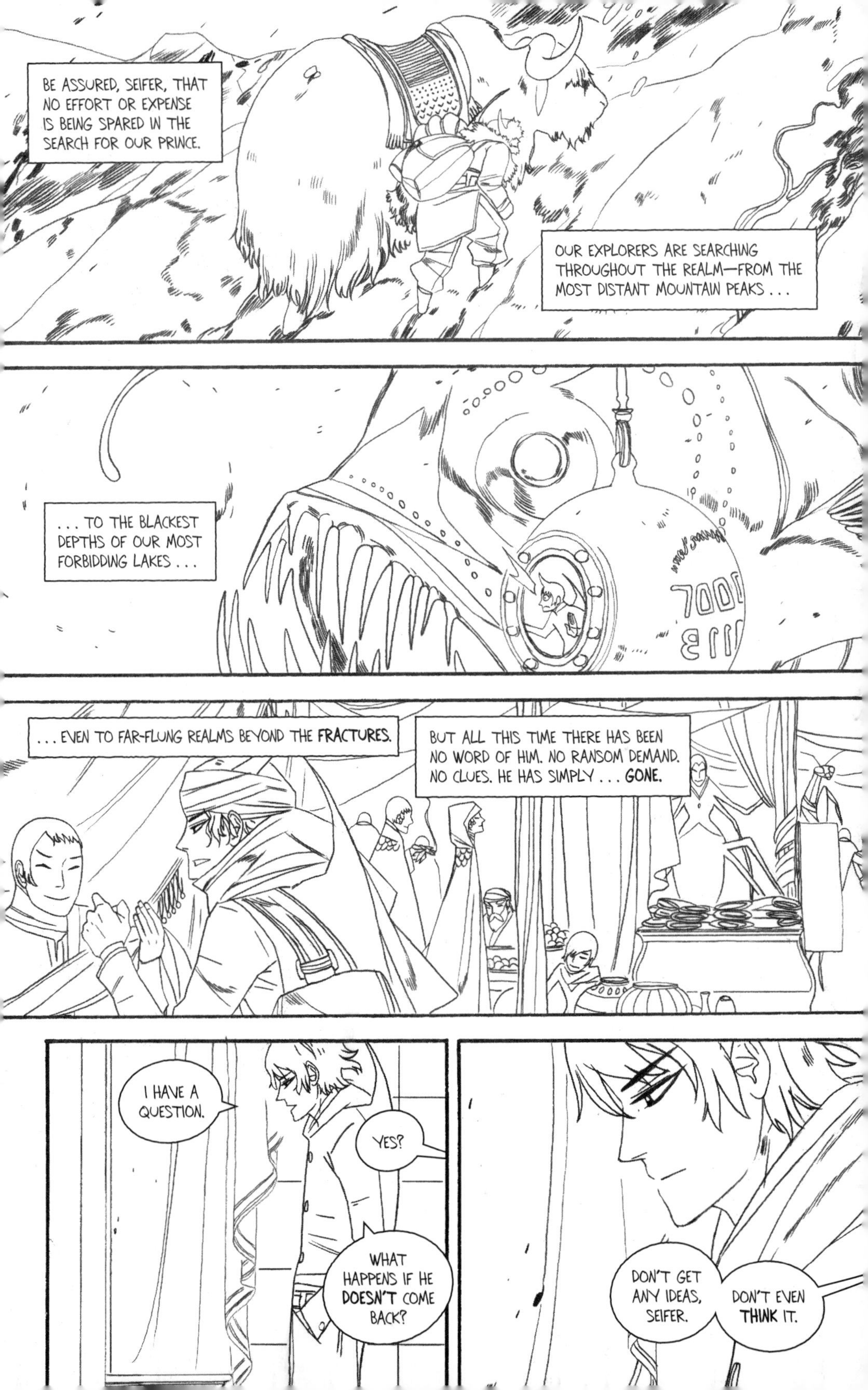

BE ASSURED, SEIFER, THAT NO EFFORT OR EXPENSE IS BEING SPARED IN THE SEARCH FOR OUR PRINCE.
OUR EXPLORERS ARE SEARCHING THROUGHOUT THE REALM—FROM THE MOST DISTANT MOUNTAIN PEAKS . . .
. . . TO THE BLACKEST DEPTHS OF OUR MOST FORBIDDING LAKES . . .
. . . EVEN TO FAR-FLUNG REALMS BEYOND THE **FRACTURES.**
BUT ALL THIS TIME THERE HAS BEEN NO WORD OF HIM. NO RANSOM DEMAND. NO CLUES. HE HAS SIMPLY . . . **GONE.**
I HAVE A QUESTION.
YES?
WHAT HAPPENS IF HE **DOESN'T** COME BACK?
DON'T GET ANY IDEAS, SEIFER.
DON'T EVEN **THINK** IT.

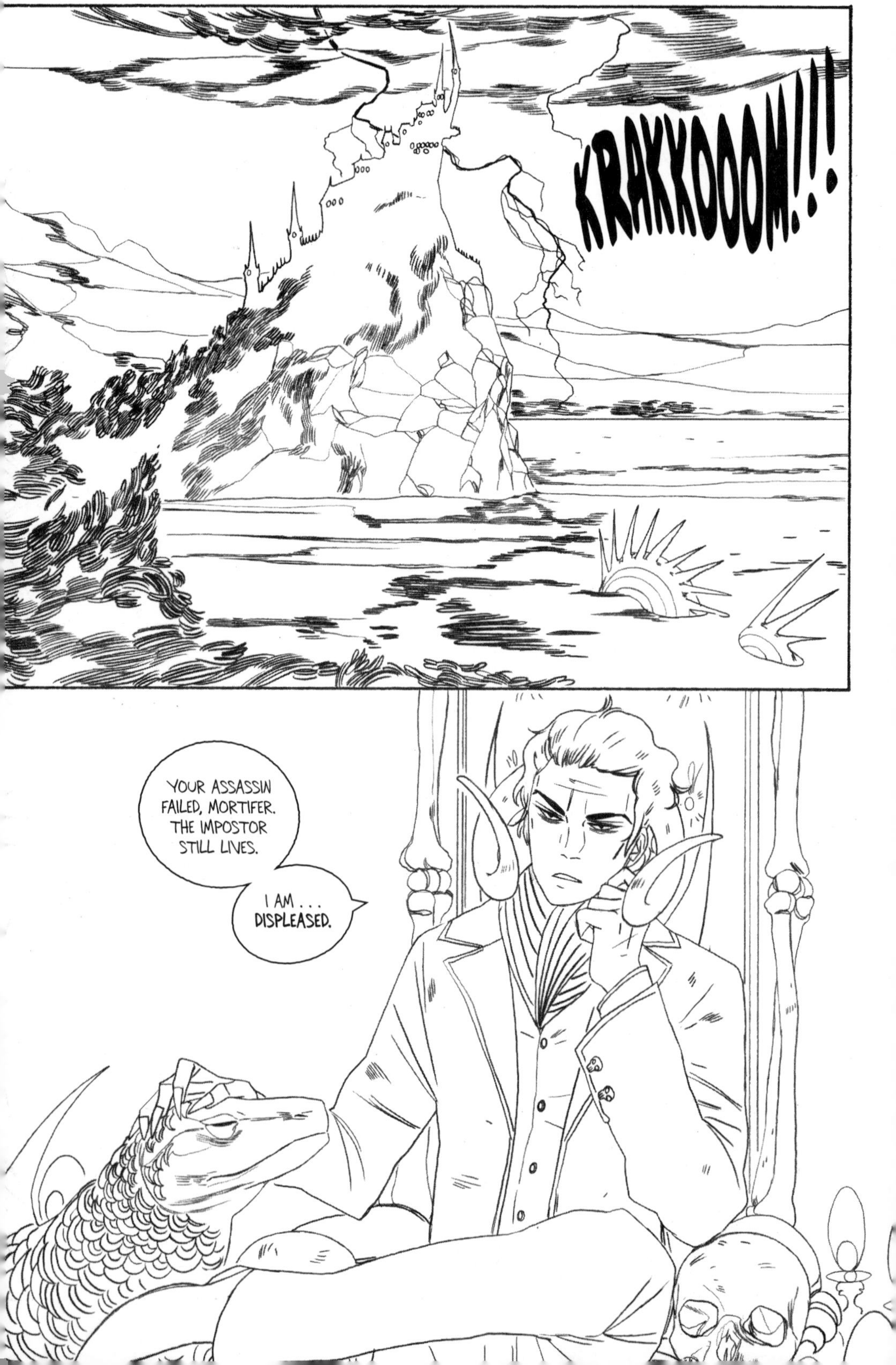
KRAKKOOM!!!
YOUR ASSASSIN FAILED, MORTIFER. THE IMPOSTOR STILL LIVES.
I AM . . . DISPLEASED.

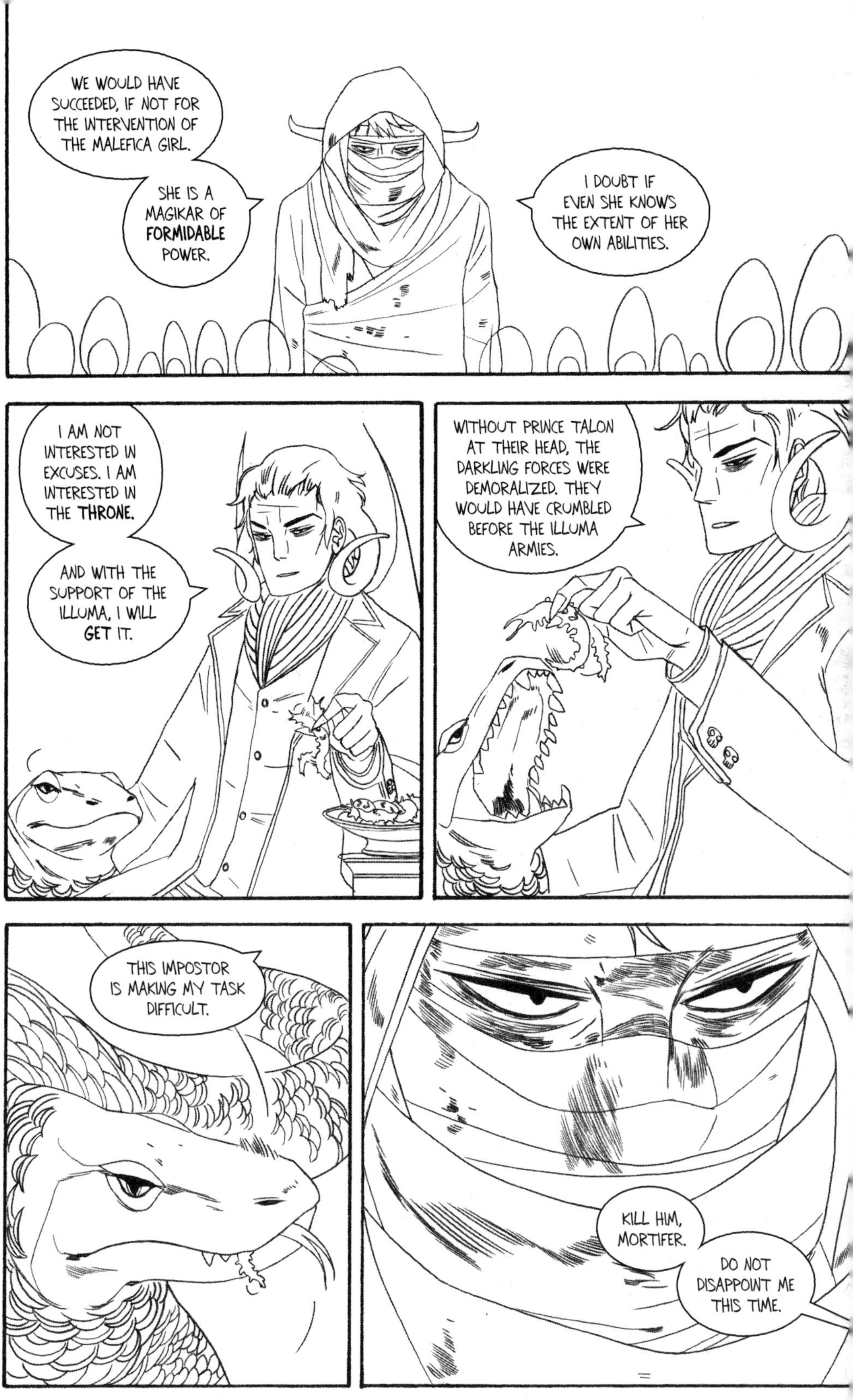
WE WOULD HAVE SUCCEEDED, IF NOT FOR THE INTERVENTION OF THE MALEFICA GIRL.
SHE IS A MAGIKAR OF **FORMIDABLE** POWER.
I DOUBT IF EVEN SHE KNOWS THE EXTENT OF HER OWN ABILITIES.
I AM NOT INTERESTED IN EXCUSES. I AM INTERESTED IN THE **THRONE.**
AND WITH THE SUPPORT OF THE ILLUMA, I WILL **GET** IT.
WITHOUT PRINCE TALON AT THEIR HEAD, THE DARKLING FORCES WERE DEMORALIZED. THEY WOULD HAVE CRUMBLED BEFORE THE ILLUMA ARMIES.
THIS IMPOSTOR IS MAKING MY TASK DIFFICULT.
KILL HIM, MORTIFER.
DO NOT DISAPPOINT ME THIS TIME.

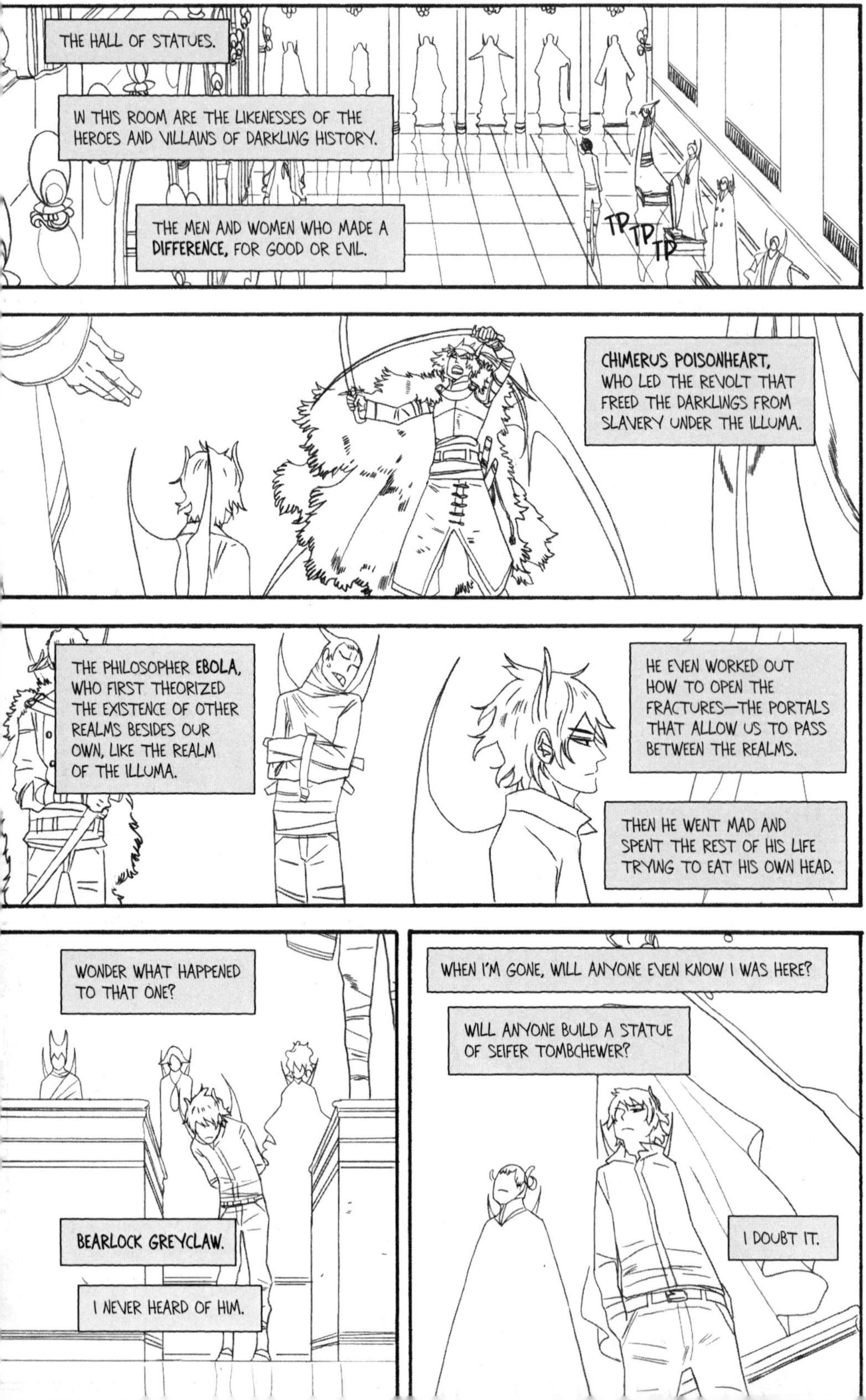
THE HALL OF STATUES.
IN THIS ROOM ARE THE LIKENESSES OF THE HEROES AND VILLAINS OF DARKLING HISTORY.
THE MEN AND WOMEN WHO MADE A DIFFERENCE, FOR GOOD OR EVIL.
TP TP TP
CHIMERUS POISONHEART, WHO LED THE REVOLT THAT FREED THE DARKLINGS FROM SLAVERY UNDER THE ILLUMA.
THE PHILOSOPHER EBOLA, WHO FIRST THEORIZED THE EXISTENCE OF OTHER REALMS BESIDES OUR OWN, LIKE THE REALM OF THE ILLUMA.
HE EVEN WORKED OUT HOW TO OPEN THE FRACTURES—THE PORTALS THAT ALLOW US TO PASS BETWEEN THE REALMS.
THEN HE WENT MAD AND SPENT THE REST OF HIS LIFE TRYING TO EAT HIS OWN HEAD.
WONDER WHAT HAPPENED TO THAT ONE?
BEARLOCK GREYCLAW.
I NEVER HEARD OF HIM.
WHEN I'M GONE, WILL ANYONE EVEN KNOW I WAS HERE?
WILL ANYONE BUILD A STATUE OF SEIFER TOMBCHEWER?
I DOUBT IT.

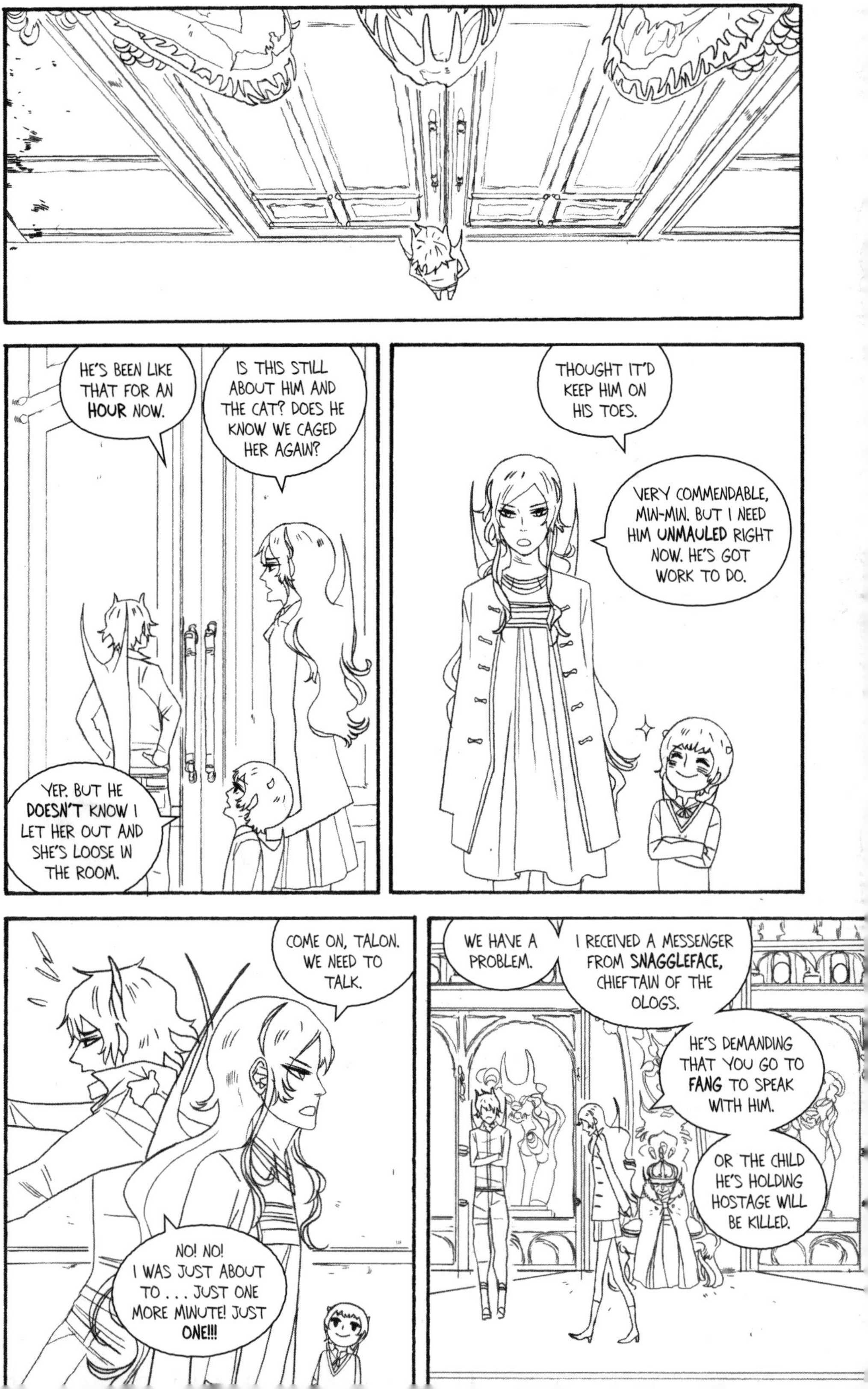
HE'S BEEN LIKE THAT FOR AN HOUR NOW.
IS THIS STILL ABOUT HIM AND THE CAT? DOES HE KNOW WE CAGED HER AGAIN?
YEP. BUT HE DOESN'T KNOW I LET HER OUT AND SHE'S LOOSE IN THE ROOM.
THOUGHT IT'D KEEP HIM ON HIS TOES.
VERY COMMENDABLE, MIN-MIN. BUT I NEED HIM UNMAULED RIGHT NOW. HE'S GOT WORK TO DO.
COME ON, TALON. WE NEED TO TALK.
NO! NO! I WAS JUST ABOUT TO . . . JUST ONE MORE MINUTE! JUST ONE!!!
WE HAVE A PROBLEM.
I RECEIVED A MESSENGER FROM SNAGGLEFACE, CHIEFTAIN OF THE OLOGS.
HE'S DEMANDING THAT YOU GO TO FANG TO SPEAK WITH HIM.
OR THE CHILD HE'S HOLDING HOSTAGE WILL BE KILLED.

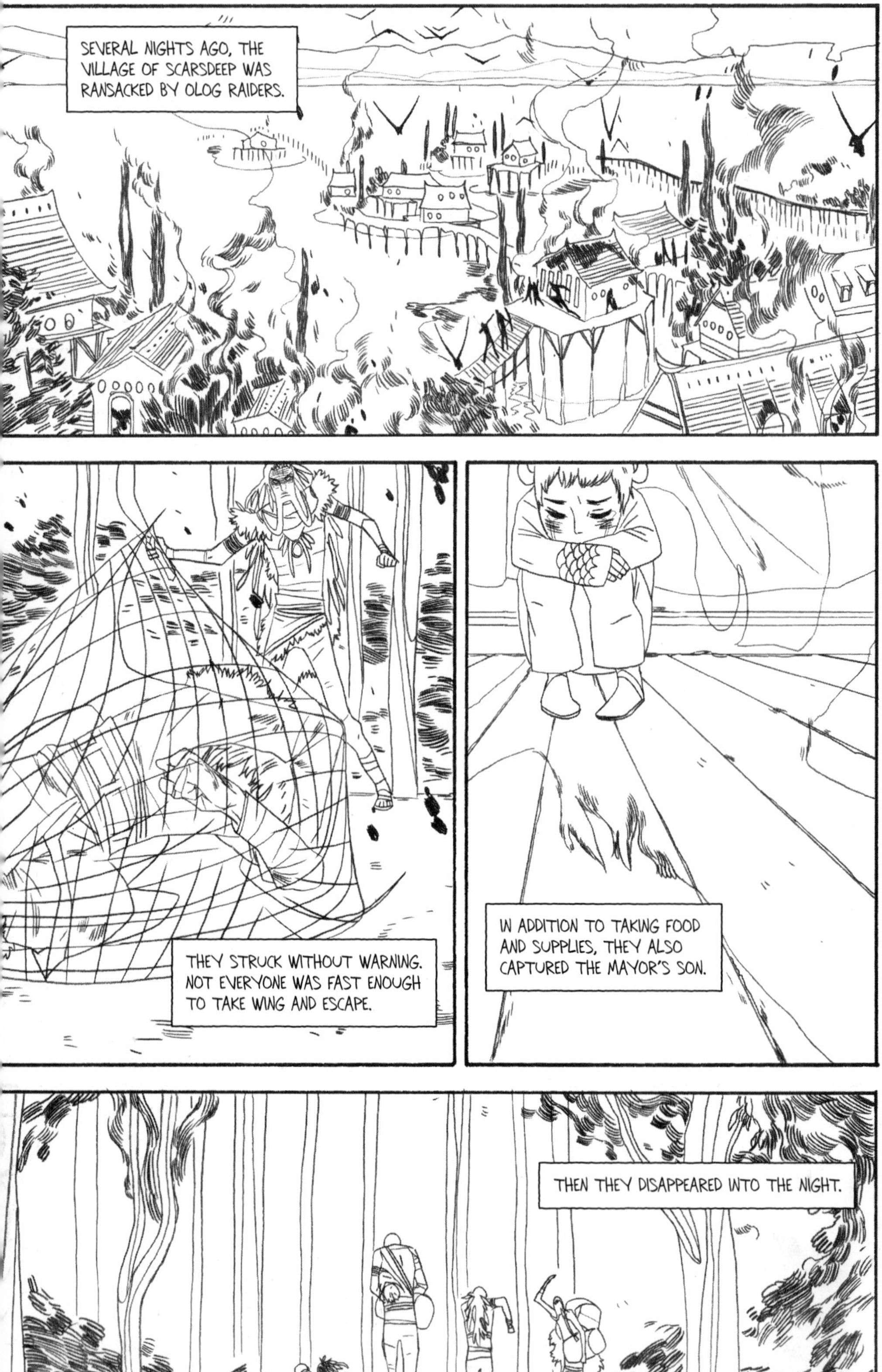
SEVERAL NIGHTS AGO, THE VILLAGE OF SCARSDEEP WAS RANSACKED BY OLOG RAIDERS.
THEY STRUCK WITHOUT WARNING. NOT EVERYONE WAS FAST ENOUGH TO TAKE WING AND ESCAPE.
IN ADDITION TO TAKING FOOD AND SUPPLIES, THEY ALSO CAPTURED THE MAYOR'S SON.
THEN THEY DISAPPEARED INTO THE NIGHT.

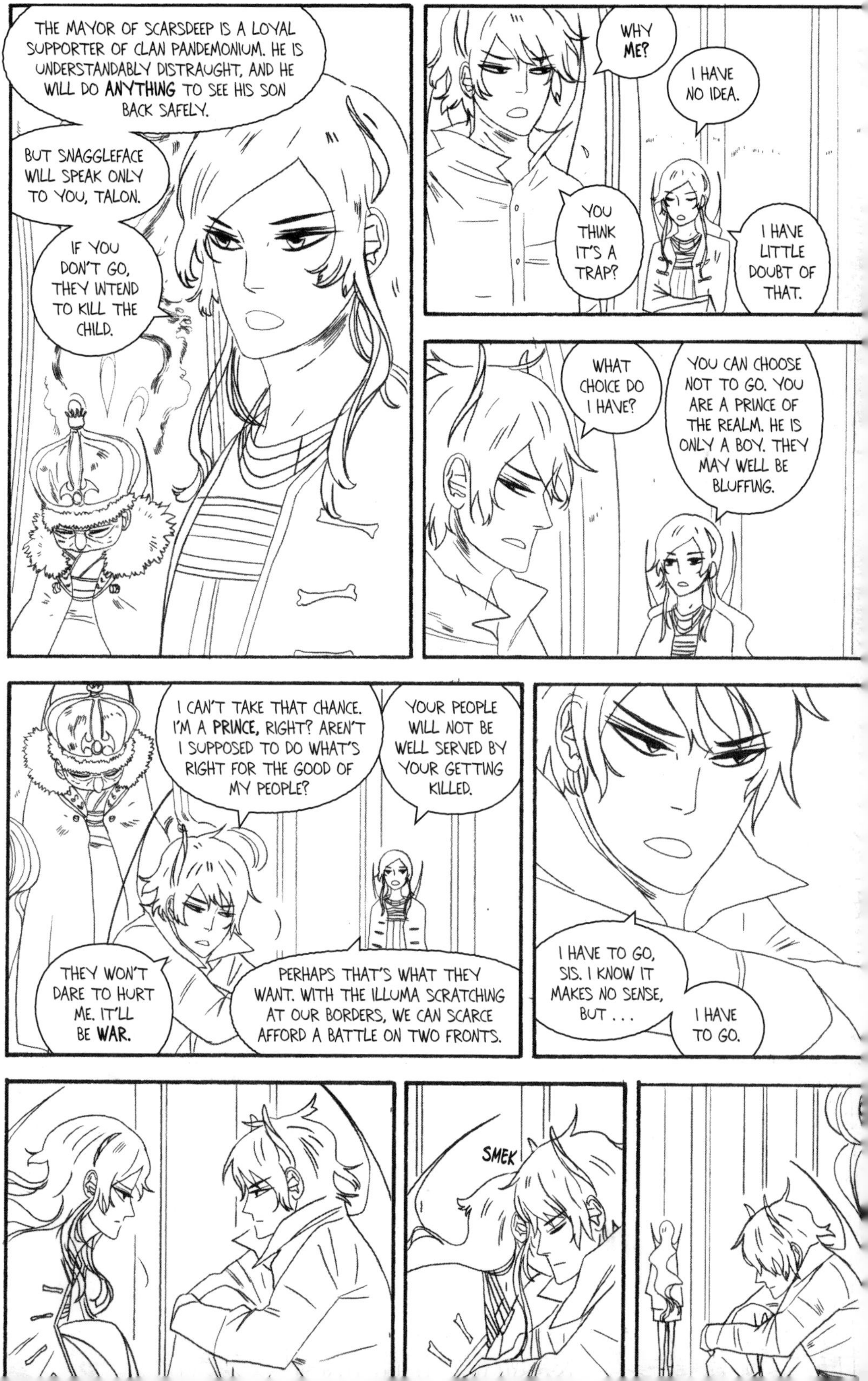
THE MAYOR OF SCARSDEEP IS A LOYAL SUPPORTER OF CLAN PANDEMONIUM. HE IS UNDERSTANDABLY DISTRAUGHT, AND HE WILL DO **ANYTHING** TO SEE HIS SON BACK SAFELY.
BUT SNAGGLEFACE WILL SPEAK ONLY TO YOU, TALON.
IF YOU DON'T GO, THEY INTEND TO KILL THE CHILD.
WHY **ME?**
I HAVE NO IDEA.
YOU THINK IT'S A TRAP?
I HAVE LITTLE DOUBT OF THAT.
WHAT CHOICE DO I HAVE?
YOU CAN CHOOSE NOT TO GO. YOU ARE A PRINCE OF THE REALM. HE IS ONLY A BOY. THEY MAY WELL BE BLUFFING.
I CAN'T TAKE THAT CHANCE. I'M A **PRINCE,** RIGHT? AREN'T I SUPPOSED TO DO WHAT'S RIGHT FOR THE GOOD OF MY PEOPLE?
YOUR PEOPLE WILL NOT BE WELL SERVED BY YOUR GETTING KILLED.
THEY WON'T DARE TO HURT ME. IT'LL BE **WAR.**
PERHAPS THAT'S WHAT THEY WANT. WITH THE ILLUMA SCRATCHING AT OUR BORDERS, WE CAN SCARCE AFFORD A BATTLE ON TWO FRONTS.
I HAVE TO GO, SIS. I KNOW IT MAKES NO SENSE, BUT . . .
I HAVE TO GO.
SMEK

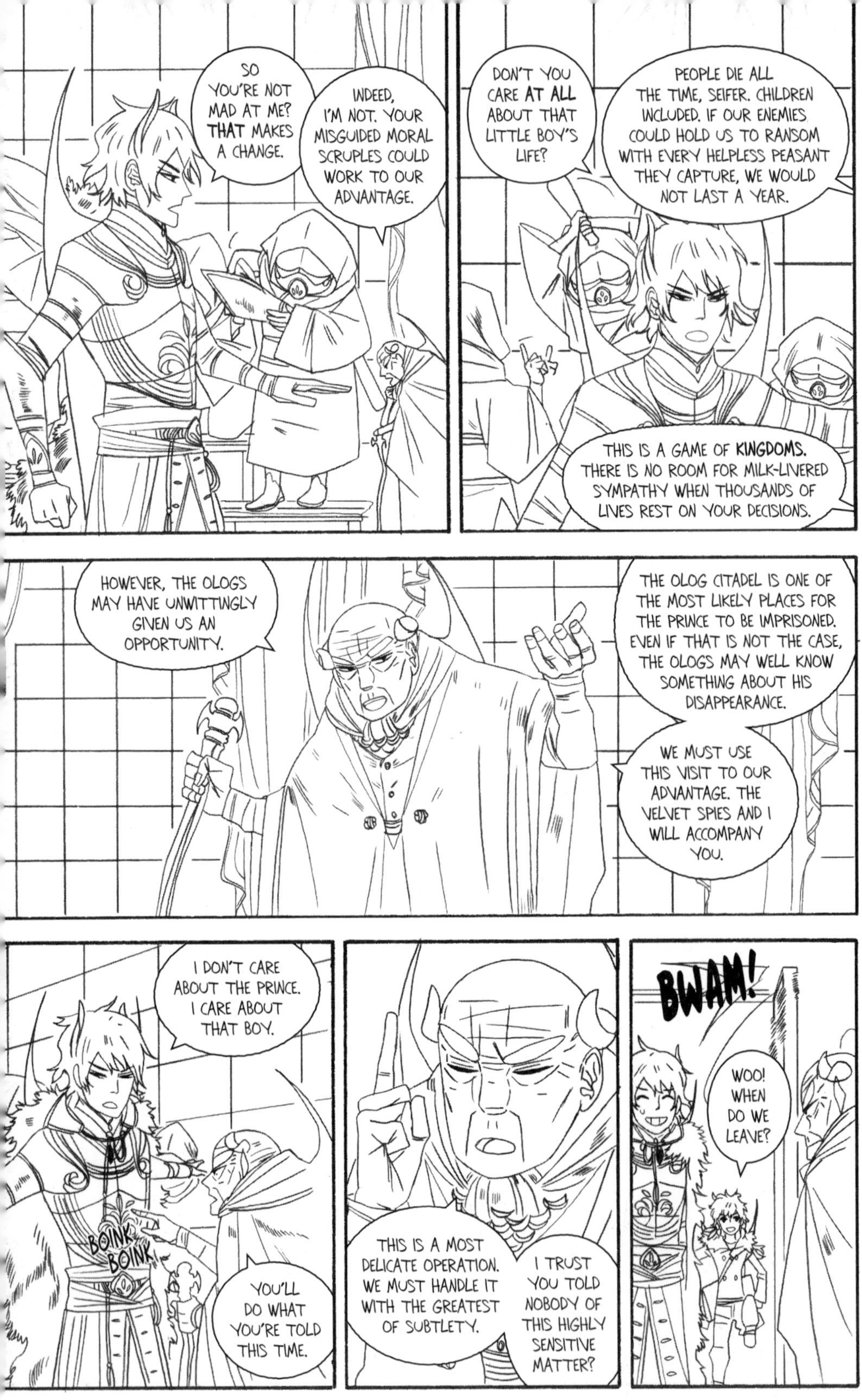
SO YOU'RE NOT MAD AT ME? THAT MAKES A CHANGE.
INDEED, I'M NOT. YOUR MISGUIDED MORAL SCRUPLES COULD WORK TO OUR ADVANTAGE.
DON'T YOU CARE AT ALL ABOUT THAT LITTLE BOY'S LIFE?
PEOPLE DIE ALL THE TIME, SEIFER. CHILDREN INCLUDED. IF OUR ENEMIES COULD HOLD US TO RANSOM WITH EVERY HELPLESS PEASANT THEY CAPTURE, WE WOULD NOT LAST A YEAR.
THIS IS A GAME OF KINGDOMS. THERE IS NO ROOM FOR MILK-LIVERED SYMPATHY WHEN THOUSANDS OF LIVES REST ON YOUR DECISIONS.
HOWEVER, THE OLOGS MAY HAVE UNWITTINGLY GIVEN US AN OPPORTUNITY.
THE OLOG CITADEL IS ONE OF THE MOST LIKELY PLACES FOR THE PRINCE TO BE IMPRISONED. EVEN IF THAT IS NOT THE CASE, THE OLOGS MAY WELL KNOW SOMETHING ABOUT HIS DISAPPEARANCE.
WE MUST USE THIS VISIT TO OUR ADVANTAGE. THE VELVET SPIES AND I WILL ACCOMPANY YOU.
I DON'T CARE ABOUT THE PRINCE. I CARE ABOUT THAT BOY.
BOINK BOINK
YOU'LL DO WHAT YOU'RE TOLD THIS TIME.
THIS IS A MOST DELICATE OPERATION. WE MUST HANDLE IT WITH THE GREATEST OF SUBTLETY.
I TRUST YOU TOLD NOBODY OF THIS HIGHLY SENSITIVE MATTER?
BWAM!
WOO! WHEN DO WE LEAVE?

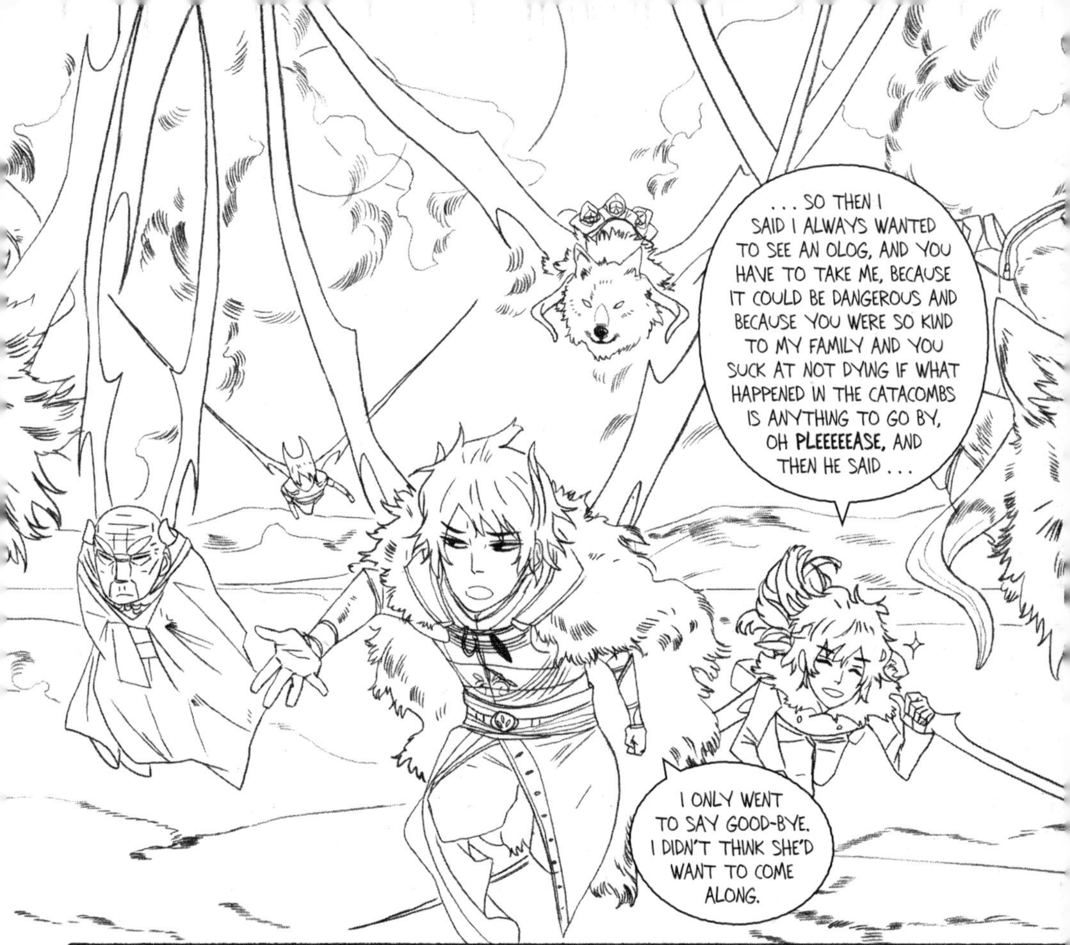
. . . SO THEN I SAID I ALWAYS WANTED TO SEE AN OLOG, AND YOU HAVE TO TAKE ME, BECAUSE IT COULD BE DANGEROUS AND BECAUSE YOU WERE SO KIND TO MY FAMILY AND YOU SUCK AT NOT DYING IF WHAT HAPPENED IN THE CATACOMBS IS ANYTHING TO GO BY, OH **PLEEEEEASE,** AND THEN HE SAID . . .
I ONLY WENT TO SAY GOOD-BYE. I DIDN'T THINK SHE'D WANT TO COME ALONG.

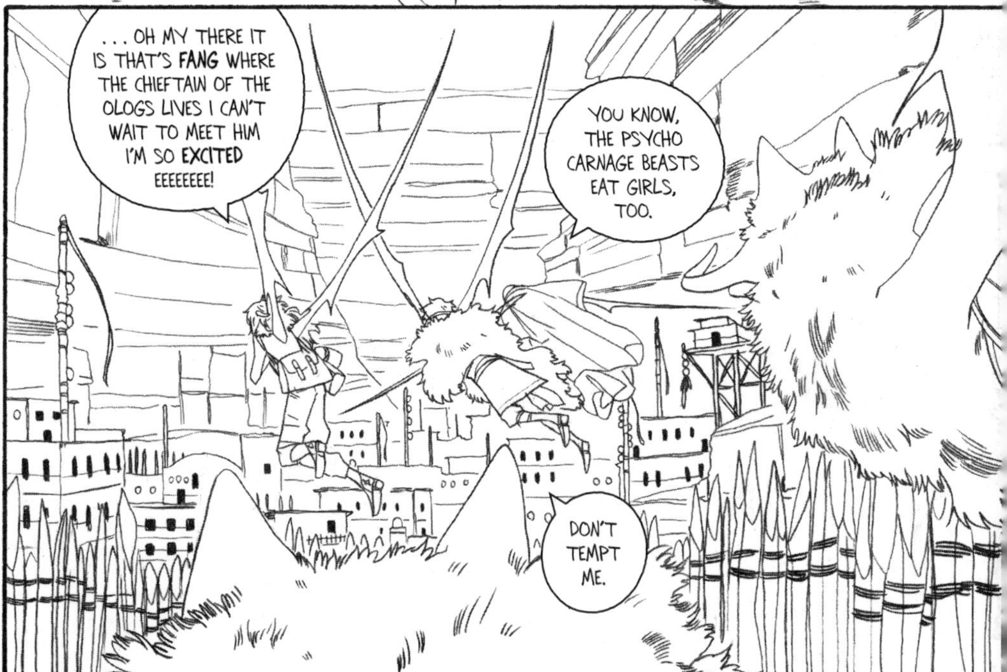
. . . OH MY THERE IT IS THAT'S **FANG** WHERE THE CHIEFTAIN OF THE OLOGS LIVES I CAN'T WAIT TO MEET HIM I'M SO **EXCITED** EEEEEEEE!
YOU KNOW, THE PSYCHO CARNAGE BEASTS EAT GIRLS, TOO.
DON'T TEMPT ME.

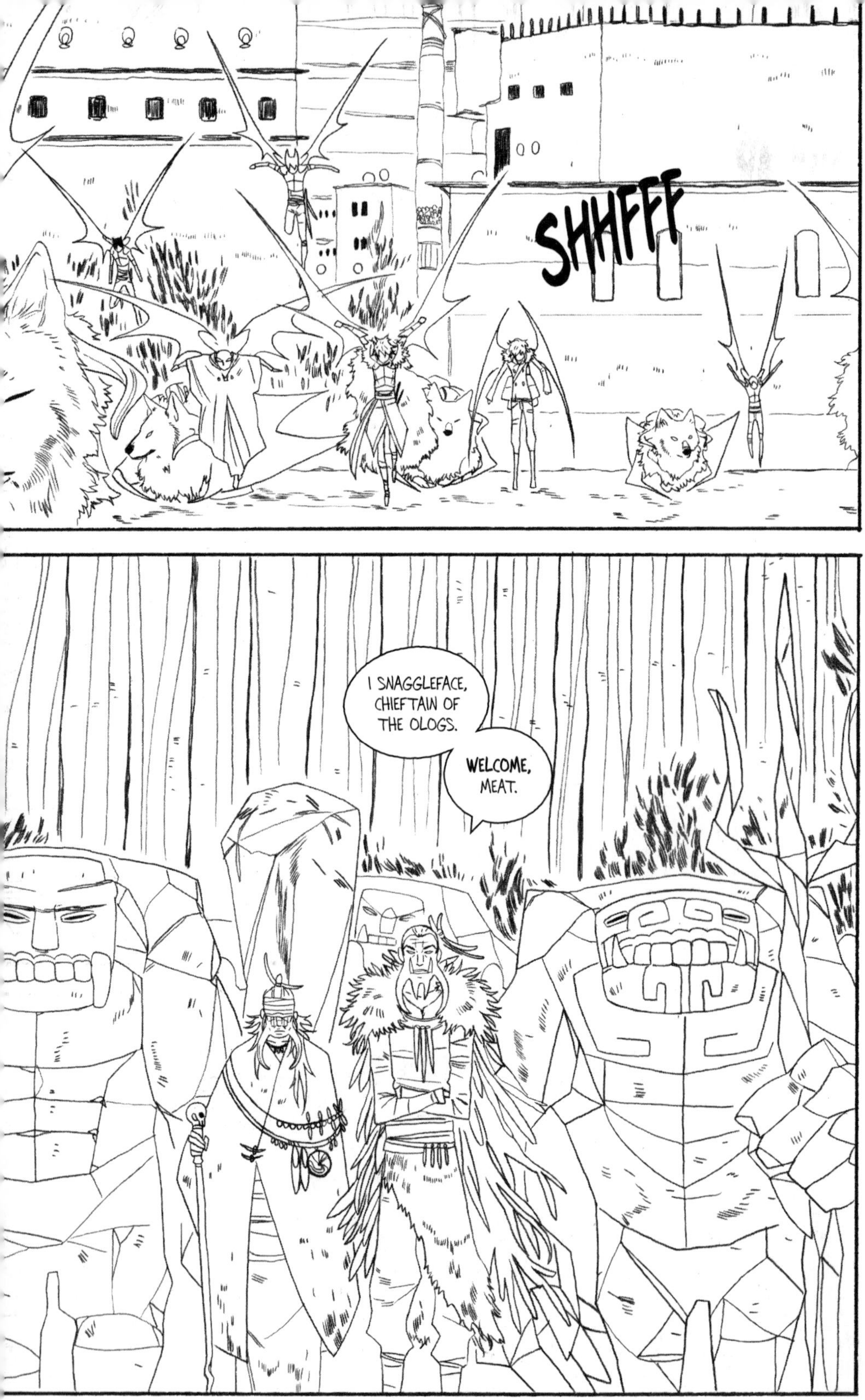
SHHFFF
I SNAGGLEFACE, CHIEFTAIN OF THE OLOGS.
WELCOME, MEAT.

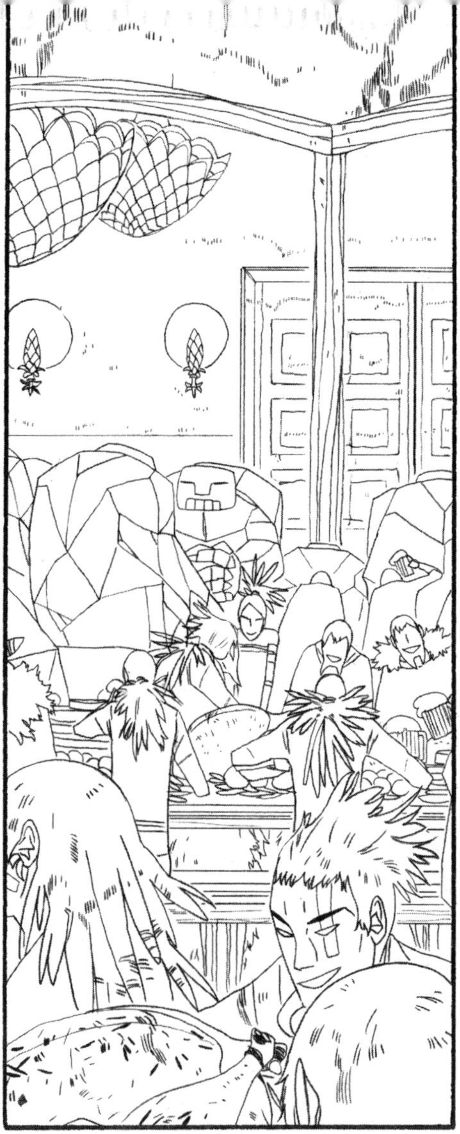
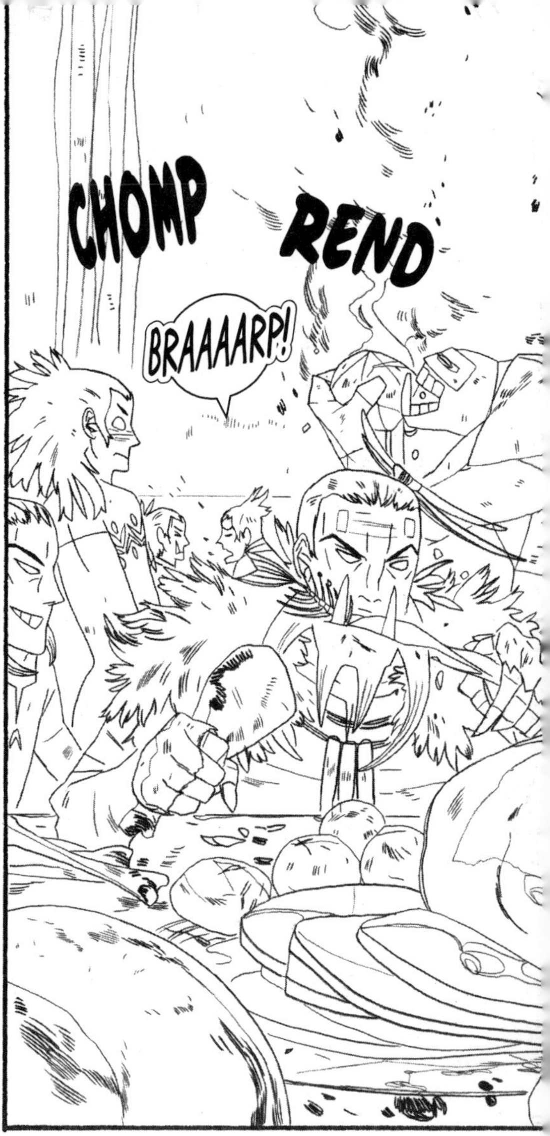
CHOMP
REND
BRAAAARP!
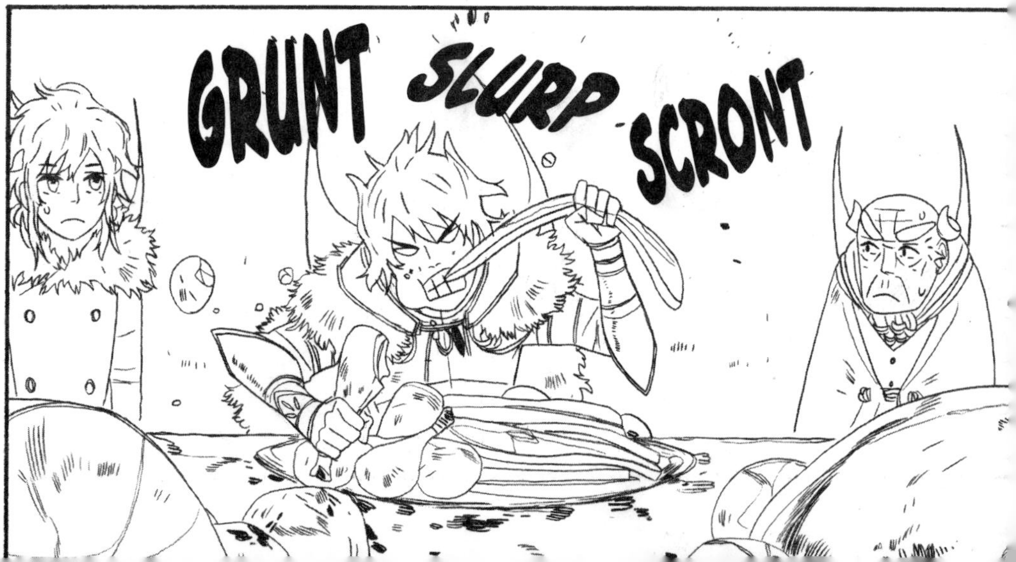
GRUNT
SLURP
SCRONT

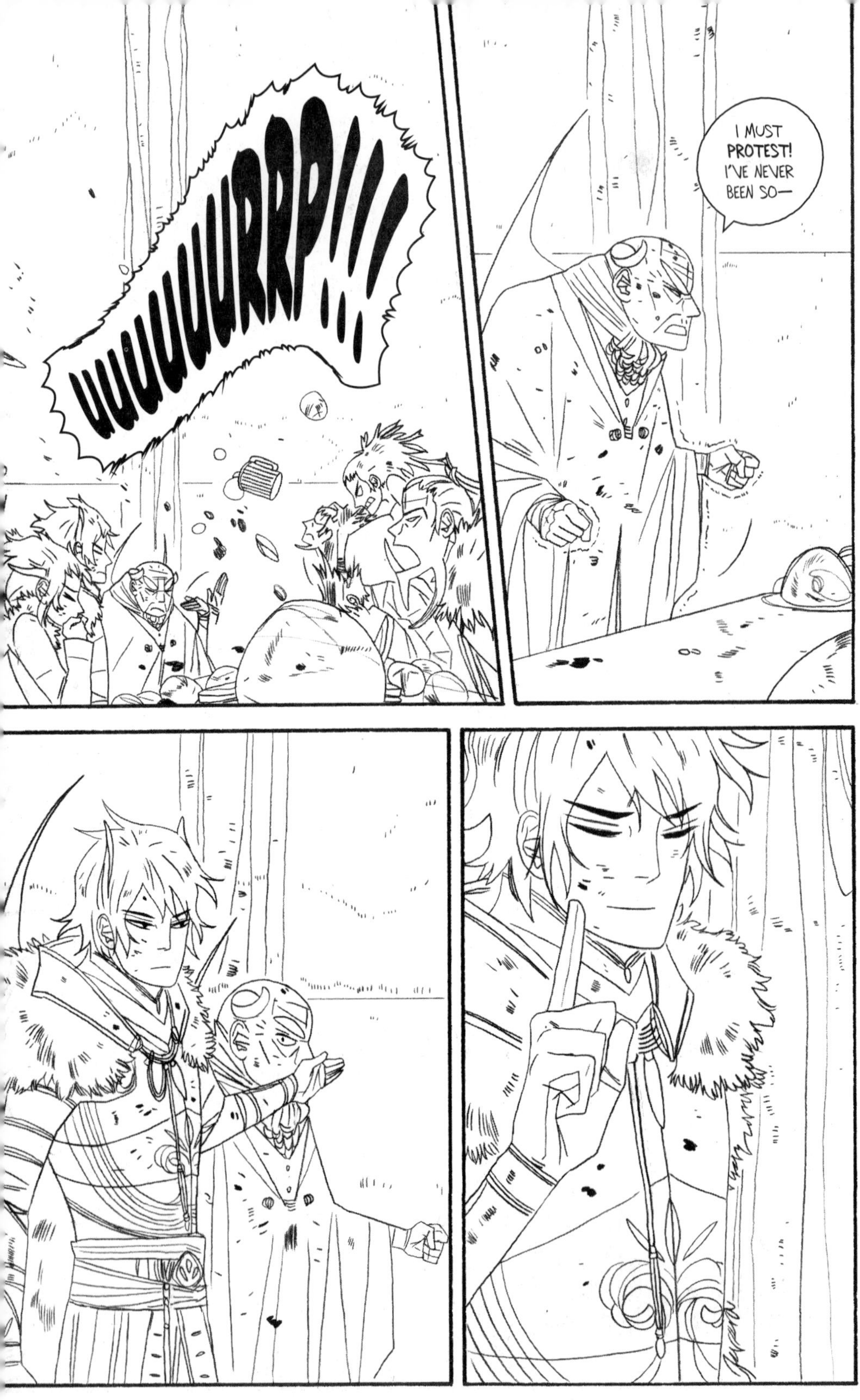
UUUUUURRP!!!
I MUST PROTEST! I'VE NEVER BEEN SO—

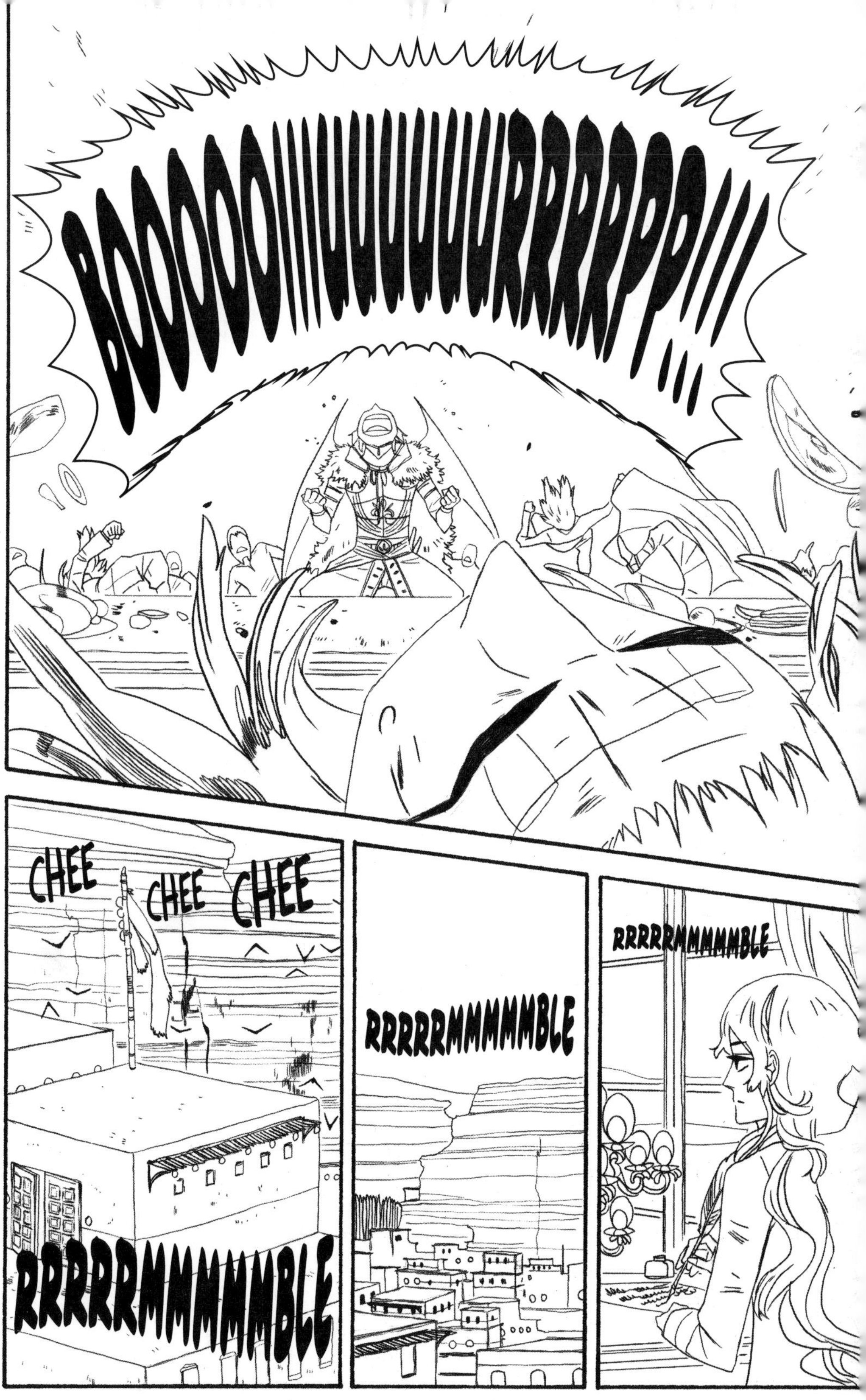
BOOOOOIIIIUUUUUUUURRRRPPP!!!!
CHEE
CHEE
CHEE
RRRRRMMMMMBLE
RRRRRMMMMMBLE
RRRRRMMMMMBLE

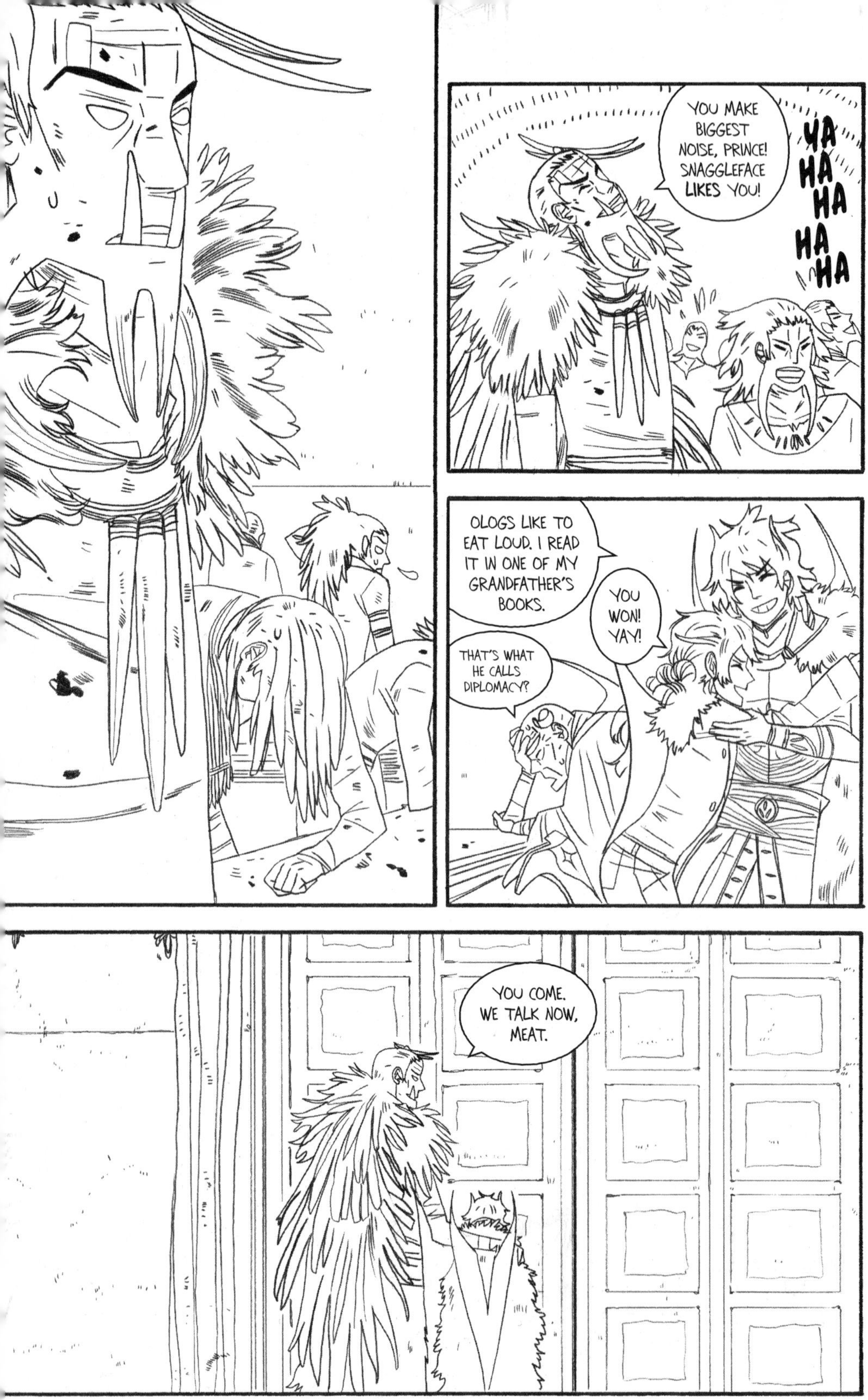
YOU MAKE BIGGEST NOISE, PRINCE! SNAGGLEFACE LIKES YOU!
YA HA HA HA HA
OLOGS LIKE TO EAT LOUD. I READ IT IN ONE OF MY GRANDFATHER'S BOOKS.
YOU WON! YAY!
THAT'S WHAT HE CALLS DIPLOMACY?
YOU COME. WE TALK NOW, MEAT.

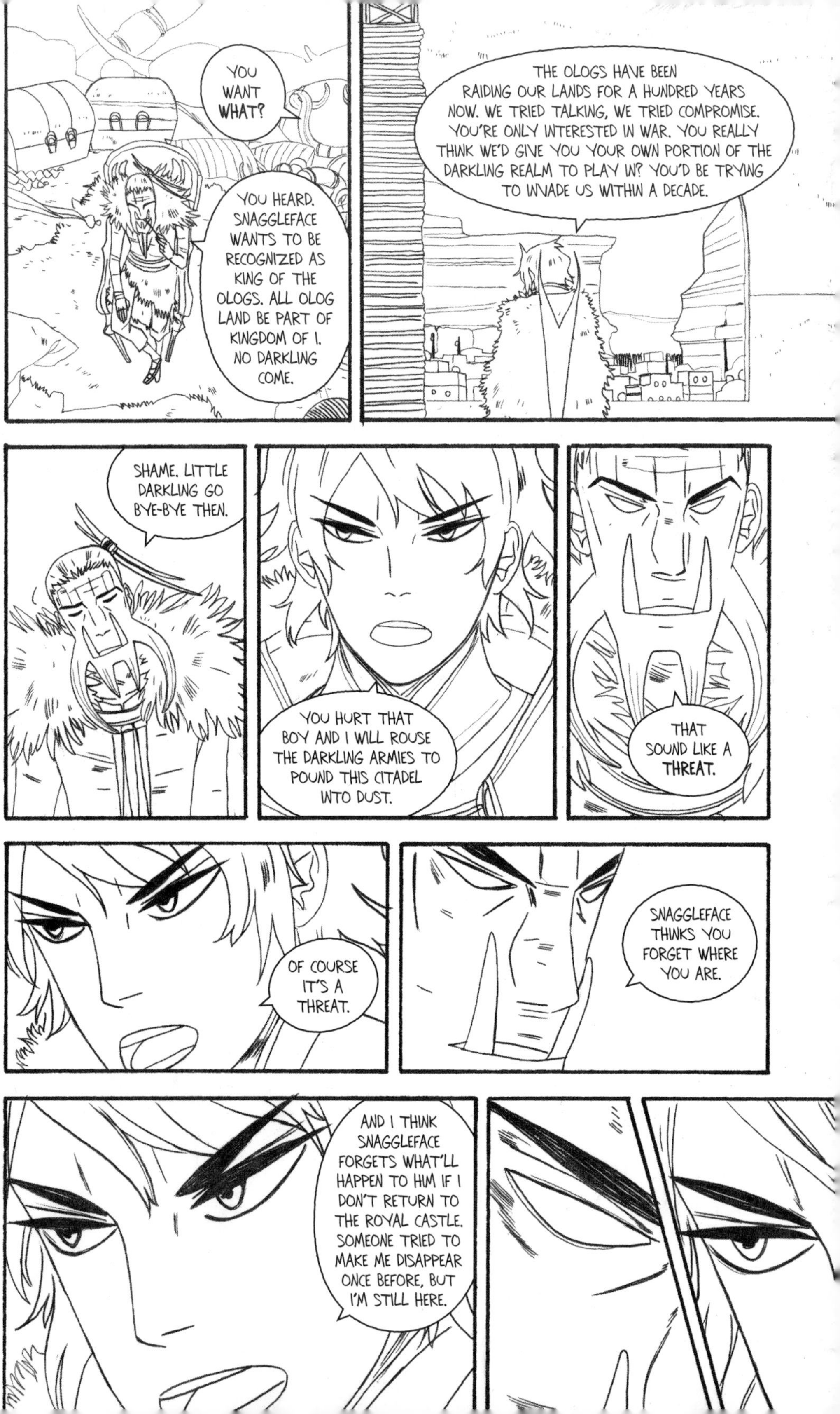
YOU WANT WHAT?
YOU HEARD. SNAGGLEFACE WANTS TO BE RECOGNIZED AS KING OF THE OLOGS. ALL OLOG LAND BE PART OF KINGDOM OF I. NO DARKLING COME.
THE OLOGS HAVE BEEN RAIDING OUR LANDS FOR A HUNDRED YEARS NOW. WE TRIED TALKING, WE TRIED COMPROMISE. YOU'RE ONLY INTERESTED IN WAR. YOU REALLY THINK WE'D GIVE YOU YOUR OWN PORTION OF THE DARKLING REALM TO PLAY IN? YOU'D BE TRYING TO INVADE US WITHIN A DECADE.
SHAME. LITTLE DARKLING GO BYE-BYE THEN.
YOU HURT THAT BOY AND I WILL ROUSE THE DARKLING ARMIES TO POUND THIS CITADEL INTO DUST.
THAT SOUND LIKE A THREAT.
OF COURSE IT'S A THREAT.
SNAGGLEFACE THINKS YOU FORGET WHERE YOU ARE.
AND I THINK SNAGGLEFACE FORGETS WHAT'LL HAPPEN TO HIM IF I DON'T RETURN TO THE ROYAL CASTLE. SOMEONE TRIED TO MAKE ME DISAPPEAR ONCE BEFORE, BUT I'M STILL HERE.

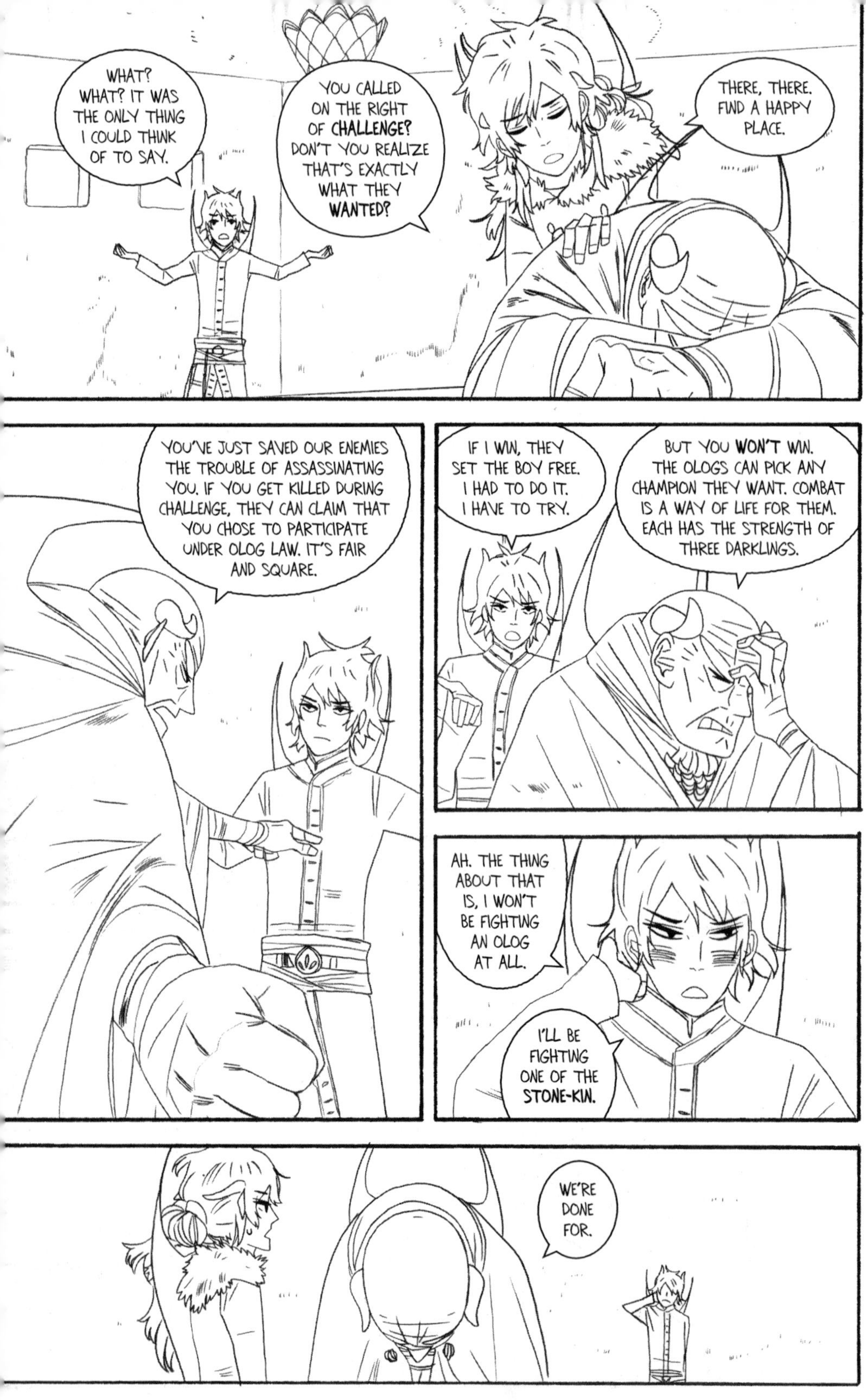
WHAT? WHAT? IT WAS THE ONLY THING I COULD THINK OF TO SAY.
YOU CALLED ON THE RIGHT OF CHALLENGE? DON'T YOU REALIZE THAT'S EXACTLY WHAT THEY WANTED?
THERE, THERE. FIND A HAPPY PLACE.
YOU'VE JUST SAVED OUR ENEMIES THE TROUBLE OF ASSASSINATING YOU. IF YOU GET KILLED DURING CHALLENGE, THEY CAN CLAIM THAT YOU CHOSE TO PARTICIPATE UNDER OLOG LAW. IT'S FAIR AND SQUARE.
IF I WIN, THEY SET THE BOY FREE. I HAD TO DO IT. I HAVE TO TRY.
BUT YOU WON'T WIN. THE OLOGS CAN PICK ANY CHAMPION THEY WANT. COMBAT IS A WAY OF LIFE FOR THEM. EACH HAS THE STRENGTH OF THREE DARKLINGS.
AH. THE THING ABOUT THAT IS, I WON'T BE FIGHTING AN OLOG AT ALL.
I'LL BE FIGHTING ONE OF THE STONE-KIN.
WE'RE DONE FOR.

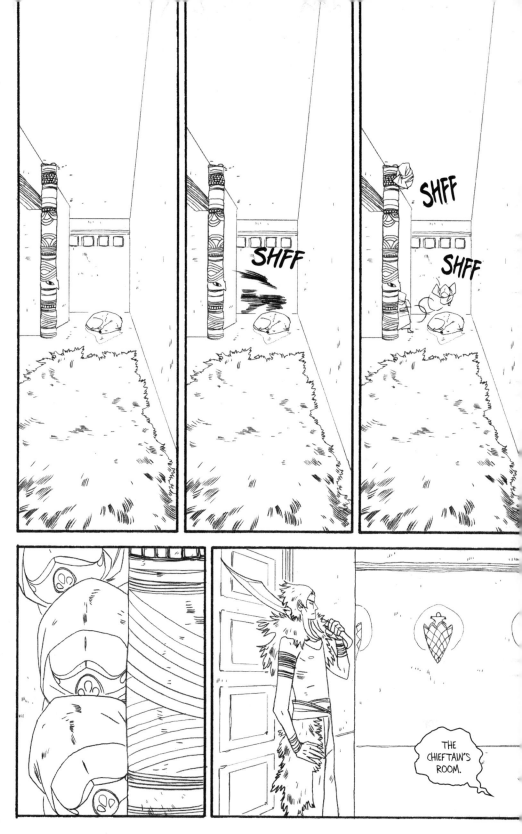

SHFF

SHFF

SHFF

THE CHIEFTAIN'S ROOM.

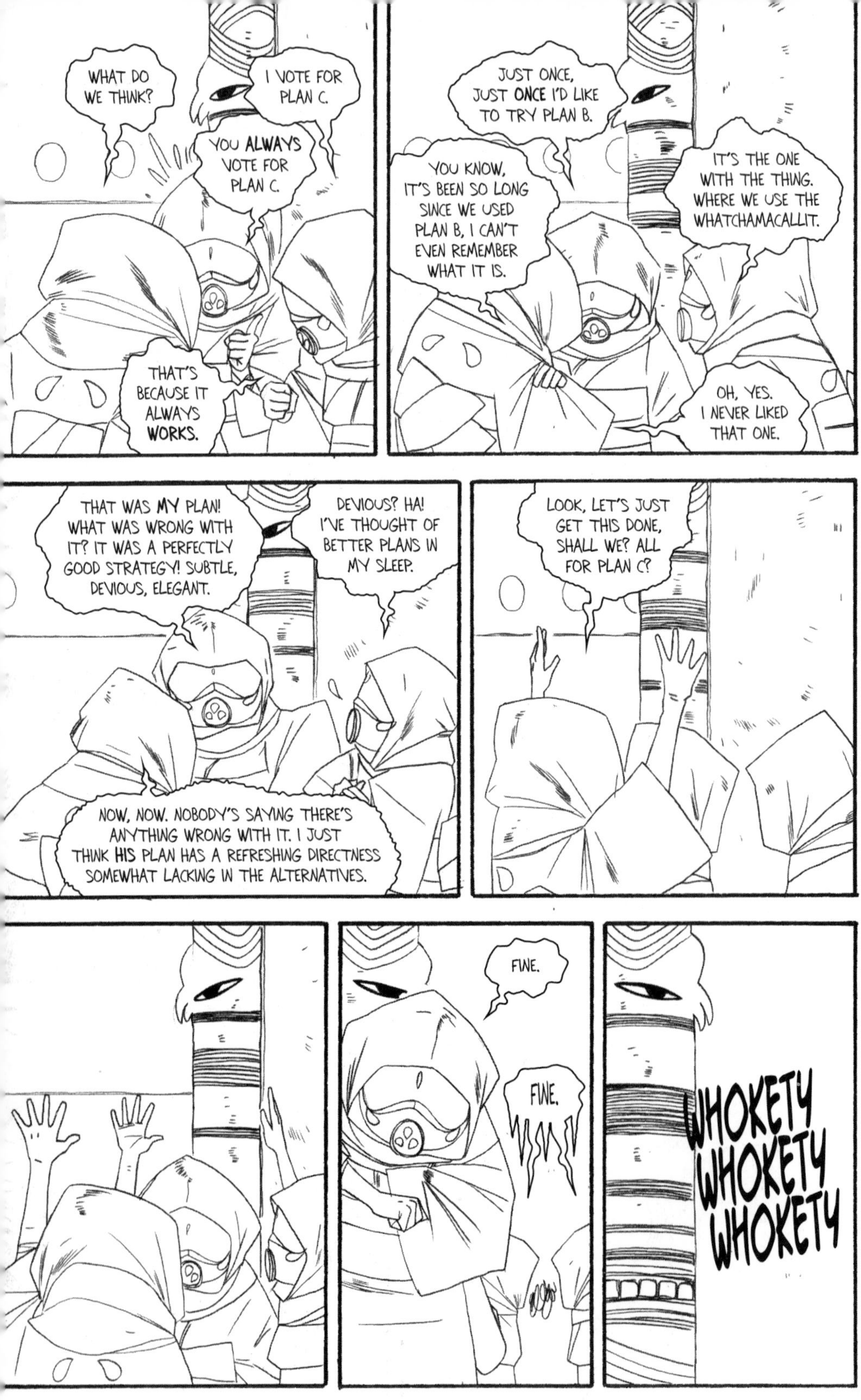
WHAT DO WE THINK?
I VOTE FOR PLAN C.
YOU ALWAYS VOTE FOR PLAN C.
THAT'S BECAUSE IT ALWAYS WORKS.
JUST ONCE, JUST ONCE I'D LIKE TO TRY PLAN B.
YOU KNOW, IT'S BEEN SO LONG SINCE WE USED PLAN B, I CAN'T EVEN REMEMBER WHAT IT IS.
IT'S THE ONE WITH THE THING. WHERE WE USE THE WHATCHAMACALLIT.
OH, YES. I NEVER LIKED THAT ONE.
THAT WAS MY PLAN! WHAT WAS WRONG WITH IT? IT WAS A PERFECTLY GOOD STRATEGY! SUBTLE, DEVIOUS, ELEGANT.
DEVIOUS? HA! I'VE THOUGHT OF BETTER PLANS IN MY SLEEP.
NOW, NOW. NOBODY'S SAYING THERE'S ANYTHING WRONG WITH IT. I JUST THINK HIS PLAN HAS A REFRESHING DIRECTNESS SOMEWHAT LACKING IN THE ALTERNATIVES.
LOOK, LET'S JUST GET THIS DONE, SHALL WE? ALL FOR PLAN C?
FINE.
FINE.
WHOKETY WHOKETY WHOKETY

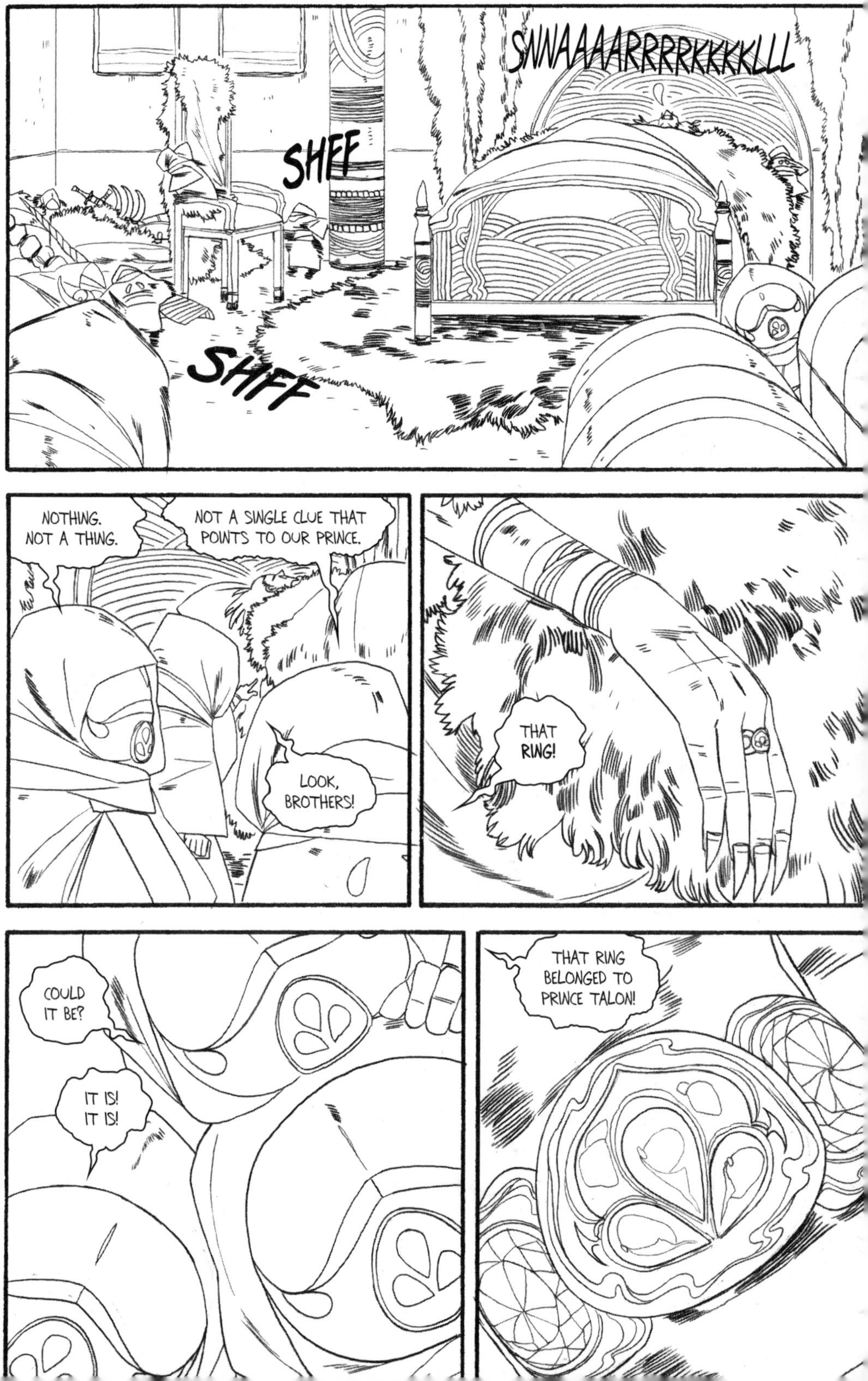
SNNAAAARRRRKKKKLLL
SHFF
SHFF
NOTHING. NOT A THING.
NOT A SINGLE CLUE THAT POINTS TO OUR PRINCE.
LOOK, BROTHERS!
THAT RING!
COULD IT BE?
IT IS! IT IS!
THAT RING BELONGED TO PRINCE TALON!

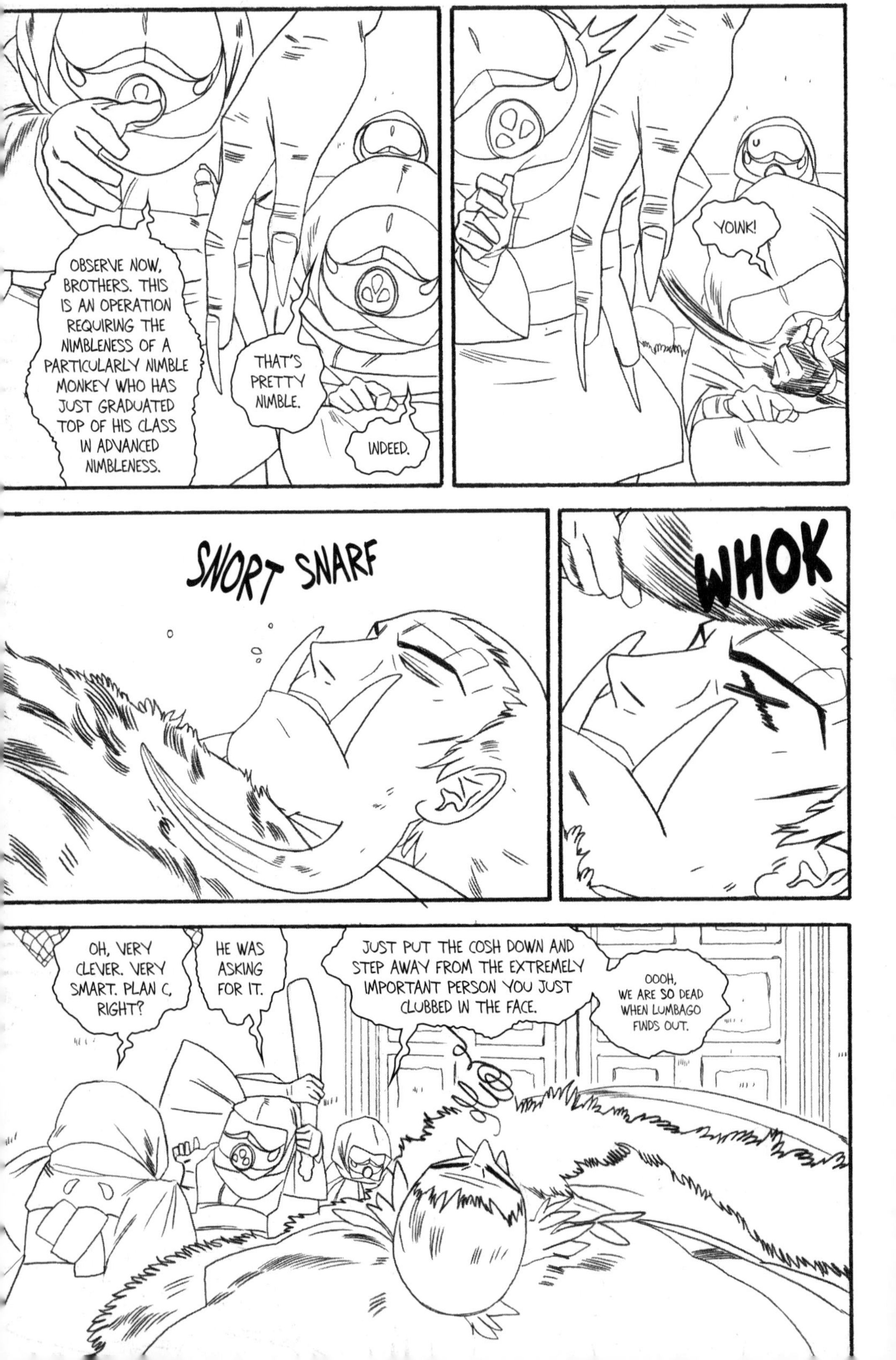
OBSERVE NOW, BROTHERS. THIS IS AN OPERATION REQUIRING THE NIMBLENESS OF A PARTICULARLY NIMBLE MONKEY WHO HAS JUST GRADUATED TOP OF HIS CLASS IN ADVANCED NIMBLENESS.
THAT'S PRETTY NIMBLE.
INDEED.
YOINK!
SNORT SNARF
WHOK
OH, VERY CLEVER. VERY SMART. PLAN C, RIGHT?
HE WAS ASKING FOR IT.
JUST PUT THE COSH DOWN AND STEP AWAY FROM THE EXTREMELY IMPORTANT PERSON YOU JUST CLUBBED IN THE FACE.
OOOH, WE ARE SO DEAD WHEN LUMBAGO FINDS OUT.

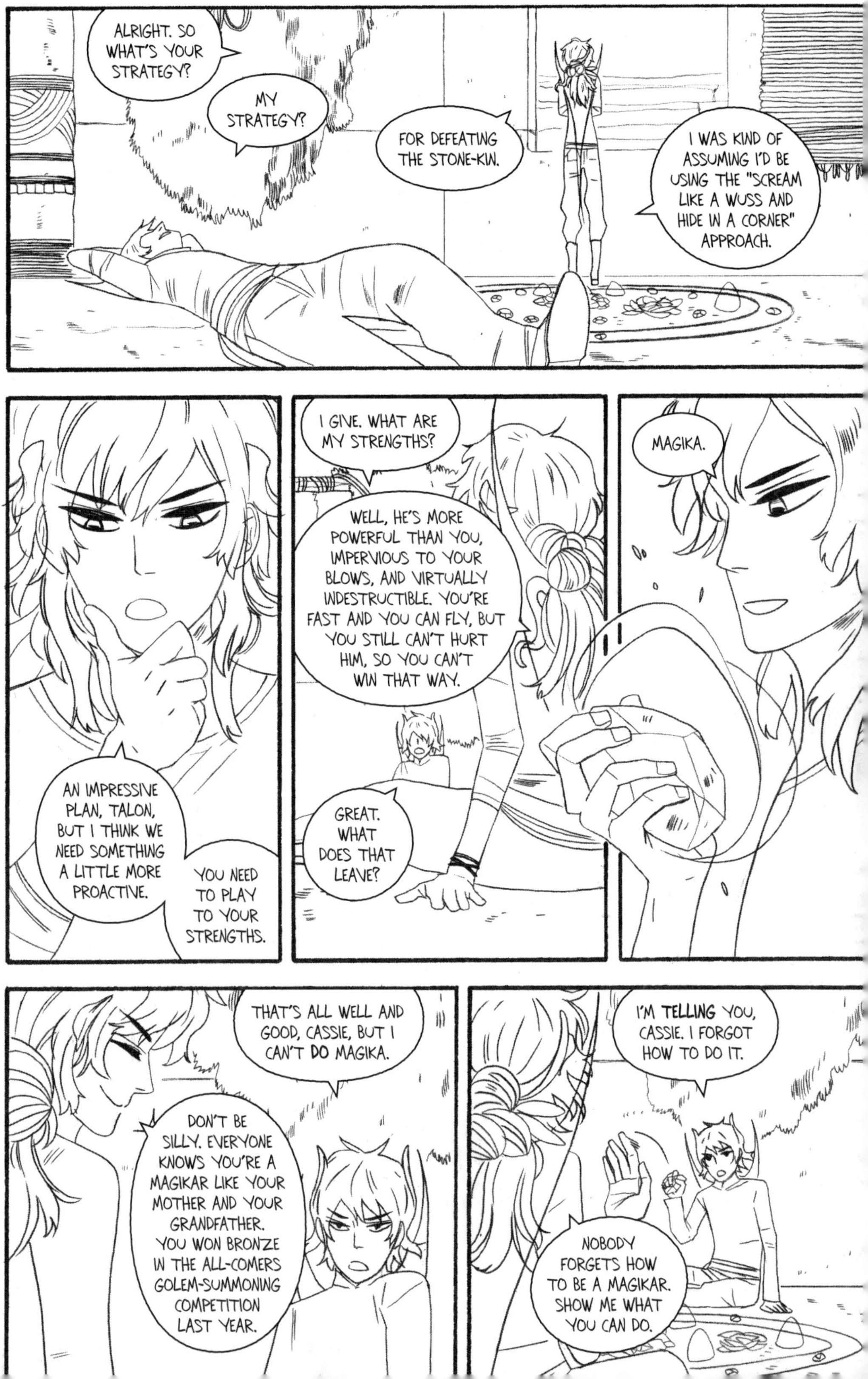
ALRIGHT. SO WHAT'S YOUR STRATEGY?
MY STRATEGY?
FOR DEFEATING THE STONE-KIN.
I WAS KIND OF ASSUMING I'D BE USING THE "SCREAM LIKE A WUSS AND HIDE IN A CORNER" APPROACH.
AN IMPRESSIVE PLAN, TALON, BUT I THINK WE NEED SOMETHING A LITTLE MORE PROACTIVE.
YOU NEED TO PLAY TO YOUR STRENGTHS.
I GIVE. WHAT ARE MY STRENGTHS?
WELL, HE'S MORE POWERFUL THAN YOU, IMPERVIOUS TO YOUR BLOWS, AND VIRTUALLY INDESTRUCTIBLE. YOU'RE FAST AND YOU CAN FLY, BUT YOU STILL CAN'T HURT HIM, SO YOU CAN'T WIN THAT WAY.
GREAT. WHAT DOES THAT LEAVE?
MAGIKA.
THAT'S ALL WELL AND GOOD, CASSIE, BUT I CAN'T DO MAGIKA.
DON'T BE SILLY. EVERYONE KNOWS YOU'RE A MAGIKAR LIKE YOUR MOTHER AND YOUR GRANDFATHER. YOU WON BRONZE IN THE ALL-COMERS GOLEM-SUMMONING COMPETITION LAST YEAR.
I'M TELLING YOU, CASSIE. I FORGOT HOW TO DO IT.
NOBODY FORGETS HOW TO BE A MAGIKAR. SHOW ME WHAT YOU CAN DO.

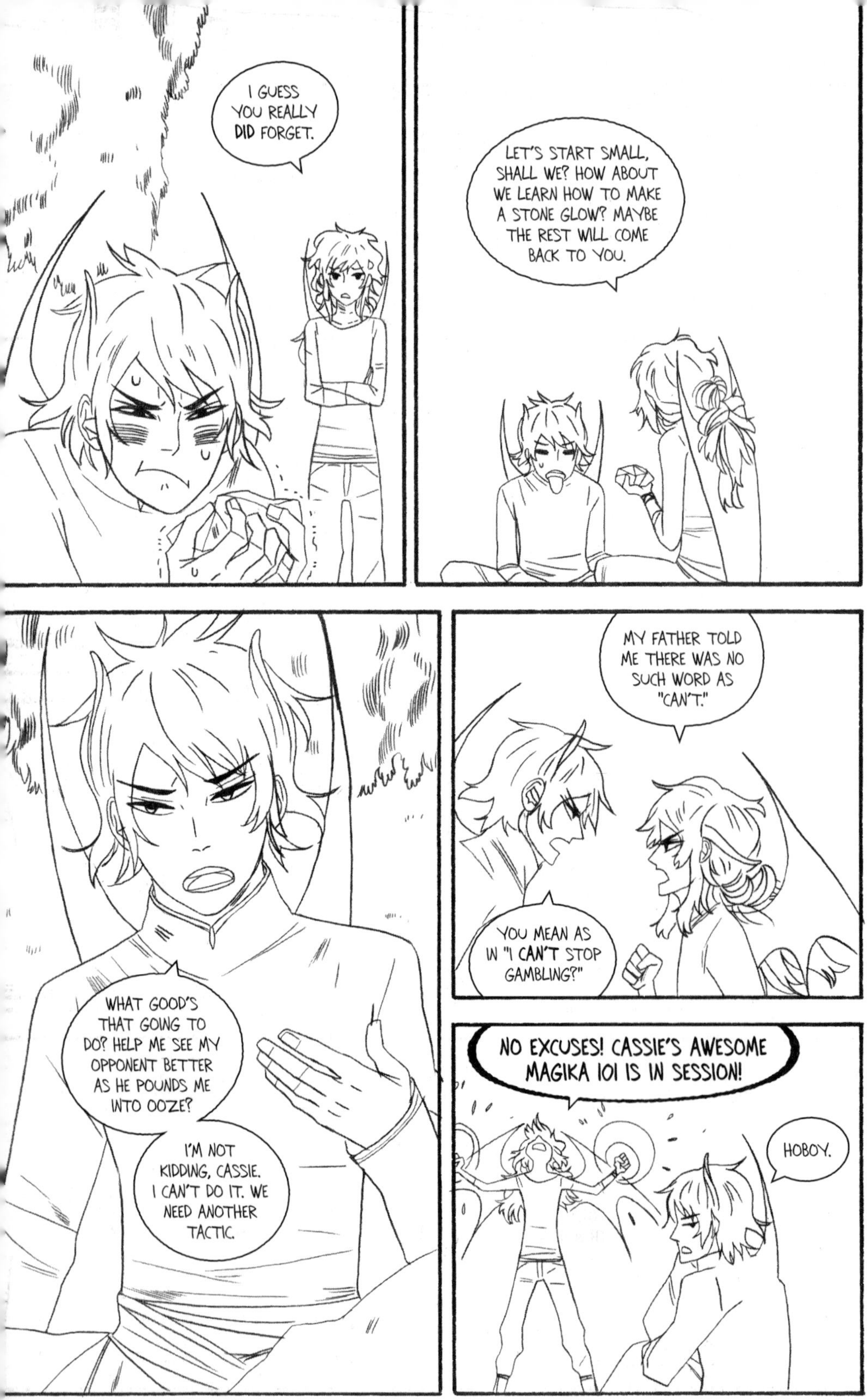

I GUESS YOU REALLY DID FORGET.
LET'S START SMALL, SHALL WE? HOW ABOUT WE LEARN HOW TO MAKE A STONE GLOW? MAYBE THE REST WILL COME BACK TO YOU.
WHAT GOOD'S THAT GOING TO DO? HELP ME SEE MY OPPONENT BETTER AS HE POUNDS ME INTO OOZE?
I'M NOT KIDDING, CASSIE. I CAN'T DO IT. WE NEED ANOTHER TACTIC.
MY FATHER TOLD ME THERE WAS NO SUCH WORD AS "CAN'T."
YOU MEAN AS IN "I CAN'T STOP GAMBLING?"
NO EXCUSES! CASSIE'S AWESOME MAGIKA 101 IS IN SESSION!
HOBOY.

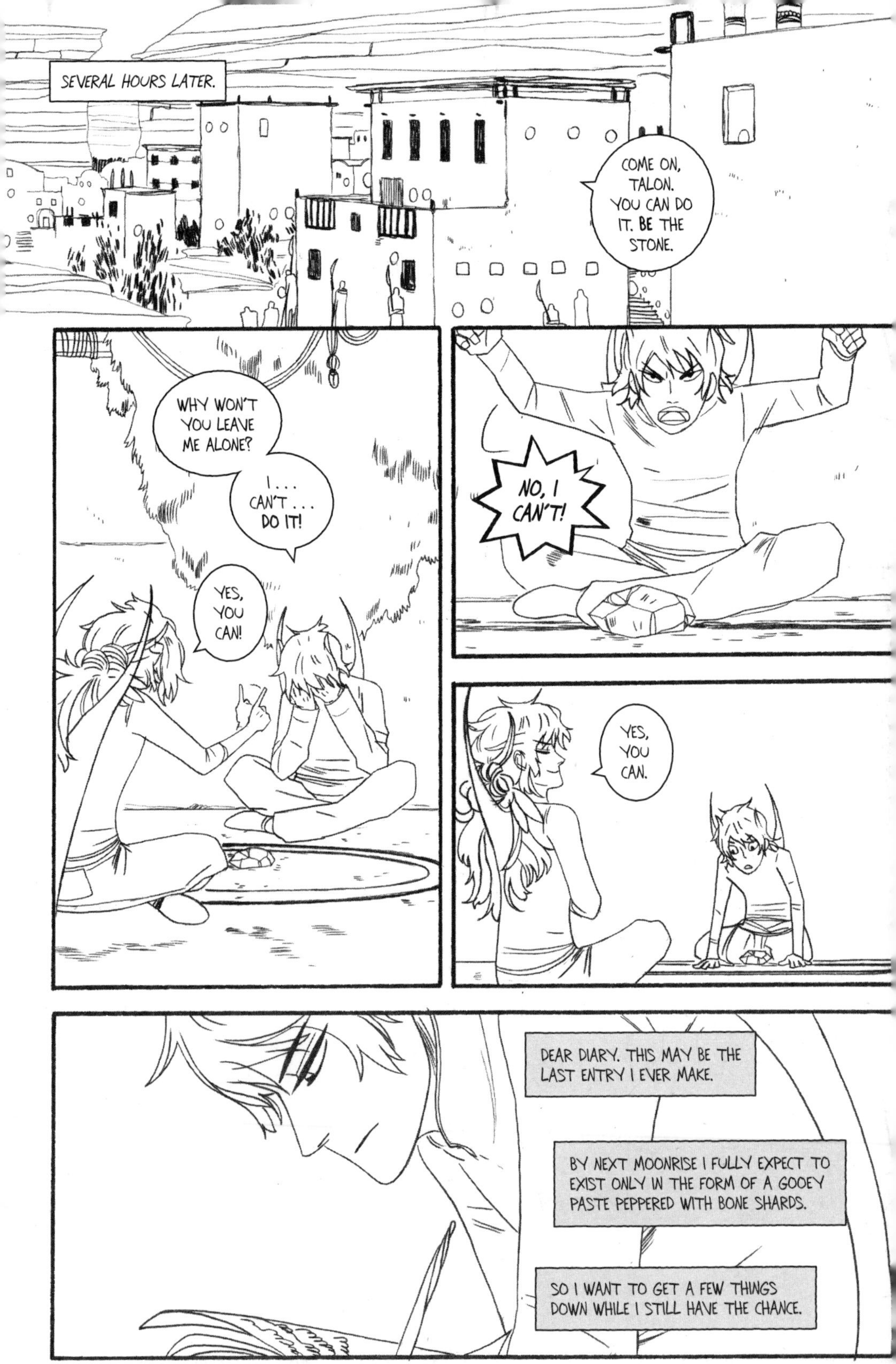
SEVERAL HOURS LATER.
COME ON, TALON. YOU CAN DO IT. BE THE STONE.
WHY WON'T YOU LEAVE ME ALONE?
I . . . CAN'T . . . DO IT!
YES, YOU CAN!
NO, I CAN'T!
YES, YOU CAN.
DEAR DIARY. THIS MAY BE THE LAST ENTRY I EVER MAKE.
BY NEXT MOONRISE I FULLY EXPECT TO EXIST ONLY IN THE FORM OF A GOOEY PASTE PEPPERED WITH BONE SHARDS.
SO I WANT TO GET A FEW THINGS DOWN WHILE I STILL HAVE THE CHANCE.

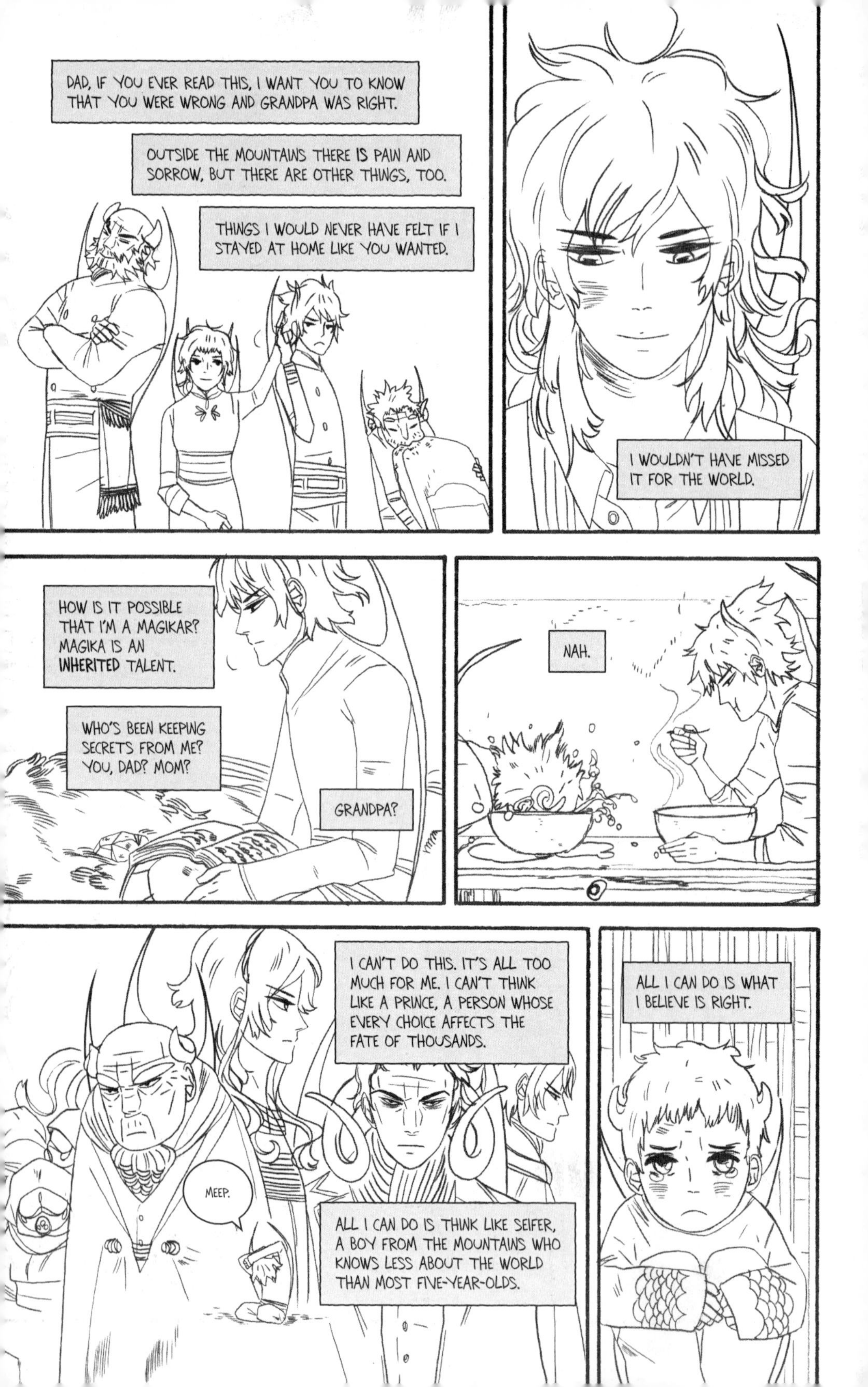
DAD, IF YOU EVER READ THIS, I WANT YOU TO KNOW THAT YOU WERE WRONG AND GRANDPA WAS RIGHT.
OUTSIDE THE MOUNTAINS THERE IS PAIN AND SORROW, BUT THERE ARE OTHER THINGS, TOO.
THINGS I WOULD NEVER HAVE FELT IF I STAYED AT HOME LIKE YOU WANTED.
I WOULDN'T HAVE MISSED IT FOR THE WORLD.
HOW IS IT POSSIBLE THAT I'M A MAGIKAR? MAGIKA IS AN **INHERITED** TALENT.
WHO'S BEEN KEEPING SECRETS FROM ME? YOU, DAD? MOM?
GRANDPA?
NAH.
I CAN'T DO THIS. IT'S ALL TOO MUCH FOR ME. I CAN'T THINK LIKE A PRINCE, A PERSON WHOSE EVERY CHOICE AFFECTS THE FATE OF THOUSANDS.
MEEP.
ALL I CAN DO IS THINK LIKE SEIFER, A BOY FROM THE MOUNTAINS WHO KNOWS LESS ABOUT THE WORLD THAN MOST FIVE-YEAR-OLDS.
ALL I CAN DO IS WHAT I BELIEVE IS RIGHT.

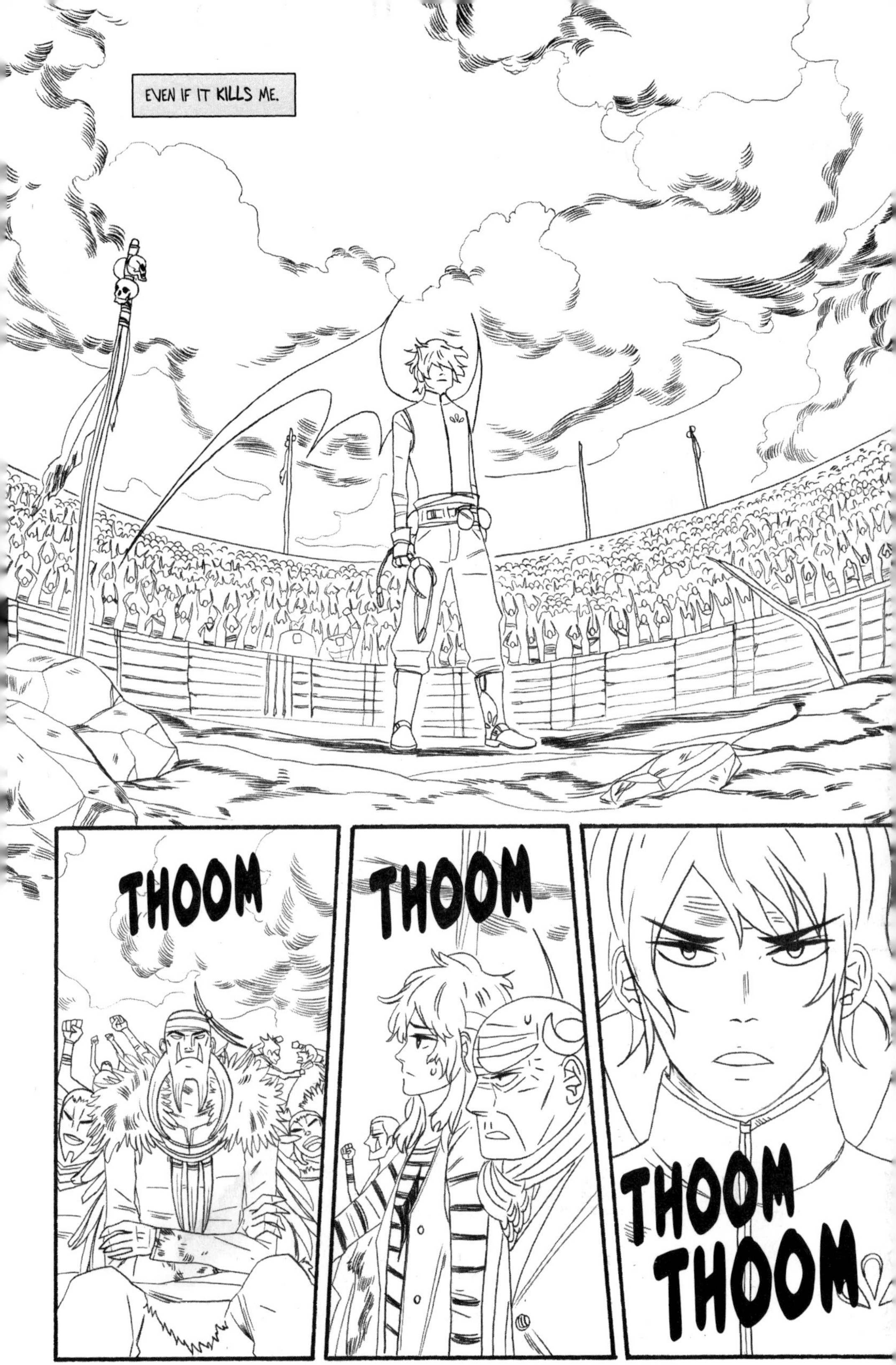

EVEN IF IT KILLS ME.
THOOM
THOOM
THOOM
THOOM

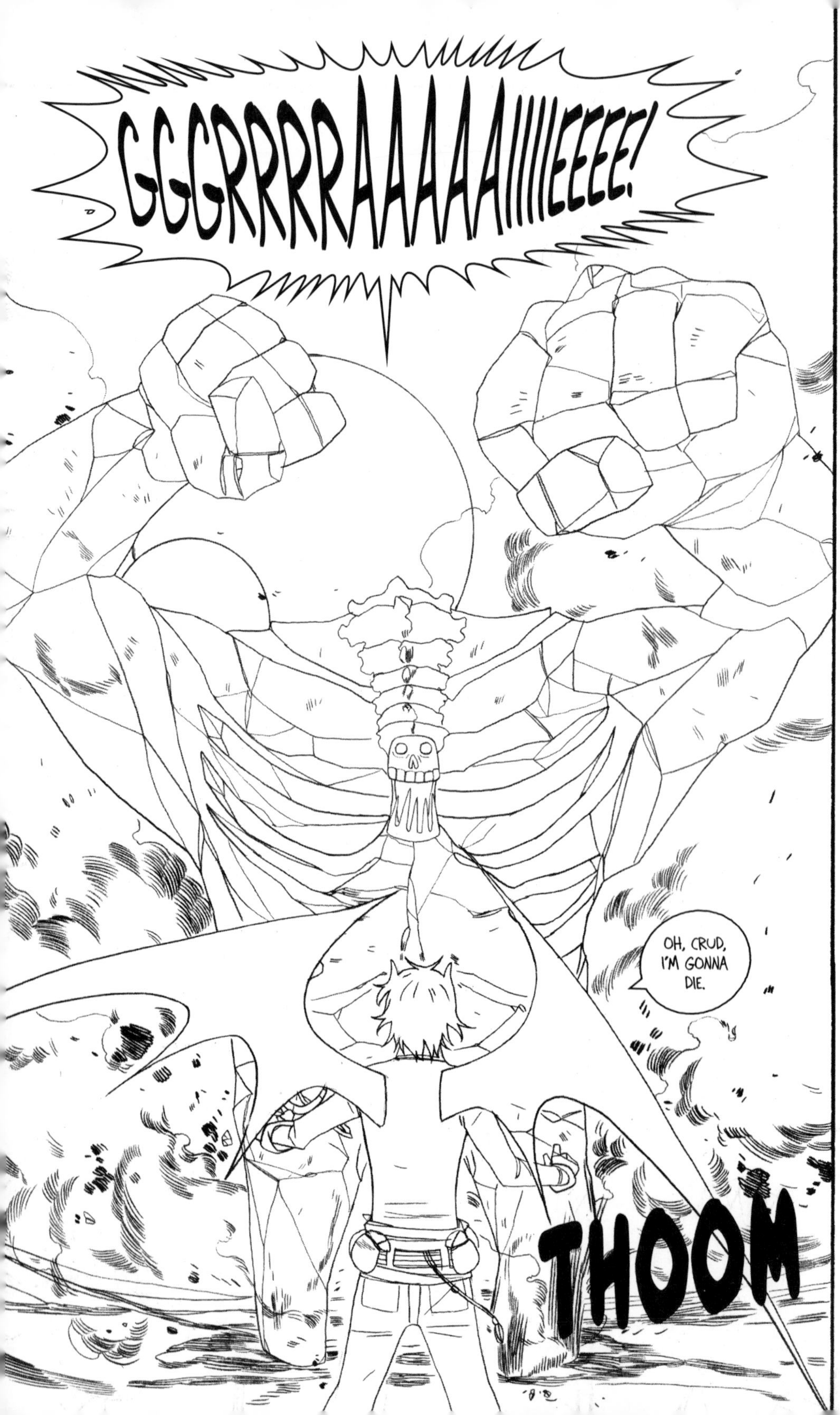
GGGRRRRAAAAIIIIIEEEEE!
OH, CRUD, I'M GONNA DIE.
THOOM

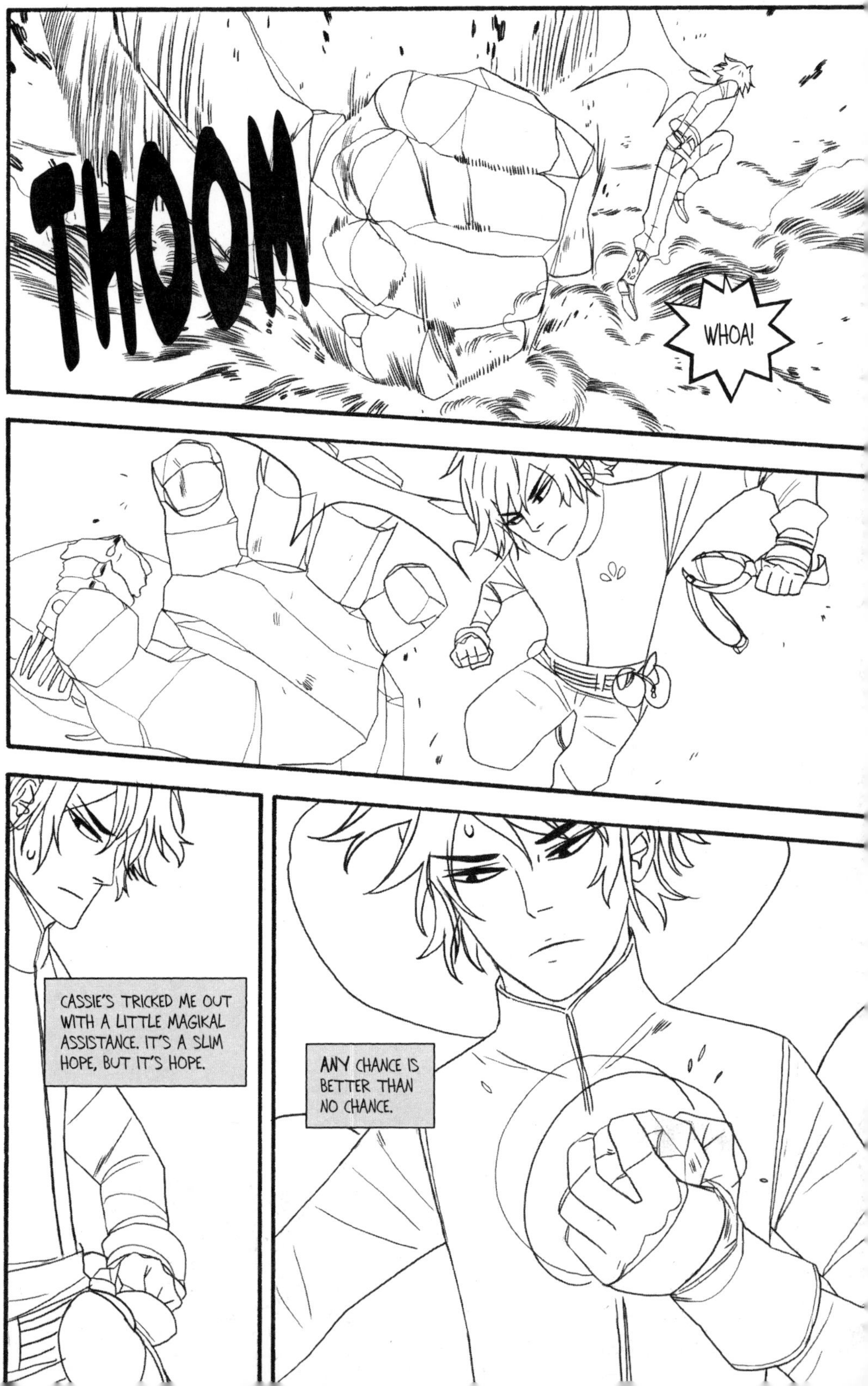
THOOM
WHOA!
CASSIE'S TRICKED ME OUT WITH A LITTLE MAGIKAL ASSISTANCE. IT'S A SLIM HOPE, BUT IT'S HOPE.
ANY CHANCE IS BETTER THAN NO CHANCE.

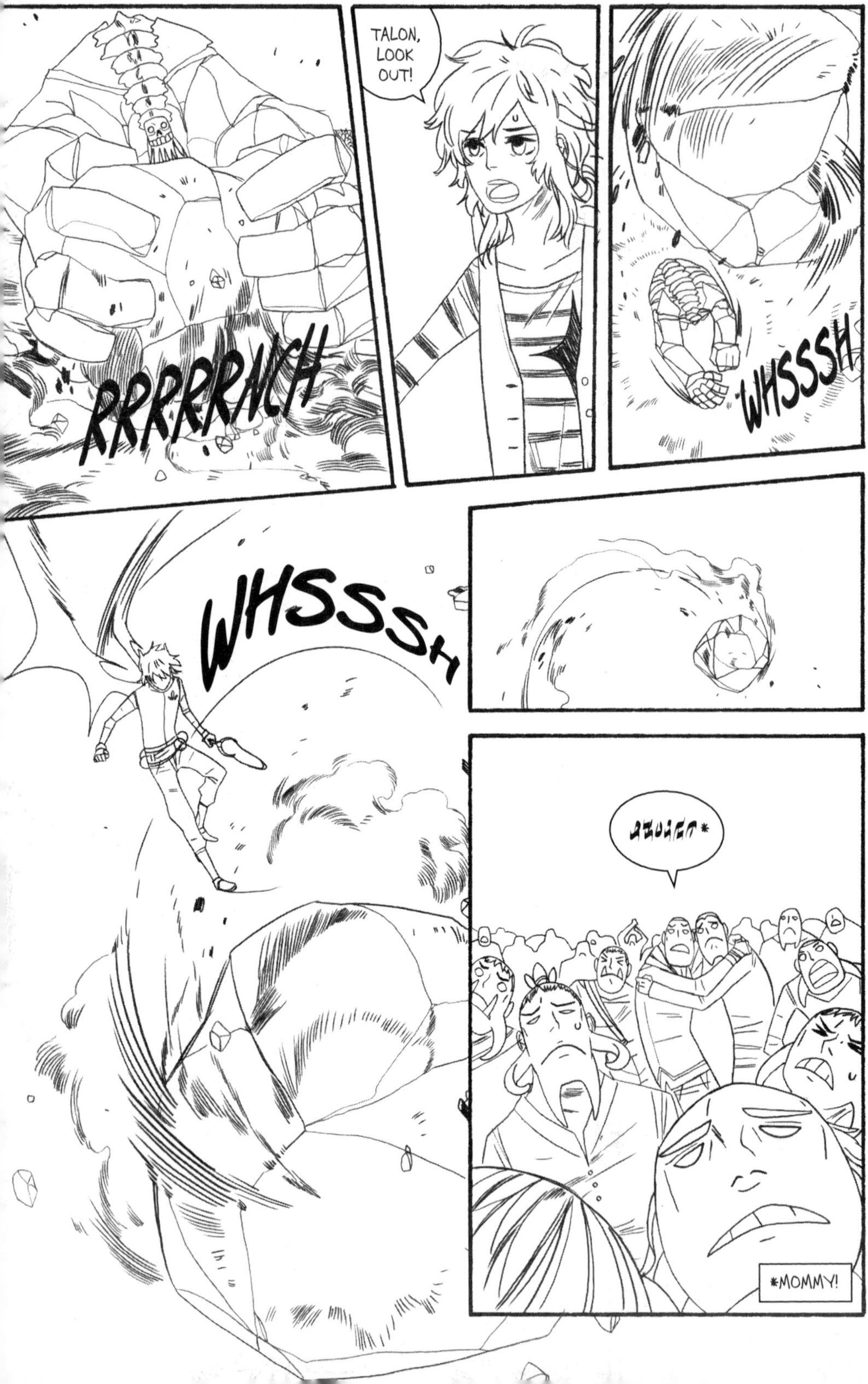
RRRRRNCH
TALON, LOOK OUT!
WHSSSH
WHSSSH
*MOMMY!

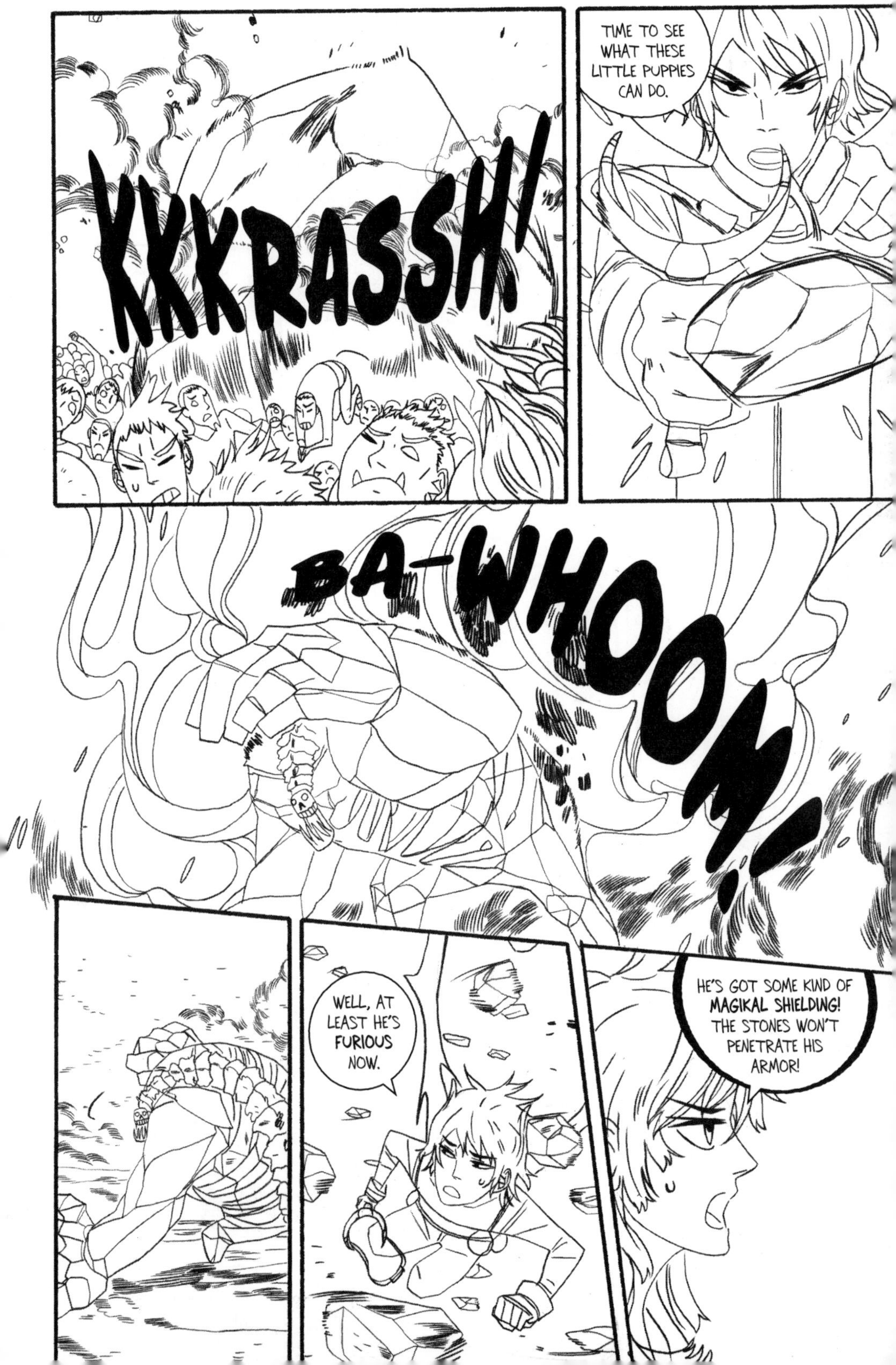
KKKRASSH!
TIME TO SEE WHAT THESE LITTLE PUPPIES CAN DO.
BA-WHOOM!
WELL, AT LEAST HE'S FURIOUS NOW.
HE'S GOT SOME KIND OF MAGIKAL SHIELDING! THE STONES WON'T PENETRATE HIS ARMOR!

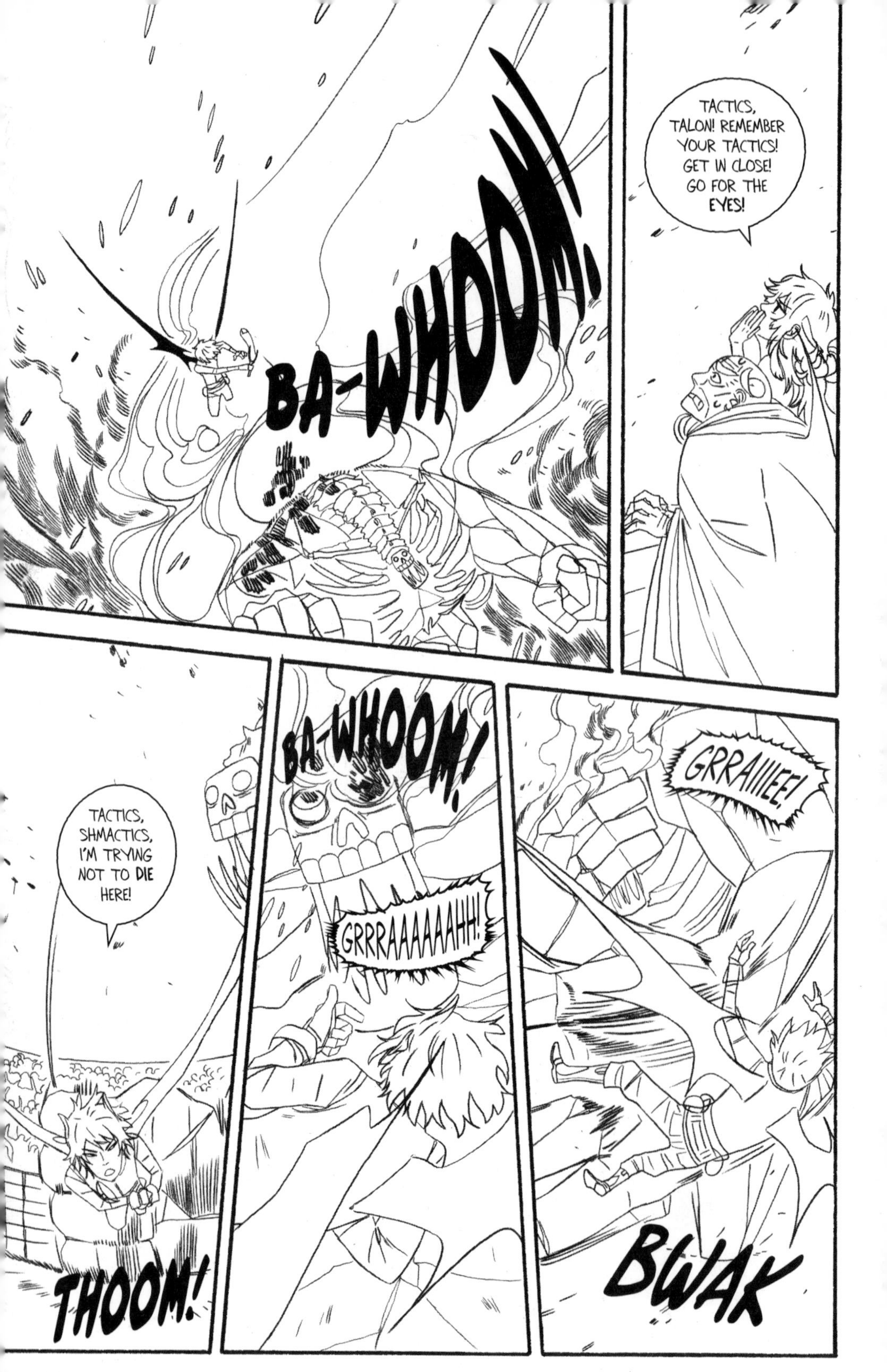
BA-WHOOM!
TACTICS, TALON! REMEMBER YOUR TACTICS! GET IN CLOSE! GO FOR THE **EYES!**
TACTICS, SHMACTICS, I'M TRYING NOT TO **DIE** HERE!
THOOM!
BA-WHOOM!
GRRRAAAAAAHH!
GRRAIIIEE!
BWAK

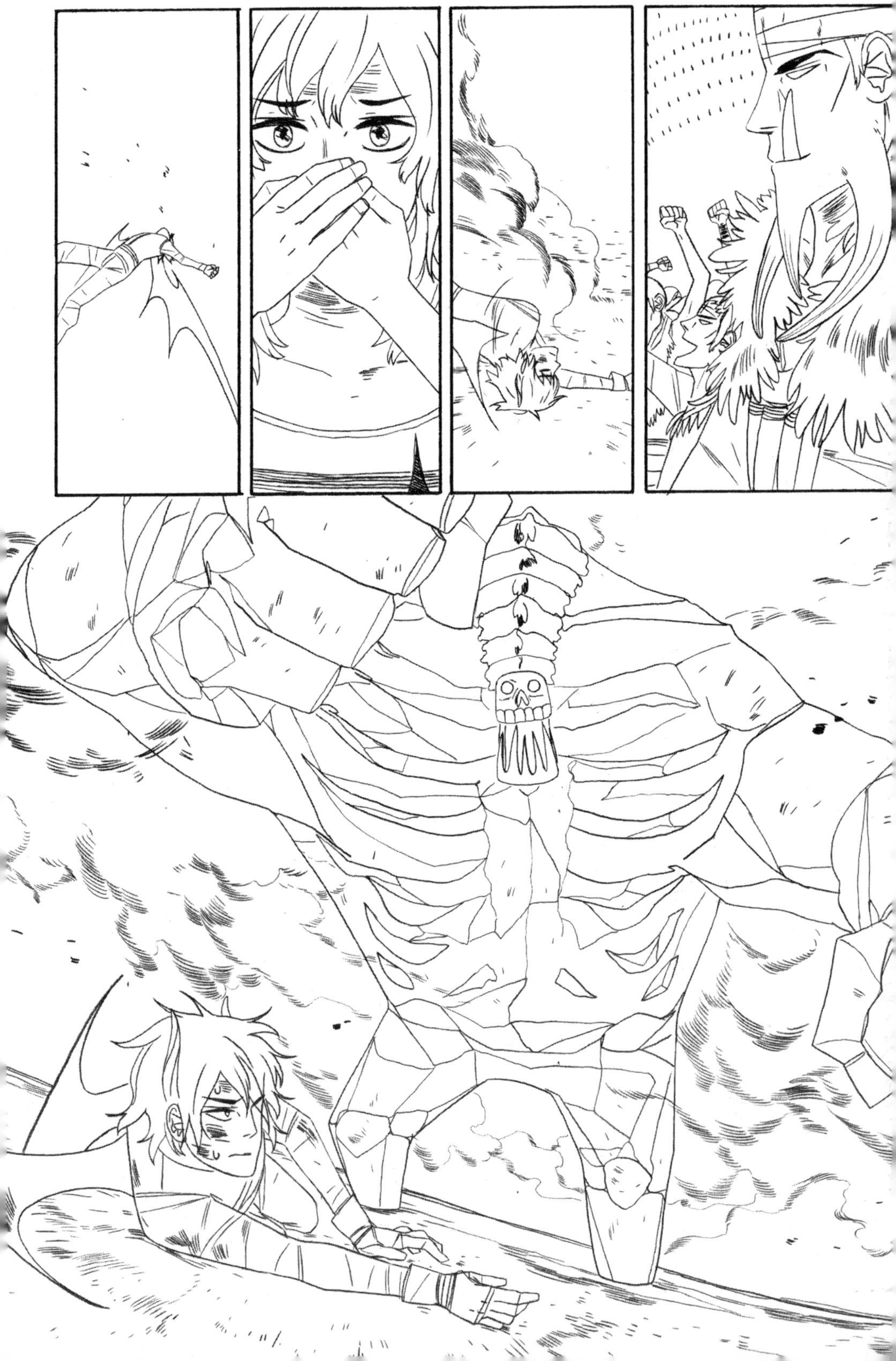

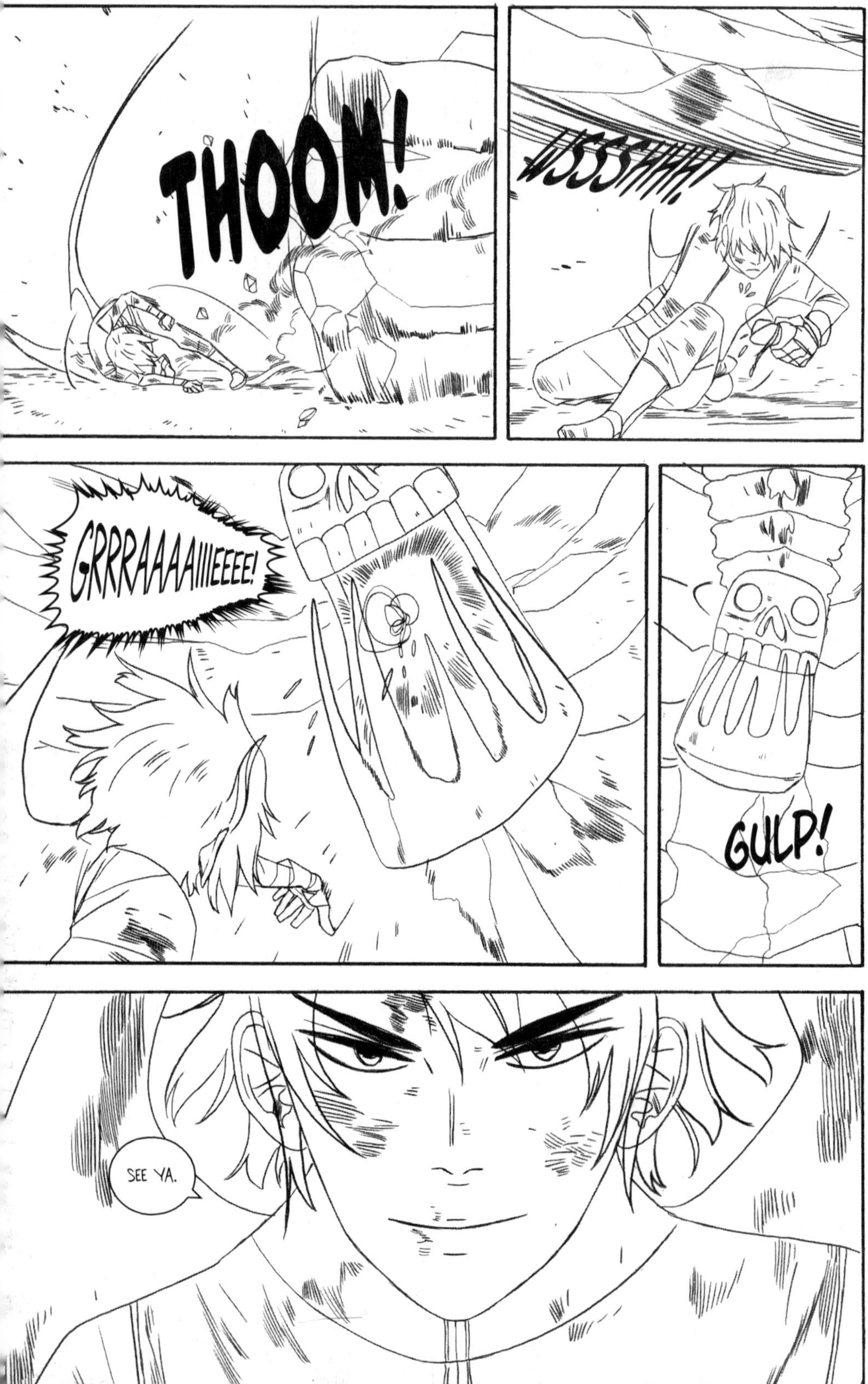
THOOM!
WSSSHHH!
GRRRAAAAIIIEEEE!
GULP!
SEE YA.

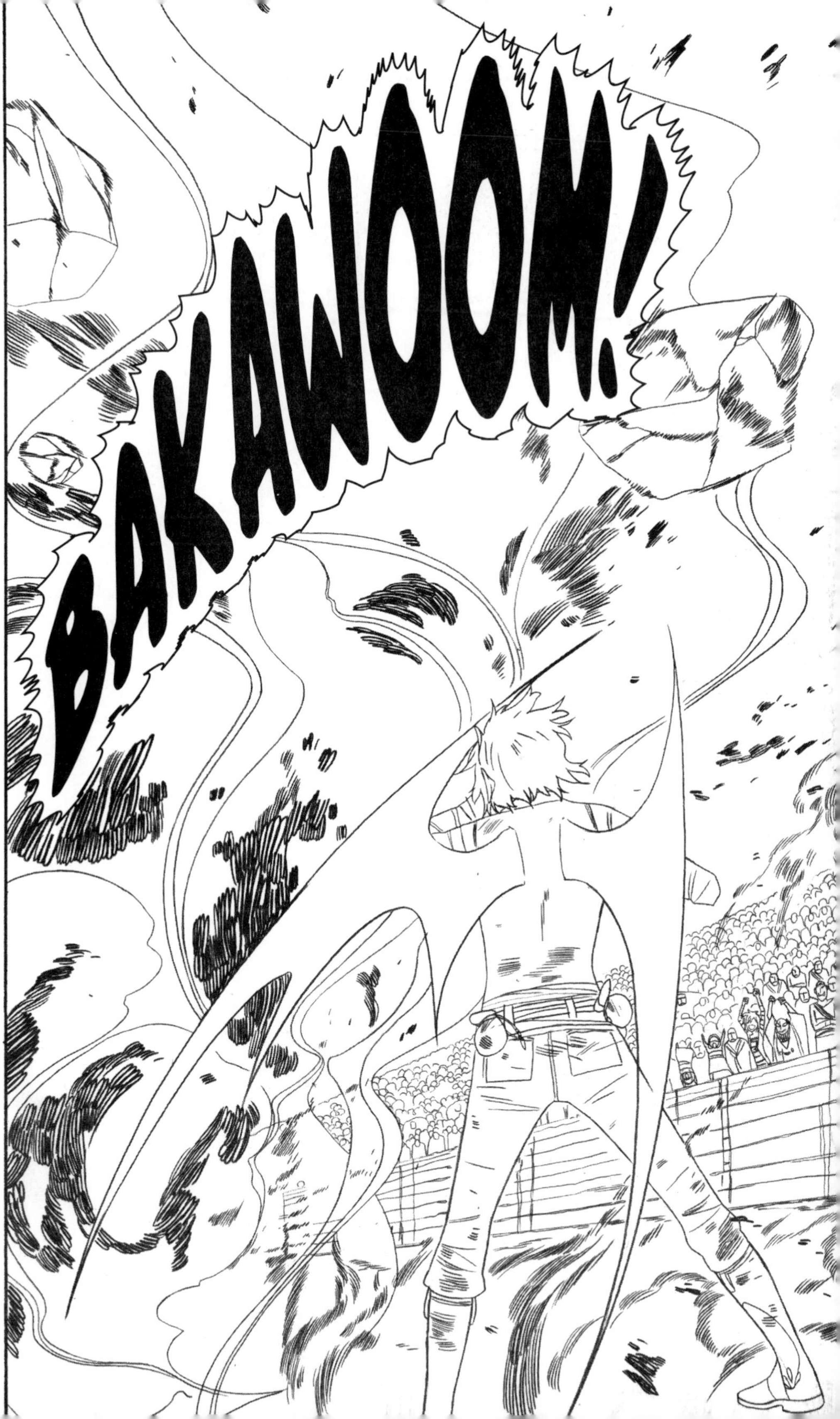
BAKAWOOM!

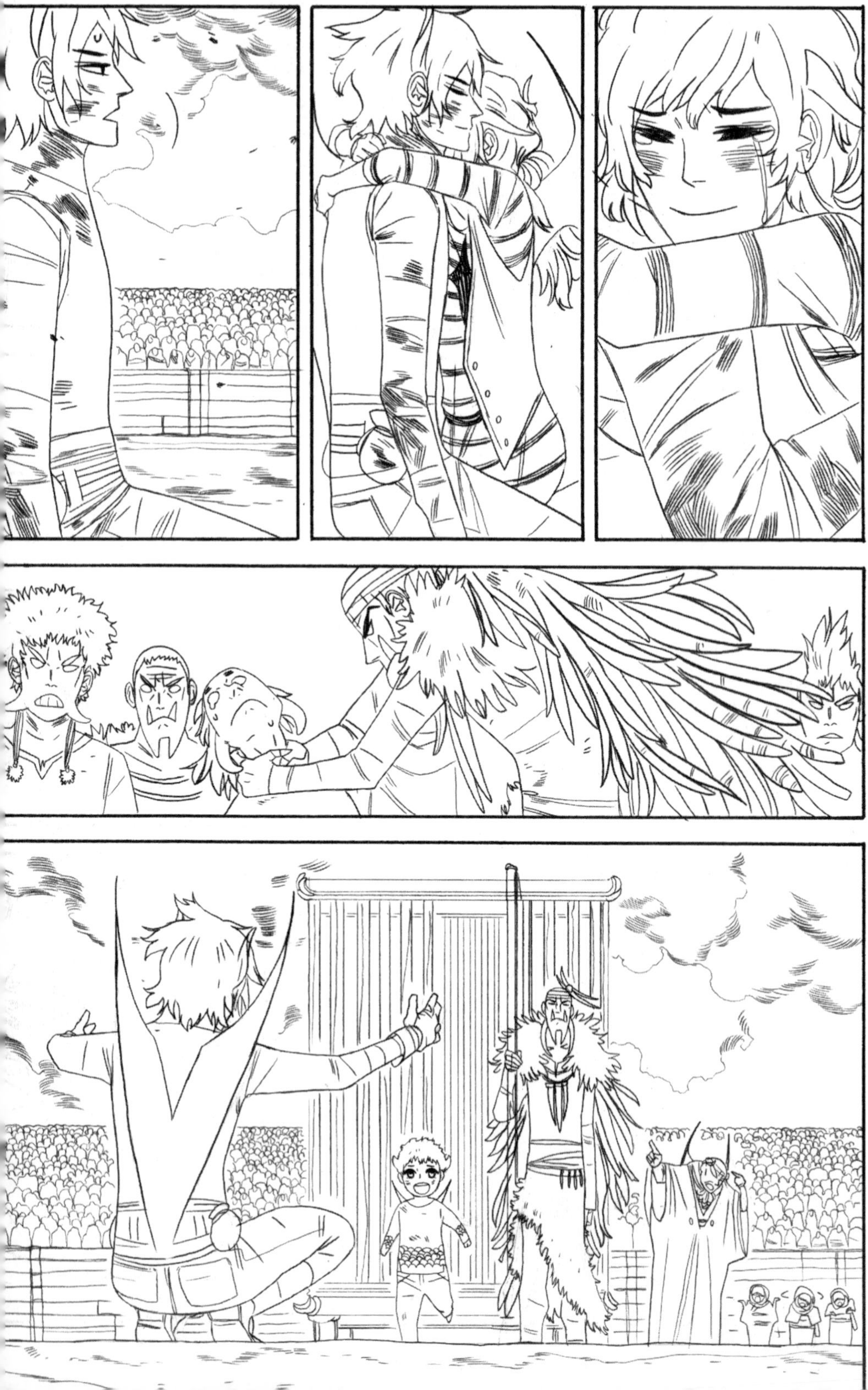

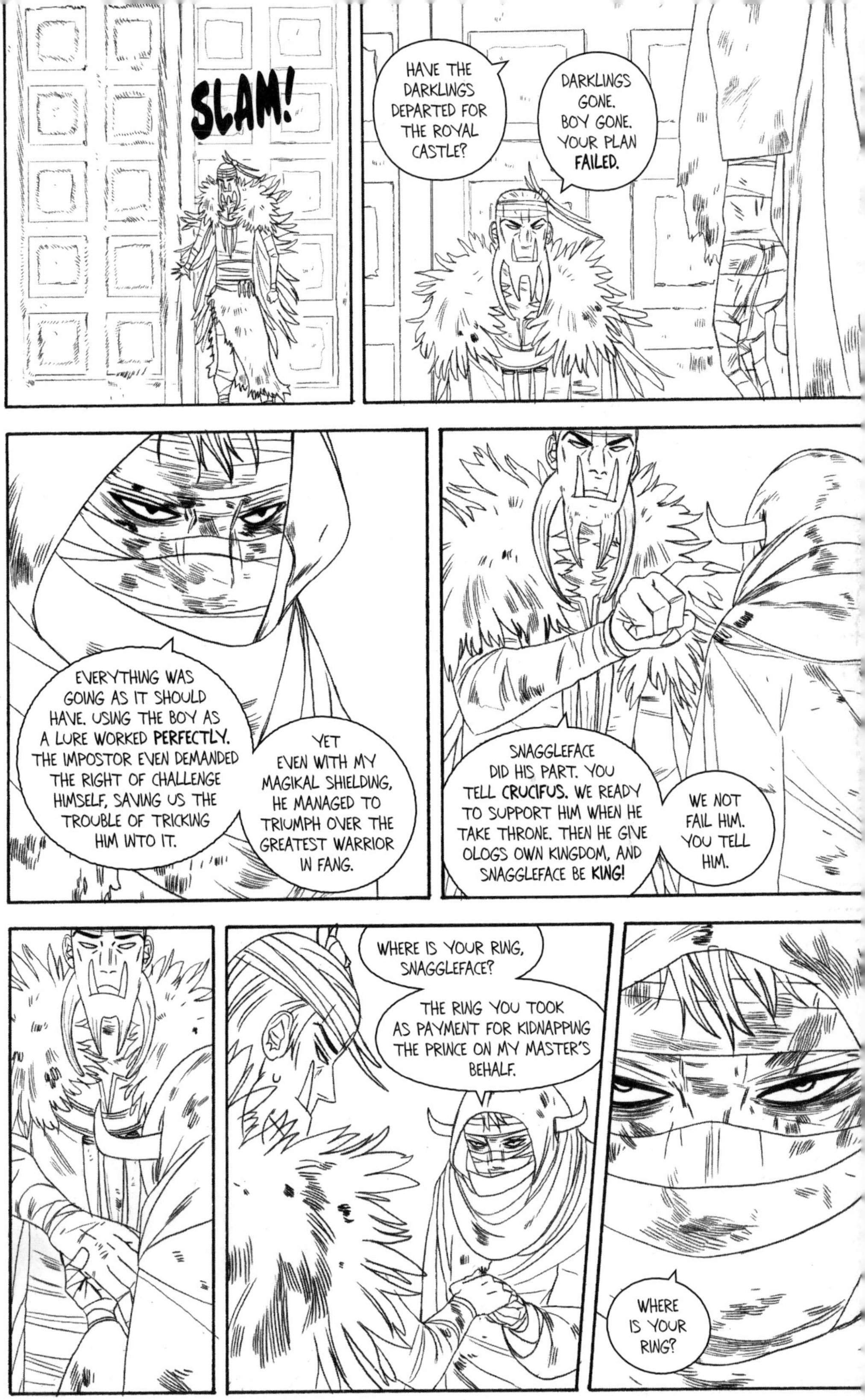
SLAM!
HAVE THE DARKLINGS DEPARTED FOR THE ROYAL CASTLE?
DARKLINGS GONE. BOY GONE. YOUR PLAN **FAILED.**
EVERYTHING WAS GOING AS IT SHOULD HAVE. USING THE BOY AS A LURE WORKED **PERFECTLY.** THE IMPOSTOR EVEN DEMANDED THE RIGHT OF CHALLENGE HIMSELF, SAVING US THE TROUBLE OF TRICKING HIM INTO IT.
YET EVEN WITH MY MAGIKAL SHIELDING, HE MANAGED TO TRIUMPH OVER THE GREATEST WARRIOR IN FANG.
SNAGGLEFACE DID HIS PART. YOU TELL **CRUCIFUS.** WE READY TO SUPPORT HIM WHEN HE TAKE THRONE. THEN HE GIVE OLOGS OWN KINGDOM, AND SNAGGLEFACE BE **KING!**
WE NOT FAIL HIM. YOU TELL HIM.
WHERE IS YOUR RING, SNAGGLEFACE?
THE RING YOU TOOK AS PAYMENT FOR KIDNAPPING THE PRINCE ON MY MASTER'S BEHALF.
WHERE IS YOUR RING?

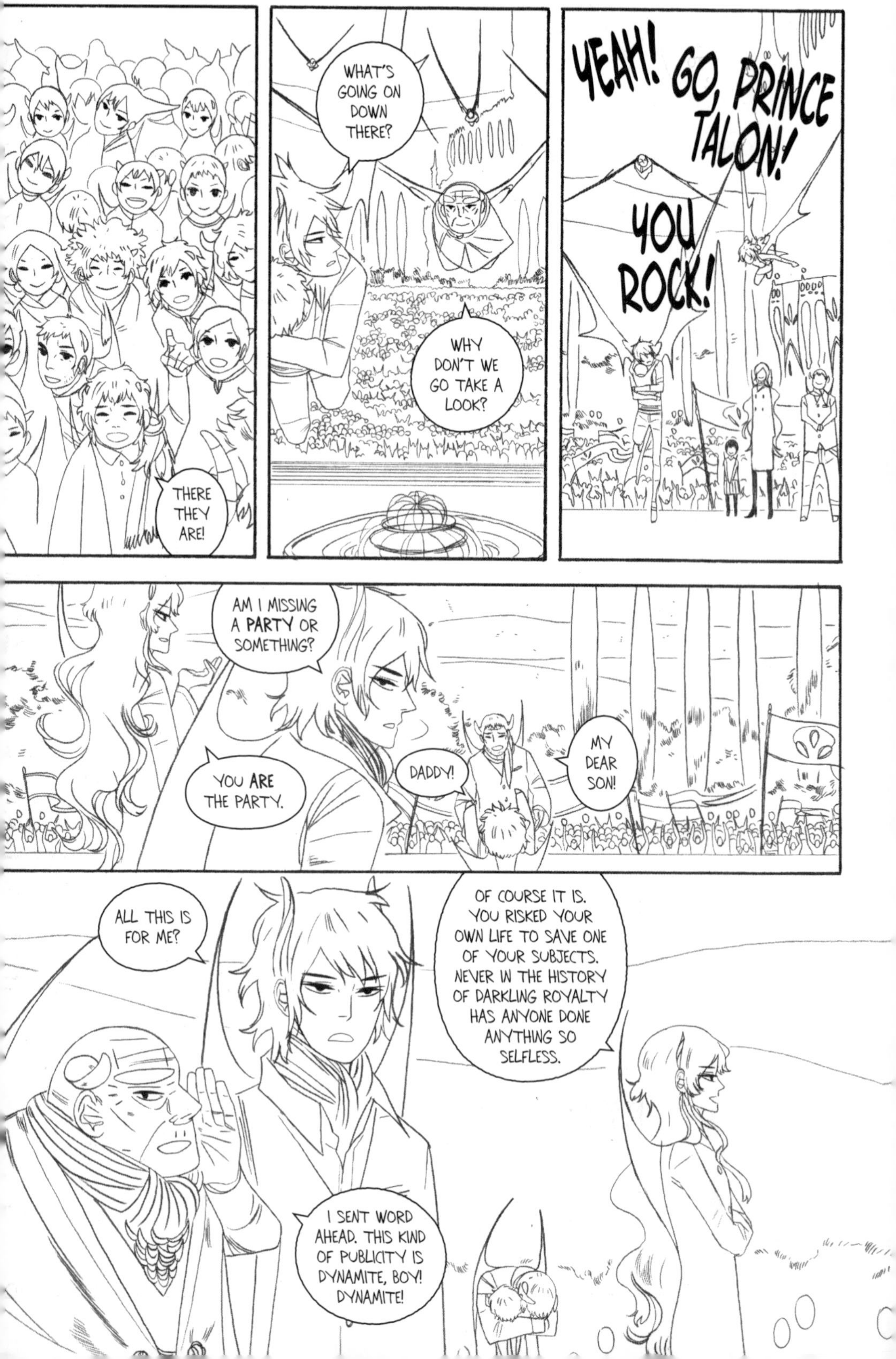
THERE THEY ARE!
WHAT'S GOING ON DOWN THERE?
WHY DON'T WE GO TAKE A LOOK?
YEAH!
GO, PRINCE TALON!
YOU ROCK!
AM I MISSING A PARTY OR SOMETHING?
YOU ARE THE PARTY.
DADDY!
MY DEAR SON!
ALL THIS IS FOR ME?
OF COURSE IT IS. YOU RISKED YOUR OWN LIFE TO SAVE ONE OF YOUR SUBJECTS. NEVER IN THE HISTORY OF DARKLING ROYALTY HAS ANYONE DONE ANYTHING SO SELFLESS.
I SENT WORD AHEAD. THIS KIND OF PUBLICITY IS DYNAMITE, BOY! DYNAMITE!

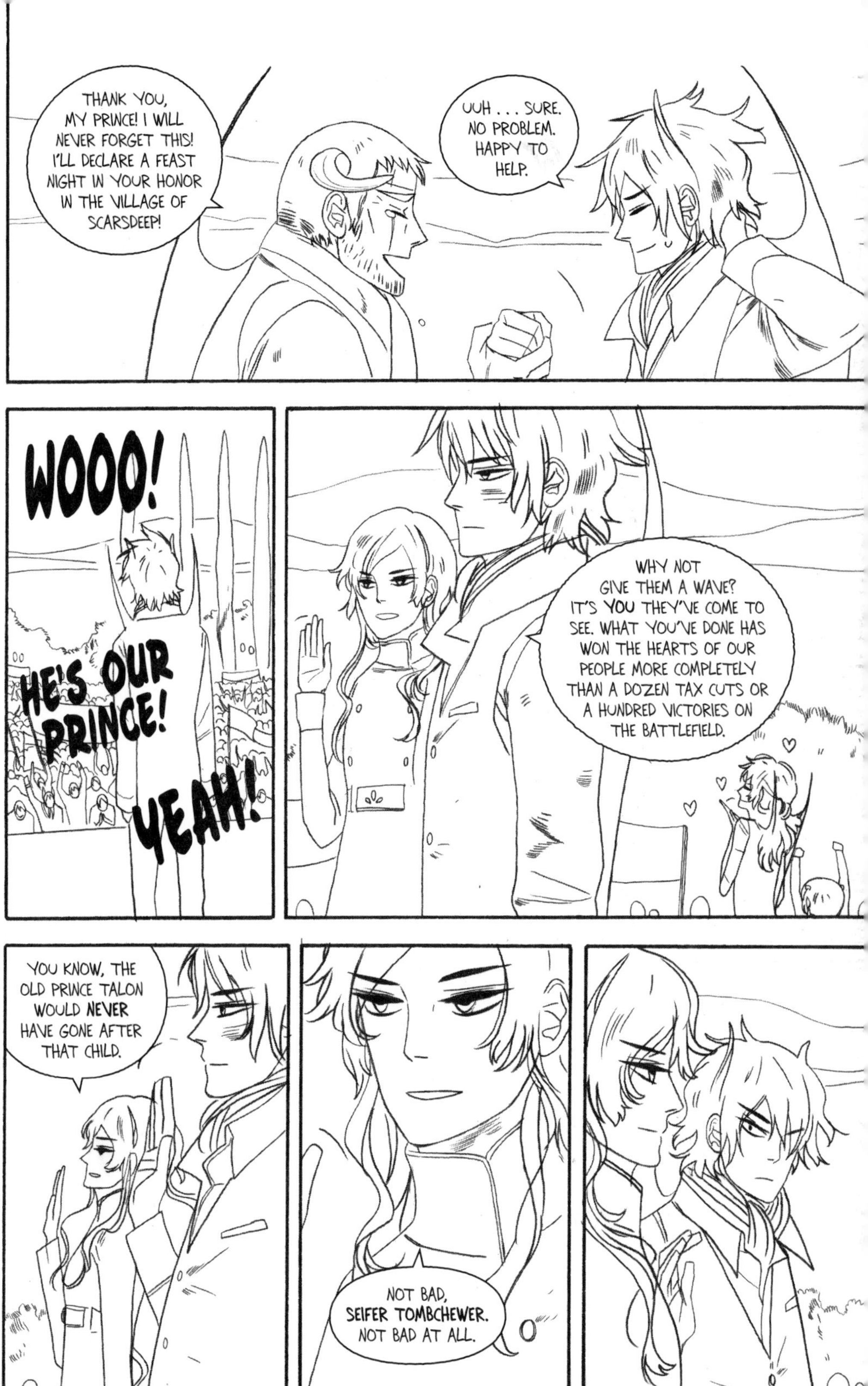
THANK YOU, MY PRINCE! I WILL NEVER FORGET THIS! I'LL DECLARE A FEAST NIGHT IN YOUR HONOR IN THE VILLAGE OF SCARSDEEP!
UUH . . . SURE. NO PROBLEM. HAPPY TO HELP.
WOOO!
HE'S OUR PRINCE!
YEAH!
WHY NOT GIVE THEM A WAVE? IT'S YOU THEY'VE COME TO SEE. WHAT YOU'VE DONE HAS WON THE HEARTS OF OUR PEOPLE MORE COMPLETELY THAN A DOZEN TAX CUTS OR A HUNDRED VICTORIES ON THE BATTLEFIELD.
YOU KNOW, THE OLD PRINCE TALON WOULD NEVER HAVE GONE AFTER THAT CHILD.
NOT BAD, SEIFER TOMBCHEWER. NOT BAD AT ALL.

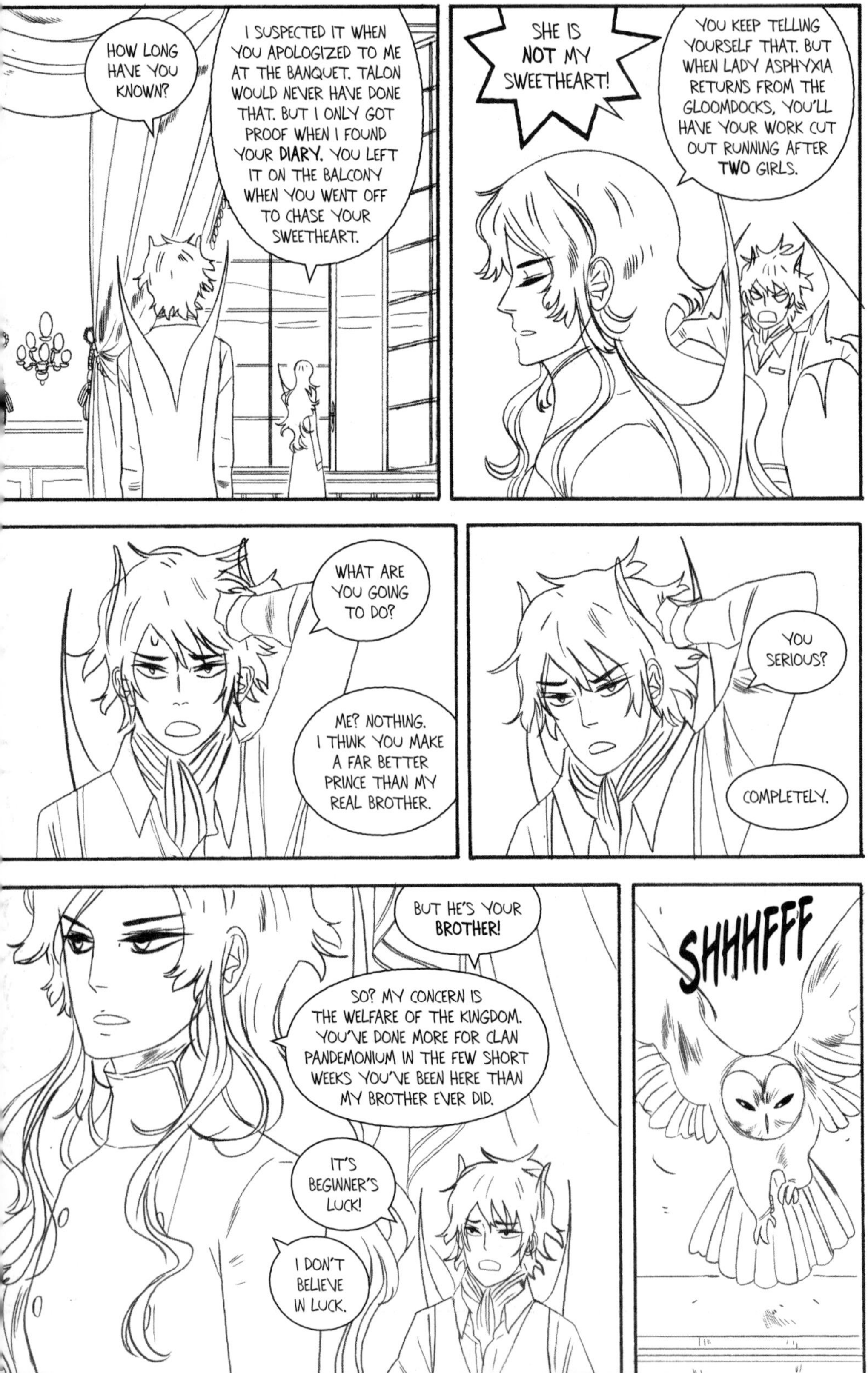
HOW LONG HAVE YOU KNOWN?
I SUSPECTED IT WHEN YOU APOLOGIZED TO ME AT THE BANQUET. TALON WOULD NEVER HAVE DONE THAT. BUT I ONLY GOT PROOF WHEN I FOUND YOUR **DIARY.** YOU LEFT IT ON THE BALCONY WHEN YOU WENT OFF TO CHASE YOUR SWEETHEART.
SHE IS **NOT** MY SWEETHEART!
YOU KEEP TELLING YOURSELF THAT. BUT WHEN LADY ASPHYXIA RETURNS FROM THE GLOOMDOCKS, YOU'LL HAVE YOUR WORK CUT OUT RUNNING AFTER **TWO** GIRLS.
WHAT ARE YOU GOING TO DO?
ME? NOTHING. I THINK YOU MAKE A FAR BETTER PRINCE THAN MY REAL BROTHER.
YOU SERIOUS?
COMPLETELY.
BUT HE'S YOUR **BROTHER!**
SO? MY CONCERN IS THE WELFARE OF THE KINGDOM. YOU'VE DONE MORE FOR CLAN PANDEMONIUM IN THE FEW SHORT WEEKS YOU'VE BEEN HERE THAN MY BROTHER EVER DID.
IT'S BEGINNER'S LUCK!
I DON'T BELIEVE IN LUCK.
SHHHFFF

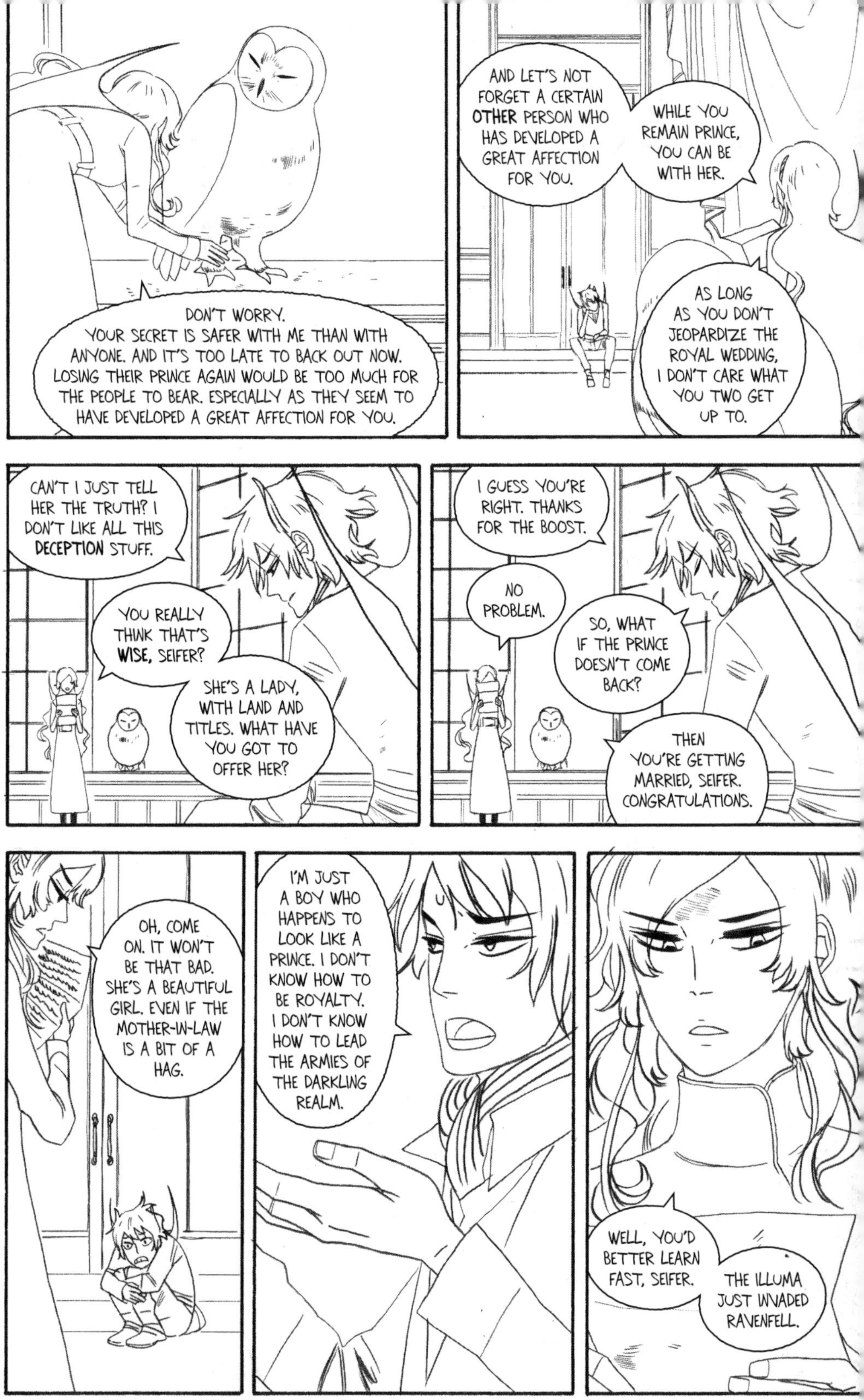
DON'T WORRY. YOUR SECRET IS SAFER WITH ME THAN WITH ANYONE. AND IT'S TOO LATE TO BACK OUT NOW. LOSING THEIR PRINCE AGAIN WOULD BE TOO MUCH FOR THE PEOPLE TO BEAR. ESPECIALLY AS THEY SEEM TO HAVE DEVELOPED A GREAT AFFECTION FOR YOU.
AND LET'S NOT FORGET A CERTAIN **OTHER** PERSON WHO HAS DEVELOPED A GREAT AFFECTION FOR YOU.
WHILE YOU REMAIN PRINCE, YOU CAN BE WITH HER.
AS LONG AS YOU DON'T JEOPARDIZE THE ROYAL WEDDING, I DON'T CARE WHAT YOU TWO GET UP TO.
CAN'T I JUST TELL HER THE TRUTH? I DON'T LIKE ALL THIS **DECEPTION** STUFF.
YOU REALLY THINK THAT'S **WISE**, SEIFER?
SHE'S A LADY, WITH LAND AND TITLES. WHAT HAVE YOU GOT TO OFFER HER?
I GUESS YOU'RE RIGHT. THANKS FOR THE BOOST.
NO PROBLEM.
SO, WHAT IF THE PRINCE DOESN'T COME BACK?
THEN YOU'RE GETTING MARRIED, SEIFER. CONGRATULATIONS.
OH, COME ON. IT WON'T BE THAT BAD. SHE'S A BEAUTIFUL GIRL. EVEN IF THE MOTHER-IN-LAW IS A BIT OF A HAG.
I'M JUST A BOY WHO HAPPENS TO LOOK LIKE A PRINCE. I DON'T KNOW HOW TO BE ROYALTY. I DON'T KNOW HOW TO LEAD THE ARMIES OF THE DARKLING REALM.
WELL, YOU'D BETTER LEARN FAST, SEIFER.
THE ILLUMA JUST INVADED RAVENFELL.

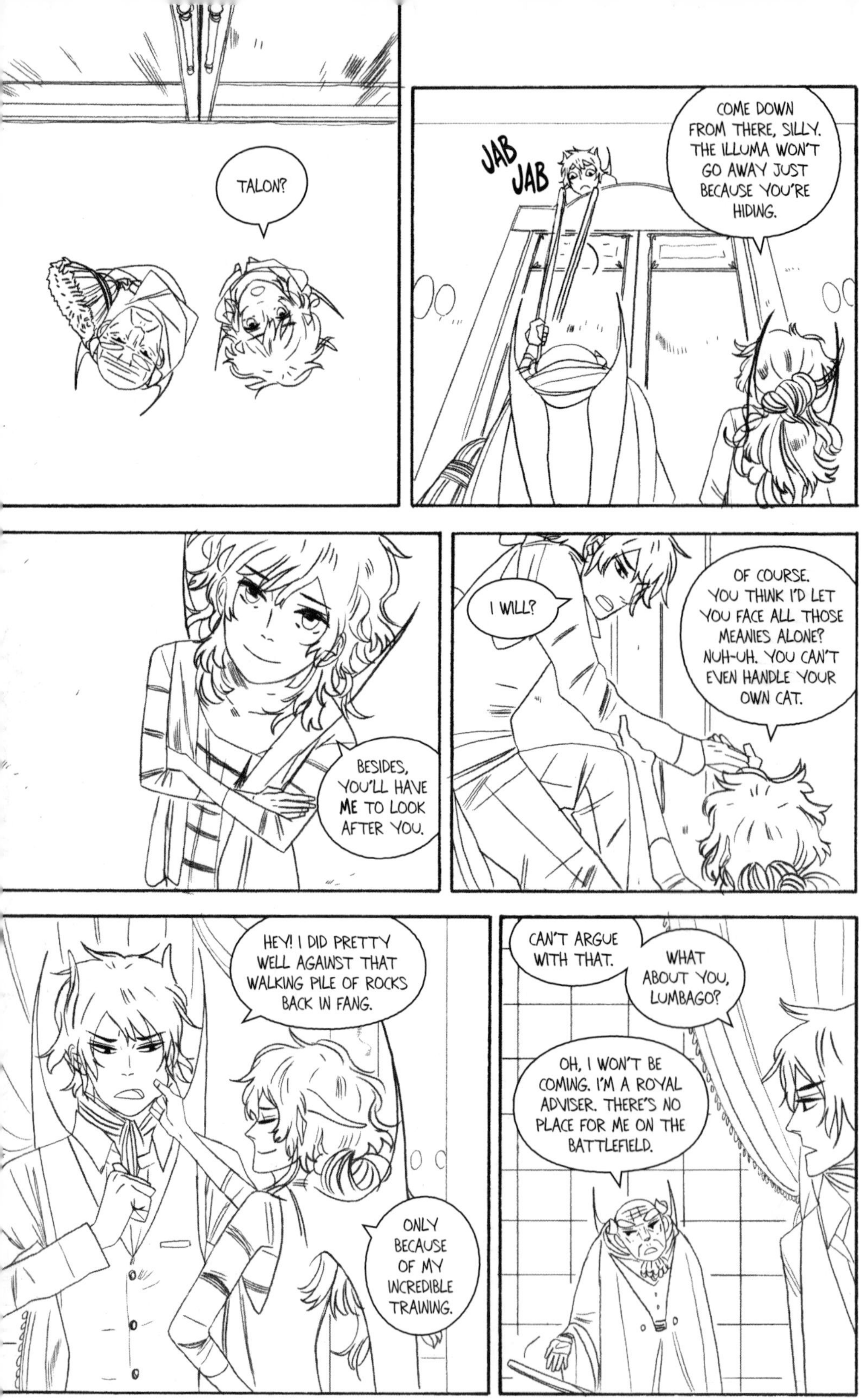
TALON?
JAB JAB
COME DOWN FROM THERE, SILLY. THE ILLUMA WON'T GO AWAY JUST BECAUSE YOU'RE HIDING.
BESIDES, YOU'LL HAVE **ME** TO LOOK AFTER YOU.
I WILL?
OF COURSE. YOU THINK I'D LET YOU FACE ALL THOSE MEANIES ALONE? NUH-UH. YOU CAN'T EVEN HANDLE YOUR OWN CAT.
HEY! I DID PRETTY WELL AGAINST THAT WALKING PILE OF ROCKS BACK IN FANG.
ONLY BECAUSE OF MY INCREDIBLE TRAINING.
CAN'T ARGUE WITH THAT.
WHAT ABOUT YOU, LUMBAGO?
OH, I WON'T BE COMING. I'M A ROYAL ADVISER. THERE'S NO PLACE FOR ME ON THE BATTLEFIELD.

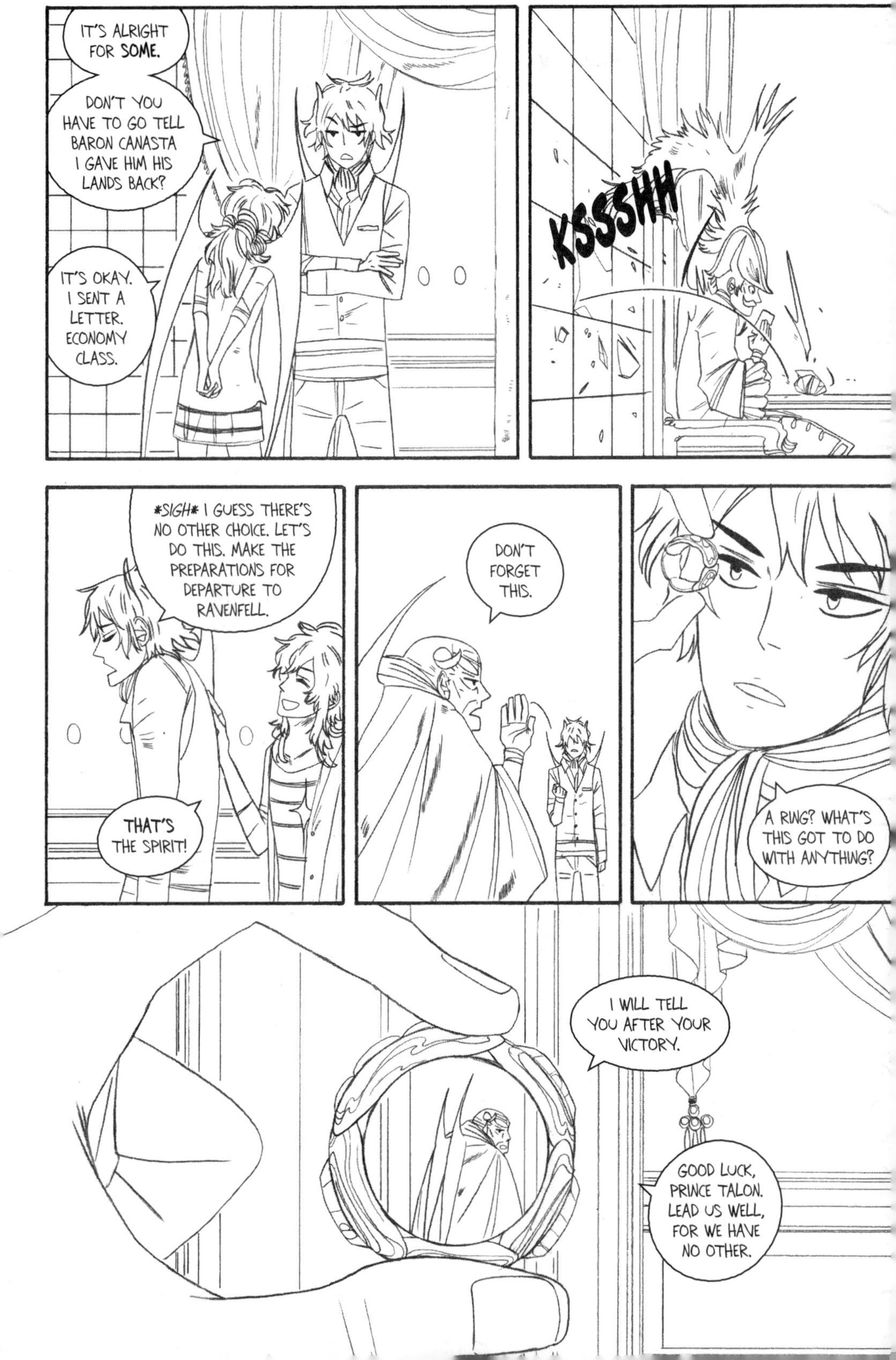
IT'S ALRIGHT FOR SOME.
DON'T YOU HAVE TO GO TELL BARON CANASTA I GAVE HIM HIS LANDS BACK?
IT'S OKAY. I SENT A LETTER. ECONOMY CLASS.
KSSSHH
SIGH I GUESS THERE'S NO OTHER CHOICE. LET'S DO THIS. MAKE THE PREPARATIONS FOR DEPARTURE TO RAVENFELL.
THAT'S THE SPIRIT!
DON'T FORGET THIS.
A RING? WHAT'S THIS GOT TO DO WITH ANYTHING?
I WILL TELL YOU AFTER YOUR VICTORY.
GOOD LUCK, PRINCE TALON. LEAD US WELL, FOR WE HAVE NO OTHER.

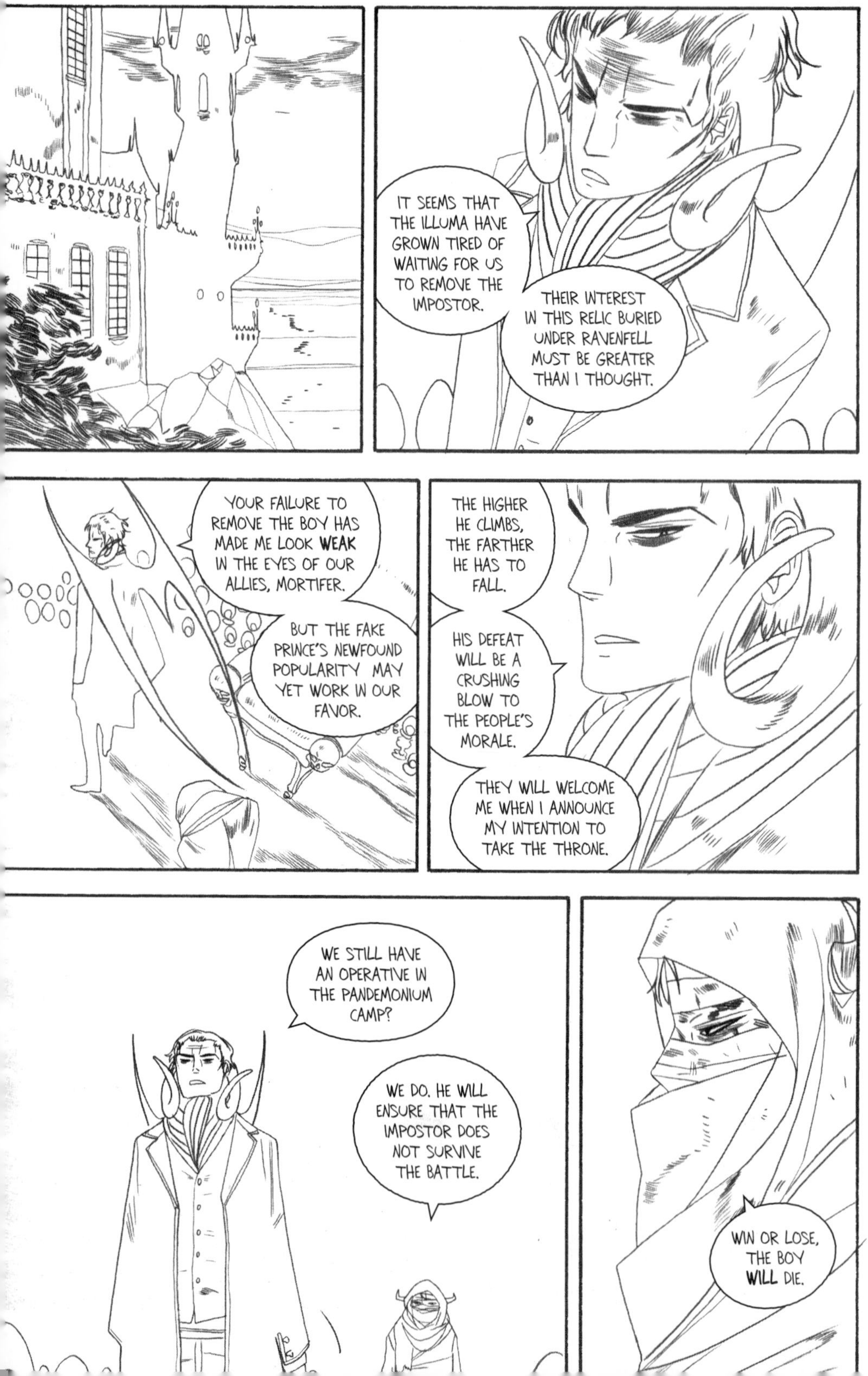
IT SEEMS THAT THE ILLUMA HAVE GROWN TIRED OF WAITING FOR US TO REMOVE THE IMPOSTOR.
THEIR INTEREST IN THIS RELIC BURIED UNDER RAVENFELL MUST BE GREATER THAN I THOUGHT.
YOUR FAILURE TO REMOVE THE BOY HAS MADE ME LOOK **WEAK** IN THE EYES OF OUR ALLIES, MORTIFER.
BUT THE FAKE PRINCE'S NEWFOUND POPULARITY MAY YET WORK IN OUR FAVOR.
THE HIGHER HE CLIMBS, THE FARTHER HE HAS TO FALL.
HIS DEFEAT WILL BE A CRUSHING BLOW TO THE PEOPLE'S MORALE.
THEY WILL WELCOME ME WHEN I ANNOUNCE MY INTENTION TO TAKE THE THRONE.
WE STILL HAVE AN OPERATIVE IN THE PANDEMONIUM CAMP?
WE DO. HE **WILL** ENSURE THAT THE IMPOSTOR DOES NOT SURVIVE THE BATTLE.
WIN OR LOSE, THE BOY **WILL** DIE.

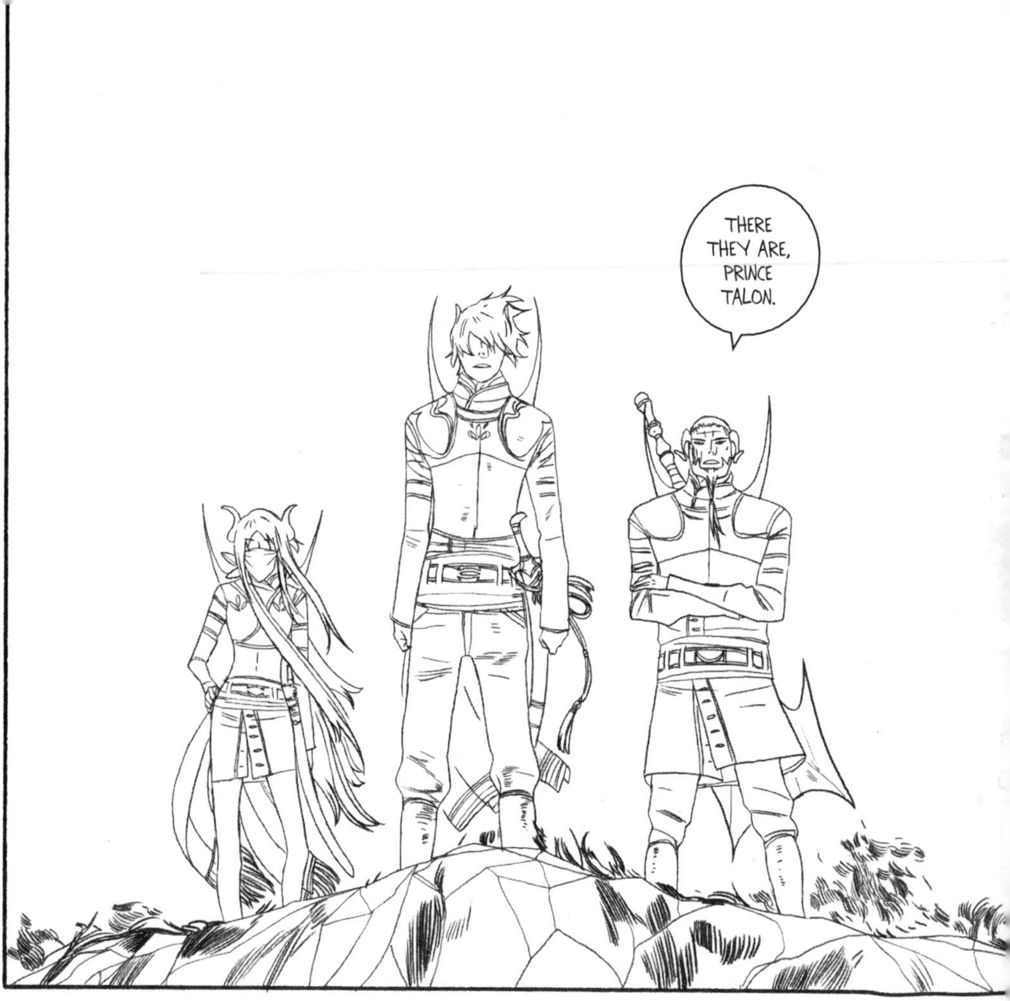
THERE THEY ARE, PRINCE TALON.

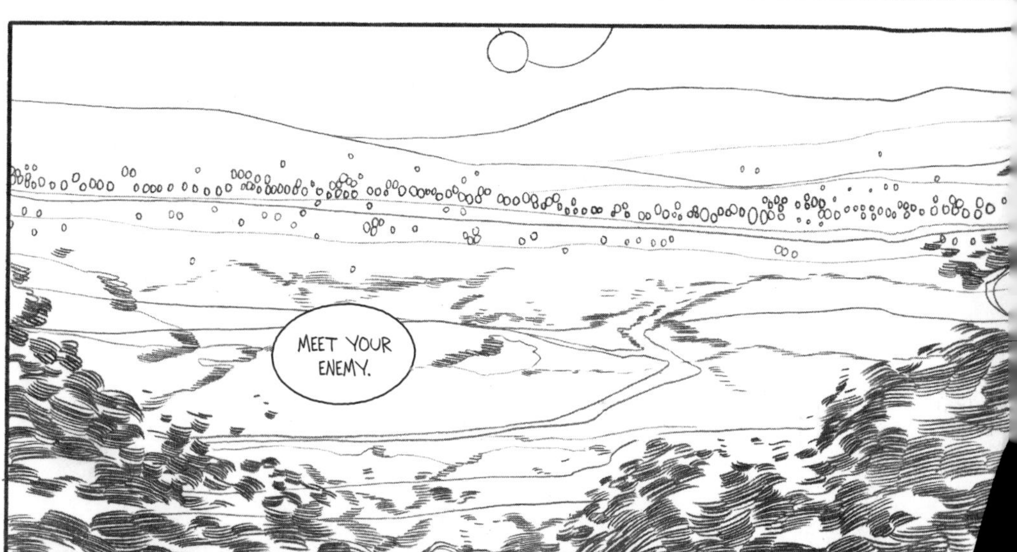
MEET YOUR ENEMY.

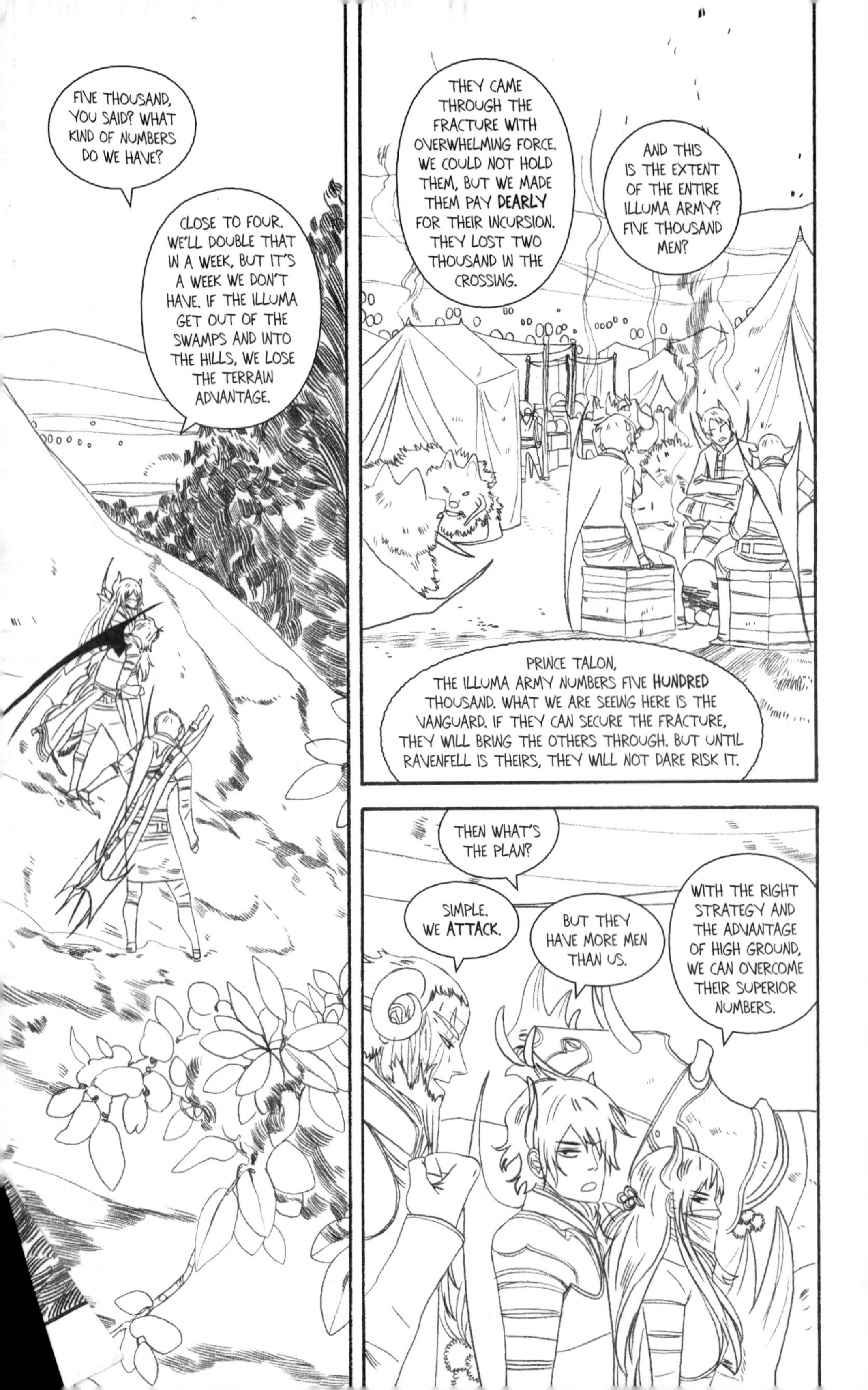
FIVE THOUSAND, YOU SAID? WHAT KIND OF NUMBERS DO WE HAVE?
CLOSE TO FOUR. WE'LL DOUBLE THAT IN A WEEK, BUT IT'S A WEEK WE DON'T HAVE. IF THE ILLUMA GET OUT OF THE SWAMPS AND INTO THE HILLS, WE LOSE THE TERRAIN ADVANTAGE.
THEY CAME THROUGH THE FRACTURE WITH OVERWHELMING FORCE. WE COULD NOT HOLD THEM, BUT WE MADE THEM PAY **DEARLY** FOR THEIR INCURSION. THEY LOST TWO THOUSAND IN THE CROSSING.
AND THIS IS THE EXTENT OF THE ENTIRE ILLUMA ARMY? FIVE THOUSAND MEN?
PRINCE TALON, THE ILLUMA ARMY NUMBERS FIVE **HUNDRED** THOUSAND. WHAT WE ARE SEEING HERE IS THE VANGUARD. IF THEY CAN SECURE THE FRACTURE, THEY WILL BRING THE OTHERS THROUGH. BUT UNTIL RAVENFELL IS THEIRS, THEY WILL NOT DARE RISK IT.
THEN WHAT'S THE PLAN?
SIMPLE. WE **ATTACK**.
BUT THEY HAVE MORE MEN THAN US.
WITH THE RIGHT STRATEGY AND THE ADVANTAGE OF HIGH GROUND, WE CAN OVERCOME THEIR SUPERIOR NUMBERS.

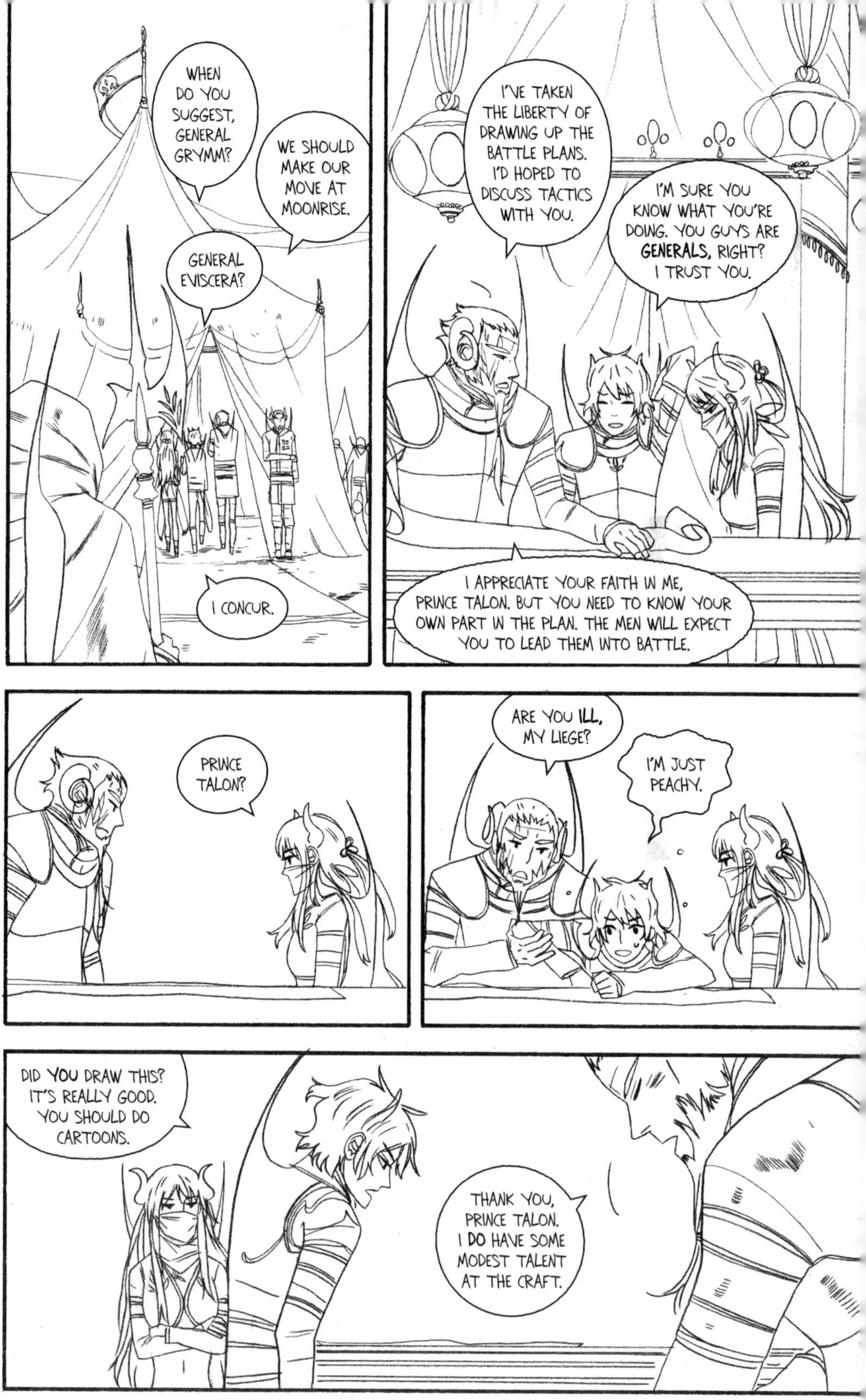
WHEN DO YOU SUGGEST, GENERAL GRYMM?
WE SHOULD MAKE OUR MOVE AT MOONRISE.
GENERAL EVISCERA?
I CONCUR.
I'VE TAKEN THE LIBERTY OF DRAWING UP THE BATTLE PLANS. I'D HOPED TO DISCUSS TACTICS WITH YOU.
I'M SURE YOU KNOW WHAT YOU'RE DOING. YOU GUYS ARE GENERALS, RIGHT? I TRUST YOU.
I APPRECIATE YOUR FAITH IN ME, PRINCE TALON. BUT YOU NEED TO KNOW YOUR OWN PART IN THE PLAN. THE MEN WILL EXPECT YOU TO LEAD THEM INTO BATTLE.
PRINCE TALON?
ARE YOU ILL, MY LIEGE?
I'M JUST PEACHY.
DID YOU DRAW THIS? IT'S REALLY GOOD. YOU SHOULD DO CARTOONS.
THANK YOU, PRINCE TALON. I DO HAVE SOME MODEST TALENT AT THE CRAFT.

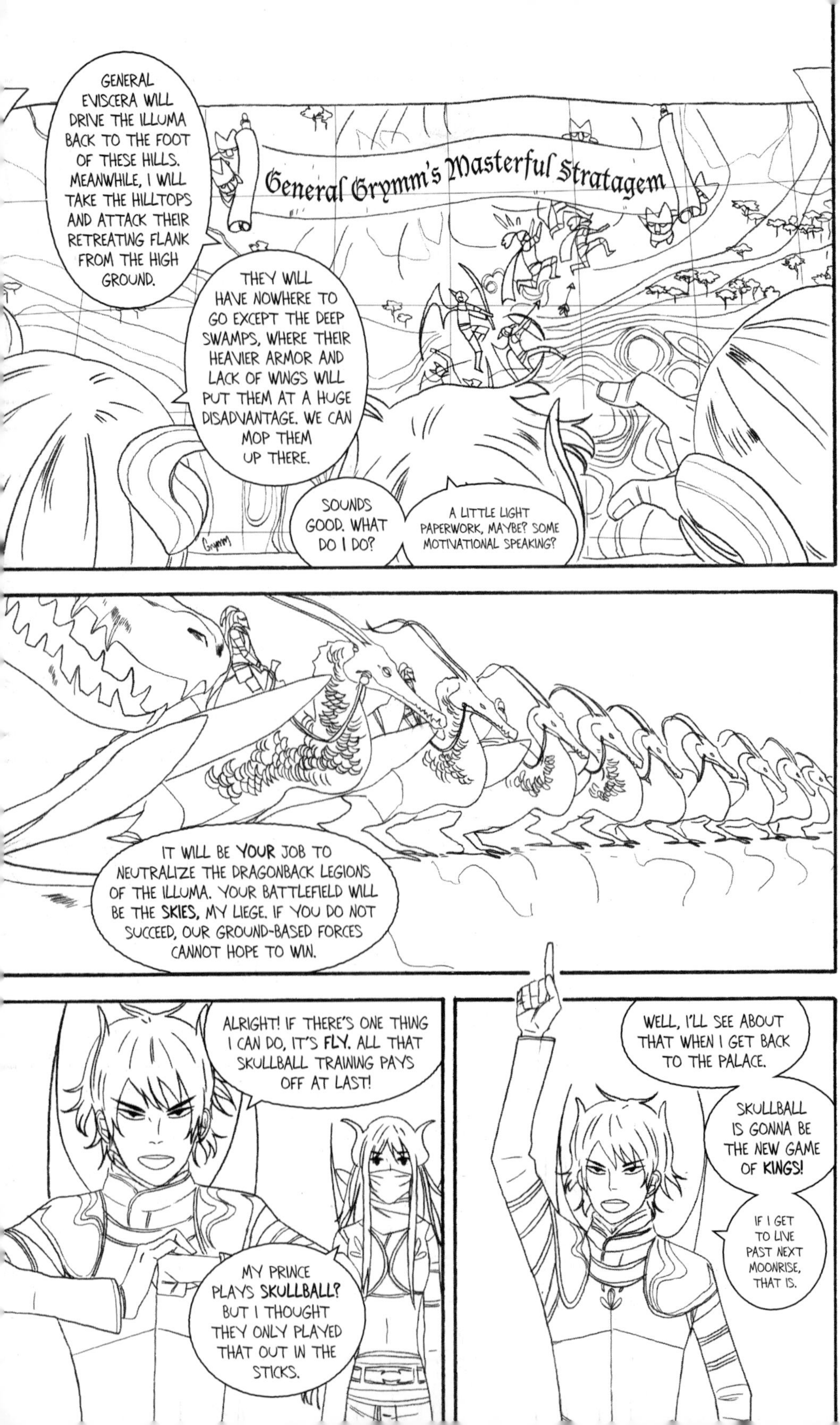
General Grymm's Masterful Stratagem
GENERAL EVISCERA WILL DRIVE THE ILLUMA BACK TO THE FOOT OF THESE HILLS. MEANWHILE, I WILL TAKE THE HILLTOPS AND ATTACK THEIR RETREATING FLANK FROM THE HIGH GROUND.
THEY WILL HAVE NOWHERE TO GO EXCEPT THE DEEP SWAMPS, WHERE THEIR HEAVIER ARMOR AND LACK OF WINGS WILL PUT THEM AT A HUGE DISADVANTAGE. WE CAN MOP THEM UP THERE.
Grymm
SOUNDS GOOD. WHAT DO I DO?
A LITTLE LIGHT PAPERWORK, MAYBE? SOME MOTIVATIONAL SPEAKING?
IT WILL BE YOUR JOB TO NEUTRALIZE THE DRAGONBACK LEGIONS OF THE ILLUMA. YOUR BATTLEFIELD WILL BE THE SKIES, MY LIEGE. IF YOU DO NOT SUCCEED, OUR GROUND-BASED FORCES CANNOT HOPE TO WIN.
ALRIGHT! IF THERE'S ONE THING I CAN DO, IT'S FLY. ALL THAT SKULLBALL TRAINING PAYS OFF AT LAST!
MY PRINCE PLAYS SKULLBALL? BUT I THOUGHT THEY ONLY PLAYED THAT OUT IN THE STICKS.
WELL, I'LL SEE ABOUT THAT WHEN I GET BACK TO THE PALACE.
SKULLBALL IS GONNA BE THE NEW GAME OF KINGS!
IF I GET TO LIVE PAST NEXT MOONRISE, THAT IS.

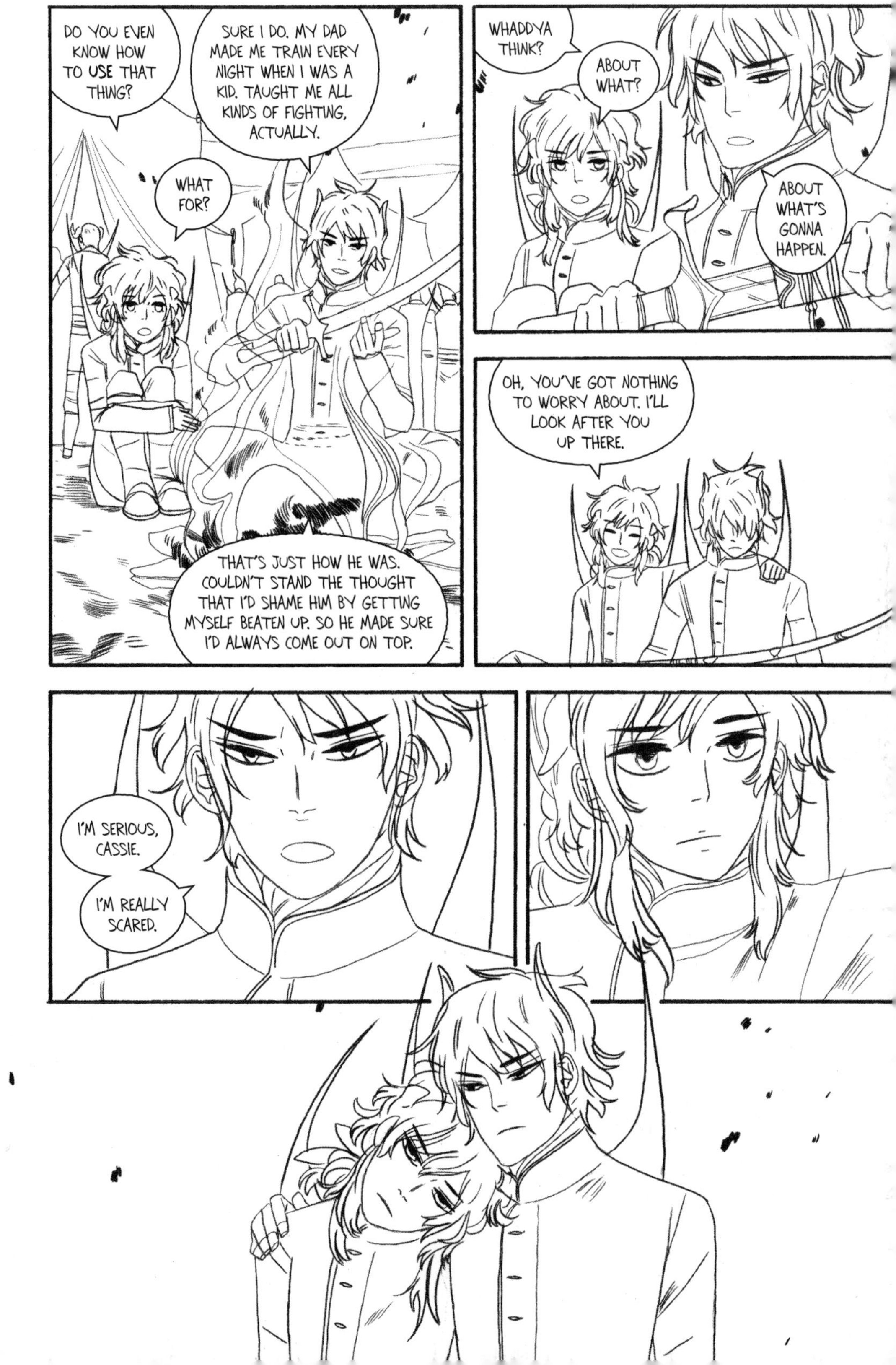
DO YOU EVEN KNOW HOW TO USE THAT THING?
SURE I DO. MY DAD MADE ME TRAIN EVERY NIGHT WHEN I WAS A KID. TAUGHT ME ALL KINDS OF FIGHTING, ACTUALLY.
WHAT FOR?
THAT'S JUST HOW HE WAS. COULDN'T STAND THE THOUGHT THAT I'D SHAME HIM BY GETTING MYSELF BEATEN UP. SO HE MADE SURE I'D ALWAYS COME OUT ON TOP.
WHADDYA THINK?
ABOUT WHAT?
ABOUT WHAT'S GONNA HAPPEN.
OH, YOU'VE GOT NOTHING TO WORRY ABOUT. I'LL LOOK AFTER YOU UP THERE.
I'M SERIOUS, CASSIE.
I'M REALLY SCARED.

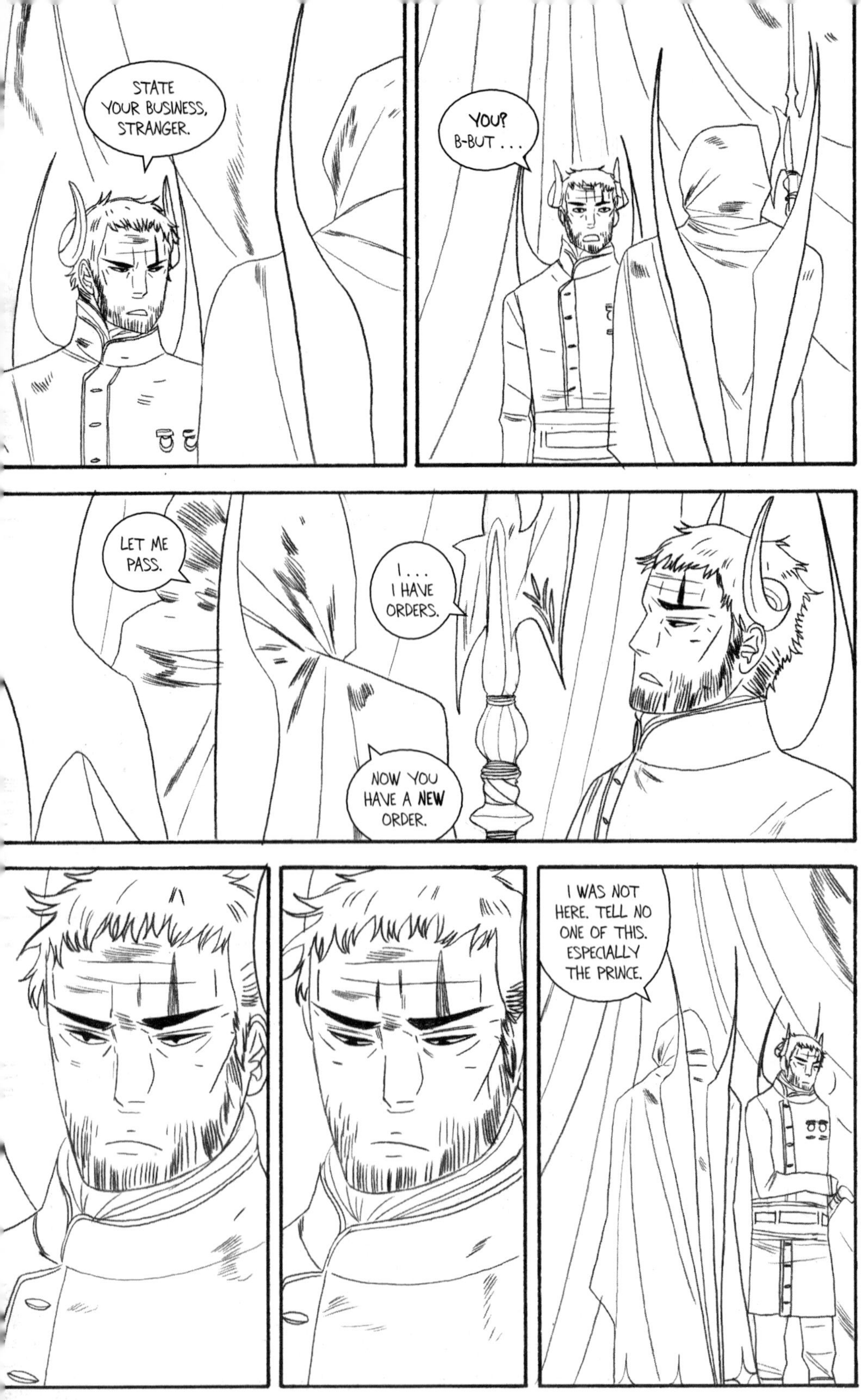
STATE YOUR BUSINESS, STRANGER.
YOU? B-BUT . . .
LET ME PASS.
I . . . I HAVE ORDERS.
NOW YOU HAVE A **NEW** ORDER.
I WAS NOT HERE. TELL NO ONE OF THIS. ESPECIALLY THE PRINCE.

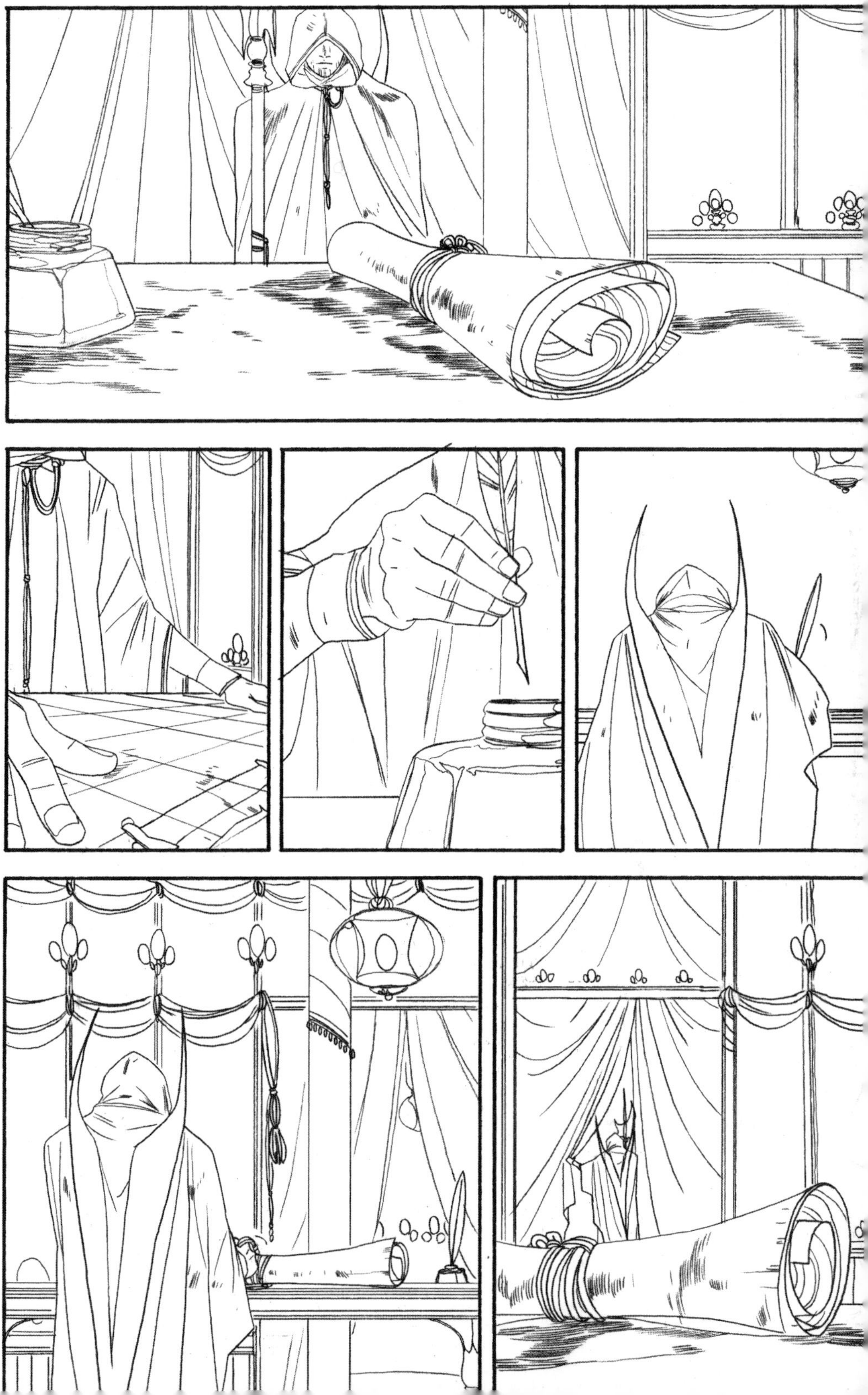

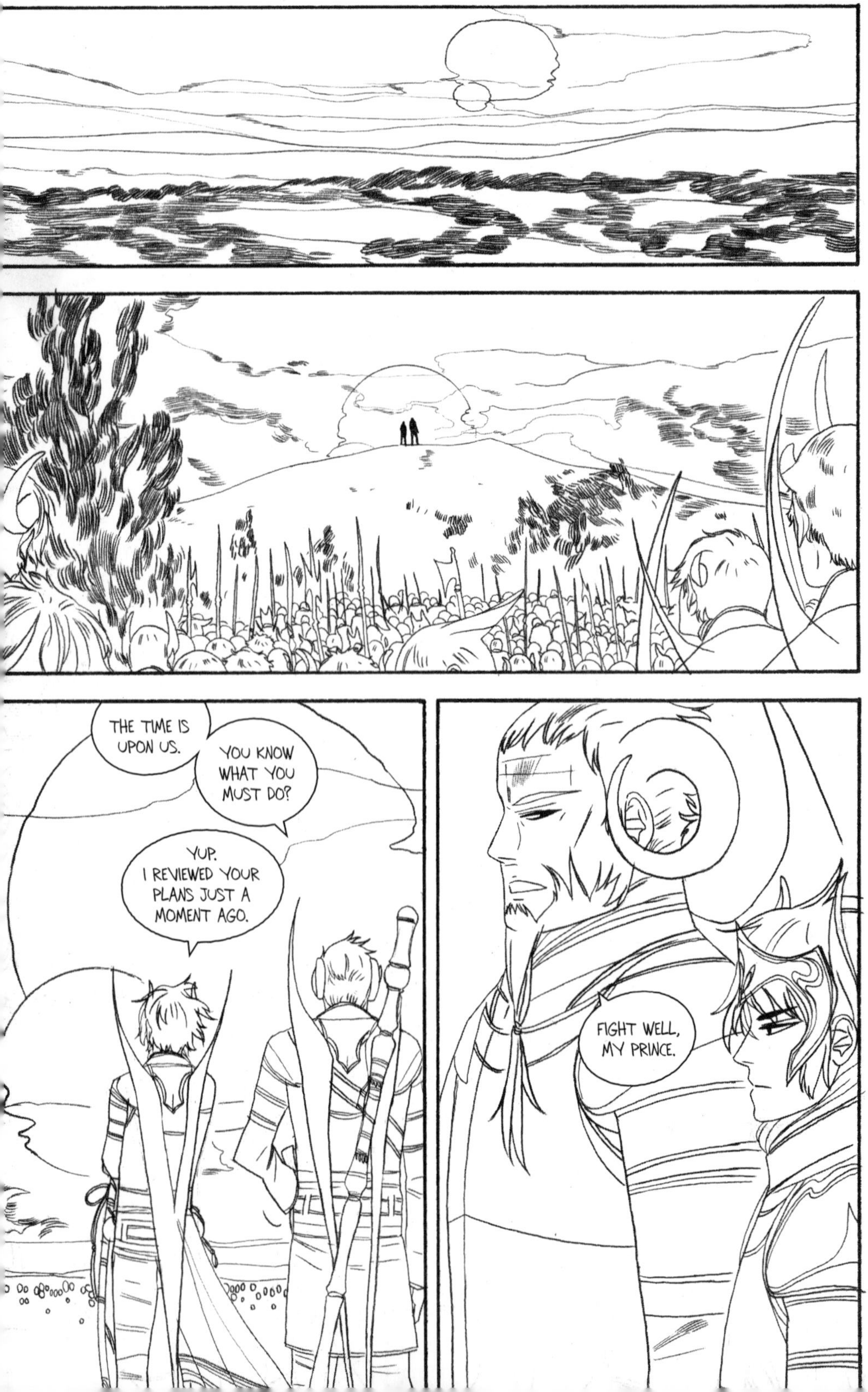
THE TIME IS UPON US.
YOU KNOW WHAT YOU MUST DO?
YUP. I REVIEWED YOUR PLANS JUST A MOMENT AGO.
FIGHT WELL, MY PRINCE.

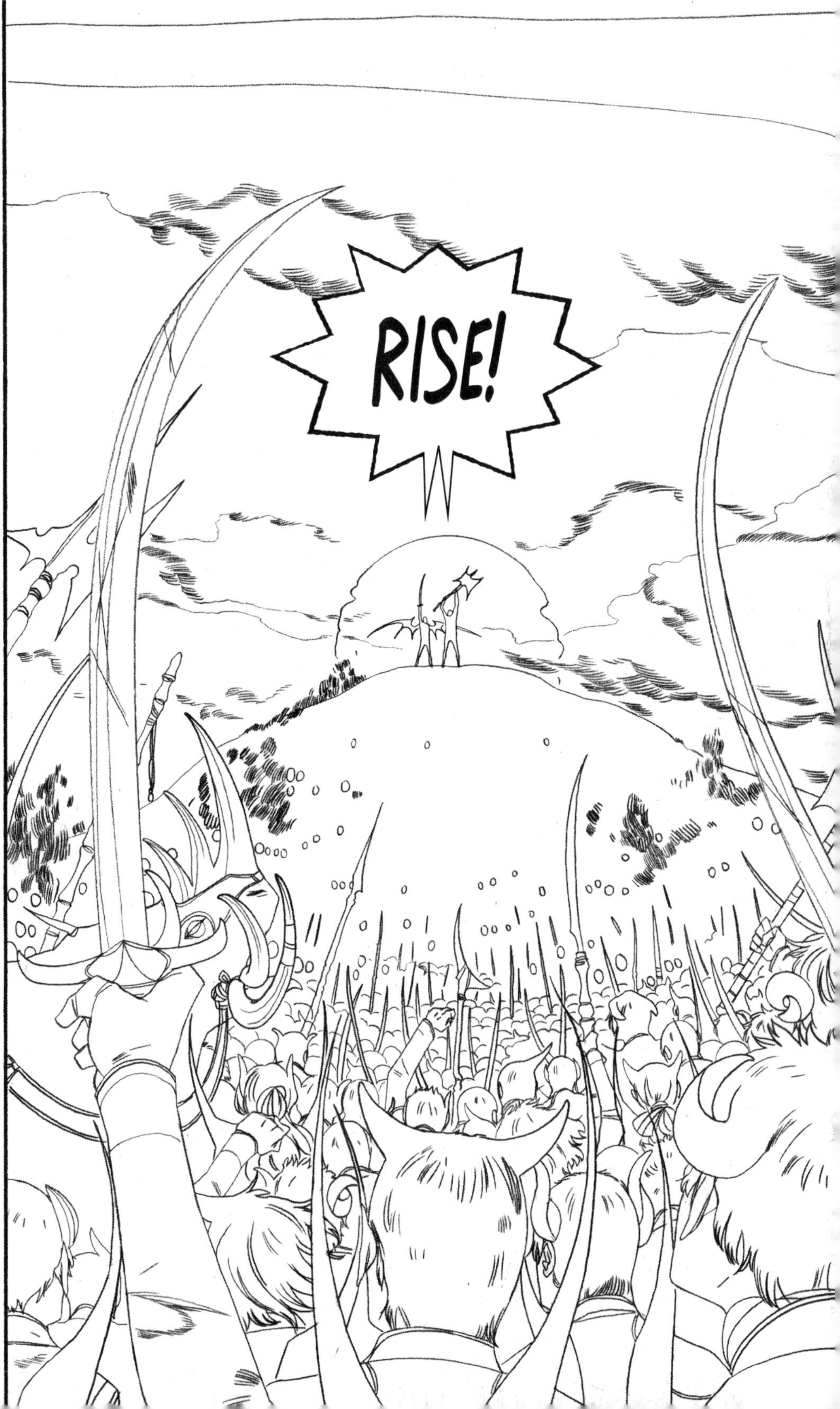
RISE!

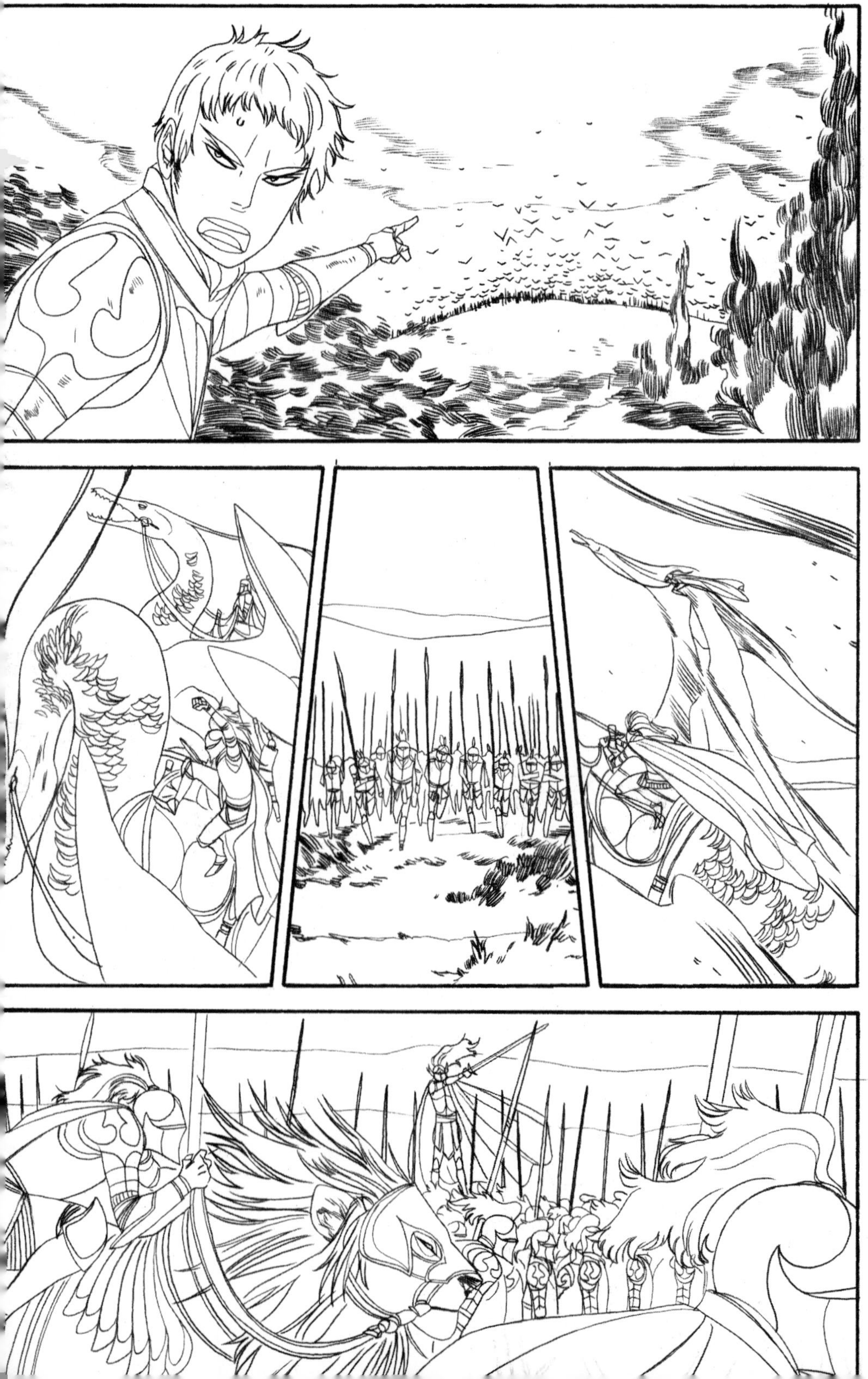

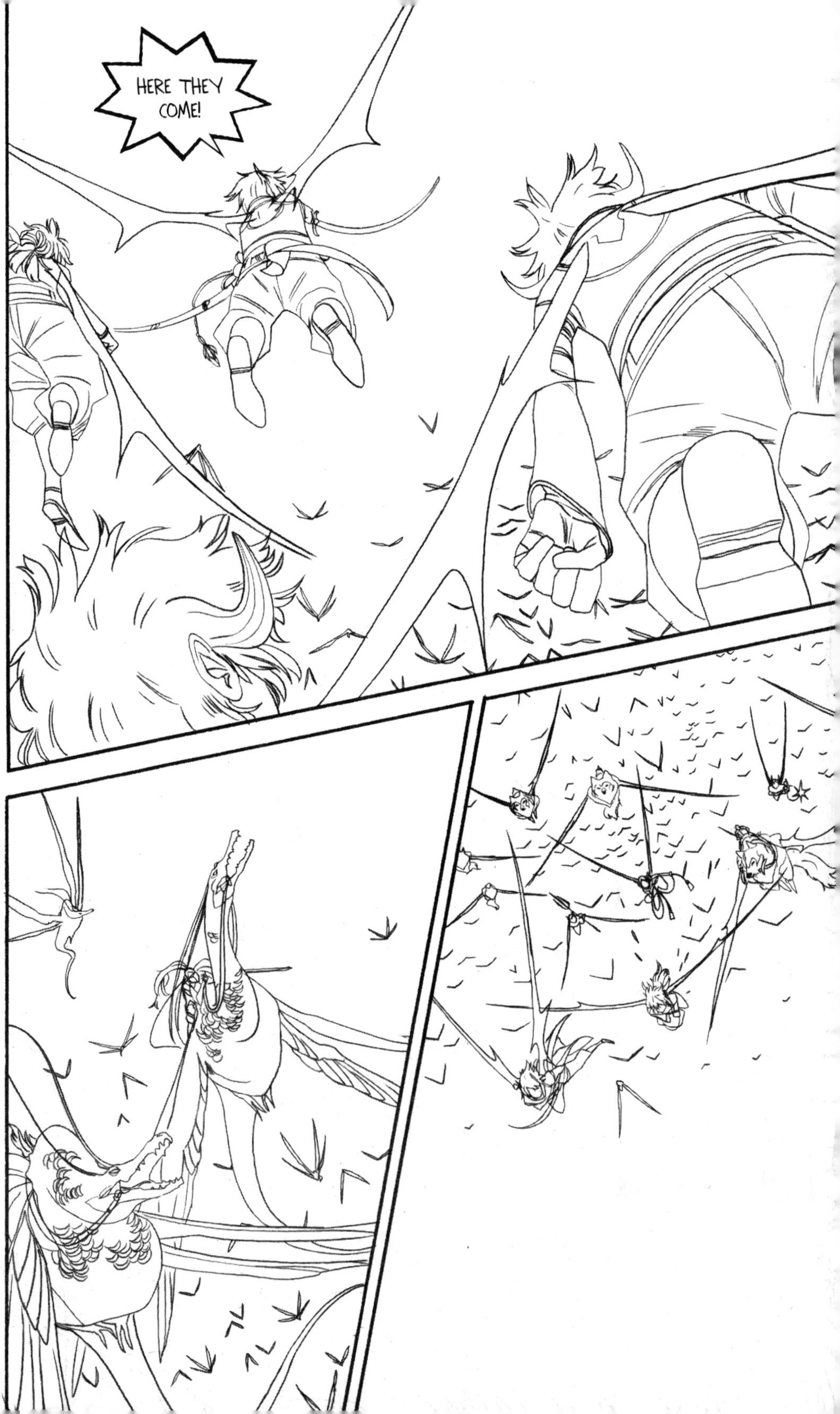
HERE THEY COME!

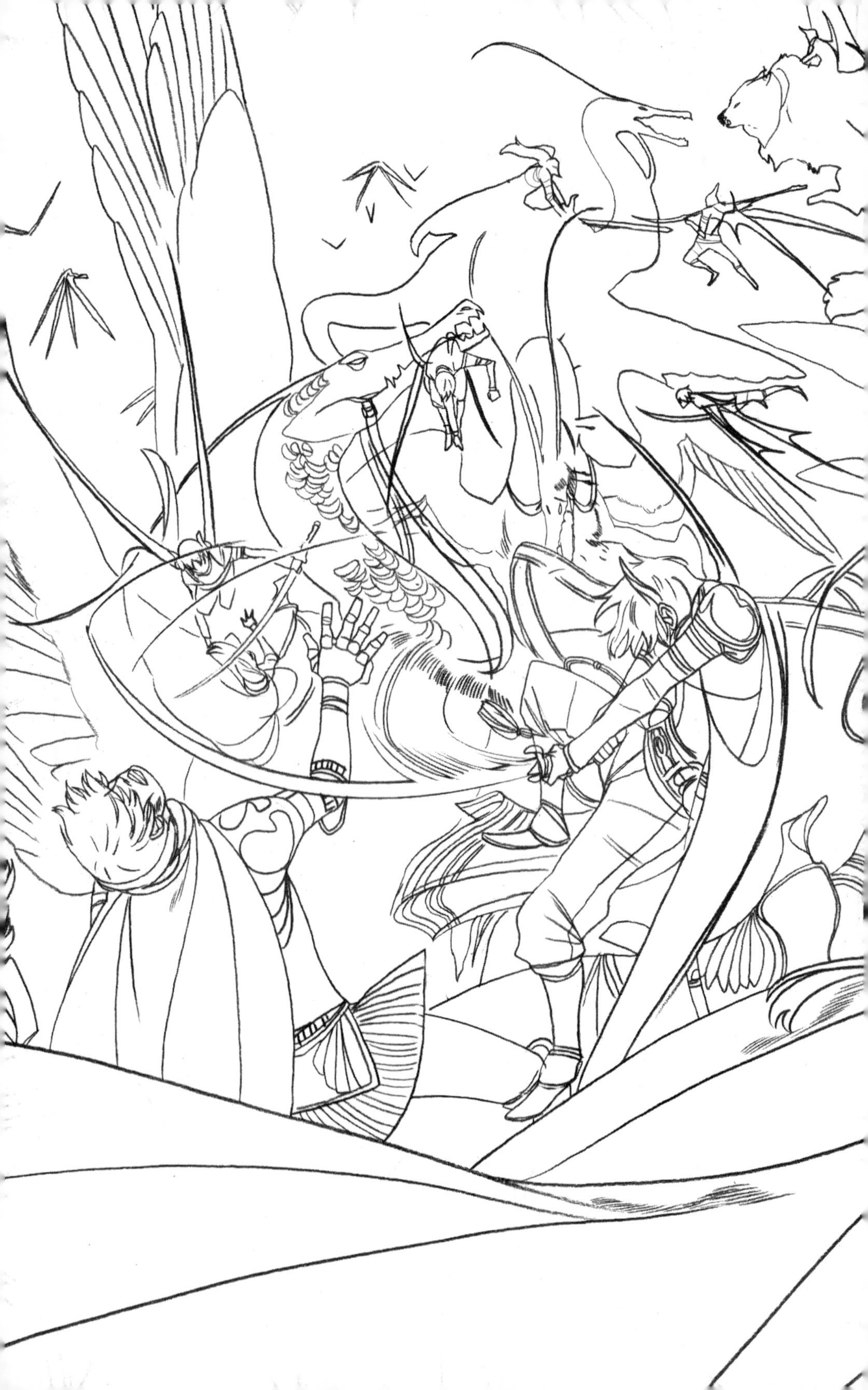

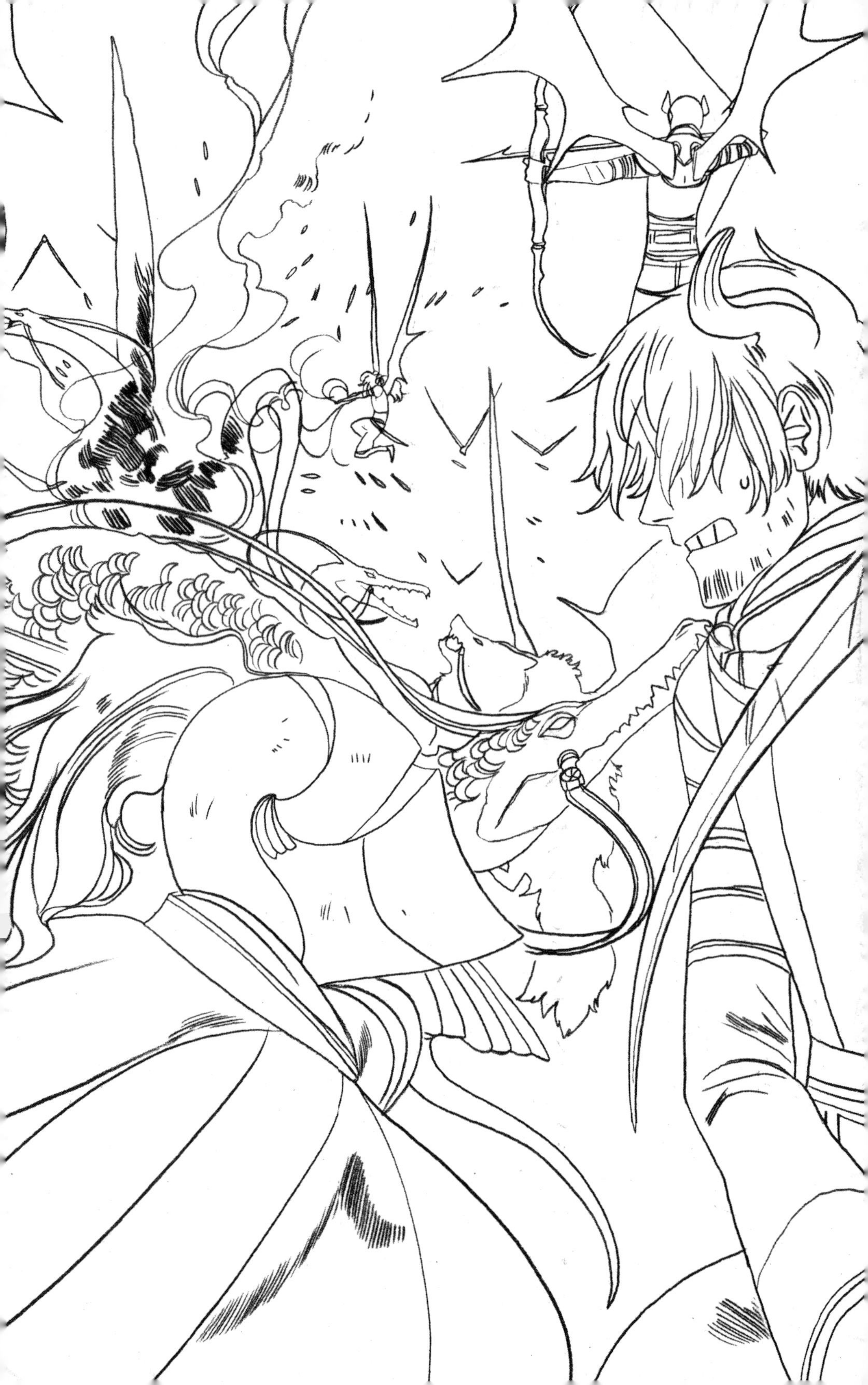

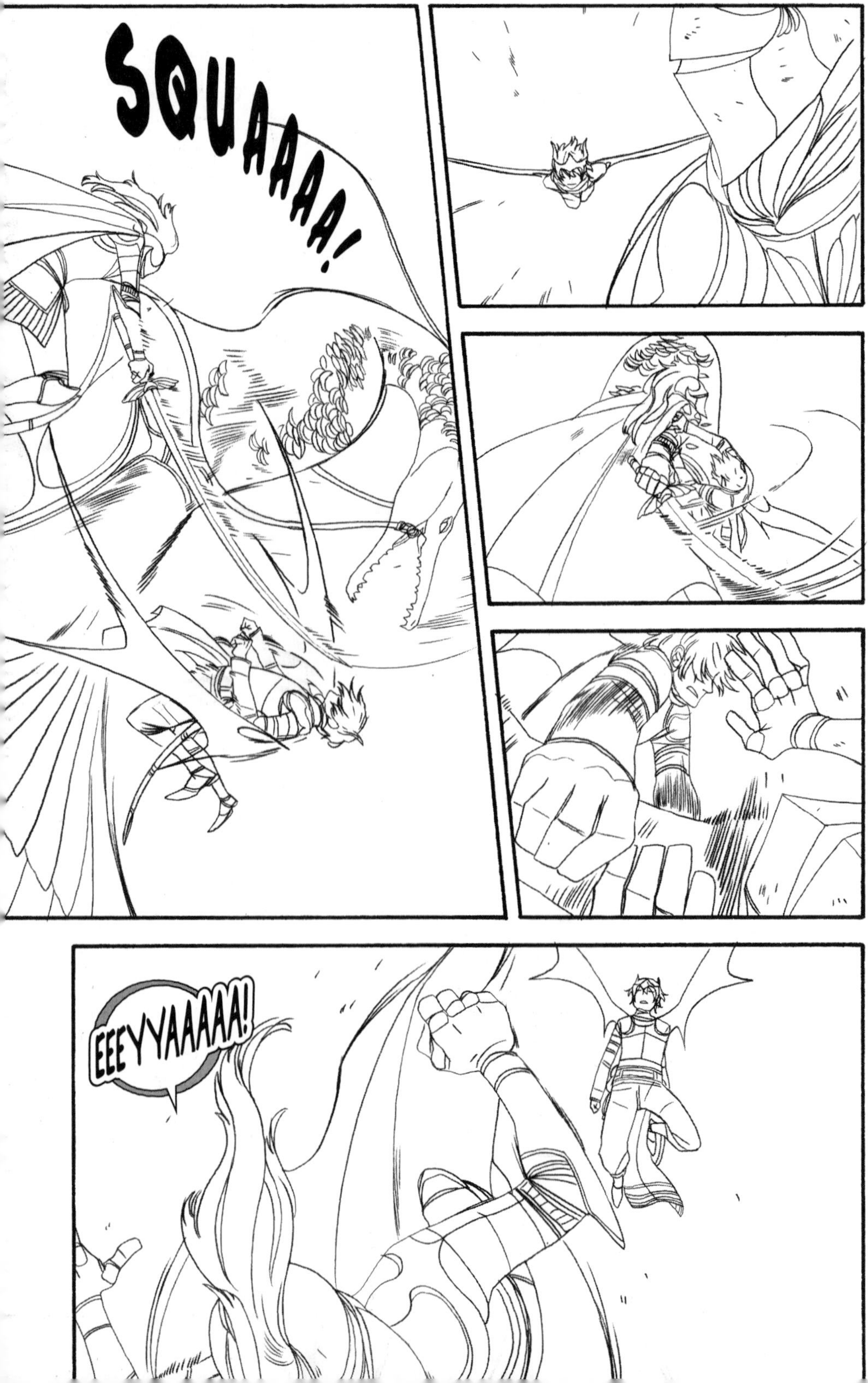
SQUAAAAA!
EEEYYAAAAA!

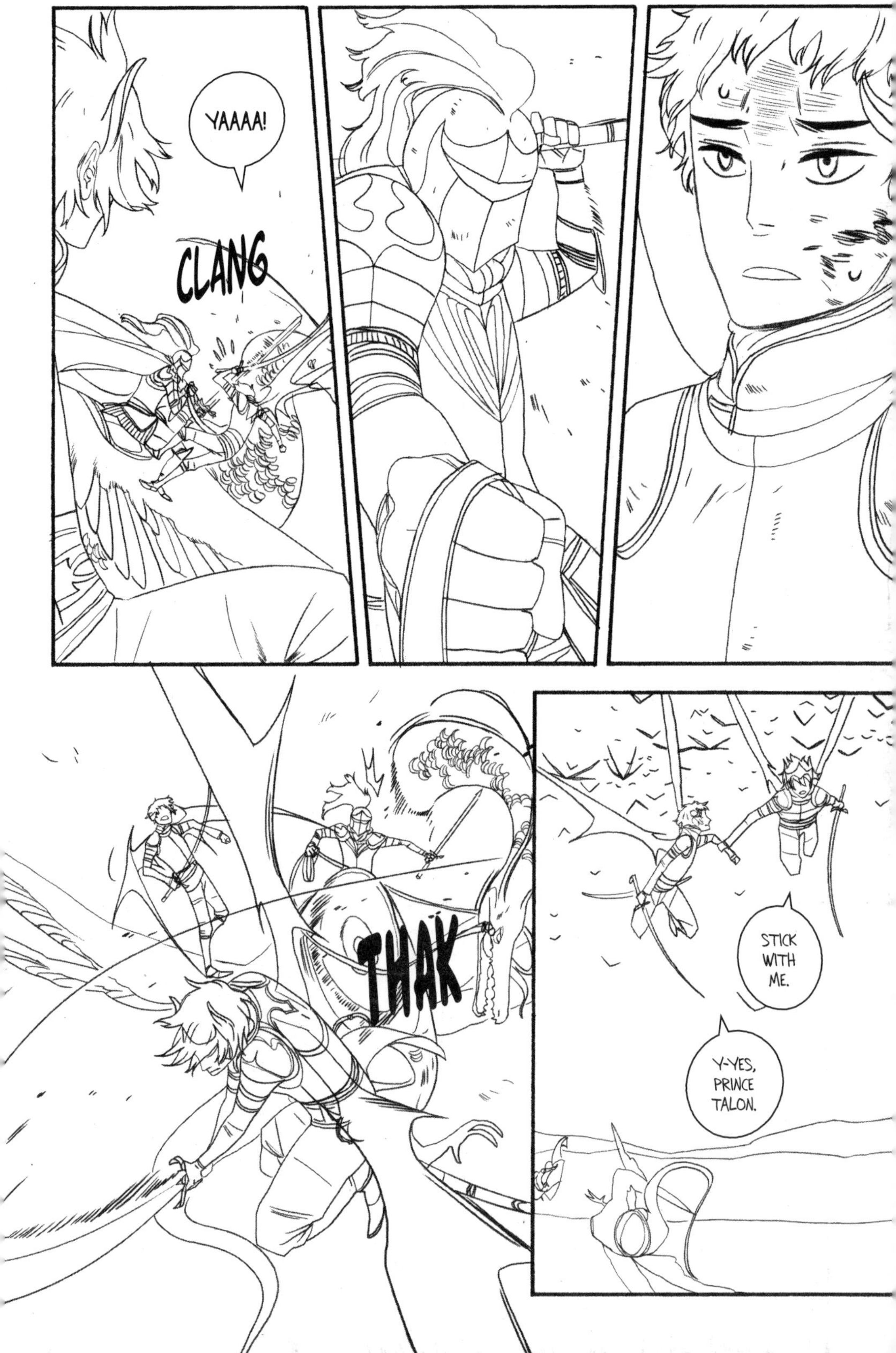
YAAAA!
CLANG
THAK
STICK WITH ME.
Y-YES, PRINCE TALON.

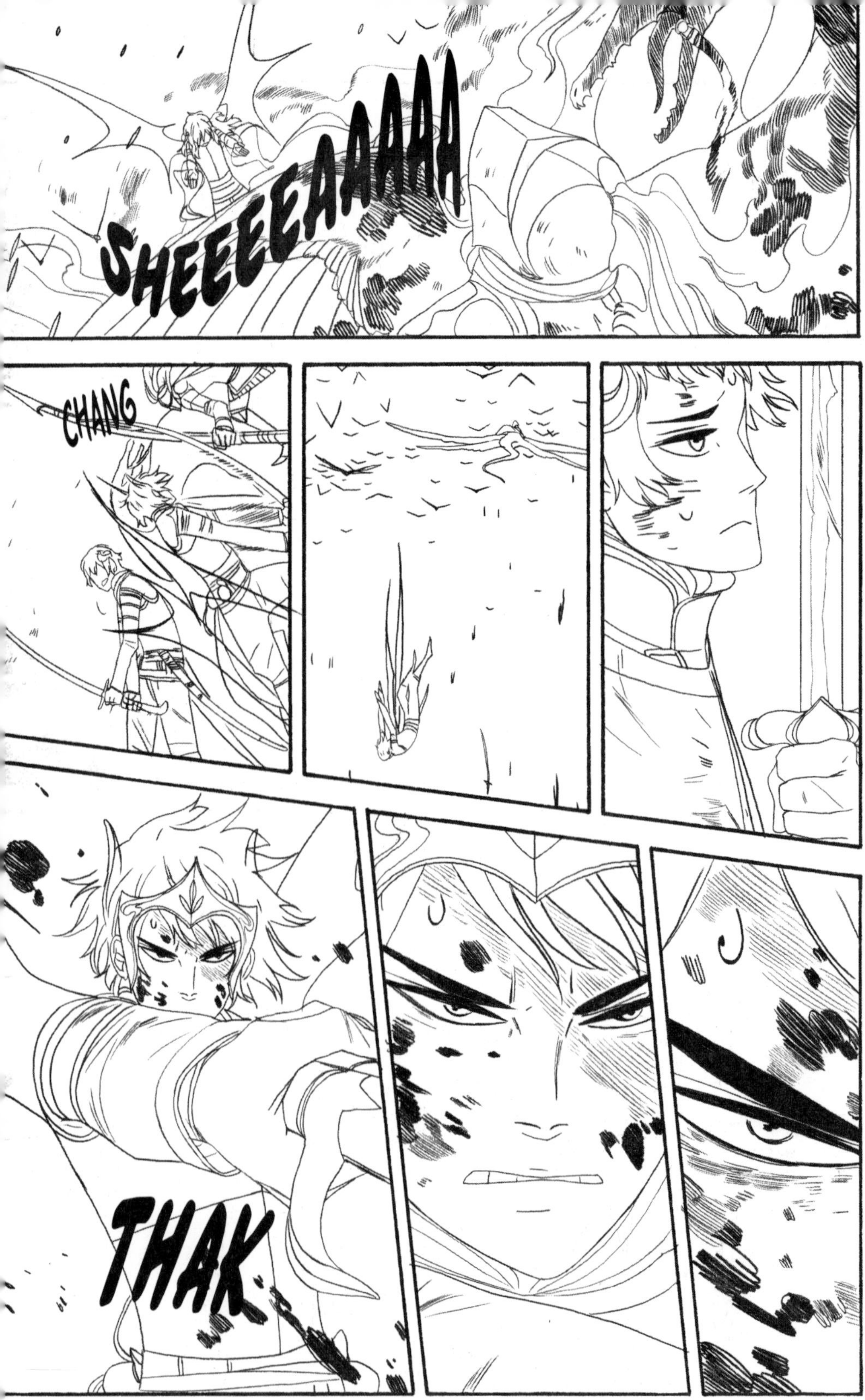
SHEEEEAAAAA
CHANG
THAK

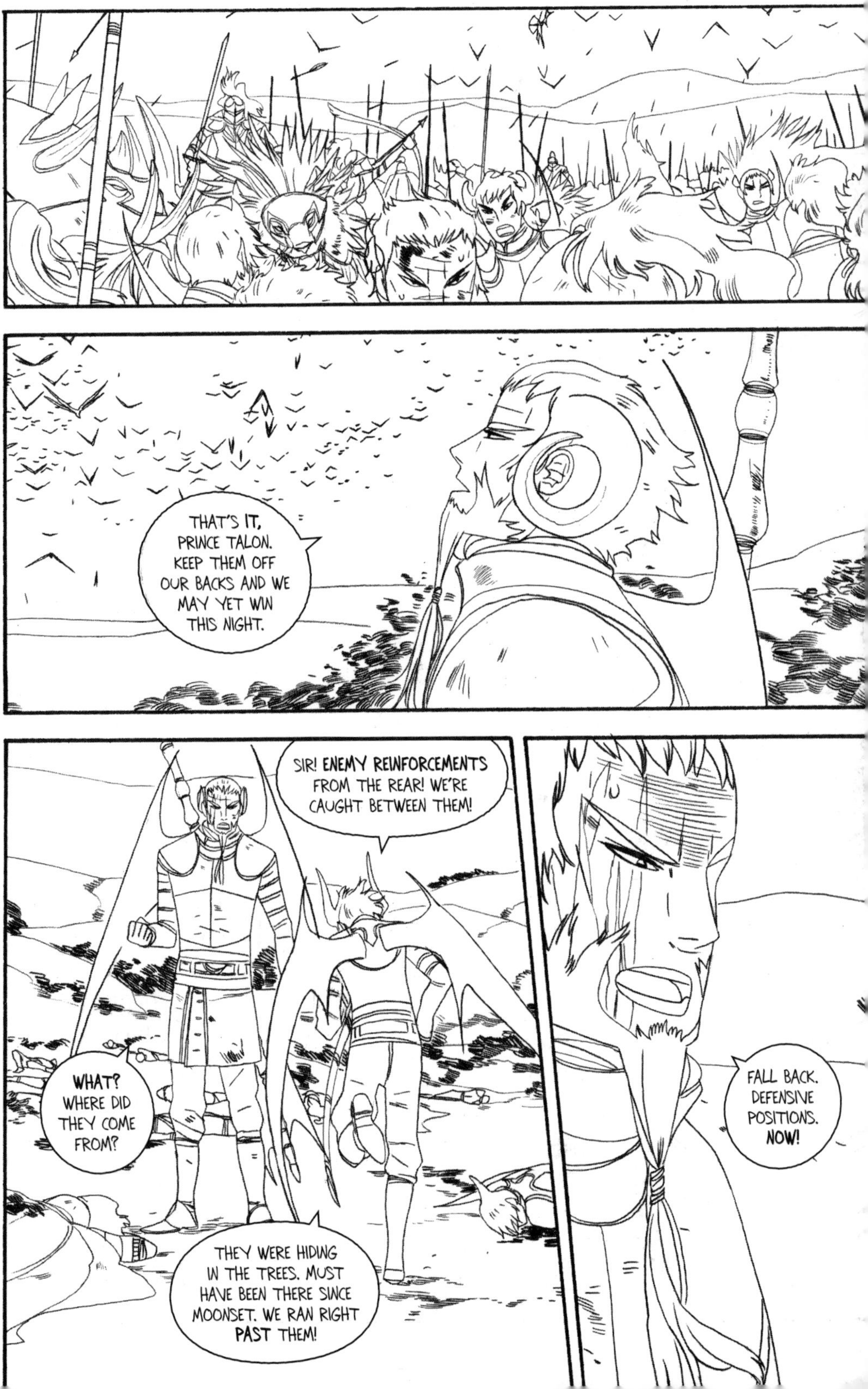
THAT'S IT, PRINCE TALON. KEEP THEM OFF OUR BACKS AND WE MAY YET WIN THIS NIGHT.
SIR! ENEMY REINFORCEMENTS FROM THE REAR! WE'RE CAUGHT BETWEEN THEM!
WHAT? WHERE DID THEY COME FROM?
THEY WERE HIDING IN THE TREES. MUST HAVE BEEN THERE SINCE MOONSET. WE RAN RIGHT PAST THEM!
FALL BACK. DEFENSIVE POSITIONS. NOW!

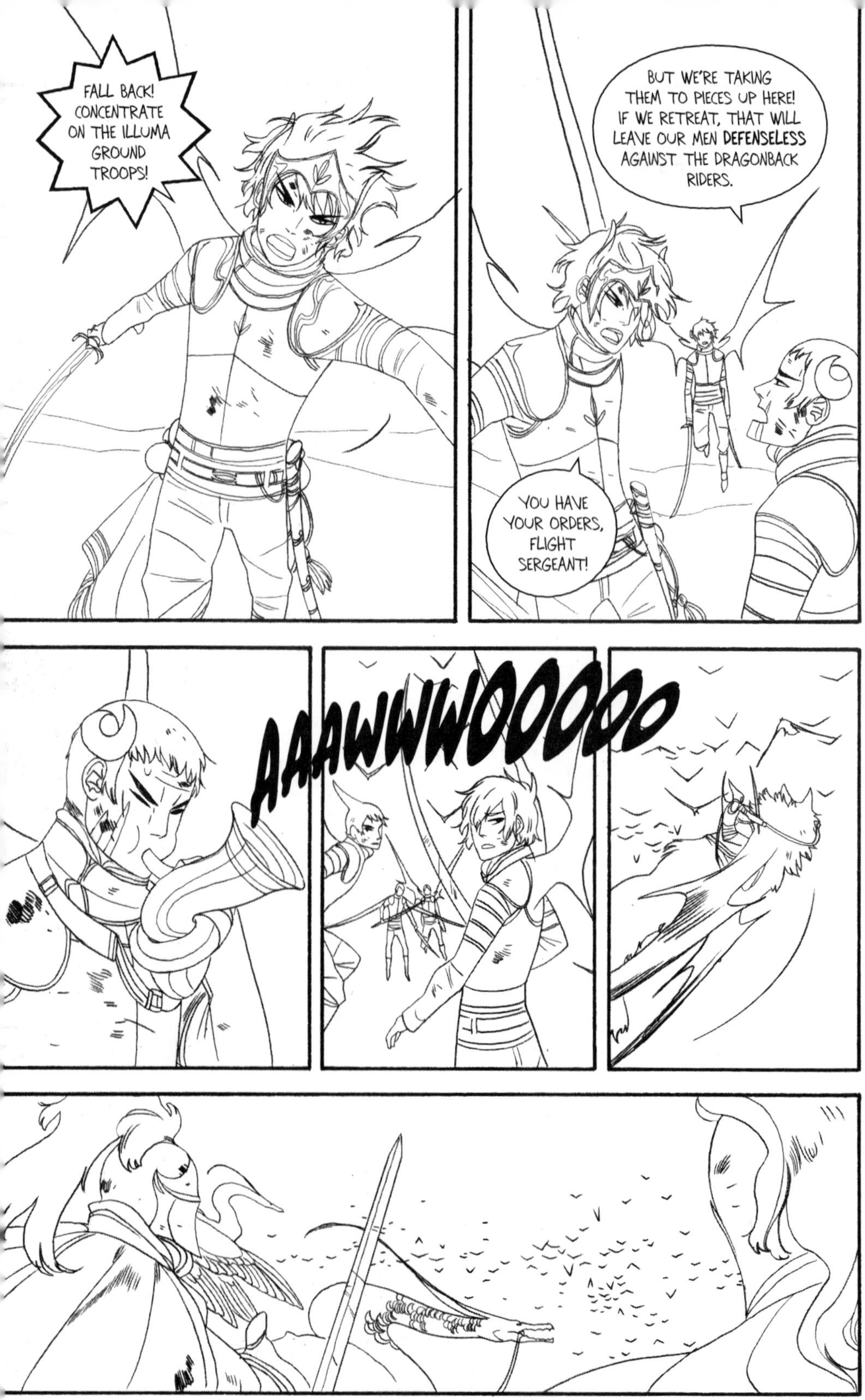
FALL BACK! CONCENTRATE ON THE ILLUMA GROUND TROOPS!
BUT WE'RE TAKING THEM TO PIECES UP HERE! IF WE RETREAT, THAT WILL LEAVE OUR MEN DEFENSELESS AGAINST THE DRAGONBACK RIDERS.
YOU HAVE YOUR ORDERS, FLIGHT SERGEANT!
AAAWWWOOOOO

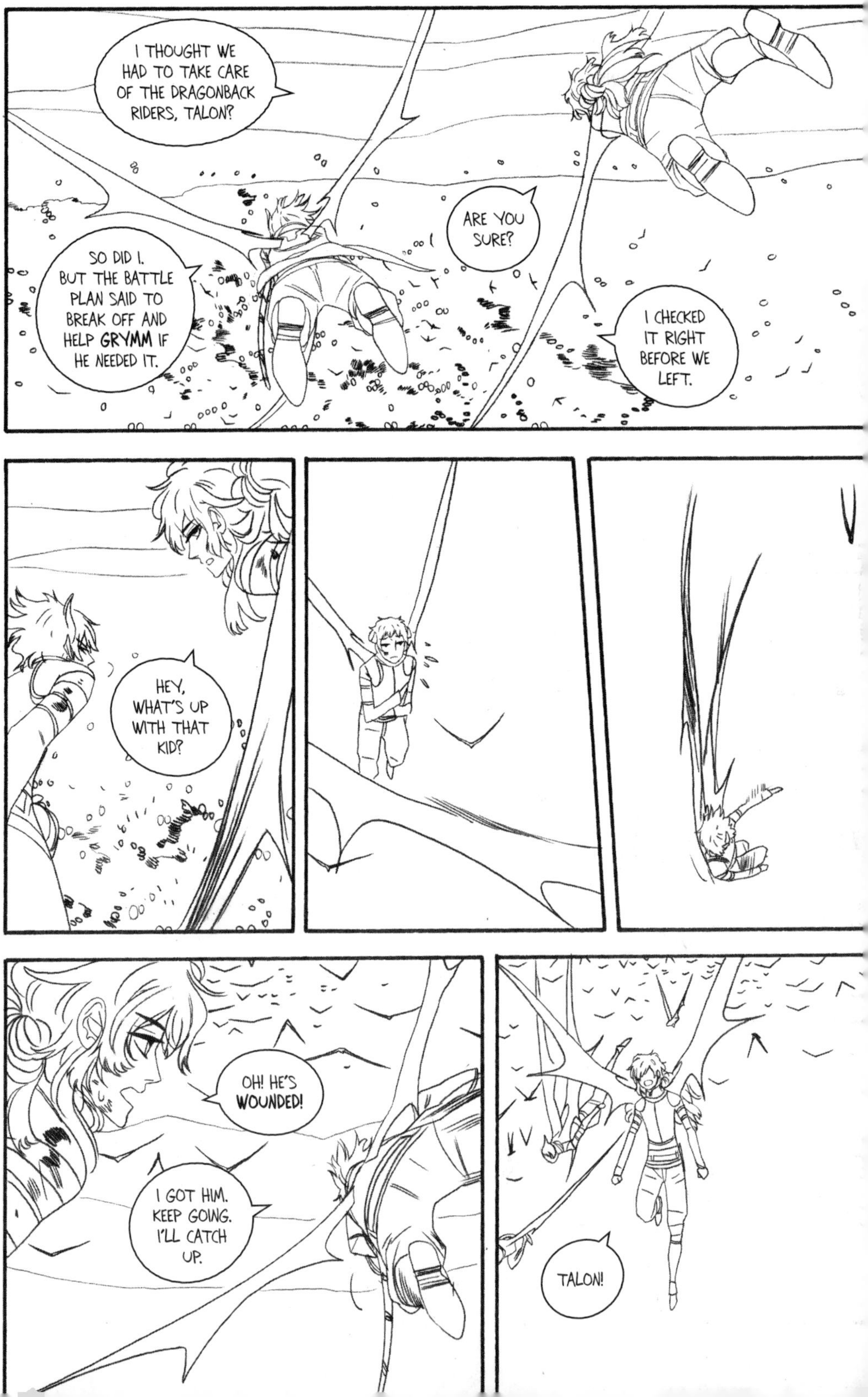
I THOUGHT WE HAD TO TAKE CARE OF THE DRAGONBACK RIDERS, TALON?
SO DID I. BUT THE BATTLE PLAN SAID TO BREAK OFF AND HELP **GRYMM** IF HE NEEDED IT.
ARE YOU SURE?
I CHECKED IT RIGHT BEFORE WE LEFT.
HEY, WHAT'S UP WITH THAT KID?
OH! HE'S **WOUNDED!**
I GOT HIM. KEEP GOING. I'LL CATCH UP.
TALON!

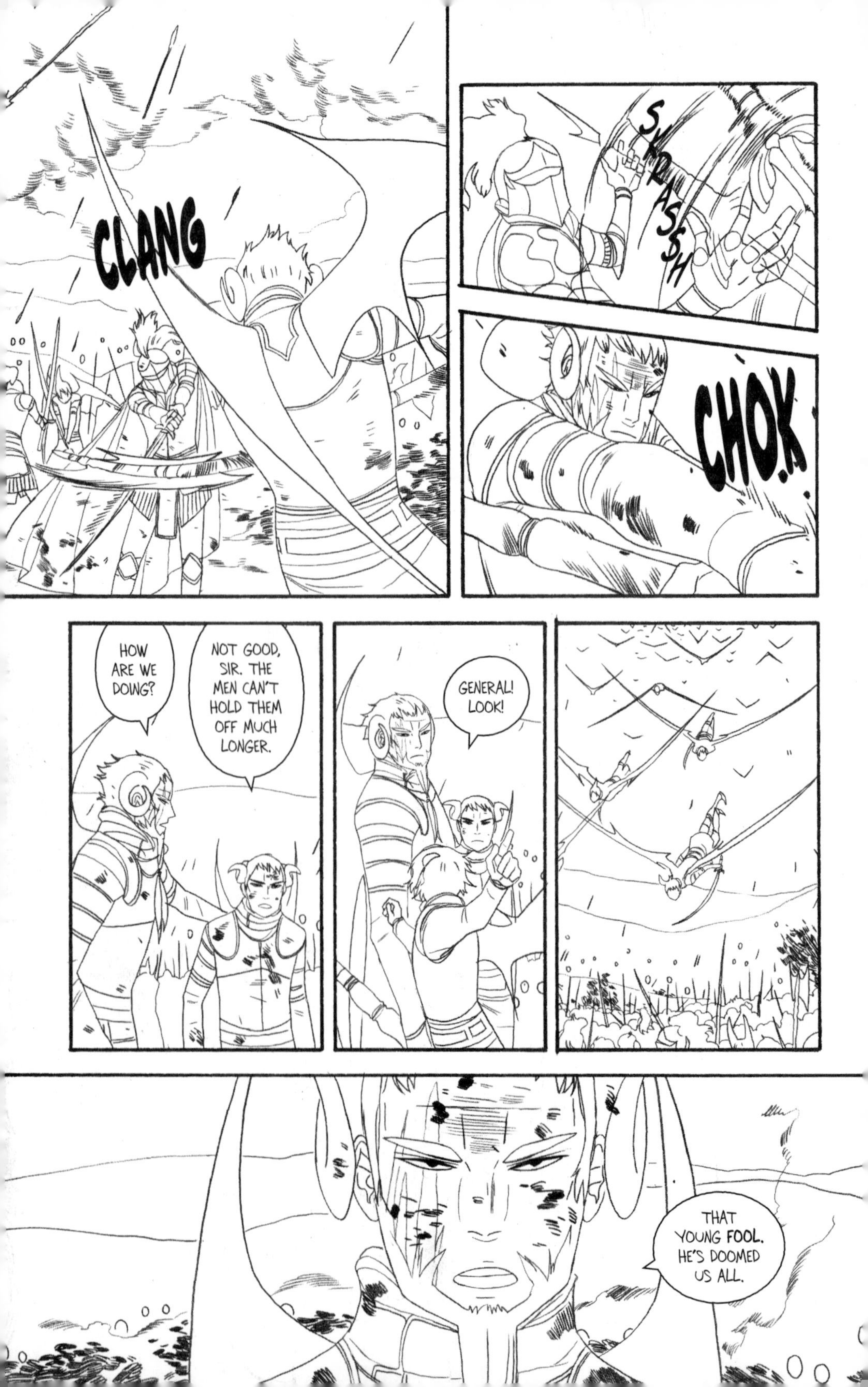
CLANG
SKRASSH
CHOK
HOW ARE WE DOING?
NOT GOOD, SIR. THE MEN CAN'T HOLD THEM OFF MUCH LONGER.
GENERAL! LOOK!
THAT YOUNG **FOOL.** HE'S DOOMED US ALL.

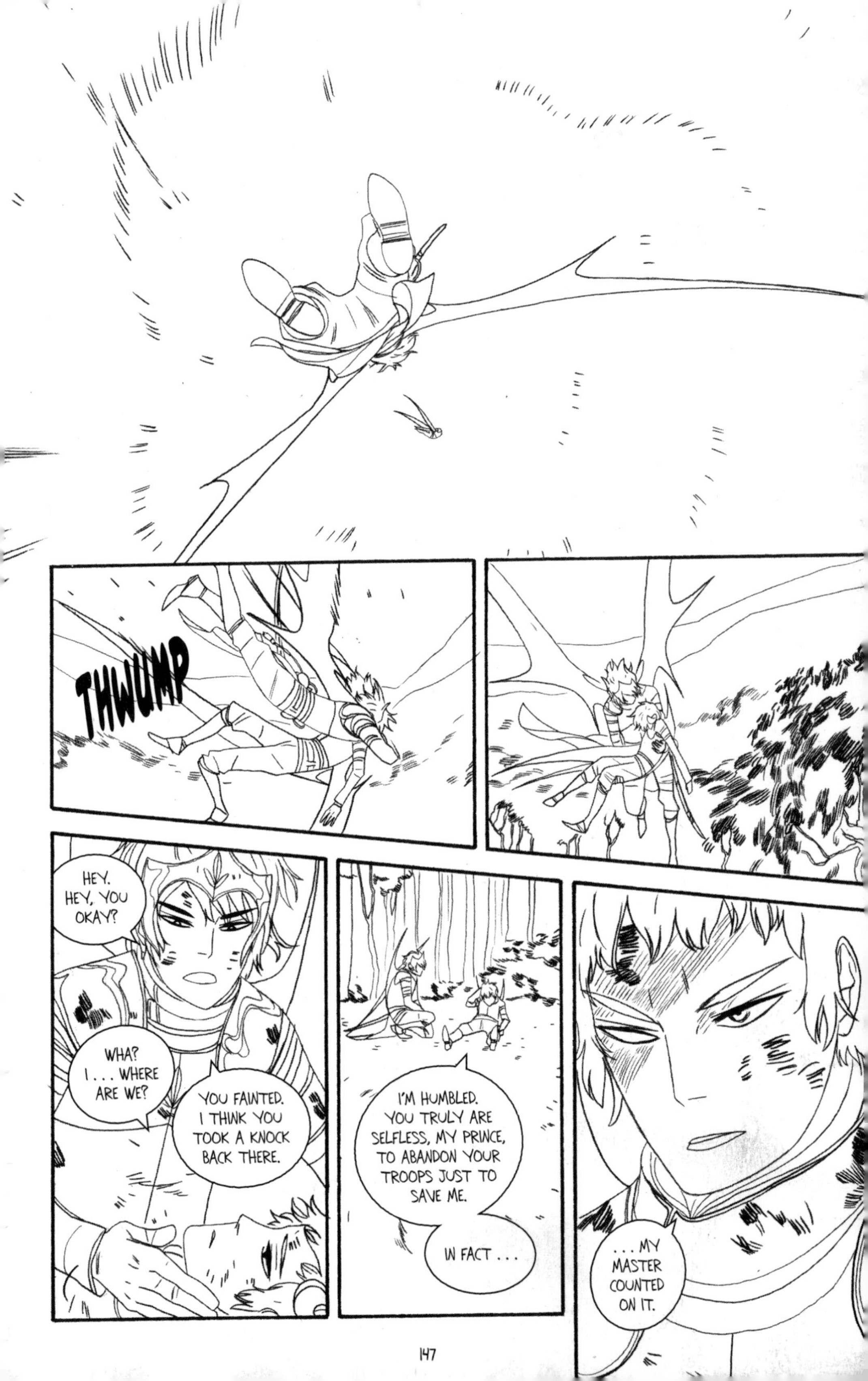
THWUMP
HEY. HEY, YOU OKAY?
WHA? I . . . WHERE ARE WE?
YOU FAINTED. I THINK YOU TOOK A KNOCK BACK THERE.
I'M HUMBLED. YOU TRULY ARE SELFLESS, MY PRINCE, TO ABANDON YOUR TROOPS JUST TO SAVE ME.
IN FACT . . .
. . . MY MASTER COUNTED ON IT.

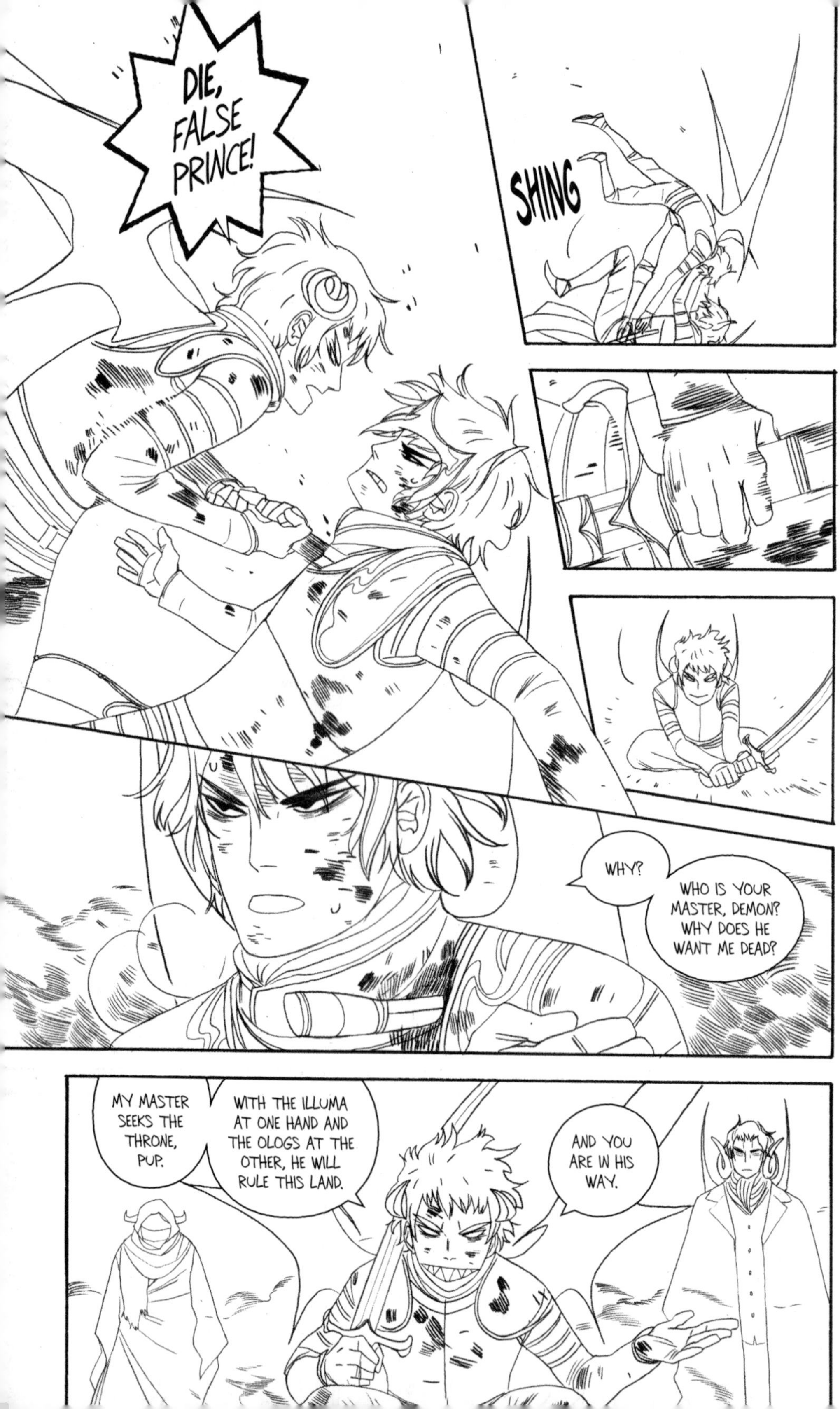
DIE, FALSE PRINCE!
SHING
WHY?
WHO IS YOUR MASTER, DEMON? WHY DOES HE WANT ME DEAD?
MY MASTER SEEKS THE THRONE, PUP.
WITH THE ILLUMA AT ONE HAND AND THE OLOGS AT THE OTHER, HE WILL RULE THIS LAND.
AND YOU ARE IN HIS WAY.

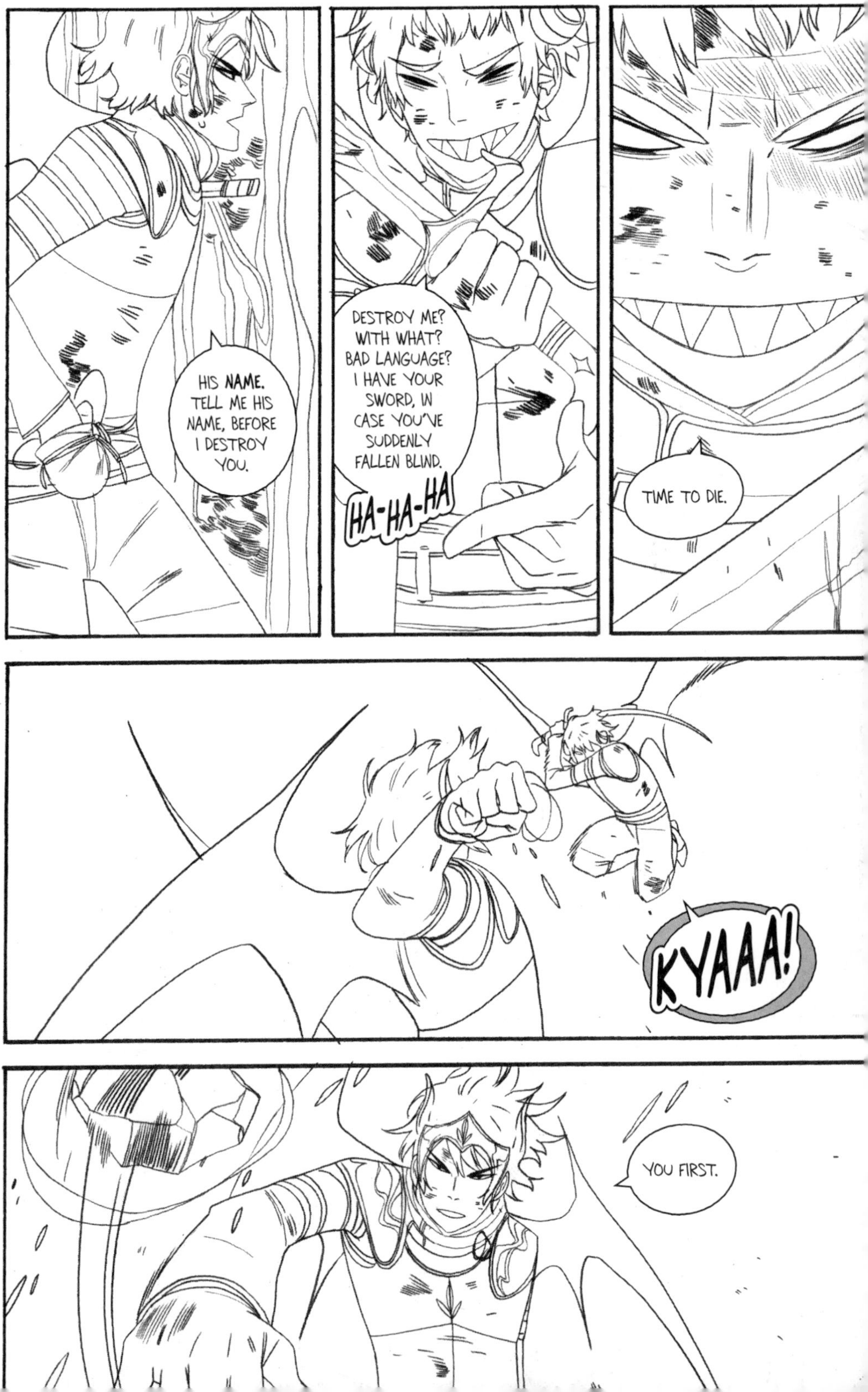
HIS **NAME.** TELL ME HIS NAME, BEFORE I DESTROY YOU.
DESTROY ME? WITH WHAT? BAD LANGUAGE? I HAVE YOUR SWORD, IN CASE YOU'VE SUDDENLY FALLEN BLIND.
HA-HA-HA
TIME TO DIE.
KYAAA!
YOU FIRST.

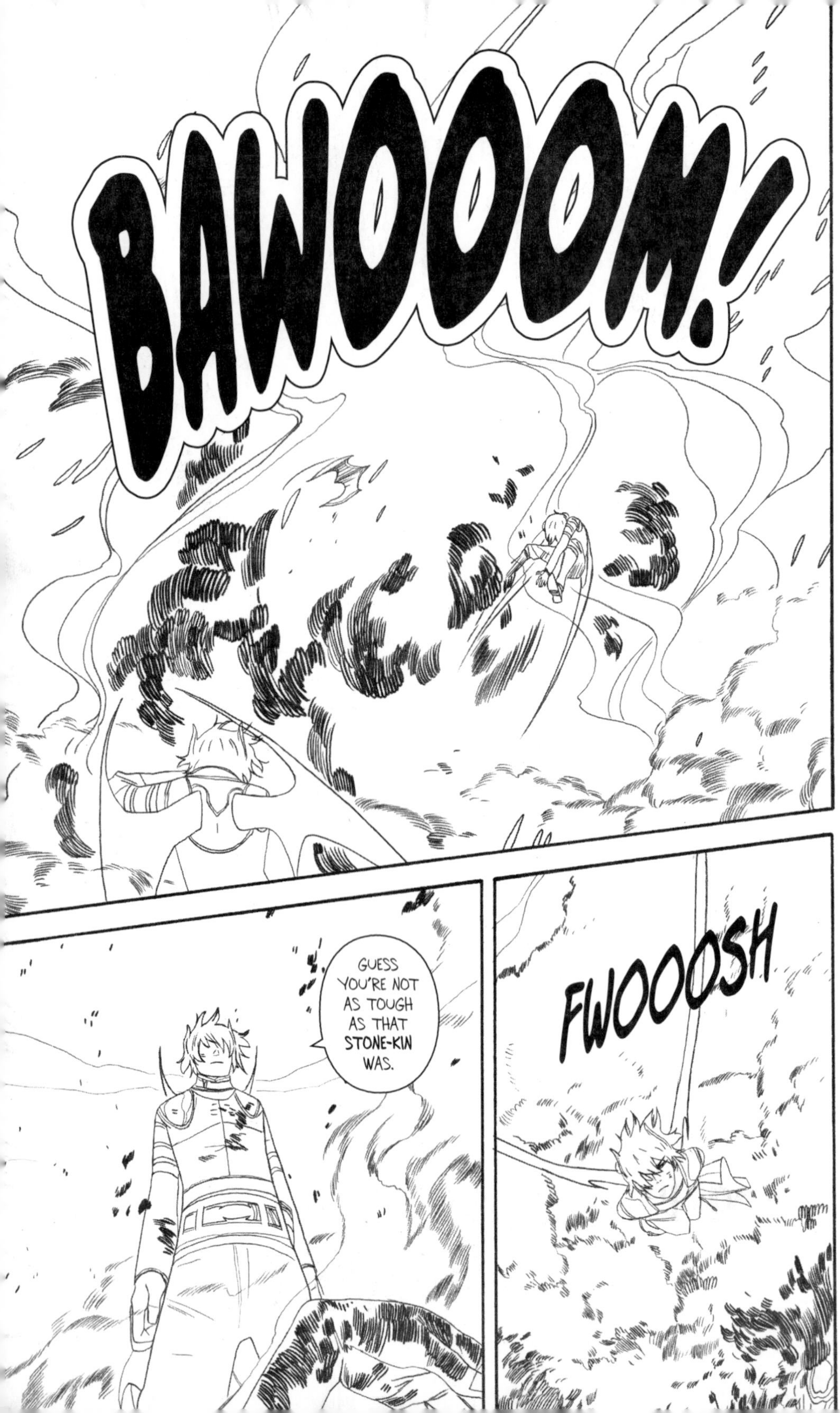
BAWOOOM!
GUESS YOU'RE NOT AS TOUGH AS THAT STONE-KIN WAS.
FWOOOSH

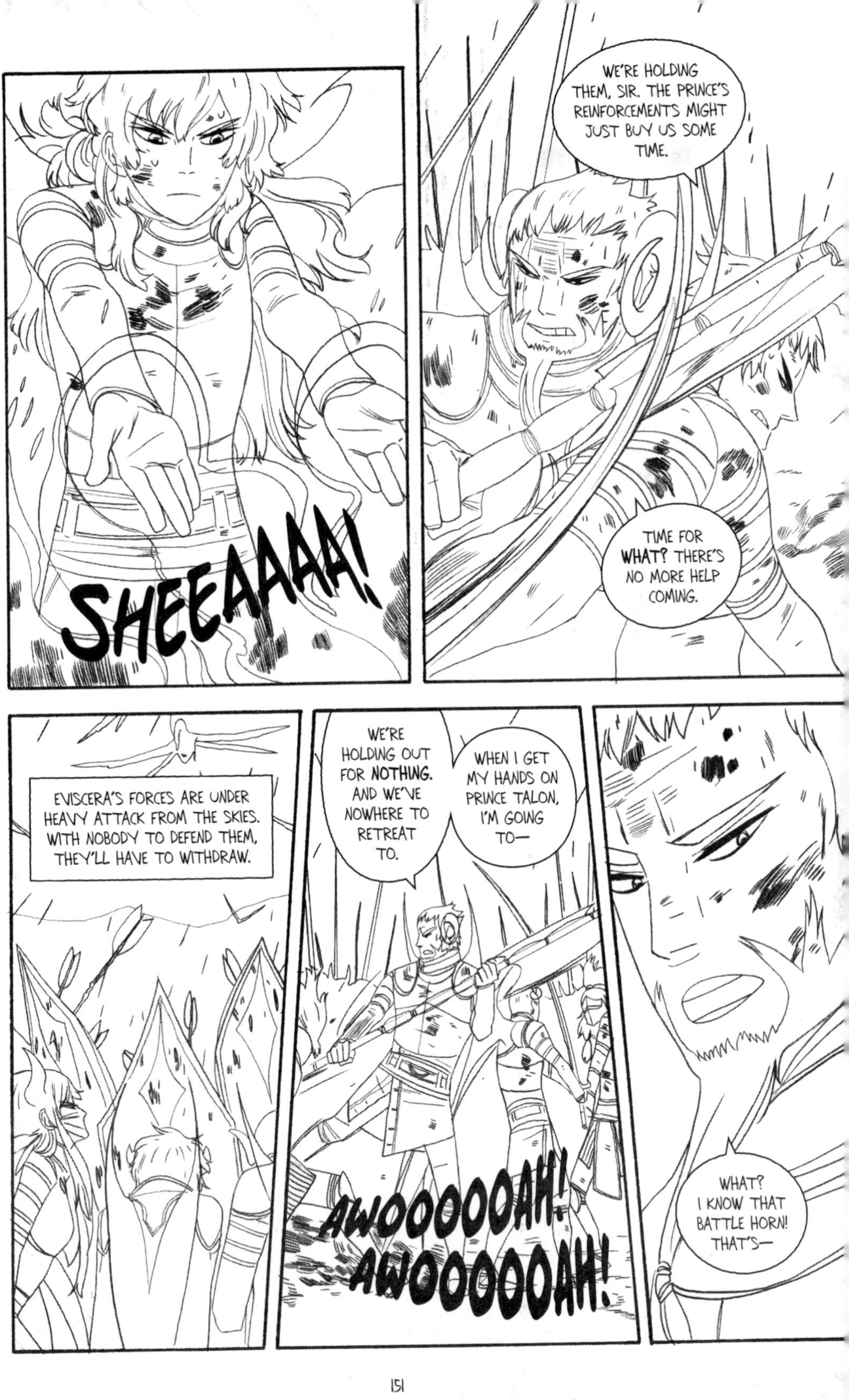
SHEEAAAA!
WE'RE HOLDING THEM, SIR. THE PRINCE'S REINFORCEMENTS MIGHT JUST BUY US SOME TIME.
TIME FOR WHAT? THERE'S NO MORE HELP COMING.
EVISCERA'S FORCES ARE UNDER HEAVY ATTACK FROM THE SKIES. WITH NOBODY TO DEFEND THEM, THEY'LL HAVE TO WITHDRAW.
WE'RE HOLDING OUT FOR NOTHING. AND WE'VE NOWHERE TO RETREAT TO.
WHEN I GET MY HANDS ON PRINCE TALON, I'M GOING TO—
AWOOOOOAH! AWOOOOOAH!
WHAT? I KNOW THAT BATTLE HORN! THAT'S—

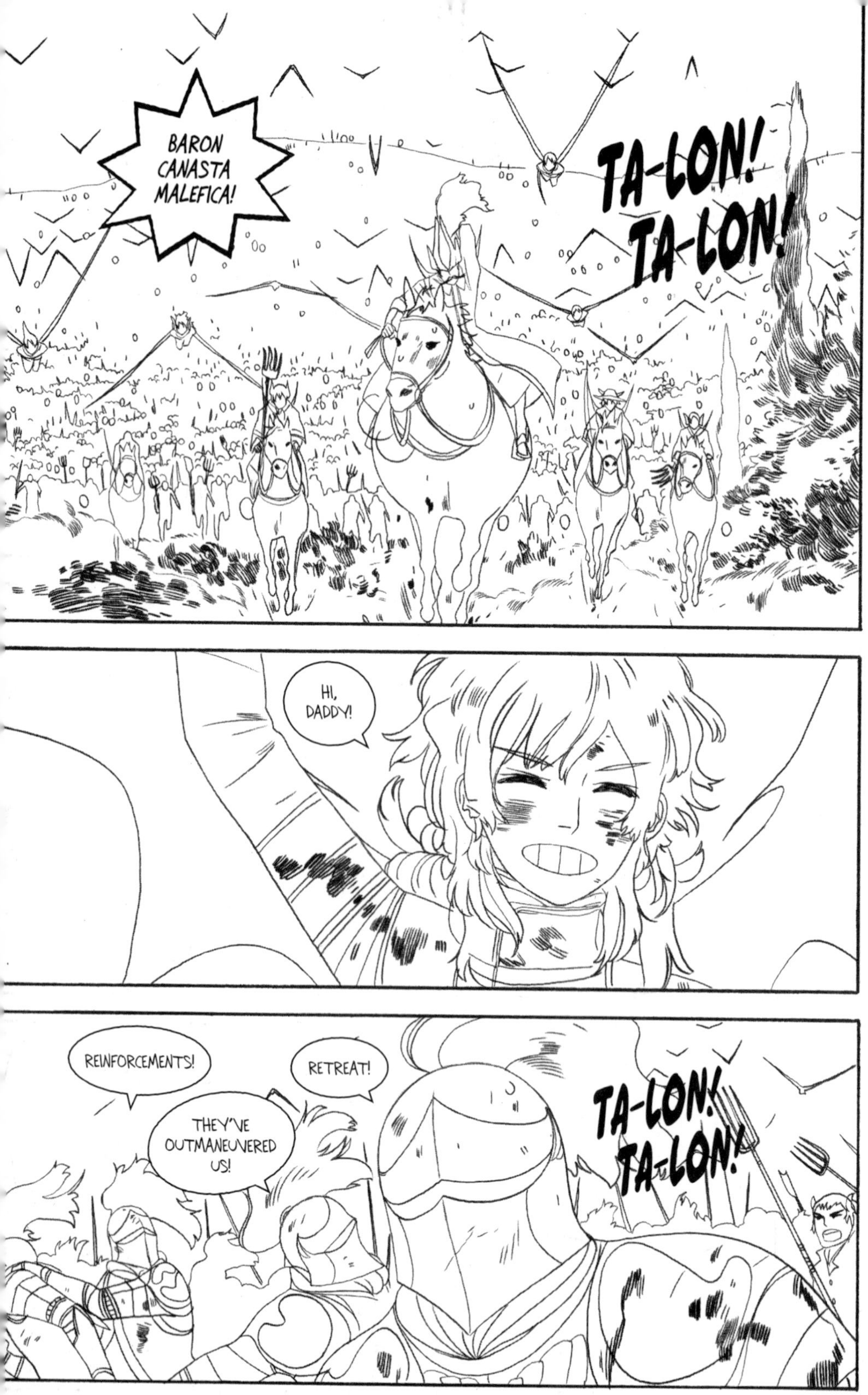
BARON CANASTA MALEFICA!
TA-LON! TA-LON!
HI, DADDY!
REINFORCEMENTS!
THEY'VE OUTMANEUVERED US!
RETREAT!
TA-LON! TA-LON!

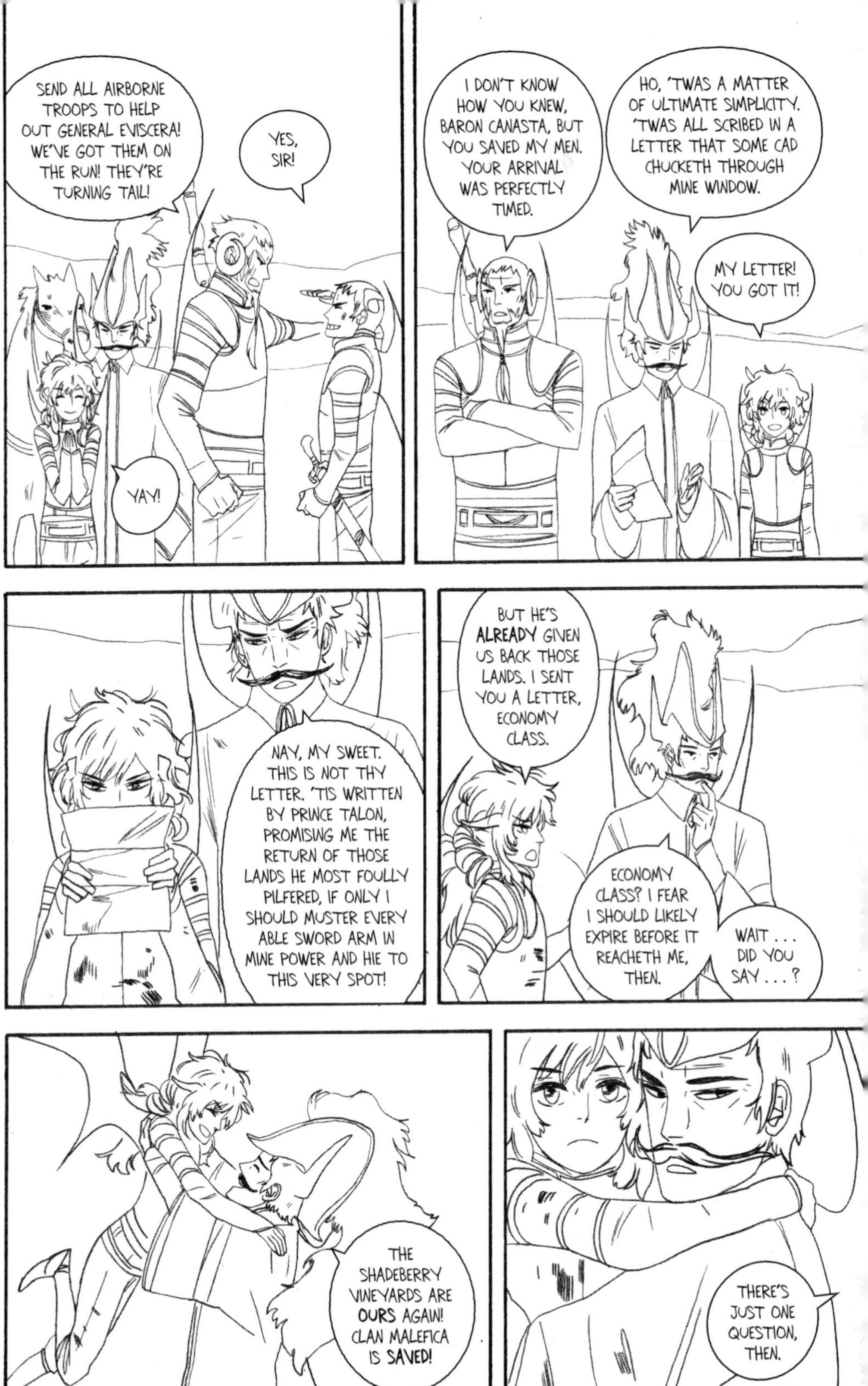
SEND ALL AIRBORNE TROOPS TO HELP OUT GENERAL EVISCERA! WE'VE GOT THEM ON THE RUN! THEY'RE TURNING TAIL!
YES, SIR!
YAY!
I DON'T KNOW HOW YOU KNEW, BARON CANASTA, BUT YOU SAVED MY MEN. YOUR ARRIVAL WAS PERFECTLY TIMED.
HO, 'TWAS A MATTER OF ULTIMATE SIMPLICITY. 'TWAS ALL SCRIBED IN A LETTER THAT SOME CAD CHUCKETH THROUGH MINE WINDOW.
MY LETTER! YOU GOT IT!
NAY, MY SWEET. THIS IS NOT THY LETTER. 'TIS WRITTEN BY PRINCE TALON, PROMISING ME THE RETURN OF THOSE LANDS HE MOST FOULLY PILFERED, IF ONLY I SHOULD MUSTER EVERY ABLE SWORD ARM IN MINE POWER AND HIE TO THIS VERY SPOT!
BUT HE'S **ALREADY** GIVEN US BACK THOSE LANDS. I SENT YOU A LETTER, ECONOMY CLASS.
ECONOMY CLASS? I FEAR I SHOULD LIKELY EXPIRE BEFORE IT REACHETH ME, THEN.
WAIT . . . DID YOU SAY . . . ?
THE SHADEBERRY VINEYARDS ARE **OURS** AGAIN! CLAN MALEFICA IS **SAVED**!
THERE'S JUST ONE QUESTION, THEN.

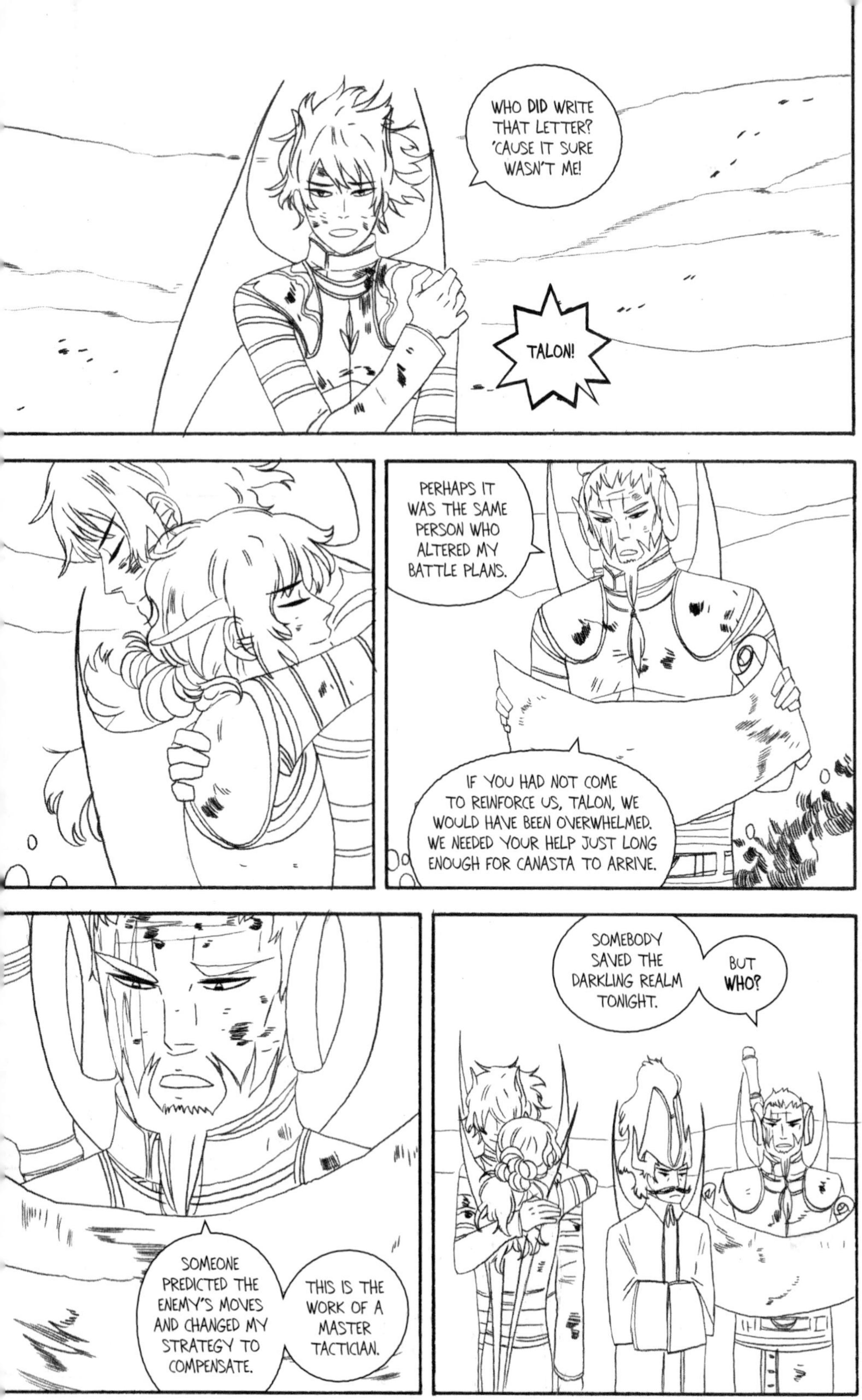
WHO DID WRITE THAT LETTER? 'CAUSE IT SURE WASN'T ME!
TALON!
PERHAPS IT WAS THE SAME PERSON WHO ALTERED MY BATTLE PLANS.
IF YOU HAD NOT COME TO REINFORCE US, TALON, WE WOULD HAVE BEEN OVERWHELMED. WE NEEDED YOUR HELP JUST LONG ENOUGH FOR CANASTA TO ARRIVE.
SOMEONE PREDICTED THE ENEMY'S MOVES AND CHANGED MY STRATEGY TO COMPENSATE.
THIS IS THE WORK OF A MASTER TACTICIAN.
SOMEBODY SAVED THE DARKLING REALM TONIGHT.
BUT WHO?

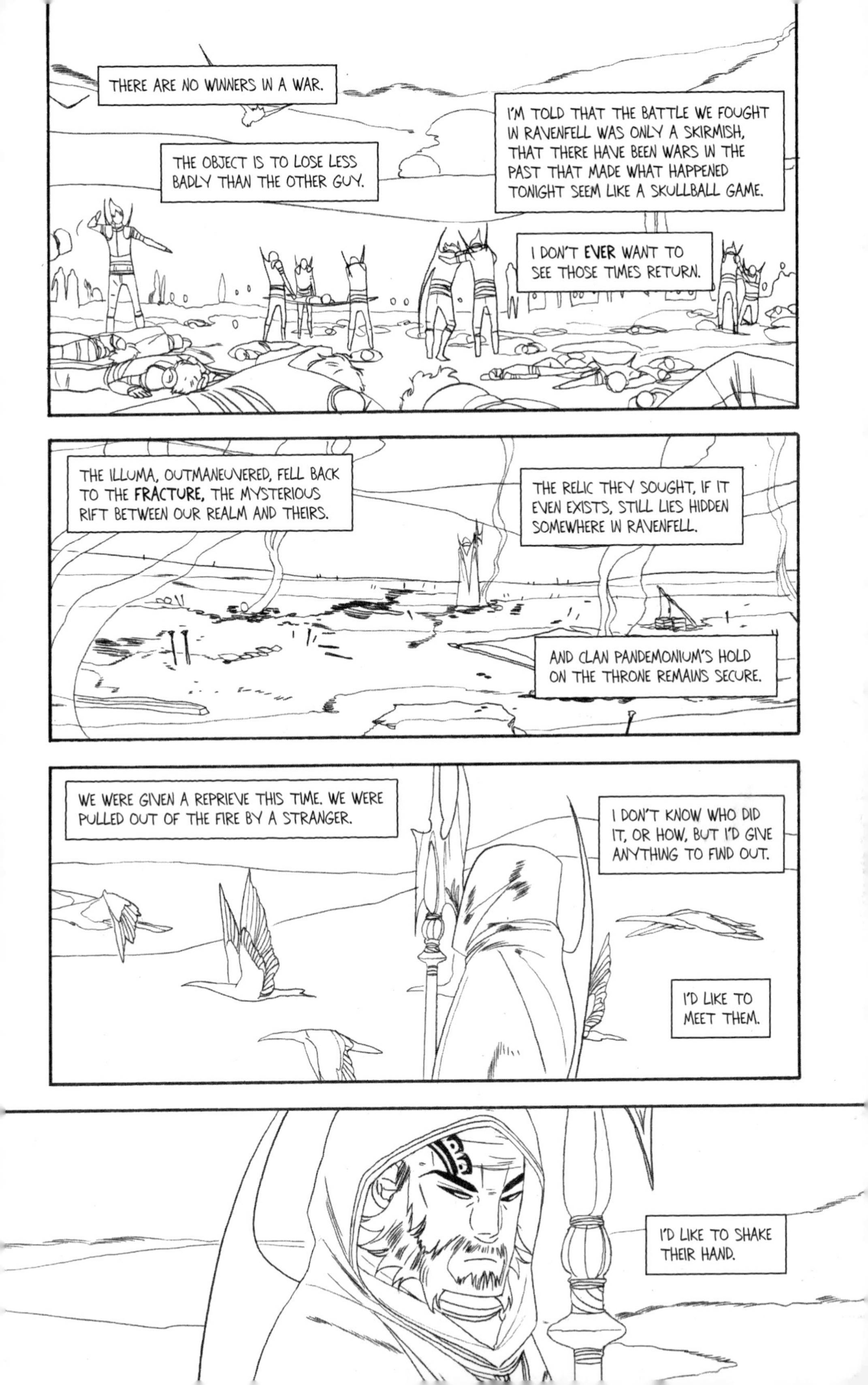
THERE ARE NO WINNERS IN A WAR.
THE OBJECT IS TO LOSE LESS BADLY THAN THE OTHER GUY.
I'M TOLD THAT THE BATTLE WE FOUGHT IN RAVENFELL WAS ONLY A SKIRMISH, THAT THERE HAVE BEEN WARS IN THE PAST THAT MADE WHAT HAPPENED TONIGHT SEEM LIKE A SKULLBALL GAME.
I DON'T **EVER** WANT TO SEE THOSE TIMES RETURN.
THE ILLUMA, OUTMANEUVERED, FELL BACK TO THE **FRACTURE,** THE MYSTERIOUS RIFT BETWEEN OUR REALM AND THEIRS.
THE RELIC THEY SOUGHT, IF IT EVEN EXISTS, STILL LIES HIDDEN SOMEWHERE IN RAVENFELL.
AND CLAN PANDEMONIUM'S HOLD ON THE THRONE REMAINS SECURE.
WE WERE GIVEN A REPRIEVE THIS TIME. WE WERE PULLED OUT OF THE FIRE BY A STRANGER.
I DON'T KNOW WHO DID IT, OR HOW, BUT I'D GIVE ANYTHING TO FIND OUT.
I'D LIKE TO MEET THEM.
I'D LIKE TO SHAKE THEIR HAND.

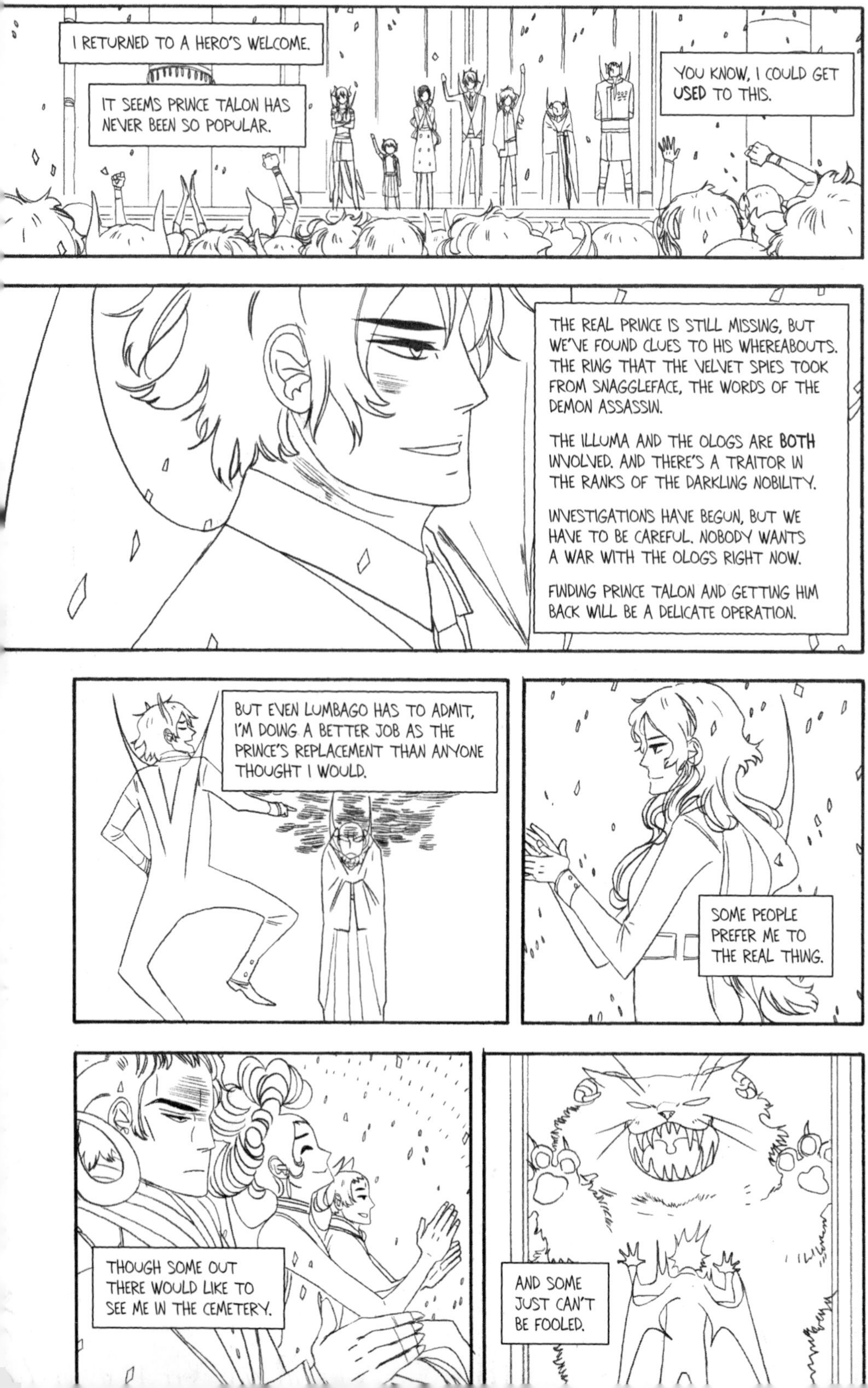
I RETURNED TO A HERO'S WELCOME.
IT SEEMS PRINCE TALON HAS NEVER BEEN SO POPULAR.
YOU KNOW, I COULD GET USED TO THIS.
THE REAL PRINCE IS STILL MISSING, BUT WE'VE FOUND CLUES TO HIS WHEREABOUTS. THE RING THAT THE VELVET SPIES TOOK FROM SNAGGLEFACE, THE WORDS OF THE DEMON ASSASSIN.
THE ILLUMA AND THE OLOGS ARE BOTH INVOLVED. AND THERE'S A TRAITOR IN THE RANKS OF THE DARKLING NOBILITY.
INVESTIGATIONS HAVE BEGUN, BUT WE HAVE TO BE CAREFUL. NOBODY WANTS A WAR WITH THE OLOGS RIGHT NOW.
FINDING PRINCE TALON AND GETTING HIM BACK WILL BE A DELICATE OPERATION.
BUT EVEN LUMBAGO HAS TO ADMIT, I'M DOING A BETTER JOB AS THE PRINCE'S REPLACEMENT THAN ANYONE THOUGHT I WOULD.
SOME PEOPLE PREFER ME TO THE REAL THING.
THOUGH SOME OUT THERE WOULD LIKE TO SEE ME IN THE CEMETERY.
AND SOME JUST CAN'T BE FOOLED.

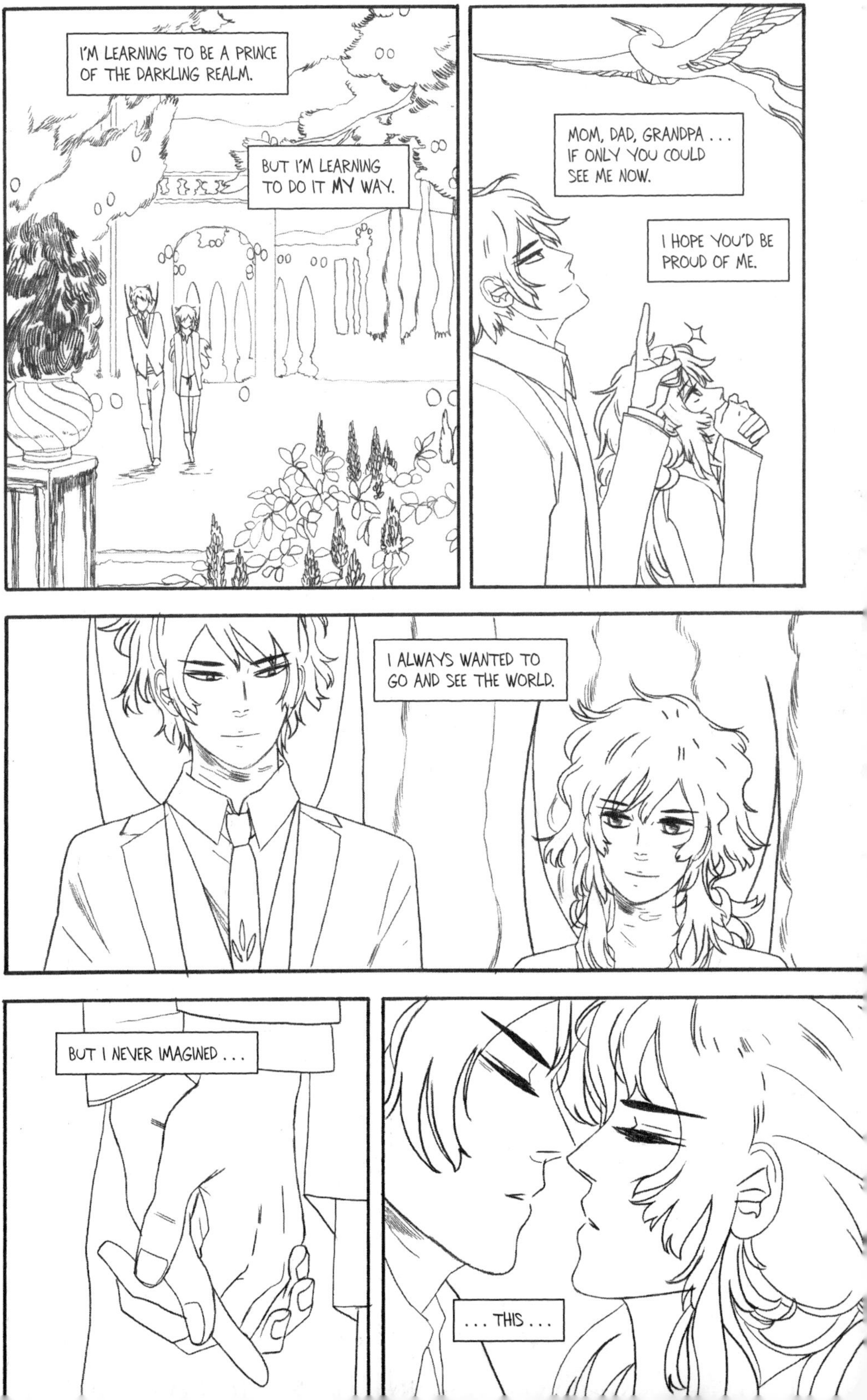
I'M LEARNING TO BE A PRINCE OF THE DARKLING REALM.
BUT I'M LEARNING TO DO IT MY WAY.
MOM, DAD, GRANDPA . . . IF ONLY YOU COULD SEE ME NOW.
I HOPE YOU'D BE PROUD OF ME.
I ALWAYS WANTED TO GO AND SEE THE WORLD.
BUT I NEVER IMAGINED . . .
. . . THIS . . .

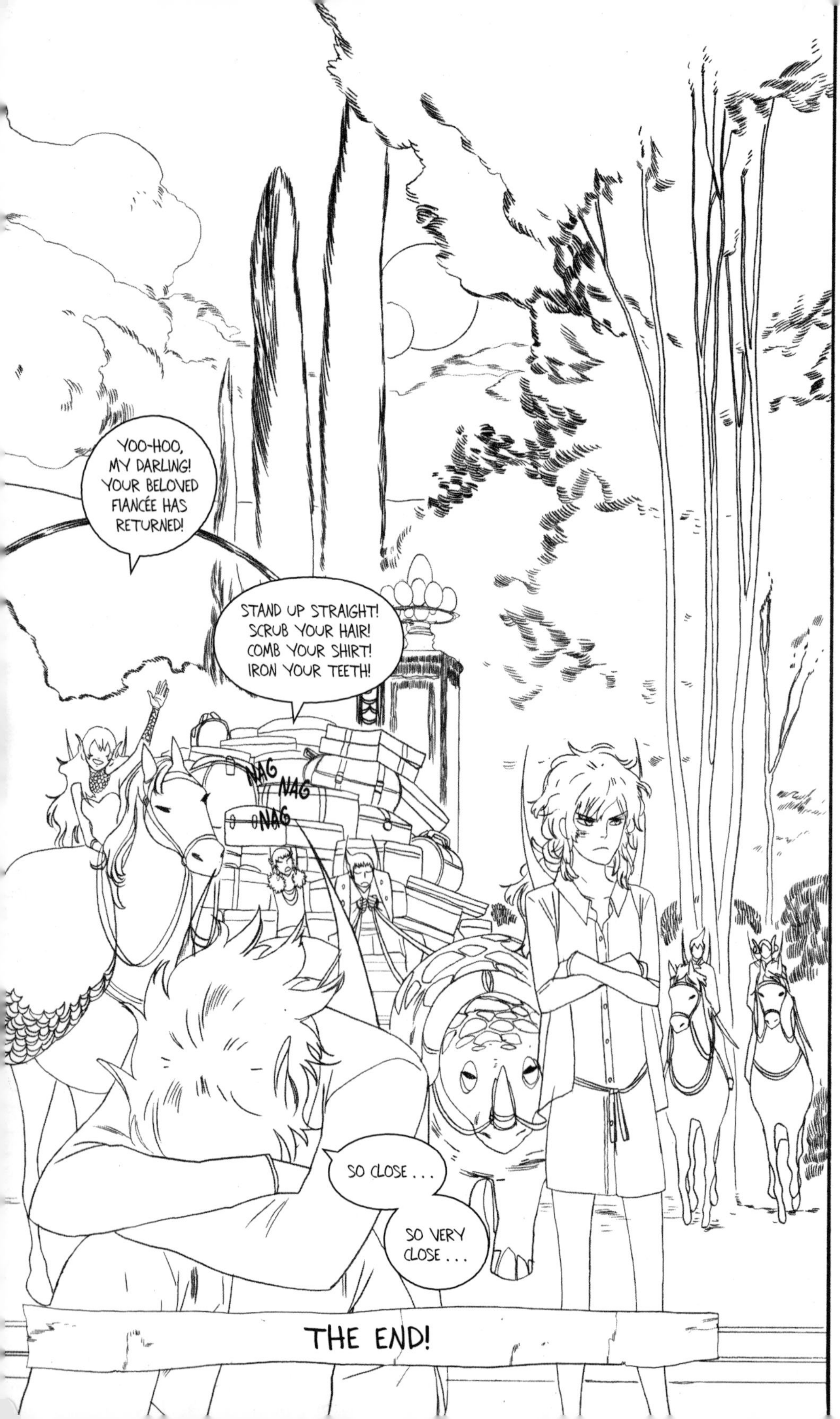
YOO-HOO, MY DARLING! YOUR BELOVED FIANCÉE HAS RETURNED!
STAND UP STRAIGHT! SCRUB YOUR HAIR! COMB YOUR SHIRT! IRON YOUR TEETH!
NAG NAG NAG
SO CLOSE . . .
SO VERY CLOSE . . .
THE END!